Isleen screwed up her

"War is not a very

to keep oneself amused."

"When dealing with mortals," Lochie countered, "I have always found it best to be blunt and to the point. No room for subtlety with them. Most important of all, the quarrel is not of my doing."

"If it is not your quarrel, why bother?"

"I learn a great deal observing mortals as they go about their business. Their behavior reminds me of my youth. And there is no better place to witness raw, unrestrained fear."

There was a pause. "I can't help myself," Isleen admitted. "I know I should be able to restrain my desires. I know I should not indulge. But I simply have no control when it comes to witnessing mortal fear. I simply have to watch.

"I will go with you, but just to observe your battle, nothing more. I won't commit to aiding you."

"Then let's be on our way," Lochie urged. "There is all sorts of trouble brewing before evening and I don't want to miss any of it."

BOOK ONE OF THE WATCHERS

THE MEETING *of the* WATERS

Caiseal Mór

POCKET BOOKS

New York   London   Toronto   Sydney   Singapore

An *Original* Publication of POCKET BOOKS

POCKET BOOKS, a division of Simon & Schuster, Inc.
1230 Avenue of the Americas, New York, NY 10020

Published by arrangement with Simon & Schuster (Australia) Pty. Ltd.

Originally published in Australia in 2000 by Simon & Schuster Australia

ISBN: 0-7434-2438-7

First Pocket Books printing March 2002

10 9 8 7 6 5 4 3 2 1

POCKET and colophon are registered trademarks of Simon & Schuster, Inc.

For information regarding special discounts for bulk purchases, please contact Simon & Schuster Special Sales at 1-800-456-6798 or business@simonandschuster.com

Front cover illustration by Yvonne Gilbert

Printed in the U.S.A.

For my Guardian Angel

Acknowledgments

I am extremely grateful to several people who gave such encouragement to me to write this novel. Selwa Anthony, my literary agent, has always been a believer in these novels and the tales I write. Without her support and friendship I would never have put a word down on paper in the first place. Thank you, Selwa, for changing my life.

Julia Stiles has edited all my novels beginning with *The Circle and the Cross*. I thank you, Julia, for your magnificent patience in dealing with my often wild rambles.

I would like to thank all at Simon & Schuster Australia but especially Angelo Loukakis who recognized the potential of the Watchers series and set about getting them published. I look forward to a strong partnership in the future.

Finally I must thank all the readers who continue to write to me through e-mail and snail mail. These many letters convinced me to continue with this cycle of stories and reminded me constantly what a joy it is to share a tale with others. If you would like to write to me to share your opinions on my novels I may be contacted through my publisher or by e-mail at *harp@caiseal.net* or by following the links from my web page. The URL is: *www.caiseal.net*.

May 2000
Caiseal Mór

Author's Note

In the gentle glow of firelight an old man, his hands hard from a lifetime of tilling the soil, warmed himself against the winter. His eyes brightened as I opened a bottle and found a seat opposite him. He told me no one listened to his stories these days.

By the time the whiskey was gone I had heard one or two of his tales, though I'm certain he kept the best stories to himself.

Music and storytelling have been a part of my life since childhood. My grandmother was a talented tale-weaver who had a gift for meshing different stories together. Her style was to overlap her tales into one long legend that explained the origins of the Irish people.

In the early 1980s I traveled to Ireland and was privileged to meet some very fine storytellers there. The legends and anecdotes I heard inspired me to record as much as possible. In my enthusiasm, I filled notebooks with wise and humorous sayings I picked up, as well as the general gist of some fascinating tales.

When I returned to Australia I put the notes away and got on with earning a degree in the arts. It was ten years before I looked at those scribblings again. By that time I had a much better knowledge of folklore and the storyteller's craft and a fascination with all the characters who appear as the supporting cast of the great dramatic sagas.

It crossed my mind that I might like to write a novel. Then by a remarkable chance, almost as if it had happened in one of those old stories, I met a mentor who would become my literary agent, Selwa Anthony. She suggested I write a story based on some of the tales I had collected.

That was how the Watchers began.

September 2001
Caiseal Mór

Prologue

I MUST WARN YOU FROM THE OUTSET. RAVENS HAVE LONG memories. So tread lightly with me or you'll finish up the worse for it. And don't be thinking any threat I offer is an idle one. I never waste my breath on empty vows, nor do I fritter my life away with fools.

I've always kept close counsel with myself. I've studied well the skill of staying silent. For I've heard it said the one who speaks with many folk may gain a trove of knowledge. But the one who knows himself is ever the wiser of the two.

I don't share your love of books—all pretense and pretty phrases. Vellum leather is too precious to squander on the pages of a gospel. A small missal of cowhide could keep me fed throughout the winter if I rationed it aright. The tales within better nourish my body than my intellect. I care not for the wit, or want of it, inked out upon each leaf. I'm suspicious of the written word, even more distrustful of the scribe.

But I know the time has come to briefly set my misgivings aside. I'll share with you what I recall so at least the story won't depart this earth along with me. I would speak to you of the old days before I journey on. For the past weighs heavy on my spirit. My thoughts are weary. Soon enough all worry will wash away in the cool gray depths of the Well of Forgetfulness.

But if you would listen to me now, I'll weave my tale into a warm cloak and fold it round your soul at Samhain tide. Let your heart be a silver Cup of Welcoming and I'll fill it with the mead brew of storytelling.

I remember everything. That's to say I don't recall if there's a part I've forgotten. Perhaps I've misplaced a memory here and there, but if so, details likely weren't important.

So where shall I begin? Shall I tell you something of myself?

I'm a bird of the green fields, the smooth rolling hills and the haunted forests. I'm a lover of the cold ocean spray. My friends are many. Some choose to dwell under the seething frozen ice floes; others build their bright palaces beneath the dark moist earth.

I'm an ancient one. I've seen bright steel flash upon the battlefield. I've heard the woeful voices of the war-fallen. I've witnessed ten thousand whispered prayers, as many mumbled curses, and countless anguished pleas for forgiveness. Only the Raven kind really listen with any interest to the dying words of a warrior.

In my long life seas have grown up from trickling springs. Mountains were transformed to gentle hills. And the once wide woods of the west were worn down to barren rocks. Through all those changes the seasons didn't touch my body. Age has not triumphed here. But there are no more like me. I'm the last.

Across the passing generations I've nurtured an appreciation for my soul's enforced solitude. These days my isolation is a joy. I guard it as I might a helpless child. And avoid all other living beings whenever possible.

I've crafted a cunning mask so as to seem content whenever I am out among the Raven kind. I can't avoid their ways if the Queen demands my counsel at her Samhain Court. So I tolerate their company. I'm courteous to them all; chattering black-hearted bitter souls they are. I'm generous to most, despite the malignant misgivings some still hold of me. I love a few as if they were my own kinfolk. But I wouldn't trust a feather of any one of them.

Ravens are carrion creatures. Count your fingers when I'm done, for I am also one of them. All scavengers know that each beating heart must take its final rest. Each bright eye will, in the end, glass over. Even you will one day cease to be.

A Raven need only wait in patience for the spirit to depart. Then Death brings us our supper. I too will soon surrender to his hospitality. So pay attention to me while I retain the power of speech.

In the days before I took on the fearful features of the black birds of battle I dwelt in the fortresses of the Fir-Bolg and the Tuatha De Danaan. I sat at the fireside with my siblings, soaking up legends in the same way an oatcake soaks up soup. The old stories are as much a part of me as bone, claw and feather. In my youth I sang songs about the Islands of the West. I chanted ancestral prayers first raised to the heavens when my mother's people left their home to seek out this land called Innisfail.

I was once a mortal, you see, ere enchantment bound me. And in my youth before these damned feathers sprouted I took a small part in the calamitous events of the age. I was still young when the ships of your people breached the Ninth Wave. I recall one Druid then who told me your ancestors were as irre-sistible as a giant wall of water rolling in from over the horizon.

No force could stop the Gaedhals, he reckoned. No wise Draoi-Craft, no chant, no spell-song, no poem would ever turn them away. Destiny decreed these folk must one day come. Fate had filled their sails to send them here.

The spirit of Danu still walked amongst us then when I was a youth of seventeen summers, eager to take up weapons and make my mark in the world. Now the Goddess of the Flowing Waters has withdrawn with all her kindred. She's but a half-remembered myth.

Your folk don't speak her name or sing her praises. They desecrate her wells, her streams, her holy mountains. They hold her sacred places to be haunted.

I could talk all night on the infamy and treachery of the Gaedhal. No treaty could ever hold them to their promises. All they understood was the sword. I still can't imagine how they thought themselves honorable.

Don't be too proud of your people. They'll turn soon enough to dust. Your voice, even the language you speak, will surely be forgotten by and by. But this tale will live, all the more surely because I've never told the whole of it to anyone until now. So listen carefully. Remember all you hear tonight for it will not be repeated.

I am called Lom-dubh. I was once a man of the Fir-Bolg. Then I grew feathers, claws and a beak. And I became a Raven.

Now at last my soul is preparing for its final flight.

Chapter 1

ON AN ICE-BLUE WINTER NIGHT FULL-MOONED AND frosty, when well-meaning folk were huddled by their firesides, a spirit of the Otherworld awoke. Roused by the scent of fear carried on a chill wind he emerged from his sanctuary in the depths of the earth.

Around the bare rocky hills a distant wretched cry echoed desperately. A delicious shiver of excitement drove off the last vestiges of the creature's long sleep. His mind now sharply alert, the ghostly shadow tarried at the entrance to the stony hill he called home and begged for another sign.

A horse neighed wildly on the far side of the forest. This dark spirit hummed with satisfaction. His senses drank deep after cold confinement within the ancient mound of rock. Eyes once shallow sparkled cool and green like two emeralds dropped in the bottom of a clear well.

For countless generations this ethereal creature had haunted the west of Innisfail. He knew every field, every valley, every lonely cairn dedicated to the Old Ones. In his time he had wandered the darkest places deep beneath the earth and the lofty mountains kissed by the clouds.

His nostrils twitched and his eyes shone bright as he tucked in his head and turned slowly around toward the fields. The midnight walker stiffened, straightened up and smiled. If he'd had a heart it would have been beating hard against his chest. A tremble took hold of him as he tracked down the disturbance that had interrupted his rest.

Through hard-driven snow a mighty drafthorse thudded down toward a stand of sturdy oak trees. Sleet and frost flew about as the animal bellowed in dismay. On the horse's back a thin weakling of a lad clung hopelessly to the mane to save himself from falling. He was only a golden-haired boy too frightened to call out and too unsteady to bring his mount to a halt. His frail frame was buffeted about on the back of the bare unsaddled animal like a sack of oats. It was all he could do to stop himself sliding off into the snow.

The spirit-walker watched in absolute silence. His prayers had been answered, and now all his dreams would surely come to pass. This was the moment the creature of the dark hills had so long awaited.

Suddenly the panicked horse charged toward a small mound of snow-covered rocks. Then just as abruptly the animal leapt high just two steps off disaster. The young rider's hold weakened as his mount lurched forward on the other side. His hands ached from exertion but the will to live was still very strong in him. By some miracle when the horse came down the lad had kept his seat.

Far behind him in the night the young horseman heard a girl call out his name. He struggled to reply but he was too breathless to speak. His head was swimming and his mind clouded as the horse turned round again to charge the trees. It was clear the animal meant to dislodge him by dragging him through low branches.

Foam streaming from its mouth, the horse ran on, making for the first great oak. The boy clung tight to the animal's neck and whimpered. In that instant, halted by an unseen threat, the mount stopped still in its tracks, and cried out in a frantic, almost human, voice. Somehow the shaken boy managed to stop himself from slipping into the snow. The horse was perfectly motionless now, breathing wild-eyed steam in the wintry air. It grunted from the back of its throat.

The lad made a move to dismount, but as he shifted position his sharp eyes caught a glimpse of something black flitting from beneath the trees. He did not have time to see clearly what was moving swiftly toward him but his heart filled with a dread such as he had never known. At last he found the breath to call out.

"Help!" It was a soul-chilling shriek.

The horse reared up, sharing the lad's terror, eyes bulging with fright. It twisted its body in one last attempt to shake off the rider, lost its footing on the icy ground and fell hard on its side. All this happened so fast the boy had no chance to jump clear. In moments the heavy animal had rolled over on top of his thin frame.

A loud gut-wrenching crack, a painful gush of air and the poor lad was pinned beneath the fallen beast. Then just as easily as it had stumbled, the horse was on its feet again, pounding away into the night.

A few short gasps, noisy, strained and desperate. A shadow passed across the snow. The lad looked up. The spirit halted not far off and waited.

"Fearna!" A girl's voice, muffled by the night, drifted across the moonlit fields. The Otherworldly creature was unmoved.

Helpless in the snow the boy uttered a dozen feeble urgent cries. He saw his own breath clouding in front of him and through the steam he glimpsed a stranger dressed in black.

"Where are you?" the girl wept in the distance.

There was defeat in her voice. Fearna heard it plainly.

Among the exposed roots of the oak grove the young rider was already beyond an answer. His lips moved slightly as they formed her name but there was no strength left to make a sound. Fearna frowned as he coughed. His mouth was full of snow and blood.

A shudder shook him, then the last breath left his body and the steam abruptly ceased.

The spirit-watcher waited for a moment longer, searching for any sign of life. Satisfied there was none, he strode directly over to where the cold boy lay on the soft white shroud of winter. There he knelt down beside the still form where it lay partly concealed in the shadows of the mighty oaks.

"Fearna!" came the cry once more.

The creature turned a nose to the breeze and sniffed, instantly judging the girl and her brother were a good distance away. To be sure the stranger scanned the line of snowy hills and the edge of the distant forest. Reassured, he turned his attention back to the young corpse before him.

The crisp white ground all round was stained red with blood. Frigid air quickly turned Fearna's skin to gray. The stranger bent over to make sure there were no stirrings of life. He caught the stench of mead on the lad's clothes and recoiled slightly.

"Well, my dear Fearna," the creature said in a low, rasping voice, "it seems you have not ended your life in an honorable way. What will your father say?"

The black spirit laughed gruffly under his breath.

"Your death has not been in vain, if that is any consolation to you. Your passing will enable me to rebuild my fortunes and save myself from an eternity of isolation and misery."

The creature turned his head sharply, senses alert, like a wild animal keeping watch for hunters. It was some moments before he relaxed and regarded the corpse once more.

"I thank you for your sacrifice," he added sincerely. "And I beg you to forgive me for taking advantage of your misfortune. But this is an opportunity I simply could not pass by. I have been waiting so long for this chance."

A scent wafted in from the hills. The stranger sniffed the air again, then he pulled back the cowl which covered his smooth bald head and closed his eyes to concentrate.

"The girl and her brother are approaching now," he announced as he leaned down to tenderly stroke the golden locks of hair away from the glassy eyes. "Soon you will rest among your own folk."

Another cry echoed into the trees. The dark-robed figure covered his head again to keep out the frost as he turned around to face the hills. Not three hundred paces away two dark shapes struggled across the thick frozen blanket of snow making a difficult headway in the icy wind.

"Your friends have come to find you, Fearna," the stranger told the boy, "but it serves my purpose they should not tarry here too long. I must make certain that pair are gone again soon. Do not fear, I will wait by you through the night and keep you company till morning."

"Fearna!"

The young woman's gray cloak flew about her face obscuring her vision. Impatiently she threw it from her shoulders to search the fields. Soon enough her copper red locks fell loose from their binding and she had to cover her head again. Her green eyes had not lost their bright light despite the seriousness of the situation.

"Aoife!" her brother Sárán begged. "Slow down. I can't keep up with you."

She ignored him, though she slipped time and again in the deep drifts of snow. Each time she struggled to her feet and trudged on as quickly as she could manage.

"I can see him!" she cried out at last. "He's standing by the oak trees."

"Where?" her brother replied, scowling.

"There," she pointed.

"Aoife, I cannot see anything. The snowfall is too heavy."

Beneath the oaks the spirit-walker let a smile curl the edges of his mouth. Then the moon passed behind a cloud and the creature melted into the trees without trace.

The young woman stopped in her tracks. "He was there!" she exclaimed. "He was standing in front of those oaks."

When her brother caught up he grabbed her hand and dragged her forward. "It was a trick of the shadows," he told her, searching her eyes for any sign of delirium. "The cold is overcoming us. We must keep moving or the frozen night will kill us both."

Aoife nodded but she knew it was not shadows she had seen.

"There is something lying on the ground near the oak wood," Sárán added, squinting to try and make out what the shape was.

"Then let's make for the trees," Aoife decided. "At least we'll find some shelter from the cold." She trudged on, cold and wet, sweating under her cloak and woolen clothes, until the grove was just ahead.

Sárán and Aoife saw the bloodstain on the snow before either of them caught sight of the drained gray features of Fearna's face, eyes wide open to the sky, collarbone shattered, neck broken and twisted. Sárán touched the boy's cheek in the vain hope of finding life but Aoife stood back staring in disbelief.

"He's dead," her brother announced with certainty.

"I could have sworn I saw him standing by the trees," Aoife sobbed in anguish. "I know I saw someone."

"There are no footprints in the snow," Sárán reasoned. "There was no one else here."

"I saw him standing beneath this tree!" she cried again as she approached the body, convinced that the boy must still be alive.

"It was a trick of the light," her brother sighed.

"No." But Aoife drew a sharp breath when she caught sight of the young man's lips, blue and swollen.

"Fearna is gone, Aoife." Sárán took his sister by the shoulders and shook her to bring her to her senses. "Do you hear me? He is dead."

"It's my fault," Aoife whispered, warm tears

streaming down her cheeks. "If it had not been for me he would be sitting by the hearth at home listening to the Bards sing their stories."

"Be quiet!" her brother snapped. "This is all your fault, I won't argue with you about that. May Danu forgive me for playing along with your game. I should have stood up to you."

"It was as much your doing as mine," she protested.

"Don't turn this on me. It was your idea to come out on this night and risk our lives for a childish prank."

"What are we going to do?"

Sárán sighed deeply as he stood up. "We must not be found with him," he decided. "If anyone so much as imagined we were involved in his death, it could mean war."

"And Father would see us punished severely," the girl added. "There is no greater dishonor than the death of a fosterling through neglect or misadventure, and he loved Fearna more than his own."

"We must keep this night a secret," Sárán insisted urgently. "You must keep quiet. Our future and that of the Fir-Bolg may depend on it."

Aoife did not answer.

"We must return to Dun Burren before anyone misses us," Sárán hissed. "Then you must banish all thoughts of this night from your mind."

"I didn't mean it to be like this," the girl cried, turning away from the corpse. "I wish I had never thought of coming out here at midnight."

"It is done now," Sárán replied. "No one knows we were here except Fearna and he won't tell. Of that you may be certain."

With that the two of them made their way as quickly as they could to the road, careful to brush away their footprints as they went. But in the event they need not have bothered. The snow began falling heavy again, and in a short while all trace of them was completely obliterated.

The two young siblings were barely out of sight and sound when the black-clad spirit appeared again from beneath the stand of ancient shadowy trees. He crouched down beside the lifeless lad.

"Only you and I know the truth, Fearna," he sighed gently. "You see what kind of company you have been keeping? I almost feel it is my duty to visit retribution upon them."

He touched the lad's hair again and there was true compassion in the gesture.

"You have no idea of the gift you have been given," the stranger whispered. "I wish you could tell me about the lands beyond life. I wish I could walk there with you."

A brief smile touched the creature's lips. Then he sat himself down amidst the snowstorm to watch over the corpse until daybreak.

Chapter 2

DALAN THE BREHON SAT DOWN BY THE SWIFTLY FLOWING stream, scooped a handful of water into his mouth and breathed in the summer fragrance of the forest air. He had been walking at a good pace all night long and he was exhausted. The Druid stretched his neck, leaned against his huge pack and traced with his fingers the shape of the bronze cauldron inside. Beside the pack sat his harp in its case, another heavy load.

"A short rest," he told himself. "Not far to go now. Why did I agree to carry both these burdens all on my own? I must have been touched with the madness."

Dalan sat up again to wash his face. The Brehon scooped up a handful of water and poured it over the crown of his head then dragged his hands down over his ears until the palms met in front of his face in the attitude of prayer. This was his silent ritual of thanks to Danu, the Goddess of the Flowing Waters. She watched over him, he knew, guiding his life from beyond the veil. The chilly droplets revived him a little. His short dark brown hair sparkled in the sunlight as if laden with dew.

Then the Brehon lay back again, propped his head against the pack and stared into the treetops, savoring the silence. During this last cycle of the moon his stamina had been sorely tested. In the Druid Assembly he had argued relentlessly as an advocate for Brocan, the King of the Fir-Bolg. Now he had been assigned to bring the Cauldron of Plenty to the west. As a gesture of goodwill by the Druid Assembly it was to be lodged in the royal house of the Burren until the next summer.

Dalan reflected on the fate of his people. So few Fir-Bolg were now under instruction in the Draoi arts that within two generations there would likely be no practitioners of the old blood left at all. He was the last traveling Brehon judge among the Fir-Bolg Druids of Innisfail. When he was gone it would be left to the Danaans alone to keep the law. In the last fifty summers his kinfolk had been driven to the barren west coast of Innisfail where the Danaans didn't care to live. Which perhaps explained why King Brocan of the Fir-Bolg was so bitterly opposed to the chieftains of the Tuatha De Danaan.

The Brehon idly brushed the smooth skin across the top of his head where he had been shaved to mark him as a man of poetry and learning. As a judge he was considered an expert in the laws and customs of his folk. He was a teacher and arbitrator, a respected adviser on matters of protocol and tradition. Yet he knew Brocan was not likely to listen to him. The king was a proud warrior and the only independent ruler of the Fir-Bolg. Dalan would be fortunate if he so much as considered a reply to his entreaty. The coming of the Cauldron might sweeten the discussion but it would not guarantee Brocan's good favor.

The Brehon's fingers searched around inside the dark blue robe he wore. After a few moments he found the little leather bag he habitually fastened about his waist. He carefully brought it out, untied the cords of the brown purse and emptied the contents into his hand.

A collection of shriveled red berries tumbled onto his palm. Dalan quickly counted them to make sure none had gone astray.

"Nine." He breathed with relief.

Then he picked up each berry and examined it closely for flaws. At last when he had inspected them all and was satisfied they were still fertile, he placed them back inside their bag and tucked the purse into his robe.

At least this part of his duty would not be difficult. As long as the berries still held the seed of life within them, his journey would have been worthwhile.

With that he stood up to stretch his legs. The stream in front of him flowed down between a small grove of trees before pouring into a wide deep sunlit pool. Dalan felt an overwhelming urge to go down and rest awhile on the warm rocks at the edge of the pool. But he still had a good way to go. He tried to convince himself he would be able to rest when he reached the battleground, but in his heart he knew there would be no opportunity.

It had been two cycles of the ever-changing moon since he had found time to be alone like this. And much longer since he had last sat down simply to close his eyes for a moment's peace, without some urgent concern springing to his mind. Perhaps if he sat here for just a short while he would be fresh and sharp-witted when he arrived at the battlefield.

Convincing himself of the wisdom of rest, Dalan made his way quickly down to the pool. There he squatted in the pleasant sunlight at the water's edge, listening to the gentle trickling of the stream as it flowed away into the thickly wooded grove beyond.

When his face was warmly tingling Dalan positioned the bag with its heavy bronze cauldron in the shade, closed his eyes and breathed slowly. Then he lay back on the rock to enjoy the feeling of the sun on his skin.

"I have spent too long in the north," he sighed to himself.

He had hardly thought these words when there was a sudden disturbance in the pool. His eyes snapped open though every other muscle froze. Directly in front of him, just under the water, a beautiful trout was sucking at the glassy surface, searching for tiny morsels of food. Dalan's stomach growled with hunger.

As if caught in some marvelous Draoi spell from the legends of old, the Brehon put aside all thoughts of his pressing duties and took a closer look. The trout stared back cheekily at him, as if challenging him to reach out and catch her. Gorgeous scales sparkled in a hundred subtle shades as she rippled her delicate body through the clear water.

Then she suddenly grew bored of Dalan and turned away. Perched on the rock the Brehon leaned over above the fish, utterly lost in thoughts of this trout and the empty space she would fill in his groaning stomach. Noiselessly, patiently, he edged close enough to strike. He lowered his hand into the water until no more than a finger length separated them. She hovered around as if unconcerned by the intruder. Dalan smiled as his palm brushed her belly. The trout did not swim away. His fingers tenderly stroked her, then suddenly he gripped her hard.

The Brehon felt the trout struggle and then she tugged surprisingly hard in a last-ditch attempt to break free. In the next instant the fisherman felt himself being pulled down into the pool. He lost his balance to tumble helplessly forward.

As the Brehon fell into the cold waters he barely had time to take a breath, but he did not let go of his prize. He panicked when his feet could not find the bottom. The mud stirred up as Dalan thrashed about and this obscured his vision. It seemed as if he had passed through some mystical portal into the Otherworld and all things had become dimmed to human sight.

A moment later he found his footing again and stood up in the water, still clutching his precious supper. Without a second thought he tossed the trout up onto the rocks where she flapped about in the golden sun, her scales reflecting light all the colors of the rainbow.

She had almost ceased her struggle by the time the Brehon hauled himself out of the pool. As if in recognition of his victory the fish gave up fighting her fate to case a steely eye upon her captor. It was then Dalan realized what a fool he was. Not only had he wasted precious time indulging himself with rest, but he had got his best cloak, his walking boots and all his undergarments wet through. He reached into his blue robe in a moment of breathless panic, then sighed with relief when he found the berries undamaged.

Now he would have to dry his clothes, he reprimanded himself crossly. He couldn't arrive at the battleground in this state. The contest didn't begin until dawn, however. As long as he did not dally too long he could have the early afternoon to himself. That should be plenty of time to dry out and tidy up.

"I'll have a fire going soon," he said aloud, deciding to make the best of things. "Then I'll eat and be on my way as soon as my cloak and robes are dry. No harm done. If I leave by sunset I'll make the battleground long before the contest is due to begin."

His heart sank a little as he wondered whether the Chief Druid, the Dagda, would approve of the break in his journey. Forget the bloody Dagda and the

Druid Assembly for a moment, he told himself. He needed to lie down with a full belly, to forget the troubles of the world for a while.

The Druid checked the position of the sun to reckon the hour. He stripped off his soaking garments, laid them out in the sunshine and went to gather enough kindling to start a decent blaze. And when the fire was good and strong he set about preparing his meal.

Dalan cooked and ate his trout before the sun had traveled a hand-breadth across the sky. His hunger satisfied, the Brehon sucked his fingers, savoring the tasty sweet juices of the slowly roasted fish. Then in a fine mood, he lay back in the sun and closed his eyes. His cloak hung on the tree behind him, his boots were by the fire and the rest of his clothes were spread out across the rocks to dry.

I'll just close my eyes for a short while then I'll be on my way again, he promised himself. It's no good for my stomach to walk a far road with a meal digesting.

The stream bubbled away nearby, the wind sighed a lullaby through the trees. In a matter of a few moments the cares of the world had dropped away from the Brehon and he had slipped into a sound and much needed sleep.

It seemed to Dalan he had hardly closed his eyes when his rest was disturbed by the sound of a woman singing in a high sweet voice.

"Why can I not have even a moment of peace?" he

hissed. "For pity's sake leave me alone for a little while longer."

The song was not a lilting sleep melody. It cut across the muttering of the gentle gurgling stream and drowned out the whispered tune of the branches swaying in the breeze. The woman's voice grew stronger and more urgent with every phrase.

Dalan refused to open his eyes.

"I am resting," he declared hoarsely. "You can sing all you like. I will not be disturbed. I'm owed a little peace after all I have been through. Come back when I am awake and I'll speak with you."

"I bathe your hands," the woman crooned in his ear, "in a cascade of mead, in the fire of my spirit, in the four elements, in the juice of blackberries, in the milk of a white cow. And I grant you nine gifts. The gift of beauty. The gift of sweet voice. The gift of endless good fortune. The gift of a good heart. The gift of gentle wisdom. The gift of merciful charity. The gift of manliness. The gift of a bright soul. The gift of fine words to speak."

Dalan smiled when he heard this. All his deepest wishes seemed to be listed in the woman's song. He opened his eyes, curious as to who had intruded on his peaceful afternoon. He sat bolt upright in shock.

The stream had become a river. The pool was a wide sea, the furthest shore of which was lost to sight in a thick rolling mist. And the rocks Dalan had been resting on were now a grassy windswept hill. All around were tall well-tended trees abundantly laden with brightly colored fruits and flowers. Strange birds sporting feathers of gold, crimson, black and yellow sang in the highest branches. These creatures looked down on him with obvious suspicion, though Dalan could not understand why the birds might distrust him.

"May you have the skill of the ancient ones who lived before the flood," the woman sang. "May talent at the harp be yours also. For you are the joy of all joys, the light of the sun, the open door of the welcome-house, the star of guidance, the swift foot of the horse, the nimble foot of the stag. You are the grace of the swan."

Dalan was entranced by the enchanting song-poem. The words shuddered through him like the rumble of distant thunder. He was sure he had heard this chant somewhere before. But he could not recall which legend tale they belonged to.

"Where am I?" he asked in a daze.

"This place is called the Islands of the West," the woman answered.

Suddenly the stranger was in front of Dalan. She was dressed in a cloak of deep blue cloth decorated with silver stars that sparkled like the eyes of a happy child. Her hair was white as chalk, though her face was youthful. She seemed no more than twenty summers old at most. Her skin was fair and delicate. Her hands were small and fine-boned.

"The best hour of the day be yours," she smiled, "and the best day of the season. May the best season of the four-fold circle be yours and the best circle of a thousand also."

"I wish these things for you also."

The woman laughed as if the Brehon's courteous reply were hilariously funny.

"Who are you?" Dalan asked with a frown.

It was at that moment he realized he was naked. Straight-away he reached up to the tree where his cloak had been hanging but the tree was gone.

"You may wear this," the woman giggled. "Consider it a gift."

As she spoke a cloak woven entirely of black feathers landed beside the Brehon as if it had fallen from the sky. Dalan carefully lifted the beautiful garment and placed it around his shoulders, surprised at the great weight of it. It fitted him perfectly, hugging close to his flesh like a second skin made of feathers. He was pleasantly warm and dry beneath this strange covering.

"Thank you," Dalan stuttered.

"My name is Cuimhne," the woman declared. "I am the guardian of the Hall of Remembrances. Some folk ascribe to me the name of Justice but only folk who do not understand my true nature."

"Justice? Remembrances?" The Brehon frowned. "I don't understand. You are the Goddess Cuimhne?"

"I'm not a goddess," she chortled. "I am merely a guardian. You have not told me your name."

"I am called Dalan Mac Math."

"Math is the old word for bear." She smiled. "Are you truly the son of a bear?"

"That was my teacher's name," the Brehon explained. "He was a Druid judge who lived in the caves of Aillwee for much of his life. He found the coat of a bear in those dark caverns one winter and he wore it ever after. That is how he came to be known as the Bear."

"So you are the son of the Bear?" she asked as she approached him. There was no sound of footfall as she moved closer. Cuimhne held out her white hand and touched Dalan gently on the chin.

"I knew your teacher," she confirmed. "You have his wisdom but you are not a bear. Your totem is the Raven."

"The Fir-Bolg people, my own folk, regard the bear as their guiding spirit."

"And like the bear in winter your kindred will sleep soon enough," Cuimhne replied. "The land of Innisfail will one day know them only in songs of past days and former glory."

Suddenly the Brehon shrank back from her, his heart beating in his chest. "I recognize you," he whispered. "I know your face. Where have we met before?"

"In your dreams and visions. In the land of memory. I am your future too. I have been waiting a long while for your return."

"Return?"

"Do not trouble yourself with such thoughts."

"Am I sleeping?" the Brehon gasped. "Is this a dream?"

"You are resting. Often what exists in the imagination is more real than the everyday things we perceive with our other senses."

"Am I imagining your beauty?"

The woman smiled sweetly. Her face shone like a lamp. "You are very complimentary, Brehon," Cuimhne laughed. "You have a good heart."

As she said that she took Dalan's hand in hers and led him to the top of the hill. When they reached the wind-blown summit she led him to the center of an incomplete circle of standing stones each of blue granite.

The woman put her hands on the Brehon's shoulders so he faced back the way they had come. A vast ocean lapped at the foot of the grassy rise. Dalan was speechless with surprise.

"That is the eastern ocean," Cuimhne crooned softly in his ear. "Your ancestors sailed across from this place generations ago to seek their new home. So many seasons have passed by since then that your people do not remember the songs of those voyages. They do not often tell the tale of their first landfall in Innisfail."

"Beyond the mists," the Brehon mumbled in a soft awed voice, "lies Innisfail?"

"Yes. The land which will one day be known as Eriu after the Danaan queen."

Then the woman turned him round again so they were walking away from the sea, passing under the impossibly tall trees which grew in an ordered wood on the other side of the hill. As they passed through the woods a new sight met Dalan's eyes. Green valleys and high-peaked mountains spread out before the disbelieving Brehon. Golden fields of wheat and oats patched a landscape irrigated by azure blue canals. As he marveled an amazing spectacle unfolded.

A great gathering of folk dressed in the same manner as Cuimhne stood in the midst of a yellow field of barley. Dalan was about to inquire the purpose of this meeting when the sound of low humming came to his ears.

A dozen men and women had stepped out from the crowd with huge bronze trumpets that curled like the horns of a cow. The sound emanating from these musical instruments was a thrumming call reminiscent of lowing cattle but much more powerful.

"Music of the Draoi," Dalan muttered. "I have never heard the likes of it."

"It is rarely heard these days in the lands before death," Cuimhne informed him. "Your folk are too consumed with their petty wants and goals. They will not rediscover this mystery until they throw off the shackles of desire. This music is the essence of the pure spirit of all people. These musicians are weaving the Draoi-Craft. If they had acted sooner their holy prayer-song might have turned events around. Alas but the melody commenced too late to save their homeland."

Once again Dalan felt his body begin to vibrate. His guts turned with the trembling resonance of the music. And then the choir of women began to sing. It was a high floating melody that danced around in delicate trills contrasting the steady low vibrato of the horns.

When the men's voices joined in Dalan began to feel very faint, as if the music held some strange power over the senses.

"I am drunk," he managed to whisper, though Cuimhne made no sign she heard him.

As the melody built to an urgent crescendo the Brehon had to drop to his haunches. He was so overcome with a nauseating dizziness he was finding it difficult to focus. A moment later a strange light began to course across the field in rhythmic pulsing beats of bright white. When this ceased and the light faded, a whirlwind formed in the middle of the field.

The choir raised the pitch of their song and the pace doubled. Dalan thought his head would surely burst if the music continued much longer. His ears were aching and his stomach convulsed in punishing spasms. Just when he was sure he was going to faint the song ceased abruptly and all was quiet again. In seconds the whirlwind disappeared, leaving behind a wide swath cut into the crops in the form of an intricate spiraling circle.

Dalan's ears were ringing and his head spun as if he had been at the very center of the twirling windstorm. But when he noticed the strange design in the barley he struggled to his feet again and stood silenced by the spectacle, arms hanging limp by his sides.

"The earth is our mother," Cuimhne told him. "Her life force is strong. In the ancient days our people knew the paths of the sacred force. They harnessed her energy for the good of all."

"Until new songs were sung," Dalan continued. "Songs of destruction, greed, jealousy and fear."

"Raising storms with the Draoi-Music will not keep the invaders at bay," Cuimhne said, shaking her head. "Even if your people could conjure the fires of the earth, as your ancestors once did, it would avail them not. The strangers will come. And these Milesians are the first of many."

"Will we be swept away?"

"Not if you learn to live with your neighbors."

"What do you mean?"

"Use the Draoi-Songs for the benefit of all," Cuimhne advised. "For the good of Fir-Bolg, Danaan and invader alike. If you all work together, the ways of Fir-Bolg and Danaan will be preserved. Share the bounty of your knowledge and the future will be a graceful dance of partnership and preservation of the land. Have compassion for your fellow beings and learn cooperation and compassion."

"What if we cannot all agree to work together?"

"Then no song will save you from the destruction that is to come. Remember the tales of the Islands of the West. The Druids of those times thought they had achieved the pinnacle of knowledge but they only brought famine, fire and flood upon their land. When their greedy melodies brought the star crashing to earth, the bowels of this world opened. Mountains spewed forth molten rock which covered their homes."

"And yet the ancients venerated the red-hot lakes of that land," Dalan continued, struggling to recall the tale, "because they believed such places were gateways leading to the Otherworld."

"You have learned your craft well." As Cuimhne spoke Dalan felt the ground beneath his feet tremble. "We must go now to the stone circle," she told the Brehon. "Do not fear. No harm will come to you there."

"What is happening?"

"The end of days has come upon us," Cuimhne explained. "You are witnessing the final moments of the Islands of the West. These lands are about to be torn asunder in retribution for the Druids' unchecked use of the Draoi-Songs. Remember well what you see here."

Dalan's eyes widened in confusion as she took his hand again to lead him back through the wood toward the summit.

"What you see before you is the past," the woman soothed. "You stand beyond the bounds of this place. You cannot be harmed."

"What can you tell me of the future?" Dalan cut in.

But Cuimhne offered no answer as she hurried him along to the top of the hill and the shelter of the stones.

"Here stand the seven," she told him. "Two more roam the world. You must take great care they do not interfere with the peace between the Danaans and the invaders. If any force in creation can bring disaster to your kindred it is those two."

"I don't understand," the Brehon said.

As he spoke the sky was ripped open by streaking purple lightning. Dark clouds blotted out the sun and the sea began to boil with fury as the elements gathered to do battle.

"I speak of the Nine Watchers of Balor who were once the greatest threat to the Danaans and the Fir-Bolg."

"Balor was destroyed in the time of my great-grandfather. Surely he poses no danger to us now?" Dalan's alarm was obvious.

"Balor is gone," Cuimhne assured him. "You need not fear. Lugh of the Many Skills put an end to him. But Balor's servants lived on for a long while after their master departed to the Halls of Waiting."

"The Watchers are still among us?" the Brehon gasped in disbelief.

"The two remaining are the most dangerous of all. They know their days are nearly at an end and they live in terror of what will become of them. That pair will stop at nothing to prolong their existence. Be careful where you place your trust. They have a longer vision than you and may act with treachery."

"How can you be so sure they will cause trouble?" Dalan asked.

Cuimhne turned and pointed to the seven stones set in an almost complete circle. "Because if they do not, they are fated to join their comrades here. This is not death. These poor souls are trapped for the rest of eternity as sleeping stones. They are aware of their surroundings but are unable to move or cry out. This is an agony worse than any death.

"Go to them," Cuimhne urged. "Touch one of the stones and you will know what I know."

The Brehon hurried over to the nearest blue granite tooth as the rain began to fall in droplets the size of quail eggs. The storm was rising to an unbelievable fury now. Birds dropped from the sky, stunned by lightning and thunder. The sea whipped up and spray was carried even to the top of this hill.

Dalan went to the first stone and stood before it.

"Place your palms flat against the surface," Cuimhne yelled above the noise of the tempest.

The Brehon did as he was told. Immediately everything that was happening around him became insignificant. A strange unearthly voice came, filled his senses, and he backed away from the granite in surprise.

"She cannot harm you," Cuimhne called out in reassurance. "Do not be afraid. It is the Watchers who are not yet clothed in stone you should fear most."

Dalan reluctantly placed his palms up against the stone again. Immediately he noticed the surface was warm to his touch. Then he heard the voice again.

"I am Sarna . . . Sarna," the voice repeated, as if singing a song with no other words.

In the tips of his fingers Dalan could feel a pleasant tingling. The feeling soon began to extend up his arms

into his shoulders. The storm around him was growing to a furious intensity but he barely noticed.

The Brehon saw in his mind's eye a tall woman
with dark skin and long black hair beautifully braided
down her back. She wore great silver half-moons for
earrings. Her arms were painted blue with intricate
tattoos laid out in geometric patterns.

"What do you want?" she demanded suddenly as if
woken from her own trance. "Why are you disturbing
me? Have you come to take me away to the land of
spirits? Is my time here done at last?"

Dalan was so shocked and surprised he could not
answer. His arms were beginning to ache now and the
stone began to glow with a gentle luminescence. A
spiral of light surrounded the base of the granite slab.
This spiral slowly began to wind its way up toward
the top. As it reached his hands Dalan felt a faintness
come upon him again.

"What should I do?" he called out to Cuimhne.

"The Milesian Gaedhals have been drawn here
through the cunning of the Watchers," she replied.
"These invaders are distant kin to the Danaans and the
Fir-Bolg. But their ancestors departed the Islands of
the West before the moon descended and the earth
erupted. Their laws and customs do not hold the
Druids of their race to account for misusing their
skill."

"How will we defeat them?"

"You will not defeat them with swords but you
may win them over with words. Convince them to

change their ways, to throw off the barbarism of their ancestors. Teach them your Brehon laws; join in partnership with their folk. There is no other way. If you attempt to defeat them in battle they will certainly prevail."

Dalan frowned deeply as he considered Cuimhne's advice.

"The Fir-Bolg and Danaans will cease to be. If they are not scattered to the four winds they will melt away from the world and disappear. Without the wisdom of your people the Gaedhals will dabble in the little Draoi knowledge they possess. In time Innisfail will fall to the same fate that came upon the Islands of the West in times long past. Do you want to see that?"

The wind whipped up the Brehon's hair as he shook his head. The gale rose suddenly in intensity, almost lifting Dalan up off his feet. He cried out in fright. Then the wind dropped again, leaving him hugging the standing stone for support.

When the Brehon's breathing had calmed he turned to face Cuimhne. But he was alone on the top of the hill, save for a strange living pinnacle of rock in his arms.

"Stay with me," the stone begged him in a seductive tone. "Tell me of the goings-on in the world beyond the circle. I will grant you a wish if you remain here with me. Anything your heart desires. I promise. Stay with me. I am Sarna."

The Brehon struggled to break free of the stone's Otherworldly grip as bolts of bright intense lightning struck the hill all about him, throwing up the turf and mud. One after another the fiery arrows descended from the heavens, each closer to him than the last, until he was sure the next would shatter the frame of his mortal body.

Then in a breathtaking purple rage the sky lit up from horizon to horizon. Dalan looked toward the clouds, tried to free his hands once more as a bolt descended toward him with a crackling, groaning roar. The Brehon had no chance to cry out as the sky fire struck him on the crown of the head.

His hands flew free of the stone, his body shook uncontrollably. The Raven-feather cloak dropped away from his shoulders. The Brehon screamed with all the force of his lungs until his strength was gone and he could cry no more. Then, sobbing like a little child, he fell back on the grass.

"Do not fear adversity," Cuimhne advised. Though he could not see the woman, her voice rang clear. "It is only through adversity you will gain wisdom, only through affliction you will discover that which heals you."

When Dalan opened his eyes again he was naked and shivering, lying on his back on the rock ledge where he had fallen asleep. The sun had set, his fire had died down and his hands clutched a heavy cloak made of Raven feathers.

Chapter 3

THREE HOURS AFTER DAWN THE THICK CLOVER GLISTENED with countless tiny beads of reflected light as a rainy squall petered out. Clouds melted away, caught up in the wind from the south. Then all the countryside around the two hills of the battleground was basked in cheering sunshine.

A youth, seventeen summers old, too young yet to dress as a warrior, crouched low in the long grass on the flat summit of one of these hills. His heart beat wildly with excitement as he scoured the countryside for any sign of the enemy.

"Aoife, where are you?" he whispered under his breath. His black hair had grown longer since the winter and he had more weight to him, but his eyes were as dark as ever. They had earned him the nickname of Brandubh, which meant Raven in the language of his kinfolk.

No more than a dozen paces away at the edge of

the hilltop lay his sister Aoife, two summers younger than he yet already wiser and bolder than her brother in many respects. Stretched out flat on her stomach on a rocky outcrop she watched intently the open plain below her. And ignored Sárán's impatient mumblings. She didn't want to be distracted for a second.

Sárán brushed the locks away from his eyes and decided it was time the two of them made their way back to their father's camp. This adventure had been thrilling to begin with, but now he was concerned they might be discovered.

"Aoife!" he hissed urgently, hoping to get her attention without giving away their position.

She ignored him. The young man breathed heavily with frustration.

"We must go now!" he grunted urgently. "Before we're caught!"

"I haven't seen any Danaan warriors yet," she hissed.

The young woman turned to face her brother and as she did so her eyes widened in surprise.

"Sárán!" she called but her warning came too late.

Before he knew what had happened a heavy blow hit the young man hard square in the middle of his back. He fell forward face first into the grass as surely as if he had been kicked down by an ox. His body hit the ground and he cried out with shock. Almost immediately the stunned youth felt a huge weight come crashing down upon him to pin him securely.

"Sárán!"

He heard his sister cry out to him but he could not see her. And in any case he was powerless to reply. Sárán Brandubh was struggling just to breathe. He strained his neck turning his head in search of his sister.

"Get up, Sárán!" the young woman cried as he caught a flash of Aoife's red hair out of the corner of his eye.

Before he could raise a plea to her for help, the confused young man heard a muffled grunt. Then suddenly the great immobilizing weight rolled off him and he could breathe again. Sárán slowly turned over onto his back and coughed until he thought he would burst.

When the fit was at its worst he felt an arm around his shoulders and his sister's hand on his forehead.

"Are you hurt?" she pleaded, but Sárán could not speak for a long while without coughing. When he eventually caught his breath and was able to look around him he saw the body of a large man lying face up in the grass.

The young man took a few moments to identify the shape. Then he jumped up in fright. He would have run off too if his feet had not been frozen to the spot with fear. A naked warrior with intricate painted designs covering his entire body was stretched out senseless. Sárán shook his head and blinked in the hope he was imagining things. But when he opened his eyes again the unconscious stranger was still there.

He was a large middle-aged man with a thick neck. A stout spear of ash and a small round shield lay beside his body. Hie head still rested against the rock that had broken his fall and rendered him senseless.

"Is he dead?" the young man stuttered.

"He is merely sleeping. He'll wake soon enough."

There were a few simple beaded adornments in the man's braided hair and around his neck. Broad blue-green painted lines snaked over his great bulky body. It was these stripes—war markings—that declared the stranger a Danaan. He was one of the enemy.

"Aoife, what happened?" Sárán gasped as he gingerly touched his ribs searching for any breakages.

"He didn't even see you," the young woman whispered with awe in her voice. This was her first taste of a real fight. She had never been near the battleground before. She gently brushed the long skeins of straight black hair from her brother's face. "The poor fool simply stumbled over you." She daubed a few light kisses of sympathy on Sárán's brow then continued speaking.

"The stranger fell over and hit his head on a stone without ever being aware that you existed. I never guessed fighting could be so easy. By the way, I'm sure Mother would like to learn that throw from you. She has often wished to be able to knock Father out before he realized she was there at all. It will come in handy when he returns home drunk late at night."

"Still your tongue. We're not supposed to be here, remember?" Sárán reminded her tersely. "I could have been killed and it would have been all your fault."

"You won't get killed if you always fight like that," she laughed, standing up to offer her hand to him.

"Father would skin us alive if he knew we were here," the young man breathed nervously. He took her hand and she hauled him to his feet.

"What is he going to do to us?" She shrugged. "We're heroes. We captured an enemy scout."

Sárán frowned, then a thought struck him.

"Oh no, Aoife," he stammered. "What have we done?"

"We have defeated a Danaan warrior. He is our prisoner."

"He is only our captive so long as he sleeps," Sárán pointed out.

"Tie him up then."

"But how will we get him back to Father's camp?"

"I didn't think of that," Aoife admitted. "Can you walk?"

"I'm not certain. I don't think I'm too badly hurt. Just shaken."

"Then we must take the captive to Father."

"It is our duty," Sárán agreed reluctantly. "But how will we do it?"

"He must weigh as much as a pony. We can't carry him."

"I am more worried about his comrades finding us before we reach safety. If we're discovered we'll have to put up a fight."

"We are King Brocan's children. What would the Danaans do if they captured us?" Aoife stuttered, fear slightly tainting her words.

"I don't imagine they'll treat us very well," Sárán

replied. "Do you think any of them might guess what part we had to play in Fearna's misadventure?"

"No. I haven't spoken a word to anyone about that night."

"Let's tie this one up," he suggested. Sárán bit his lip as he considered admitting to his sister that he had not kept the details of Fearna's death from Lom. "And then we'll go and fetch some of Father's warriors."

Aoife nodded but she was not really taking any notice. Her thoughts were off with Fearna. She sat back down against a rock and stared off into the distance as her brother took the leather straps from his small basket to make some strong restraints.

Sárán had just wrapped the sinews round the Danaan's wrists when he heard the sound of footsteps running up the hill.

"Lay down your weapons!" came a firm and threatening command. "If you do so now you will not be harmed. You are trespassing on Danaan land."

Sárán looked at his sword which lay in the grass just out of reach. He swallowed hard before answering boldly, "It is you who is trespassing on Fir-Bolg territory."

A young naked warrior stood up out of the grass. His honey-colored hair was knotted into long braids. His eyes were mellow blue, determined and expressive. He had obviously earned his right to stand with the warriors of his people. The designs painted on his body were not as many or as intricate as those of the other Danaan, but they marked his profession.

The terrifying sight of this savagely arrayed stranger sent Sárán diving into the grass for his short-bladed weapon. The Danaan spoke again as Sárán stepped forward to defend himself.

"You are wrong. This part of the battleground was given to my people to defend. You are trespassing."

"The whole of the west of Innisfail belongs by right to the Fir-Bolg from the days of our ancestors. The Danaans are invaders. Wherever you go you are trespassing," Aoife declared as she drew her own sword.

The siblings moved slowly closer to each other until their shoulders touched.

"I will take him on," Sárán told his sister. "You must run to get help."

"I'll stand by you," she snapped, annoyed at the suggestion. "I am a better fighter than you in any case."

"If anything happens to you, Father will murder me," the young man whispered.

"To say nothing of what I will do to you," Aoife quipped.

Her brother shook his head. "If you know what's good for you, you'll leave us be," he challenged the warrior, but the threat sounded hollow. The Danaan laughed.

"You are trespassing," he repeated. Then he turned his attention to Aoife. As his eyes met hers she felt the resolve melt away from her. Suddenly she was shaking.

"Throw down your blades and no harm will come to you," the stranger ordered.

Aoife had never seen a Danaan painted for war before this morning and this strange barbaric fellow fascinated her.

"You are my prisoners," he went on. "You must not refuse to give up your swords or you'll be breaking the truce," he added in a tone of friendly advice.

"Where will you take us?" Aoife demanded.

"To the King of the Danaans. He is an honorable man. You will be well treated and cared for until you are free to go home."

"When would that be?"

"After the battle of course. You were caught trespassing. You must withdraw from the field so you can't take part in the fight tomorrow. As soon as the conflict is decided you will be set free."

Sárán swallowed hard. His mind was buzzing with possibilities, any idea that might save him the dishonor of capture. He was going to fight tomorrow and no Danaan was going to stop him.

Sárán turned to his sister and mouthed a word.

"What?" she asked.

"Run, Aoife," he said calmly.

"Run?"

"Run!" he screamed.

She was so startled by the power of his voice that she turned and took a dozen steps before she came to her senses. Then she stopped and turned around. She would have gone back to stand at her brother's side but it was already too late. The stranger had leapt forward to lunge at Sárán with a leaf-shaped blade. In a very short while Sárán was already retreating, driven back by the relentless attack.

The stranger was very light on his feet. Every move he made was like a step in an intricate dance. There was a gentle grace to him, thought Aoife. He was relaxed, almost playful about his task. He was not a warrior at heart, she decided.

The stranger may not have possessed the spirit of a warrior but he had the experience of one. And he was not about to let his opponent escape. With sword raised high the Danaan advanced two paces then brought his weapon down hard at his opponent's skull. Sárán blocked the blow and pushed the enemy blade away, but he hardly had time to recover before a driving thrust was aimed at him

The young man parried the sword but struggled to keep the stranger's weapon from tearing into him. His fine saffron shirt tore at the sleeve with one stab from the Danaan. And before he had time to bemoan the damage to his precious shirt another blow came down. The young man blocked it well but lost his balance on the uneven ground.

In the next moment Sárán was hastily ducking away to avoid a wide sweep from the Danaan's sword. The blade came so close to his face that he felt the rush of air as it passed. He had not recovered before the enemy made another sweep. This time Sárán was not fast enough. The very tip of the weapon caught him just above the eye. Blood trickled down his cheek into the corner of his mouth and the taste of it frightened him more than anything he had ever known.

Sárán had often wondered what it would be like to fight in a real battle. Now the only thought on his mind was to stay out of the swinging arc of that fearful blade.

The stranger struck two more blows well parried by the young Fir-Bolg. Then the Danaan took a few paces back to rest. Sárán recovered his composure and raised his blade again.

"Since you won't come peacefully," the Danaan panted, "I will have to teach you something of the ways of the warrior."

"Stay away from him!" Aoife yelled defiantly. "He is my brother!"

She strode forward to stand by Sárán in a show of boldness but there was a tremor in her voice that betrayed her fear.

The Danaan let his blade dangle point to the ground for a moment. He looked her square in the eye, smiled and lifted his sword, extending the point to her brother. Aoife was caught in the Danaan warrior's stare.

"There are two of us," she ventured, unblinking.

The stranger laughed, circling the point of his sword in the air in front of Sárán. Suddenly he froze, then lowered his blade.

"He is your brother?" the Danaan asked, indicating Sárán with a brisk nod of the head.

"Yes."

"You are both too young to be on the battlefield. You can't be older than fourteen summers."

"I am sixteen," Aoife replied indignantly. "And my brother will be eighteen at the next full moon."

"You're sixteen?" the Danaan asked with a smile.

She nodded.

"Since you are so young," the stranger declared, "I will allow you to go back to your own people and tell them exactly what happened here this morning."

Aoife breathed a sigh of relief and dropped the point of her weapon, returning his smile. "Thank you," she sighed. "We don't really want to fight with you."

"What are you talking about?" Sárán yelled. "He is the enemy! It is our duty to capture him and take him back to Father's camp."

"This was a mistake," Aoife replied. "We should be grateful he is letting us go. I don't want Father to know what we've been up to. He expressly forbade us to follow the warriors out here. I can't imagine he'd be too happy if we ended up as guests of the Danaan king."

Sárán grumbled under his breath but he knew she was right. This was a chance to walk away from what could have been a very embarrassing encounter.

"Very well," Sárán conceded, addressing his sister. "I agree with you. Perhaps it would be best to accept this warrior's offer."

"You have misunderstood me," the Danaan cut in. "The young woman may go. She is not of warrior age.

Under the rules of war I am not permitted to take her captive. But you"—the stranger turned to Sárán—"you are just old enough to be considered a warrior. And you have defended yourself well. You must come with me to answer for this intrusion."

With that he picked up his sword again and leveled it at the young Fir-Bolg.

"You will have to take us both then!" Aoife declared. "I will not abandon my brother."

"Then I am sorry to say we will have to fight," the Danaan sighed.

Aoife raised her blade as he spoke and lunged forward to strike. But the stranger effortlessly blocked her attack.

Sárán moved around to strike from behind while his sister kept the Danaan's attention. The stranger was obviously impressed with her skill. She held the blade lightly so that she could swing, parry or stab with as little effort as possible. But that was also her weakness.

When the Danaan struck her blade her grip weakened and the weapon flew out of her hand. It flew swishing over the top of the long grass to land ten paces away. She swiftly moved to pick it up but the stranger blocked her with the point of his sword. Then he quickly knelt down to retrieve the blade himself.

"Submit to me or I will strike you down without mercy," the fair-haired stranger advised in a serious tone. He watched her intently as he sheathed her sword in his belt. Aoife's eyes were twin fires of rage. She looked as if she would leap at his throat if he dropped his guard. Sárán hovered to the enemy's right, searching for an opportunity to attack.

The Danaan seemed entranced by the young woman who stared him down so defiantly. Copper red hair was rare among his people. He had only once before seen anyone with such long locks of it. He was fascinated.

"Will you submit?" he asked after a long pause.

"I will not submit to a dead man," Aoife replied.

"What do you mean?"

No sooner had he asked the question than he understood her meaning. Remembering Sárán the Danaan spun around to face him. "You slipped my mind for a moment there," the warrior conceded. "That was careless of me."

In the next breath he thrust six swift stabs which had Sárán Brandubh gasping to avoid them. While the young Fir-Bolg was still reeling from that attack the enemy warrior ran forward, grabbed his opponent's sword hand and knocked the weapon out of his grasp. Sárán fell backward in shock and disappeared from his sister's view in the soft net of the long grass.

As her brother fell Aoife's rage boiled over. Before she knew what she was doing she had emptied her lungs, screaming at the stranger in fury. He took no notice of her. The warrior did not want to be caught off guard again.

"Get away from my brother!" the young woman

bellowed with all her strength and would have stepped forward to lay her fists upon the Danaan had something not happened to distract her.

She distinctly heard the voice of her brother calling out her name. This confused her for a brief moment because the call came from well behind her. Sárán had fallen ten paces in front of her. Aoife turned, keeping an eye on the enemy in case he should rush at her. Then she caught sight of someone a short distance down the hill. Her eyes widened.

"Oh no!" Aoife cried. "Now there will really be trouble."

The stranger watched the color drain from the young woman's face. Intrigued, he followed the line of her stare. When he realized what she was looking at his mouth dropped open.

Now it was his turn to feel fear tingle against his skin. The Danaan warrior shook his head as he looked down at the unconscious form of the young dark-haired man in the grass before him. Then he looked back up at the youth who was now charging toward him with clenched fists and fury in his eyes.

These two Fir-Bolg youths had the same face. It was more than that, they were the very same man. The Danaan shook his head.

Their eyes were as black. Their hair brushed back the same way. They both wore saffron and brown. Though this one had his shirt tied about his waist.

"Fir-Bolg trickery," he stuttered. "I must have fallen for one of their illusions."

The young Danaan well knew these folk were capable of subtle disguises, clever ruses and confusing spells to take advantage of their opponents. All the old stories spoke of these skills. His warrior's resolve faded. His enthusiasm for the fight waned. He dropped the point of his sword and took a step back.

This was just enough to give the charging youth a slight advantage. He was able to get close enough to his shocked enemy to punch him hard in the stomach and wrestle the sword from his hand. Before the Danaan could react he took another heavy blow across the jaw and lost his balance. When he landed on his back he lay still on the grass, unable or unwilling to move. And the thought never crossed his mind that this apparition might be his opponent's twin.

"Lom! How in the name of heaven did you find us?" Aoife demanded.

"When you didn't invite me on your adventure I decided to follow you anyway," Lom replied. There was a tremble in his voice that made her feel ill. She had never seen him so frightened before.

"I've been tracking you all morning and you had no idea." Lom tried to laugh. "You'll make a fine pair of scouts."

"What hit me?" Sárán grunted as he tried to get up.

"A Danaan who will soon be asking the same question," Lom answered, indicating the warrior. "I would rather be elsewhere when these two regain their senses." He moved to help his twin stand up. "I suggest we make a run for it in case there are any more about like them."

"We can't just leave them here!" Aoife protested. "We should take one of them back to Father's camp. The information they could provide might prove valuable."

"We are going to have to help our brother home. He has been badly beaten. How do you imagine we are going to carry two Danaans on our backs as well?"

The question was never answered. At that moment the first and larger of the two enemy warriors began to stir. The huge man rubbed his head and shook it as he rolled over onto his side.

"We must hurry!" Lom insisted. He took his twin brother by the shoulder then picked up Sárán's sword. At the same time the large Danaan warrior got to his knees.

"Fir-Bolg!" he shouted when his eyes fell on the scene before him.

And not far off there was an answering call. A long low howling horn blast that rose in pitch as it petered out.

Immediately there was another call followed by yet another, blown in short sharp urgent bursts. From all along the little valley the Danaans were gathering to the aid of their comrades.

Lom grabbed Aoife. "Run for your life!" he yelled but the words had barely left his mouth before his sister had broken away from him. By the time Lom turned his attention back to Sárán she had sprinted across the top of the hill out of sight.

And as she disappeared from view a cold wind arose from the south hugging the top of the summit. Swirls of dust, grass and leaves sailed spiraling high into the air. Then as quickly as it had appeared the wind dropped again and Lom was left with a terrible feeling of foreboding.

He handed the blade to his brother as a frightening sound fell on his ears. Somewhere nearby he could hear laughter. It was dark and entirely without joy. It was the kind of laughter he imagined might have suited one of Balor's legendary demons for it froze his heart with despair.

Then the laughter too was gone and Lom was helping his brother to his feet.

One hundred thousand paces from the battleground in barren land, where only mosses thrived, stood three circular gray-green earthen mounds perfectly shaped and finely wrought. In ancient days within these stone-lined hills dark chambers were constructed to give shelter to the gods and goddesses on their journeys through the land. In later times the chambers became the center of ritual activity. Each clanhold put a great deal of effort into enticing their deities to tarry near their settlements. But the minds of mortals change constantly. That which is considered sacred today may be forgotten within two generations.

And so it was with the stony hills. Countless summers burned away to winters. The chambers within lay empty and neglected. Until in the end they provided sanctuary for only two restless Fomorian souls.

The last of the Watchers.

At the end of a long irregular rock-hewn passage deep within the largest mound there was a massive flat circular stone. A single oil-burning lamp was positioned on one side of this slab. Its slowly pulsing flame painted the chamber in a golden glow.

Damp walls glistened, sharpening the details of countless spiral carvings. The interior of the chamber was completely covered in these motifs. Over the ceiling, across parts of the floor and on every upright stone the spirals twirled their way. And in the lamplight the designs seemed to be dancing.

Two figures dressed in long dark traveling cloaks sat on small stones at opposite sides of the flat table rock. They both stared at the flame of the oil lamp and leaned their chins on their hands in silent contemplation. Neither spoke nor so much as moved. They could have been mistaken for rocky outcrops.

On the table before them cut into the stone were carved bands of decoration. The pattern these straight lines described was a gaming board. And on this perfect square were laid playing pieces of bone and blackwood.

The Danaans knew this game as Fidchell. The Fir-Bolg called it Brandubh. Raven. The dark pieces were named after the great black carrion birds because they swarmed around the edge of the board devouring any piece venturing too close.

In the days before the flood the Brandubh was held sacred. The subtle moves, potent symbols and secret numbers crafted into the game concealed all the mysteries of the earth. So holy was the pastime that it had been preserved by every race who had ever inhabited the Islands of the West.

The lamp spluttered a little. One of the figures twitched then touched a finger to her lips. Her opponent shifted in his seat and straightened his back. He ran the palm of his hand across the top of his perfectly bald head and yawned.

"You play a challenging round when you have a mind to," he said eventually.

"Playing this game was my greatest joy in the old days," the other figure answered in an enticing feminine voice. "That is to say, it was *one* of my greatest joys."

She looked up from under the hood covering her head. Fine brown locks fell around her face as she drew back her cloak. Her eyes were bright green and vibrant, her skin the color of buttermilk. She smiled, hoping to discern some sign of life in her companion's eyes.

"Of course that was long before I met you," she added. "What were you doing, Lochie, before we went to Balor?"

"I don't think of those days," her companion mumbled, not wishing to discuss this matter. "I find it better to stay in the here and now. If I dwell on the past I begin to suffer from remorse."

"What's wrong with nurturing a few regrets?"

"They are a waste of precious energy," he answered gruffly. "There are more important matters for me to concentrate my mind upon."

"I was happy then," Isleen confided. "Before the war and all the strife that followed. In the days before Balor. I have never known such happiness since, despite all the fine promises we were made."

"Do not speak so!" Lochie snapped and his voice echoed in the stone chamber. "I do not regret anything I have done. That is what has kept me from falling into the Great Sleep. You would be wise to learn to put aside all remorse and might-have-beens. Such thoughts will only bring sorrow to your heart."

"My memories are mostly pleasant," she sighed. "For I enjoy the sad feeling which accompanies them. It reminds me that I once was mortal."

"How many seasons have gone by since Balor was killed?" Lochie asked, trying to change the subject.

"I ceased to keep a tally after three hundred," Isleen replied. Then she reached out with long nimble fingers to lift one of the gaming pieces from the board. She held it in her palm for a second before placing it carefully on a new square. She kept her hand on the piece until she had made absolutely certain the move was safe.

Her companion watched her intently.

"Let's say a thousand summers have gone by," he ventured. "Isn't it time your memory was beginning to fail you? Aren't you ready to gather in some new recollections? Why do you always talk of the days before Balor as if it were some charmed time when everything was perfect? It wasn't perfect, you know. There was a war and a famine to deal with."

He stared at the ceiling to avoid her eyes.

"Lochie," she asked, ignoring his annoyance, "are you saying you never find yourself thinking about the old days?"

"Never." Lochie brushed the knee of his traveling breeches and lifted a silver cup to his lips, hoping his companion would not pursue this questioning.

"Do you ever wonder what might have become of us if we had not entered into Balor's service?"

"Never."

"Never?"

"I told you," Lochie repeated clearly, losing his patience, "I don't think about such things. What use is there in wondering what may have been? The past cannot be changed. We are as we are. The future will unfold in its own sweet time. We must live for now, for today. And we must discover a way to avoid our fate. That's all I know."

"I often wonder what might have been," Isleen pressed.

"You and I live now according to the results of our own wishes," Lochie reminded her, his temper already cooling. "If we had chosen otherwise it may have been different, but who's to say? Did the ones we left behind have better lives?"

"I wonder," Isleen replied.

"You are a fool," Lochie told her. "We are very fortunate. When Balor asked us for our wishes, you and I spoke the wisest of all the Sidhe-Dubh, though perhaps we didn't realize it at the time."

"I feel sorry for the others. Their pleasures were so easily sated. Then they had to live with them for the rest of eternity. At least you and I have something to look forward to each day."

"We were very fortunate." Lochie nodded in whole-hearted agreement. Then he reached out a long bony hand and picked up one of the dark pieces from the gaming board. He held it up to the light to inspect the craftsmanship.

"This is a fine set." Lochie smiled. "Where did you get it?"

"A gift."

"From the Danaan king?"

"Yes."

"Cecht is an outstanding warrior and a just ruler," Lochie stated. "His court is rich and his craftsmen among the best in the land."

"He has always had the good of his people at heart," Isleen agreed.

"But what reason could he have to gift you this set of gaming pieces?"

Isleen shifted uncomfortably in her seat.

"Don't tell me you accepted it as a reward for the granting of some favor!" Lochie hummed, delighted at the prospect of some relaxation in his companion's strict code of conduct.

"No. It wasn't that," Isleen countered.

Lochie placed the black piece upon the board, Isleen watching his move attentively.

"I was playing against Cecht," she went on, "and the king insisted on a wager. He promised me I could have anything my heart desired if I beat him. I quickly outmaneuvered him. It wasn't difficult. I have been playing this game for a lot longer than he has. I know all the moves."

"Is the Danaan king not wed to a queen?"

"His wife has been dead these seven seasons," Isleen answered quickly, then realized she had spoken a little too warmly.

"And if you had lost the game," Lochie asked, intrigued, "what would you have paid the king for your wager?"

"Cecht wanted to hear the tale of Balor."

"Are you saying the king knows what you are?" Lochie gasped in shock.

"He does not!" Isleen insisted. "I am posing as a wandering Bard from the North Country. That tale is a favorite of his."

"You should be careful."

"King Cecht has no notion of my real purpose. I am certain of that."

"And just what is your real purpose, Isleen?"

The woman blushed and pulled the hood back over her head.

"You mean to wed him, don't you?"

"Nonsense." Isleen laughed unconvincingly. "We

enjoy each other's company, that's all. What good would come of such an arrangement?"

"If you had lost the game," Lochie pointed out, "you would have had to tell him everything you know of Balor and the downfall of the Fomorians. You are far too honest to omit any detail. You surely know much more of the tale than any of the mortal Bards. The king would have immediately known you are not of his people. A fool could have concluded you are a Watcher. And the Danaan king is no fool."

"Cecht is wise but I am a much better player than he is." Isleen smiled. "There was really no chance he could win." With that she picked up one of the white pieces and deftly skimmed it along the surface of the stone board until it came to rest in a new square.

"You must have desperately wanted to possess this set." Lochie squinted. "But you are not usually one to let desire or passion rule your life. I have never seen you place yourself in peril of discovery before. Are you beginning to become bored?"

"Not at all," Isleen snapped and her eyes flashed a deeper green. "I had grown tired of the old gaming pieces. I don't know how long I carried them round. They are crude and poorly made compared to these. And some of the old set are chipped and worn with all the traveling I have done."

"This is the start of the boredom," her companion warned, fear obvious in his tone. "The first twinges of weariness are eating at your soul. We have both seen it too many times in our fallen comrades. It begins with something small. A wish that does not seem unreasonable. A desire to possess some unusual and interesting object. Or to bed some fascinating mortal being. But we both know how it ends, don't we?"

"My soul is not suffering from the wasting sickness!" Isleen laughed, but she was not convincing Lochie. "I am in no danger of joining the others. I have a necessary part to play in the future of this land. And my wish will keep me from harm."

"That's why you're pursuing the king." Her friend giggled. "Admit that you're bored."

"That is not true," she insisted hotly. "I have learned a lot from Cecht. He has become a good friend. Beyond the sensual temptations of his company I appreciate his wit and good sense."

"You are a very good player." Lochie nodded with a wry smile. And Isleen knew he was not simply referring to the Brandubh. "I am glad we have stayed friends through all the hardships and grief. Truly we have shared the bitter with the better. I don't wish to think of what it would be like to have to go on without you."

"I never tire of my work," she assured him. "The wasting sickness will not take me."

"I feel that way now too. But how can we be sure we won't be struck down? Remember Sarna. She fell to the blight so unexpectedly that she was lost to us before we could guess what was happening."

"I don't want to change into that kind of a creature." Isleen shuddered.

"Nor do I," Lochie cut in quickly, "so we must keep an eye on each other. We must make sure we are kept busy so the rot cannot set in. Both of us like to rest now and then to forget the troubles of the world, it is true. But we cannot risk falling into indolence."

Then a thought came to him. "When did Cecht's people begin to play the Brandubh again? It has been generations since they bothered to compete among themselves."

"I reintroduced the game to them," Isleen replied. "It suits my purposes to have them playing and pondering the results of their actions." She nodded toward the board. "It's your move."

Lochie regarded the pieces carefully then rubbed his eyes. "It seems once again I am beaten," he conceded. "One day I'll discover your trick."

"It's no trick," Isleen countered indignantly. "It is an art much more subtle than simply countering the moves of one's opponent. Over the seasons we have known each other I have learned to read you and your intentions merely by the expression on your face or the way you flick dust from your breeches."

She smiled with delight to be letting him in on her little secret. "I have spent so many months seated opposite you I know without thinking what strategy you are about to employ. Once in a while I let you play out your tactics, just to see if I have the skill to rescue the situation at the very last."

"And you usually do." Lochie smiled. "We would be worthy opponents in the outside world."

"No."

"It would be a challenge," Lochie argued, seeing a glimmer of interest. "No different from sitting down to a game of Brandubh. Imagine what we could achieve if we set our minds to it."

"Or what we could destroy," Isleen rejoined, shaking her head. "The lives of mortals are not to be played with. They are not soulless pieces of bone or pottery we can move at our will. If we're not careful we could set in motion the beginnings of our own destruction. I will not take up your challenge and I beg you not to broach the subject again. We have discussed this matter many times. I cannot with any conscience turn my craft to my own petty entertainment. We have a great responsibility to endure."

"Shall we play again?" Lochie asked her.

"One more round," Isleen conceded with a smile.

The two players reset the Brandubh pieces and played on long into the night. Lochie was determined to give his opponent a worthy challenge. But Isleen was too quick-witted for him and he often found himself desperately filling the gaps in his defense.

"Your play has improved," she congratulated him as the sun rose in the world outside and the latest match drew to its conclusion. "But I have won this round."

"It is not over yet," Lochie countered.

"Yes, it is." Isleen picked up her white high-king and made her move. Then she sat back and smiled with contentment.

"I can't believe I didn't see that move coming," her companion marveled.

"If you had seen it you would have done something about it. That's part of the trick," she explained. "Always plan effective covering moves. Hasty decisions come to nothing. Patience nurtures good strategy. Never let your opponent guess for an instant what you are really up to."

Lochie smiled back at her, catching a sparkle in her eyes. "We had a lot of fun together when we first met," he remembered wistfully.

"Yes, we did," she agreed in a subdued tone, turning her head away so that Lochie would not be able to look into her eyes.

"We caused a lot of havoc among the Danaans," he went on.

"That is true."

"I will always look upon those times with fondness."

"So will I," Isleen sighed.

"Then why don't we work together again? As we did when we were young. It would certainly brighten us both up to have some renewed purpose in our lives."

"I refuse to interfere with the fortunes of mortals just to amuse myself," she informed him. "Those days are ended for me."

"If you won't do it for amusement," Lochie countered, "then do it for your survival."

"What do you mean?"

"You are slipping. I can see it plainly. But you're too stubborn to admit it."

Isleen laughed nervously and waved a hand in dismissal.

"I am firm. I will not slip away. I am content as I am."

"Contentment is the first sign of trouble," Lochie warned. "Remember our brothers and sisters who have not been so fortunate. Every one of them found contentment before they began to slip away. What must their existence be like? Do you want to end up like them? Empty? Passionless? Bored? Is that what you want?"

"I have no time for boredom," Isleen replied nervously. "I have a duty to fulfill, not to Balor but to myself. I have plenty of work to keep me occupied. I watch over a few individuals who have become my favorites. And I make a point of ensuring no one suffers from my gentle meddling. The Danaan king is a perfect example."

"There is no such thing as gentle meddling." Lochie laughed. "There is only deliberate interference."

"I don't expect you to understand," she snapped. "Your purpose has taken a path quite different from mine."

"Over the years we have grown apart," Lochie admitted. "When we first started out we had a common goal. The nine of us were specters of fear to our enemies. Our assembled company was an unbeatable force."

"Until the Danaans defeated us," Isleen quipped.

"It was Balor of the Evil Eye who let us down," her companion snapped back. "You and I were never defeated. If Balor had not allowed his pride to rule his decisions, the Danaans would have been overrun and the world would be a different place. The Children of Danu are still our enemies."

"There are no more Fomor," Isleen said slowly. "You and I represent the last of the sea folk. We have been very fortunate to survive this long. Perhaps you are right, it is time to consider our future. No good will come of dragging up the past and using it to justify our actions. The Danaans are not my foes."

"We are the Fomor," Lochie stated. "The last of our people. We have a duty to our ancestors which must be honored. And we have an obligation to ourselves to outlive the scheming mind of Balor who abandoned us to our fate. How would our forebears judge us if they could hear this conversation?"

"Perhaps they can hear it," she whispered, regretting her hasty words. "You seem to forget," Isleen went on, "we forfeited the right to dine with our ancestors in the Otherworld when we made our oath to Balor."

"I hope to find a way around that yet," he told her. "But I'm not quite ready to give up this existence. I know my soul will be liberated one day. And I am determined to discover the means to set it free. Until then I have a duty to myself to keep active and not to risk going to sleep. You have seen our comrades. They are prisoners for eternity in a circle of stone."

"I am beginning to see your argument," Isleen whispered, unwilling to make the admission. "But in the end you must follow your path as I must try to find my own. We worked together once but that was long ago. You must pursue this destiny without me."

"I need your help!" Lochie blurted desperately.

Isleen caught the hint of panic in his voice and she carefully scrutinized his expression. Suddenly she understood what was behind their conversation. "Are you worried you might be about to slip away like the others?" she asked. She placed a hand tenderly on her companion's shoulder to comfort him.

"I am frightened," Lochie admitted. "Aren't you?"

"I have never been so afraid." She nodded.

"I will fight against this fate," Lochie vowed quietly, his eyes to the floor. "I chose my path long ago. My passion will not burn out. I will not become an empty soul like the others. There will dawn a day when this spirit is set free."

"I would dearly love to be free," Isleen admitted.

"Then you must join with me for your survival."

"I cannot," she replied. "Not if there is a chance of any mortal being hurt. I do not wish to bring any more sorrow into the world."

"That is our nature. Does an oak refuse to give acorns? Does a cow refuse to give milk? Does a warrior ask whether it is right to defend his kinfolk with the sword?"

"We don't have to bring misery into the world. I have become compassionate."

"Compassion!" Lochie spat. "Have you been playing compassionate Brandubh matches with King Cecht? It was passion not compassion that led you to his bedchamber in the middle of the night to ply the gaming board with his playing pieces."

"I am sure I detect the pungent scent of jealousy," she shot back. "I told you earlier I have a good friendship with the Danaan king. I am passing on to him many lost and forgotten customs."

"What value is all your compassion now?" Lochie hissed. "Your argument is empty if you can't show compassion to the one who has known you the longest. What use is your high-minded idealism if you can't bring yourself to aid the only other living soul on this earth who understands you?"

Lochie paused to gauge Isleen's reaction. "We are in danger," he pressed. "If either of us succumbs to the Great Sleep it will be the end of the other as well. There is nothing we can do to avoid that. I need you and you need me."

"It is true then?" Isleen asked. "You feel you are drifting away?"

"I fear that I am." Lochie nodded.

Then he looked up and locked eyes with his friend. "You simply must help me. As I must help you also."

"I will consider what you have said," Isleen agreed as she slowly bowed her head.

"Perhaps you'd like to view a little of the work I've been engaged in," Lochie offered. "If you saw what I was arranging you might be inspired to lend a hand

and perhaps slow your own decline in the process. We are both in limbo, neither of this world nor the next. And as each new day dawns we come closer to that state which has claimed our seven friends."

"What work have you been doing?" Isleen sighed in a defeated tone.

"A battle." Lochie beamed. "Shall we go to watch it? There is still time."

Isleen screwed up her nose in disgust. "War is not a very subtle way to keep oneself amused."

"When dealing with mortals," Lochie countered, "I have always found it best to be blunt and to the point. No room for subtlety with them. Most important of all, the quarrel is none of my doing."

"If it is not your quarrel, why bother?"

"I learn a great deal observing mortals as they go about their business. Their behavior reminds me of my youth. And there is no better place to witness raw unrestrained fear."

There was a pause. "I can't help myself," Isleen admitted after a moment's internal struggle. "I know I should be able to restrain my desires. I know I should not indulge. But I simply have no control when it comes to witnessing mortal fear. I am fascinated. I simply have to watch."

"I know what you mean. That is Balor's legacy to us. We feed on fear and so we live. It's our nourishment and to a certain extent we are slaves to it. For now."

"What are you talking about?"

"I intend to find a way to free us both from this bondage," he explained. "But if my plan is to succeed we will both need to build up our strength in a way we have never done before."

"And that is why you think we should work together to interfere in the lives of mortals?"

"Precisely. There will be sorrow in the world whether we guide it or not. Doesn't it make sense to turn the suffering of mortals to our advantage? When we have built up our strength we will be able to break free, change our fate and escape the end Balor had planned for us."

His companion found herself warmed by the hope in his voice. "But how can it be right to feed from the discomfort of others?" she argued.

"We will turn their fear into our freedom," Lochie explained. "We will transform an unfortunate reality into a healing release."

"I will go with you," Isleen agreed softly, her eyes betraying her interest. "But just to observe your battle, nothing more. For the time being I won't commit to aiding you."

"Then let's be on our way," Lochie urged excitedly. "There will be all sorts of trouble brewing before evening. And I don't want to miss any of it."

Chapter 4

AOIFE SCRAMBLED DOWN THE HILL IN PANIC, ALL THOUGHT of her brothers banished. Terror had a grip on her heart, blurring her vision, heightening all her other senses. She heard every twig snap beneath her feet, smelled the strong scent of her own sweat and tasted the dry salty flavor of fear in her mouth.

She was so distraught that every bush seemed to be a forest where many Danaans lurked in ambush and she soon became disoriented. Her one hope was to reach the encampment of her father, King Brocan of the Burren, but such was her terror that she had no idea in which direction the camp lay.

Panic swept over her in a wave of rising shudders. Her legs moved faster, feet flying, barely touching the ground as she ran. Halfway down the hill Aoife tripped over an exposed root. She tumbled headlong for ten paces, rolling over and over on the soft grass until at last she ended her descent face down near the bottom of the hill.

The young woman did not know how long she lay there like that before she heard herself sobbing. When she realized her face was wet with tears her resolve suddenly hardened. A bitter determination took over, enclosing her soul in its armor.

Aoife sat up to catch her breath. Her clothes were wet with perspiration, her head ached with a hot thudding at the temples. But she found herself strangely calm. As the young woman stood up to brush the grass off her clothes, she suddenly remembered Sárán and Lom. She was their only hope. It was her duty to find the Fir-Bolg camp and bring help to her brothers. She dare not tarry for too long. In a short while enemy warriors would likely be swarming all over the hill searching for her.

Soon she was stumbling on her way again with visions of a horde of Danaans in pursuit. Along the rough path to the bottom of the hill she darted this way and that, searching for cover. In her confusion she found herself barreling down a bank of earth overgrown with flowers and long grass. Somehow she managed to keep her feet without falling again. Then abruptly she came to a halt, her way blocked.

Doubled up breathless, Aoife found herself at the foot of a hill, a stand of trees forming the edge of a little wood. Thick strong bushes blocked her path in every direction. Birds sang in the trees and butterflies blundered along oblivious to the disputes of Danaan and Fir-Bolg. It was shaded and peaceful here. No sign of war.

It briefly occurred to the young woman that the woods might be full of the enemy, but she dived in among the underbrush anyway hoping to find a way through. She stumbled on with frantic haste between the trunks, running from any sounds she heard. At last, almost dropping from weariness, she realized she had lost all sense of direction. Exhausted, frightened and alone she leaned up against a tree to catch her breath.

After a moment she became aware she was hugging her right arm tightly against her chest. Then she noticed a twinge of pain. Aoife realized she must have bruised herself when she leapt into the forest. She had already forgotten her tumble down the hill.

Shortness of breath was making her head spin and her eyes were full of tears. Her mind was sharply aware of the danger all around her. She struggled to bring her breath under control.

It was a long while before she was feeling any better. She sat down against the tree trunk and threw back her head to look up at the canopy of leaves spread out above her.

"What will Father say when he finds out all three of us are here?" she asked herself, hardly knowing whether she spoke aloud or not.

"All of you!" a deep voice repeated in dismay. "May you find a speedy ship and have a strong wind in your sails if that is true. For your father will chase you down until he has spent his wrath for this stupidity. You foolish child. Where are your brothers?"

"Fergus!" the young woman cried as an old Fir-Bolg warrior held out his hand to assist her. "Uncle, you must help Lom and Sárán. They are up there with two Danaans." She pointed back in the direction from which she had come.

"They're on the hill, my lord Brocan," the man repeated, passing on the message. A dozen warriors abruptly stood up out of the bushes. The Fir-Bolg war party had been concealed close around her all along. And she hadn't realized.

"We'll not risk the lives of other warriors on those two boys," the king answered and Aoife did not miss the coldness in her father's voice. She was ashamed of herself. She should never have convinced Sárán to come with her on her adventure. Now both her brothers were in deadly danger with no one willing to rescue them. If anything happened to them she would be responsible.

Her father did not rebuke her, but his silence stung her worse than any words.

"You must help your sons!" she pleaded. "The Danaans will kill them!"

Brocan did not speak but instead turned to Fergus and slowly shook his head. The old warrior looked away with sadness in his eyes. They had silently agreed to do nothing.

"We would be safe at home awaiting the return of

the war band if it had not been for me," Aoife pressed. "This is not their fault. Don't blame them for my stupidity."

"That is quite an admission, daughter." The king turned away and stared into the forest. "But those two wouldn't be the first of our bloodline to find themselves in deadly peril at the whim of a woman. All the males of our line are weak-willed. I know I am."

"Father . . ." Aoife began but he cut her off.

"You have too much of your mother about you, young girl. You're willfully contemptuous of tradition, custom and the wisdom of your elders. And like my wife you always have an elaborate argument to present. You at least can see when you have committed some wrong."

"What about Lom and Sárán?" she breathed, shocked he could calmly leave them to be murdered by the enemy.

"If they are killed," her father told her, "you will have to answer for their deaths. And if they live, they will have learned an invaluable lesson. They will take more care for their safety in future. And they will not so easily be swayed by the speech of a pretty woman, whether she be their sister or their mother."

Aoife wondered whether her father would be acting differently if it were Fearna's life that was at risk. Brocan had openly favored his enemy's son over his own flesh and blood. She blushed with guilt at the thought and drove all memory of the dead boy from her mind.

Brocan turned to face her again, his black eyes hard and emotionless. "You will go immediately to my camp under escort and wait until I return there this evening. There is to be no battle until tomorrow. The ground is too wet. If the clouds stay away it will take the rest of this day to dry out. We will meet the Danaans in the morning."

"Are you really going to leave your sons to be captured?" she gasped.

"If they survive this trial I may allow them to join the battle tomorrow. However, you ran from the enemy, abandoning your brothers in time of need. You will not fight this year. You have too much to learn. You can't even follow a simple order to stay at home to help defend the clanhold. What would have been the result if I had lost the fight and the Danaans had decided to march on our home? Who would have been there to defend it?"

Aoife hung her head.

"You must think hard on the consequences of your actions," Brocan went on. "You are born to a royal house. You have no right to indulge your sense of adventure if it puts the lives and livelihoods of others at risk. Do you understand?"

The young woman nodded.

"Well, go and do as I tell you," her father huffed.

"Yes, Father," she replied but as she moved a sharp, urgent pain ran up her right arm. Aoife looked down at her numb hand. "I can't feel anything in my fingers," she said in shock.

"You've broken your arm," the king informed her without any hint of sympathy in his voice. "You're lucky I thought to bring Fineen along with me. He is the finest healer in the west. Go to him. He is sitting by my fireside turning the spit for our feast tonight. He'll do what he can. It's a miracle you did no other damage to yourself. You might have been killed and that would have been an end to the female line of the family. You are the last. Remember that well."

Aoife swayed as shame and pain began to overwhelm her.

Fergus put an arm gently around her waist to support her. "I'll take her back to the encampment," the old veteran offered.

"Thank you, foster-brother," Brocan replied. "We will return at sunset."

With that Fergus led Aoife away through the woods until they found the path which led to the camp.

"You don't want to take too much notice of your father," the veteran told her kindly as they walked. "He is just relieved you are safe, even though he may seem very angry."

The pain in Aoife's arm had intensified before they had gone too far. Scorching fire of agony spread down from her shoulder and ended with an uncanny lack of sensation in her fingers. She was unsteady on her feet. Her head was heavy; her feet ached. With every step her awareness faded until, before they had walked two hundred paces, she slipped into unconsciousness.

So Fergus carried the young woman the rest of the way to the Fir-Bolg camp. It was a long, slow journey but the veteran's burden was not great. It was late afternoon when Fergus laid the young woman down among her father's fine collection of bed furs then went off to find Fineen the healer.

By the time the old warrior returned with the Druid physician, Aoife had started to stir. Through tired, sore eyes she glimpsed the fair-haired man in the long blue cloak. Fineen was renowned for his skill. He was a friend to Brocan and Fergus, even though he was a Danaan. As a healer and a traveler on the sacred path he put himself above all disputes.

"She broke her arm tumbling through the trees," Fergus told Fineen.

"How long ago?" the healer inquired urgently, observing carefully the color of her eyes and tongue.

"This morning," replied the veteran with uncertainty. "No more than four hours after the dawn, I'd say."

"The evening meal is about to be preapred!" the Druid exclaimed. "I may already be too late if the blood has become poisoned. Is the flesh torn?"

He gently lifted Aoife's wounded arm, carefully cut away the sleeve of her tunic with his knife and inspected the break.

"She is lucky," Fineen sighed. "The king's only daughter may one day be able to swing her sword arm again."

"Bless your wisdom," Fergus offered.

"You will have to hold her down while I reset the break," Fineen told the old veteran. "When I move the bone she will go wild with agony." The physician took a large leather pouch from the belt hook at his waist and emptied the contents onto a low table.

The girl looked up at Fineen and blinked to clear the haziness from her vision. He smiled back, his white straight teeth gleaming against the tanned skin of his face. It was his fair locks that set him apart from those bred of Fir-Bolg stock. Few of Brocan's folk had hair as honey golden or eyes as blue as the tribes of the Tuatha De Danaan.

"You are lucky, Aoife," the healer told her. "I have a good supply of herbs and extracts to calm the pain. And I have an expertise in setting bone. I would expect you to be using that arm again by the next waxing moon after this one."

"I won't lose my fingers?" she asked with worry.

"Your fingers?"

"I can't feel anything in my fingers," she sobbed.

"I'll see to that," Fineen soothed. As he prepared his remedies the physician kept up a conversation with the young woman to calm her.

"How did you come to be out this morning?" the healer asked. "I thought we left you with your brothers at home."

"We were commanded to remain at Dun Burren," Aoife admitted. "But Sárán and I passed by the watchman before dawn and followed the warriors out here.

In the early morning fog we became lost and strayed onto the battleground."

"Fergus tells me you started a fight with a Danaan scout party. That would have been truce-breaking. It could have turned out to be very nasty, you know. Did you see any of my people?"

"Two of them. One fell over Sárán and knocked himself senseless. The other warrior appeared out of nowhere brandishing a bright blade."

"Warriors of the Danaan are dangerous folk to cross. They are highly skilled and their tempers run hot," Fineen told her solemnly.

Aoife tried to raise herself up on her good elbow as she replied. "I have—"

"Stay where you are!" Fineen barked. And Aoife was shocked at the change in his voice, which had gone from soothing and gentle to commanding in an instant. Hurt that he would talk to her in this manner, she sank back down among the furs without a sound.

"If you want to have the use of those fingers and that wrist in old age, I suggest you keep perfectly still until I am ready to set the bone," he advised her more gently.

Fineen went over to the fire in the center of the house and returned with a bronze jug of hot water. He poured some into the king's gold cup and crushed some bark into the steaming liquid. Then he stirred the water with his finger until he was satisfied with the infusion.

"Drink this," he told Aoife and, handing the cup to Fergus, added, "Make sure she swallows every drop."

A short while later the healer had finished preparing his splints and bandages and was ready to perform the bonesetting. He went to the furs and knelt down at Aoife's side.

"Are you feeling sleepy?" he asked her.

She nodded drowsily.

"Good." He wiped the strands of copper hair from her face. "Sleep then. Sleep heals bodily ills and cures the soul of all afflictions. When you awake it will be the morrow and the troubles of today will already be no more than a fading memory."

The healer watched the young woman for a few moments as the infusion took effect and she slipped into a deep, sound rest. When he was certain she had drifted off he turned to the veteran.

"Fergus, I want you to hold her down. If she starts kicking, you will have to throw your weight on her. If she becomes too violent she'll strain the break and I'll not be able to guarantee the recovery of her sword arm."

The warrior nodded as he sat down beside Aoife, waiting anxiously for the physician to do his work. He need not have concerned himself. Fineen's infusion put the girl beyond pain and the healer's skill at bonesetting was such that she did not stir at all.

As the splints were placed around the bone to protect the arm from further injury Fergus stood up to take his leave.

"I've never seen a healer work like you, Fineen," he said in awe. "The girl was hardly aware you were touching her. You are rare among the Danaans."

"The break was not too bad," Fineen answered humbly, ignoring the implied insult to his kinfolk. "And the tea I gave her was probably a little too strong. I'm not very good with guessing the right dosages for each patient."

"I'll check on her this evening before the king returns," Fergus said.

"They'll be back after sunset then?"

"Today was supposed to have been spent scouting out the best positions and discussing strategy," the veteran explained. "But we were distracted. I don't expect to see them here before dark."

"If she is asleep when you return, don't wake her," Fineen advised as he gathered up his herbs and packed them back inside his leather pouch. "She may want to sleep until tomorrow night."

"Would you have time to come and see to her too?" Fergus asked respectfully. "I would feel easier if you could. I would like to report to the king that all is well with her."

"I will make time before sunset," Fineen sighed after a few moments' thought. "I'll come after I've visited some folk from the nearby hillfort," he added as he turned to face Fergus. But the veteran had already left to go about his other duties.

Chapter 5

TWO SHADOWS PASSED BETWEEN THE TREES AT TWILIGHT. No more than a pair of blue-gray wisps caught in the draught of a spring breeze. But they were not the last remnants of an early morning fog retreating into the woods.

And they were not ropes of smoke spreading out fingers from the campfires.

These shades were a favorite form of the Sidhe-Dubh, the fabled and once-feared spirits of the dark. A sharp eye might glimpse their human form behind the veil of enchantment, but most folk would never even notice them.

That was the nature of the Watchers, a gift given them by their lord and master, Balor of the Evil Eye. This talent for remaining unseen coupled with a pro-longed lifespan made them perfect tools in the ancient war between the Fomor and the other peoples of Innisfail.

None of the Watchers had been a warrior. They had all been Druids tutored in the arts of law, music, poetry, history, healing and storytelling. Their weapons had been words. That is how they had spread discord between the Tuatha De Danaan and the Fir-Bolg to destroy their alliance against Balor.

Old habits die hard. The Watchers had been defeated so long ago their treacherous ways had become nothing more than fable, only half believed by most folk. And yet these two Sidhe-Dubh still plotted to get the better of their ancestral enemies.

"This morning," Lochie explained to his companion as they moved silently through the forest, "King Brocan's three children were discovered trespassing on the Danaan part of the field. An undeniable breach of truce, that is. It will be interesting to see what comes of it."

"How did these two peoples come to be at war this time?" Isleen asked suspiciously. She knew her companion could not resist interfering in the affairs of others.

"That's a very long story," Lochie replied evasively, drifting away from her a little.

"Long stories make the best tales in my experience," Isleen replied quickly.

"We don't have time for the whole thing."

"Lochie, we have more time than we know what to do with. Tell me the story."

"Very well then," he answered as he turned to glare at her. "I'll tell you on the way to the king's tent. It's only a short walk."

"Walk?" Isleen frowned.

But before he could answer he had begun his transformation. Isleen watched as a body took solid shape around the spirit form of Lochie.

"Walk with me," she heard him beckon in her thoughts. "It's a beautiful night for a stroll."

She smiled to herself and had to admit he was right. A few hours in the company of King Brocan and his court might be an enjoyable way to spend a warm spring evening. She began to weave a solid appearance about herself, and in a remarkably short while had taken on a new shape.

Isleen stretched her arms up to the sky and breathed deep draughts of air to fill her lungs. She hummed lowly, enjoying the vibrations spreading across her new body. But she dared not look at the world just yet. First she wanted to listen, breathe and hear her own voice crooning. Eventually she noticed a strange dull ache in her stomach and realized with surprise that she was hungry. She opened her new human eyes and before her was a dark-haired stranger.

The man smiled broadly. "Isleen, is that you?" a familiar voice asked.

"Lochie?" she whispered.

"Indeed, it is I," he declared. He held his arms wide as his green eyes twinkled with gentle mischief. "Do you like it?"

"Yes. I do."

"Won't this be fun?" Lochie teased.

"I think it might," Isleen replied, mimicking his tone. She took a few strands of her own locks in her fingers to examine the color. "I am very fond of red hair," she sighed.

"I am so glad you chose it. It's very becoming. And it reflects your true nature, don't you think?"

"You've met my Seer many times," she scolded him, "and you've never commented before."

"Your Seer has never been quite this gorgeous before," he shot back. "So, this is the traveling Druid who spends so much time playing Brandubh with King Cecht? Little wonder he doesn't mind being defeated continually and then willingly gives a fine gaming set as a prize."

"It is marvelous to breathe out in the open fields again, isn't it?" Isleen luxuriated, deliberately changing the subject.

"It is so good to laugh again too," Lochie added, "and to feel your whole body shake with mirth."

"The colors seem so much more vibrant when I have this form," Isleen marveled. "And I'm hungry!"

"Let's go to the king's tent."

"And along the way you can tell me the long story."

"The long story?" Lochie countered as he wiped a piece of dust from his eye and held it up on the tip of his finger to marvel at it. "What long story?"

Isleen came close to him and put her arm through his. Then she pushed him forward gently and they started walking. "The long story about how these two peoples came to be at war." She smiled.

"Why do you want to know that?" he asked her in mock innocence.

"Because I have a notion you might be involved somehow."

"Myself?" Lochie gasped. "I merely took advantage of circumstances as they arose. In truth I have had no part but as an occasional observer of this little tale."

"Just tell me how it happened." Isleen groaned.

"How what happened?"

"The war."

"I'll give you the quick version," he conceded, lowering his voice to a whisper. "When Cecht submitted to Brocan five seasons ago, the Brehon judges decreed that the Danaan king's youngest son Fearna would go into fosterage at Brocan's court."

"Why did Cecht give in so easily to the Fir-Bolg?"

"He was tired of the war. The conflict has dragged on for generations, ever since the days of Balor. The Danaans have never trusted the Fir-Bolg since they entered alliance with our folk the Fomor in the ancient days."

"They soon enough changed sides again when the mood took them," Isleen noted with bitterness.

"The Fir-Bolg have inhabited Innisfail longer than any other folk. Brocan and his people are proud. They have never accepted conquest. And they continue to resist the Danaan domination of the Druid Assembly. But that is another story."

"What part has Fearna to play in the tale?"

"Fearna was given over to Brocan as a hostage in

the hope that his presence in the Fir-Bolg court would help smooth relations with the Danaans. The ploy worked. Fearna was not a strong lad but he had a good heart and a determination which the Fir-Bolg king appreciated."

Lochie squeezed her hand to emphasize his next point and Isleen savored the sensation of being touched by another living being.

"Brocan is renowned for his stubbornness," Lochie continued, "not to mention his bitter temper and his insufferable pride, but gradually he began to soften. After two winters the King of the Fir-Bolg was treating the young Danaan like his own son. Better, some said. And by that time Fearna had no desire to return to Cecht's court and the peace was sealed. So it seemed the Brehons had been very wise in their judgment."

"Why would Fearna have been content to live among the stone huts of the Fir-Bolg?" Isleen scoffed. "Cecht is a good father and his halls are warm and dry. The Danaans want for nothing, whereas Brocan's folk scratch out an existence on a barren tract of land where even the grasses struggle to survive. Their houses are beehive hovels without even mortar to hold the walls together."

"Fearna was content to stay because he had lost his heart to red-haired Aoife, the daughter of King Brocan," Lochie explained. "Poor lad, there was never a more hopeless match. For you see Fearna was—how shall I say it?—an untried lad. Aoife is somewhat wiser in the ways of the world and she was very cruel to him. She manipulated him into several embarrassing situations. She goaded him to take foolish risks. And all for her own entertainment."

"Did Brocan let her get away with this?"

"The king became harsher with his own children as the moon cycled through two seasons. The royal offspring soon became quite jealous of all the attention Fearna was receiving. Riona, Brocan's queen, stood by her children but their father was unswayed by any entreaties for forgiveness. That was the beginning of the trouble between husband and wife. Before long Aoife's brother Sárán gladly joined her in her tormenting ways. And the little tricks they played upon Fearna soon became more dangerous and elaborate."

"And you inspired them to their mischief, I suppose?" Isleen interjected.

"As a matter of fact I did not," Lochie replied. "Sárán encouraged his sister to continue her ways and she took strength from his support. I'm going to be watching that lad very carefully over the coming seasons. He has a bright future, that one."

"Go on," Isleen gently urged.

"So one night in the middle of winter, when the snow was thick on the ground and sensible folk were seated by their firesides, Sárán and Aoife took Fearna to the forest with a horse and a jug of mead."

"What for?"

"To get him drunk."

"The horse?"

"No. Fearna, the son of the Danaan king," Lochie answered, exasperated. "Please listen carefully. Have you not heard what happened? I thought you and King Cecht often played Brandubh together."

"I have not been to see him for a few months," Isleen told him crossly. The jibes about King Cecht were beginning to irritate her. "I am enchanting the Danaan ruler with short visits timed well apart. What were Aoife and Sárán going to do with the lad when he was drunk?"

"They intended to coax him into riding the horse through the snow."

"I don't understand." Isleen frowned.

"They wanted to watch him fall off."

"That's all?"

"All they wanted was to see him tumble off the horse's back into the snow," Lochie confirmed. "For a laugh."

"A laugh?" Isleen asked in disbelief. "And how does this tale end in a war?"

"They got him very drunk. So befuddled he could barely stand. How he got up on that poor frightened creature I'll never know. In any case, Fearna climbed on the horse's back, fell off before he realized he was in the saddle, and cleanly broke his neck when he landed."

"Dead?"

"Sleep without breath in the frozen forest. Young heart unfettered now by the grief of the world. Strife will follow hard after you," Lochie recited.

"A pretty verse."

"That is how the Bard spoke the eulogy at the parting feast," he explained. "It's quite good, isn't it?"

"One of yours?"

"Yes it is, actually."

"Naturally the Danaan king was devastated by the loss of his son," Isleen guessed, refusing to be distracted by Lochie's high opinion of his own poetry.

"Indeed so." He smiled. "Apparently Fearna charmed most folk. He was a favorite child of Cecht. And the Danaan demanded reparations. He demanded the lad's honor price in full from the Fir-Bolg as recompense for the negligent loss of his dear boy."

"But King Brocan was too proud to pay the fine, and so the two peoples came to be at war?"

"You are right. Except to be fair to Brocan he has no idea of the part his children had to play in Fearna's death. When the two mischievous siblings realized the lad was dead, they decided to say nothing about the incident. Fearna was missed the next morning and his body was soon discovered. They had made no attempt to conceal his corpse."

"And so it was assumed Fearna met his death while riding alone in the forest, completely drunk on a jug of mead?"

"That's it, Isleen." Lochie snapped his fingers. "That is precisely what happened. Sárán and Aoife kept quiet, and if they both came down with the winter chills, no one thought to ask them how they had caught them seated safe by the fire."

Lochie sighed.

"When the matter came before the Brehon judges they decided the dispute should be resolved in a trial by contest. So here we are on the battleground of Mag Slécht."

"And what part have you had to play in all this?" Isleen pressed.

"None," Lochie responded. "I swear to you I have not interfered in any way. But that is about to change."

"What do you intend to do?"

"The king must know of his daughter's misdeeds," he told her.

"What good will come of that?" Isleen demanded. "The war has already started. The Brehon judges have made a decision, one which is unlikely to be reversed even if this revelation comes to light. Surely there is no point in telling King Brocan the truth. The story will come out eventually."

"These two peoples are not destined to fight today," Lochie explained. "Well, not very much anyway. A certain Brehon is on his way here even now. He has been charged by the Dagda to order Brocan and Cecht to lay down their arms. This Brehon is the key to our salvation for he has a great knowledge and he is a Seer."

"How can he help us?"

"I have scrutinized the Druid Assembly. This Brehon is our only hope. He has the talent to take the office of Dagda one day. And when he does we must be ready."

"Does the Brehon know Aoife and Sárán were responsible for Fearna's death?" Isleen frowned.

"He does not," Lochie replied, shaking his head. "There are other reasons for canceling the fight. You will have to be patient until all is revealed."

"I don't see what you hope to achieve."

"I wish to shame King Brocan, if not publicly then privately. That will soften his attitude enough so he will readily agree to the compromise the Brehon is about to offer."

"And that compromise is the hub of your mischief?"

"It is not mischief, Isleen. This sort of thing ensures I do not become stale. It keeps me alive. We have a chance to defeat our fate. And if we are careful we will gain great strength from the conflict about to descend on Innisfail."

"What conflict?"

"I'll let you know all about that by and by." He winked. "It's my little surprise. A piece of work I have been planning for many seasons. I'm quite proud of my efforts too."

"You seem to be going to a lot of trouble for rewards that are not immediately evident to me."

"I haven't done anything yet." Lochie laughed. "The Danaans and the Fir-Bolg have managed this mess thus far on their own."

"Who are you?" bellowed a Fir-Bolg sentry high in the branches above.

The two Watchers ended their conversation immediately, instantly becoming the characters they were portraying—two travelers from the north.

"We are Druids," Lochie stated, looking up. "My name is Lochie. I am well known to your king and people. And this is my wife, the renowned Seer Isleen." He gestured toward his companion.

"Your wife?" she hissed under her breath as she punched him on the arm.

"We have come to witness the battle at Mag Slécht and to preserve the memory of it in song," he went on, ignoring her protest.

"You are always welcome, Bard," the sentry replied enthusiastically. "King Brocan is out scouting. But we expect the warriors to return soon. You may go and wait by the great fire if you wish. Fergus is in camp. You may remember him. He is the king's steward and foster-brother."

"Thank you," Lochie replied graciously. In a moment he was nimbly adjusting the position of a heavy harp case which appeared out of nowhere to hang over his left shoulder.

"I will not pretend to be your wife!" Isleen whispered as soon as they had passed the sentry.

"You don't have to do anything," Lochie grumbled. "Just enjoy yourself. We don't get as many opportunities to have fun as we used to in the old days."

"Why did you tell the sentry we are married?"

"Because that way it's easier to explain your presence. Most Druids travel alone, you may recall. It might be suspicious if we arrived together and were not husband and wife. It will instantly earn you the trust of the king and his people."

Isleen was silent, unwilling to concede that he might be right. Then a thought crossed her mind. "We aren't likely to have any dealings with the Danaans, are we?"

"I hardly imagine that will be possible," Lochie laughed, "as we are taking dinner with their bitter enemies."

"I've never heard you play the harp," Isleen went on with a sigh of relief, changing the subject smoothly.

"I took up the craft ages ago," Lochie told her proudly. "The harp keeps me out of mischief. It reminds me of my youth. And I have composed some touching ballads. I must sit down and play a few for you."

"There were no harps like that when you were a lad." She laughed.

"Why must you insist on spoiling everything for me?"

At that moment Lochie noticed Isleen staring off along the path ahead of them, breathing in very deeply. Then he too smelled something on the air and was immediately reminded of his empty belly. His companion was already pointing to the great fire where Fergus the veteran was methodically turning the carcass of a pig on the spit.

"It is a wonderful thing to have possession of the full five senses again," she said in a whisper. "To feel the breeze against my skin, to hear the wind in the trees and to catch the aroma of slowly roasting meat in the evening air."

"Just beyond that fire is the king's tent," Lochie stated. "That is where we begin our work."

"Have we time for a small bite to eat first?" asked Isleen hopefully, her mouth watering.

Lochie somehow managed to restrain his joy at hearing those words. "Of course we do." He smiled broadly.

Despite the soothing infusion Fineen had given her to drink Aoife awoke time and again, unable to fully rest. Her head swam with drowsiness and her limbs ached from exhaustion but her thoughts were alive with worry.

And the nagging pain in her arm made it impossible to relax. Soon after the sun had set the young woman was still drifting in and out of consciousness, overhearing voices from her past in the busy conversations just outside the hut. She began to experience vivid visions of that terrible night in the snow last winter. Her blood began to pump loud at her temples as the memory of her fear returned. She'd thought they'd all be lost in the storm, for when she and Sárán had left Fearna by the oak grove, they'd had no idea where they were.

In the deep falls of snow the landscape had altered dramatically. Before brother and sister had realized something was amiss they were heading in the wrong direction, clambering among unfamiliar rocks.

Now the agony in Aoife's aching limbs reminded her of that night. Of the slow trudge into the white night for what seemed an eternity. Aoife had felt as if she was fit to drop from the effort. As her thoughts wandered, her legs somehow kept time, taking up a slow monotonous rhythm. A steady thud began to course through her as her feet marched on. Then a female voice rose from nowhere to fill the air. A woman was singing in a clean somber tone. It was a tale of her own long march in search of her true love. Aoife was astounded when she realized she knew the words to this song even though she had never heard it before.

In her imagination Aoife was in the snow again, yet on the night of Fearna's death she had not heard any music or song. She was starting to feel confused now. This vision had seemed like a dream reminiscence at first. Now it was strangely distorted.

A goatskin bodhran picked up the beat as the mysterious performer's song melted away. And instantly Aoife was walking again in the rocky uneven snow-fields of the Burren searching for the way home. She was humming the sweet melody under her breath, keeping up with the beat of the bodhran. Ahead of her she thought she could see her brother keeping a strict pace so she followed his example until the ground became flat and even. The music of the tiny bronze bells she always wore on her boots rang in her ear.

Her whole being was tramping through the icy white making toward the Dun of the Burren, yet part of her also knew she was wrapped safe in her father's furs. Suddenly a chorus of men and women joined in the drumbeat with a soothing chant. Whenever their voices ceased the melody was taken up by other instruments and a droning hum which she could not name. And then as she watched the world began to change slowly.

The snow and ice were melting from the ground. Winter retreated and the spring buds appeared on every tree as if time was rushing by in a torrent as the swelling voices rose in intensity.

The choir hummed a soft but potent melody punctuated with the lilting voice of the woman who had started the song. Aoife had no choice but to surrender to the haunting call. The chant went on as the wheel of the year turned full circle before her eyes. Winter disappeared. Then as spring came round all the voices dropped gradually away until there was almost complete silence. The woman's voice continued to hover delicately in the air until she was barely whispering.

And then with a sudden burst of color the earth exploded into vibrant heady summer.

Every hue of the rainbow was daubed on the trees, rivers, fields and sky. Aoife was not marching anymore. She was dancing joyfully in time with the glorious entrancing beat of a drum she could not see. She closed her eyes to soak up the compelling music as if it would seep into the wellspring of her soul.

Swaying to the merry tune she allowed her hands to reach out far ahead of her and high above. It was then she sensed the warm, inviting presence of another soul nearby. She opened her eyes and recognized the man she was dancing with straightaway.

He was the young blue-eyed Danaan who had challenged her brother and herself on the hill that morning. The choir returned to hum their drone once more and Aoife was drawn to approach this stranger.

His eyes flashed with fire, caught her gaze, and in unspoken agreement the two souls let themselves fly with the rhythm as their bodies transformed into a pair of dancing green dragonflies. Their faces were unchanged but their flesh was the same color as the holly leaves at Samhain.

She stared in wonder at the bright red tips of her partner's legs and the delicate golden lines across his belly. But most astounding of all, more incredible than the six pairs of feet they both now possessed, were the limbs which sprouted from their backs.

Aoife and her partner each sported two pairs of translucent silvery wings. Flimsy they seemed and yet when she had the mind to beat them together they lifted her up and around until she laughed for the joy of her flight. The Danaan flitted about her gracefully. Throughout their beautiful dance they never said a word to each other. Nor did they touch for even the briefest moment. But those two dancers spoke to each other with their spirits.

As the pair fluttered about each other the great unseen choir moved away, gradually allowing the song to fade and die. The intensity of their performance never once waned until the last moment when the entrancing drumbeat was swallowed up by the warm night.

The words of an old poem came into Aoife's mind, then it was her dancing partner who was speaking them in a deep soothing tone that sent shudders of excitement rippling through her body.

"In love the greatest king becomes a slave. Dust becomes gold. Soured milk turns to honey. Pain is joy. Small faults forgiven. The dead come to life. Love is the elixir to cure all ills. Drain the Cup of Desire then fill it up again. The Well of Passion is unquenchable."

Aoife sat up a little with a start. Instantly she was back in her father's hut. It was summer, her arm ached and the young Danaan spirit dancer had fled back from whence he had come.

The enticing aroma of cooking food filled her senses now. She opened her eyes and her attention was drawn to the weight restricting her arm. The young woman looked down at the splints wrapped by bandages and straightaway recalled falling heavily on the hillside as she made her escape.

She raised herself on her good elbow and looked around the hut, which was little more than a low circular stone wall with hasty thatching thrown over the top. She was alone. She reached out to pick up a jug of water then drank deeply. After a few moments the effort of staying upright proved too much so she put the jug down and lay back in the furs, rolling carefully onto her side so she could nurse her wounded arm.

As she started to relax again a movement, caught out of the corner of her eye, abruptly distracted her attention. She looked up at the doorway. A man was standing there. His shape was outlined by the firelight outside and she could not discern the features of his face.

"Fergus?" Aoife called. She had no idea how much time had passed since that morning. "Is that you? You don't have to watch over me, you know."

The man laughed.

Aoife gasped. This was not the old veteran. "Who are you?"

The stranger took a few tentative steps forward.

Aoife was beginning to feel very frightened now. There was something familiar about this young man's shape, his walk, even his sniggering laugh.

"Who are you?" she repeated with more urgency.

He came swiftly closer, his feet making no sound on the floor.

Aoife made a move to get out of bed but to her dismay her body would not respond. Her terror increased tenfold when she found she could not move her eyes, nor could she speak or utter any sound at all. She was trapped and she could barely breathe.

The stranger shuffled out of her line of vision and sidled up to the furs. Aoife's heartbeat thundered through her body as she lost sight of him. Now she was certain she was dealing with a malevolent spirit.

"Do you not know me?" came the hissing taunt.

At the sound of that voice Aoife would have

jumped out of bed and run all night with fear if she could have persuaded her body to do her bidding.

"I know *you* well enough," the man whispered and she felt his breath on her face. It smelled of mead and it was as cold as a snow wind.

"Fearna," Aoife managed to stammer.

"Fearna," the stranger confirmed.

"Why have you come?"

"I loved you. You teased me. You taunted me. You mocked me. You murdered me." There was no emotion in the voice. The words were uttered as if they were the obvious answer to her question.

"We meant you no harm," she protested but she didn't sound convincing even to herself.

"No harm?" the spirit repeated with distaste.

"Sárán and I were just thinking of fun. We only wanted to have a laugh."

"A laugh?"

"We didn't know you'd get so drunk you'd fall off the drafthorse and break your neck," she sobbed. "No one was meant to be hurt."

"You lied to your father about your part in my death."

"We were frightened," Aoife told him. "Sárán was sure your father would use our involvement as an excuse to end the old truce."

"As it is there is war anyway. You were more afraid of your own father than you were of mine."

"Yes," she admitted. "Our father would surely have taken leave of all restraint in his rage if he had known what we had done."

The figure moved to stand in front of her again. He had his back to her as he spoke.

"You have done a great wrong, Aoife. You owe me recompense and one day I will ask to be repaid the debt."

"Your eric-fine should have been handed over immediately. I don't know why Father opposed the payment."

"I am not talking about giving over my value in cows!" the spirit cried. "You owe me for what you have done. You stole the rest of my life away from me. How will you repay me for forty good summers?"

"I don't know. I'll find a way if you can forgive me."

"The next time I come to you," Fearna's ghost told her, "it will be time for me to claim my fine. And then you will give me whatever I ask of you."

The spirit turned around and Aoife could see the features of his face clearly. She recognized the youngest son of the King of the Danaans immediately, even though his skin was gray and his hair spattered with blood and soil.

"That's how you looked when they brought you in," Aoife sobbed. "Your lips were blue and your eyes glazed over with snow."

"May you never forget me, Aoife."

"I won't," she replied. "The tears I cried for you were real enough."

"You weren't crying for me," the spirit huffed. "You were crying for yourself, for your own guilt."

And with those parting words the ghost of Fearna,

son of the Danaan king, melted into the air and was gone. In his place stood Fergus, Brocan's foster-brother, and there was shock on his face.

Aoife shook her head a little. "Is that you, uncle?" she asked nervously.

"It is," he replied solemnly.

"How long have you been standing there?"

"Long enough to know how Fearna came to be riding alone and drunk in the forest after a heavy snow-fall."

"What?"

"I heard everything, Aoife," Fergus told her. "It was as if you were speaking to someone who never answered. I thought for a while you imagined yourself to be talking to Fearna himself, come back from the dead to haunt you."

"It was him!" she cried. "He has returned to torment me!"

"It is your conscience that's tormenting you," the old veteran told her with raised eyebrows. "But that'll soon be put to right. I must tell the king of this."

"This is a portent of death," Aoife whispered. "Fearna came to summon me after him."

"I did not see Fearna," her uncle assured her.

"Am I going to die?" she cried. "I don't want to pass over to the Halls of Waiting yet."

"You're not going to die," Fergus soothed.

"But when folk are visited by a tormented spirit it is a sign their life is ended." Her frightened eyes stared out past Fergus toward the doorway.

"Death is the least of your concerns," he told her. "There are worse things than death that can befall you in this world."

"What is worse than losing your life?"

"Loss of dignity. A compromise to your honor. When you have to endure those things, death can be a welcome visitor."

Aoife thought about the veteran's words before she fully understood his meaning. Her father would be held responsible for Fearna's death, even though she had committed the crime. He would suffer the loss of dignity to a greater extent than she.

"Uncle Fergus, I beg you, don't say anything to Father."

"I must tell him," Fergus answered wearily. "I could never lie to my king. He is my brother. It is right he should know. This will put an end to the battle contest. Many lives will be saved tomorrow."

"But our people will face a heavy eric-fine."

"It would be a terrible injustice if this fight were to go on. Your father will reconsider his position. If Brocan is willing to accept the terms the Danaan king offers, then we might be able to walk away from this contest with some dignity."

"It will cost us so dearly," Aoife repeated in a tearful voice.

"Your father's reputation will be torn to shreds," the veteran agreed. "And yours also. No man among our people will likely ever consider joining with you in marriage since you have proved so dishonest.

Other costs can be easily borne. But poor reputation is not easily mended."

"My kindred will forget in time," she said defiantly. "I will earn my good name back."

Another figure came to the doorway and stood for a moment before entering the hut.

It was Fineen.

"How are you feeling?" the healer asked.

"My arm feels much better," she told him.

"Nevertheless you should be resting."

"But I have had a visitor."

"Who was it?" Fineen frowned in confusion. "Has your mother, the queen, decided to join us after all?"

"There was no visitor," Fergus stated. "She imagined she saw——"

"Someone was here," the healer cut in as he surveyed the hut, using all his senses. "She is telling the truth."

"It's about time she got into that habit," Fergus mumbled under his breath.

"It was Fearna's ghost," Aoife sobbed, crying fresh tears. "I am responsible for his death."

"You?" Fineen asked, scratching his head. Then he held up a hand to silence her and his frown deepened. "Wait," he whispered. "Don't make another sound. I can feel a strange presence in the air."

The healer turned his head this way and that, taking careful note of the coldness in the room. He brushed the golden stubble on his chin thoughtfully. At length he turned to the young woman again.

"I believe you," the healer assured her. "You have had a visitor of some kind. Though I can't say if it was Fearna."

Fergus shuddered and edged toward the door. The veteran had fought in bloody battles, witnessed men and women suffer agonizing deaths, and always led the charge at the front of the Fir-Bolg warriors. But matters of the Otherworld gave him an intense feeling of unease. He preferred to leave such mysteries to the Druids.

"Is there any danger?" he demanded.

"I don't believe so," Fineen reassured him. "Whatever was here is gone now."

"In that case I will go attend to the preparations for the feast," the veteran excused himself. "And I must consider how I will break this news to the king."

"Have you been visited before by this apparition?" Fineen asked Aoife when they were alone.

"No."

"Are you certain?"

"Yes," she insisted. "I've never experienced anything like it."

"I see," Fineen said, half to himself. "I do not feel it was a ghost which visited you this evening. I'll have to ask the advice of Dalan the Brehon. He knows of these things. He has studied the lore of the Otherworld."

"Where is Dalan?"

"In the east. Attending the great gathering of the harpers. I expect him to return before the turning of the moon."

"Healer!" Fergus bellowed from outside. "The Bard, Lochie, has returned to us. And he has brought his wife along with him at last."

Fineen was distracted. "His wife?" the healer called back but received no reply. "If you receive another visitation such as that one," he warned Aoife, "you must let me know immediately. If I am not available, someone else must sit with you. Do you understand?"

"I do."

"Very well," the physician sighed, "I will leave you to rest. It might be best if you were not awake when your father arrives home. I have heard he is extremely displeased with you as it is. This news will not improve his mood."

"How will I sleep?" she sobbed.

"I will arrange for someone to watch over you through the night," Fineen promised. "Now it is time to rest again. Tomorrow you may talk as much as you like. Tonight you must rest."

"Thank you," Aoife said, already making a show of shutting her eyes. "But I doubt I will take another peaceful night of slumber for the rest of my life."

The healer hushed her, then patted her head like an indulgent parent and departed.

As soon as he was gone Aoife sat up again as best she could. "Please leave me in peace," she prayed.

But if Fearna heard her he did not acknowledge the entreaty.

Chapter 6

OUTSIDE THE HUT FERGUS AND LOCHIE WERE LAUGH-
ing uproariously at something the storyteller had
said.

Fineen rolled his eyes. Lochie was a Bard who
loved being the focus of all attention, so he was very
well suited to his profession. As the healer approached the fire Fergus turned to him, obviously
cheered by the arrival of the storyteller and his wife.

"I was telling him of the intrigue I have just uncovered and complaining that I would have to tell the
king about it." Fergus coughed and laughed again.
"And he told me about the time he was frolicking in
the river with a chieftain's daughter—"

"Just a silly tale to cheer you up," Lochie cut in
quickly. "How is young Aoife?"

"Do you know her?" Fineen asked and he felt the
same feeling of coldness about his body he had experienced at the young woman's bedside.

"That is her name, isn't it?" the Bard asked innocently. "The one with the fiery red hair?"

"Yes, Aoife is her name," the healer confirmed. He had spent many evenings in this Bard's company but he had never noticed anything unusual about the fellow before. Now that Fineen looked closer, however, his attention was drawn to the man's unusual fingernails. They were perfectly shaped for playing the harp, long and rounded at the tips to catch the strings lightly without dampening the sound too much. Fineen could not help wondering how the musician had managed to keep them in such wonderful condition.

"You must have had a very hard journey," the physician suggested.

"Why do you say so?" Lochie inquired.

"Because the gathering of harpers ended only two days ago," Fineen said. "You could not possibly have traversed the distance from the eastern shore of Innisfail in so short a time without experiencing some hardship."

"He had a good woman to drive him on," Isleen laughed, approaching the group.

"Your husband has mentioned you many times," Fineen offered with a bow. "But his description does you no justice."

"Many husbands do little justice to their wives," she replied, shrugging her shoulders and holding out her hand in greeting.

"King Brocan will be pleased to see you," the healer assured them. Isleen's gaze lingered a little too long on him. He felt decidedly uncomfortable. "Will you stay to witness the battle tomorrow?" he asked, his voice cracking slightly under those enticing eyes.

"That is our intention," Lochie replied as he moved between the two of them. At that very instant he stopped speaking and spun round in his tracks. In two breaths he spotted what had alerted him.

Three men, the first taller than the other two, appeared in the firelight beneath the watchman's tree. And there they halted.

"Fergus!" a man's voice bellowed from high in the trees. "Come here."

The old veteran stopped turning the spit, wiped his hands clean, picked up his sword and calmly walked out to the watchtree to see what the fuss was all about.

Fineen followed after him, gesturing at Lochie and Isleen to remain by the fire.

"It is Mahon," Lochie whispered to his companion as soon as they were out of earshot.

"The son of the Danaan king?" she scoffed. "What would he be doing here tonight?"

"He was captured by Sárán and Lom," he confirmed.

"I am supposed to be the Seer, not you," she hissed. "In any case, I don't believe you."

"It is Mahon!" Lochie hummed with delight. "I can feel his outrage in the air. This is too wonderful. I never dreamed this would come to pass."

"I . . . I don't want him to see me," Isleen stammered.

"Why not?"

"I will go to sit with Aoife." She coughed nervously.

"I would let her sleep if I were you. I have just given her a scare and she really should be allowed to recover."

"Put your hand to turning the spit and make yourself useful," Isleen advised sharply.

"She is a pretty one," Lochie commented. "I wonder whether Mahon will fall in love with her."

"She could do no worse!" Isleen shot back. "He is ignorant of the Bardic skills. Would she be content with a warrior who knows little of music, poetry or storytelling?"

"True enough she is destined for the Druid path," her companion noted, shaking his head. "But none of her own kin will ever consider taking her to bride when her full story is known. A marriage to Mahon would be quite an attractive option for her, I imagine."

"Aoife is too intelligent to be attracted to one such as he," she answered flatly. "The girl would quickly become bored. Though I must admit he has some skill in the bedchamber, which compensates slightly for his lack of education."

"Does he indeed?" Lochie beamed, overjoyed to have caught his companion out. "So you have been busy at the court of the Danaan king, have you?"

Isleen glared at him, then disappeared into the round hut without another word.

In those days the rules of war were many yet they were straightforward enough. This fight had been arranged three moons earlier. A chieftain or a king who felt his people had been wronged in some way could call on the Brehons to withhold judgment until a trial by combat had been completed. Merely defeating the enemy in the resulting battle did not necessarily secure the victor's claim, however. The judges looked at the entire fight from start to finish, read the auspices of the conflict and presented a ruling in accordance with their observations.

Thus a king who wielded a superior force could not be certain of winning the trial even though the battle might surely be his. Honorable action, valor and abiding by the conventions of warfare were the goal of each combatant. For this reason it was rare for large bands of warriors to face each other down.

In most cases the kings or chieftains chose champions who fought the lawsuit in single conflict. This minimized the possibility of a breach of custom by either side and, more importantly, saved lives. But the tension between Fir-Bolg and Danaan had been building for a long while. A contest of champions would not have satisfied anyone.

Besides, the Brehons were growing impatient with the stubbornness of both parties in the dispute. It was clear Cecht and Brocan wanted to indulge in a good fight. So this battle on the ritual ground of Mag Slécht was to be one of those infrequent occasions when many warriors would join the fight to preserve the dignity of their people.

Everyone hoped it would settle matters once and for all. But one breach, one minor disregard of custom, could easily spell defeat for either side. Fergus marched purposefully to the watchtree to find Sárán leaning against it to steady himself. The young man had a small gash at the side of his head and his hair had some flaking blood caked in it. Nearby a tall golden-haired stranger sat cross-legged in the middle of the path, his long hair over his face.

"What's going on here?" the veteran demanded.

"The watchman will not let us come into the camp," Lom explained.

"Why not?" Fineen gasped, confused.

"Because of our prisoner," Sárán hissed, pointing at the seated warrior. He tipped up a waterskin hanging at the tree and washed his face. Diluted blood ran down his neck in little streams to stain his shirt and tunic.

"Prisoner?" Fergus grunted as he stepped forward to get a better look at the captive.

When the moonlight shone on the young stranger's skin the veteran could plainly see battle markings painted in blue. The spirals and zigzags were Danaan designs. There was no doubt about it.

"Where did he come from?" Fergus demanded. "The truce is not yet ended. You have no right to be taking captives."

"He and his companion attacked us," Sárán protested, turning his head to show off his injury. "They broke the truce. We could have been killed."

"Not even the Danaans would dare attempt to take a life while the truce held," Fergus reminded him. "If you had died it could have only been by your own stupidity. As it is, it might have been better if you had fallen. This is a flagrant violation of the rules of warfare."

The captive chose that moment to lift his eyes to Fergus, whose jaw fell open in shock.

"Do you know who this is?" the veteran spluttered when he could master his tongue.

"We didn't get a chance to ask him, uncle," Lom stated, trying not to sound too disrespectful.

"His name is Mahon mac Cecht," Fineen interrupted in a low voice. "He is the eldest and last remaining son of the Danaan king."

"I don't believe it." Sárán laughed, certain the healer was joking.

But no one else smiled. It was obvious Fineen was telling the truth. The repercussions of bringing their prisoner to camp began to dawn on Sárán. He moved away from the watchtree, wiping his hands on his tunic as he did so.

"I beg you to forgive this terrible misunderstanding," the veteran began, addressing the Danaan.

But the enemy warrior did not utter a sound, nor did he show any sign he had heard the apology. Mahon touched a hand to his left brow where a dark bruise was rising.

"This warrior will be our honored guest," Fergus declared. "Help him to his feet. He will walk into the camp a free man and sit at table with the king tonight. He is a prince and we are expected under the terms of the truce to offer him hospitality until the agreement expires at midnight and the contest begins."

Lom was at Mahon's side in an instant, unbinding the prince's hands and wrapping a cloak around him to cover his nakedness. But the young warrior shrugged away the covering. Sárán stumbled over, ready to help the Danaan to his feet. As he passed by, the veteran leaned in close to reprimand him.

"Bad enough you had to break the truce," Fergus hissed furiously at Sárán. The old warrior didn't realize he was speaking loud enough for everyone to hear. "But did it have to be with the capture of the son of the enemy king? What in the name of Balor's black heart will Brocan say about all this?"

"You're about to find out," the lookout high in the trees announced. "There's a small party approaching us through the forest."

"We had better get this young Danaan seated by the fire," Fergus commanded in an urgent voice. "I don't want the king seeing him like this."

In a moment the Danaan was standing unfettered.

"I offer my apologies," the veteran began. "What more can I do? A great wrong has been done to you this day. And you would be within your rights to claim recompense for the grave insult to you and your people. There will be no more insult heaped upon you, I promise."

Mahon, Prince of the Tuatha De Danaan, remained silent, staring straight ahead of him as if he had heard nothing.

"I'll send Sárán ahead to gather some clothes for you," Fergus offered.

"I am dressed for war," Mahon answered firmly without shifting his gaze. "I will die that way."

"You're not going to die!" Fergus cried. "What is this fascination all you young folk seem to have with death?"

"I will wear a cloak," Mahon conceded. "I have no wish for anything more and it is fitting if I am to be seated at the feast table."

"Very well," the veteran agreed, snapping his fingers at Lom who draped the cloak around the young warrior's shoulders.

In a very short while they were all seated by the fire, apprehensively awaiting the arrival of King Brocan. Only Lochie offered Mahon a friendly greeting as he took his place.

Despite the lookout's report the scouting party was a long while, so Fergus offered the prince a choice cut of the roast boar.

Mahon shook his head. "I would rather wait for the king if you don't mind," he told him sternly.

Fergus tried to calm himself but he could not stay seated while he waited for the scouts to come in.

There were simply too many thoughts running through his mind. He closed his eyes and said a short silent prayer to the Goddess Danu, begging her to intervene in some way, if only to cool Brocan's usual fiery temper.

It would complicate matters beyond repair if the king did not immediately realize the implications of Mahon's presence. Fergus was still wording the prayer in his mind when the sentry at the watchtree called out again.

"Queen Riona is approaching the camp!"

Fergus stopped breathing. "Danu," he whispered to himself, "have you deserted me? Let the watchman be mistaken. Please don't send the queen to us now!"

As Queen of the Fir-Bolg and a former warrior herself, Riona was expected to attend such gatherings. But on this occasion she had decided to stay behind at Dun Burren. She had explained her actions to no one but Brocan, so most folk reasoned she must have had another fight with her husband.

The king and queen had quarreled day and night ever since Brocan had formally adopted Fearna as his own son. This action had outraged her so much she had hardly spoken a kind word to the king since. Her own sons, Sárán and Lom, did not enjoy the privileges young Fearna had enjoyed. Indeed, once the young Danaan boy had won Brocan's heart, the two of them had become inseparable. Riona had acted as an advocate for her children until the king suggested Fearna might be a good match for Aoife.

That had been too much for the proud queen to bear. In her fury, she had thrown a bronze jar at her husband, which had broken his nose and bruised his eye. And from that moment their partnership had begun slowly to disintegrate.

Riona was a queen who boasted a royal lineage stretching back to the noblest clans of the Fir-Bolg. By marriage, her mother Eriu was Queen of the Tuatha De Danaan of the East. So Riona was used to her opinions being heard and her wishes respected.

After Fearna's death, relations between the queen and her king had chilled considerably. To be in the presence of both of them at once had become an uncomfortable experience for all involved.

Fergus sighed to think that lately Riona and Brocan enjoyed arguing more than they had once reveled in their lovemaking. As these thoughts passed through the veteran's mind a tall red-haired woman with striking green eyes walked confidently toward the fire. Everyone, including Fergus, bowed low before her as she approached.

The queen's clothes were practical: warrior's breeches, a saffron shirt such as her husband often wore, walking boots and a dark rust-brown cloak to contrast with the copper shades of her hair.

"Welcome to the camp of Mag Slécht," the veteran piped up, offering her his hand.

Riona smiled as her eyes quickly scanned the faces around the fire. "Thank you, loyal Fergus," she replied formally, her gaze falling on Mahon. "I see you have an honored guest at the royal fire. Isn't it unusual to invite the enemy to dine the night before a battle?"

"Mahon mac Cecht," the veteran introduced the warrior, "this is Riona ni Eriu, Queen of the Fir-Bolg of the Burren."

"It is my great honor to meet you, my lady," the Danaan replied politely, standing to take her hand in his.

As the young warrior sat down again Fergus came closer and whispered in the queen's ear. "What are you doing here?" he asked urgently under his breath.

"It is my duty to witness any battles fought on behalf of my kinfolk."

"The king told me you would be staying at Dun Burren."

"That was a week ago." She shrugged casually. "I waited to arrive until this evening because I wished to miss my husband's temper tantrums. In the days before a battle he is unbearable."

"Do you know what sort of trouble this could cause?" the veteran pressed.

"By the looks of your company tonight there'll be plenty of other upsets to distract Brocan," she quipped. "He won't have time to antagonize me."

"I wish you two would settle your differences," Fergus hissed. "If only you realized what it is to be around you both when you're fighting, you would surely end your feud immediately."

"Brocan should apologize then."

"The pair of you are worse than two young children quarreling over a slab of honeycomb. Neither is willing to give in." With that the veteran coughed loudly to signal his disgust.

"How did the scouting go today?" Riona asked.

Fergus coughed again as he nudged his head in the direction of Mahon.

"There's your answer."

He noticed the slightest trace of a smile begin to form on the queen's lips. And suddenly the veteran was certain the queen would not let this opportunity pass her by. Her husband had argued strongly in favor of this fight though she had refused to be a party to it. Now it seemed Brocan should have taken her advice.

"Mahon," she went on, "your father is a true gentleman to have sent you here to feast with us on such a night."

Fergus rubbed his forehead and tried to think clearly. "Mahon is not visiting our camp," he explained in as polite a voice as he could muster. Riona was enjoying this immensely. He could sense it.

"Don't be silly." The queen laughed. "He is here on the eve of a battle. What else would he be doing but visiting the camp to offer his father's good wishes?"

"Your sons captured him on the battlefield," Fergus admitted quietly.

Riona frowned and shook her head.

"The battle was today?" she asked, feigning confusion.

The veteran wondered why she loved to play with

people in this way. "The fight is arranged for tomorrow," he informed her tersely.

"Then this fellow was trespassing on our territory?" Riona hummed, wagging her finger at the young warrior as if he were a child of three summers who had had been caught stealing butter.

"It transpires that Sárán and Lom were the ones trespassing. They captured the prince on Danaan ground."

Riona cast a brief glance of silent reprimand toward her two sons but gave no other sign of anger. Sárán dropped his head to avoid her gaze. Lom could not meet her eyes either.

The queen knew her sons' actions could not possibly reflect on her. The lads were almost of warrior age. They were their father's charges. Brocan would have to wear the responsibility for their foolishness, she thought with satisfaction.

"And you've let this prince sit naked by the fire after such a breach of custom was committed against him?" Riona noted as she turned back to Fergus.

"I am waiting for the king to return," the veteran explained. "The prince has a cloak."

"And all this while Cecht is searching for his son, probably frantic with worry," she went on. "That to me is a much more severe breach of the law. Shouldn't you send word to Cecht that his son is in no danger?"

"I thought it best to wait," Fergus repeated tersely. "And Mahon will share in our feast."

"Any young man will take the opportunity to eat at a hearth other than his own." Riona laughed. "But that doesn't mean it is always right to invite him. In this case I am sure Mahon did not consider how worried his father might be."

"You're right," the young Danaan agreed rather hastily. "I should have gone straight back to my father. I will go now."

Fergus cursed the chance that brought these two together at this moment. The Danaan was obviously a naive lad with little experience of the world. Riona, on the other hand, was a wily mischief-maker when she set her mind to it. The veteran prayed to the private deities of his heart that the queen would just be quiet.

Mahon stood up but Fergus placed a firm hand on his shoulder and pushed him back to his seat.

"Wait here, lad," the veteran advised. "Believe me, there'll be more trouble if you leave now than if you just tarry awhile longer until the king returns."

"I should go," the Danaan insisted, shoving the veteran's hand away.

Fergus struggled with the young man for a moment but in the end relented. As Mahon rose again the cloak covering him dropped away.

Riona smiled at the naked young man standing before her. "I wish you could stay," the queen hummed. "Surely your father would forgive you this one visit."

Fergus rolled his eyes.

"If you think my father would understand my

predicament," the Danaan retorted, "then you obviously don't know him."

"I've never met King Cecht," Riona replied. "Is he anything like you?"

Fergus brushed the sweat from his forehead with the back of his hand. Suddenly it seemed a very good idea to send Mahon back to his father's camp as soon as possible.

As it happened the decision was quickly taken out of his hands. As Fergus was wrapping the cloak around the Danaan's shoulders again the lookout announced the arrival of King Brocan and his warriors.

"Danu preserve the peace at this fireside," the veteran prayed with sincerity. "I have never before been more sincere in a request. Grant this and I will not neglect the rituals again as long as I live."

"Perhaps our guest would appreciate a mead cup, Fergus," Riona suggested.

The veteran was just handing the cup to the Danaan when Brocan stepped into the circle of firelight, flung his cloak aside and called for the jar himself.

The king had noticed his wife's presence as he'd approached and was determined to stay calm in front of his warriors whatever the cost. But then he saw young Mahon seated by the fire. His twin sons stood beside their guest. There was dried blood on the side of Sárán's head.

Fergus could see the expression change on his foster-brother's face and he expected the worst. But

Brocan quickly sized up the situation. It was obvious some breach of custom had occurred, but the king realized he could not afford to show any sign of anger toward his sons in front of the Danaan. He did not wish to add a breach of hospitality to the list of his crimes. And most of all he did not want his wife to have any excuse to rebuke him later.

"Welcome to my hearth," the king began. "I am Brocan, King of the Fir-Bolg."

"I am Mahon, son of Cecht, who is King of the Danaans of the West. Your queen has already graciously welcomed me to this fireside."

"I hope you will convey my respects to your father," Brocan answered placidly, observing the bruise above the young man's eye.

"You may do that yourself on the battleground tomorrow," was the cold answer. "After he has defeated you he may at last have earned your respect."

"How came this warrior to be among us?" the king asked Fergus, refusing to be drawn by this challenge. Likely the lad's outrage was well justified.

"This is the man Aoife and Sárán came upon on the hill," Fergus explained.

"They were trespassing on territory assigned to my people in this fight," Mahon corrected. "They are truce-breakers."

"When Aoife withdrew from the fight," Sárán went on, taking up the part of the tale Fergus had not yet heard, "Lom and I wrestled with Mahon and the other Danaan warrior until we had overpowered them. We could only bring one of them back with us as a prisoner. We chose Mahon."

"A senseless act!" his father spat, instantly cursing his inability to keep his mouth shut.

"We overcame two Danaans without a drop of blood being spilled."

"Without a drop of valuable blood being spilled," the king noted, pointing to his son's head wound. "The rules of war simply must be obeyed," he stressed.

"The first lesson a warrior has to learn is to keep within the law," Fergus agreed.

"The laws of battle ensure death and injury are kept to a minimum," the king continued. "You broke a fundamental rule. You disregarded a truce."

"How were we to know we were in enemy territory?" Sárán complained.

"What sensible warrior is not aware of when he is walking his opponent's ground?" Fergus laughed.

"This whole arrangement of formal battle," Brocan explained, "is meant to settle a dispute. That is why there are rules and conventions. The Danaans could easily claim victory by the simple fact that you breached the law."

"He attacked us," Sárán protested.

"And there was another warrior with him," Lom added.

Fergus raised an eyebrow and laughed. "You pair overpowered two Danaan warriors?"

"It was a lucky blow rendered me their prisoner," Mahon explained. "At sword point they took me when I had recovered a little. My companion dared not intervene for fear they would kill me."

"Have you been given anything to soothe your bruise?" Riona inquired.

The young man shook his head as he touched a hand to his left brow. "The injury is not serious," he stated coldly. "I have recovered."

"This is all your fault, Brocan," the queen spat, turning on her husband. Fergus stepped back out of the way, fearing the worst. "Don't berate the lads for your own failings. You should have taught them properly."

"Stay out of this," the king hissed. "You are not a warrior."

"I was a warrior before I married you," she reminded him. "And I will be until the day I die."

"We've done nothing but fight these last six moons," Brocan conceded sarcastically. "You're right. You are a warrior."

"Your sons put up a good fight," Mahon cut in.

"What?" the king asked, distracted.

"They both fought like honorable warriors," the Danaan went on. "If they had meant to kill me, I am sure they would have used their swords with more skill. I am as much to blame for this incident as anyone. I should have retreated when I stumbled on them. But my pride would not allow me to withdraw."

Brocan frowned in confusion until it struck him that Mahon probably expected to be reprimanded by his own father for the breach. It was in everyone's interest the whole matter be brushed aside.

"Perhaps we are making too much of this unfortunate episode," the king ventured.

"You are very likely right," Mahon added quickly. "I am not going to pursue the matter. I hope we can forget all about it."

Brocan could not believe his luck. "You will feast with us as our guest," the king declared with relief. "And you will be escorted to your own people this night before the end of the truce."

"Thank you," Mahon replied, bowing his head.

"We will say nothing more of this?" Brocan pressed.

"Nothing," the Danaan replied.

"As usual my husband has found a solution which avoids the need to consider honor," Riona noted dryly.

"How is Aoife faring?" the king asked Fineen, ignoring his wife.

"It was a clean break and will likely mend well," the healer assured him, unhappy that attention was now focused on him. "But she is still suffering from the shock of her fall. I have ordered her to rest this night."

"In the future she will perhaps think twice before going off in search of adventure," Brocan sighed.

"Was the young woman hurt?" Mahon cut in, surprised. "I didn't mean to injure her."

"She broke her arm in her rush down the hill," Fergus told the young man. "It was none of your doing."

"It is my fault," Mahon admitted. "I shouldn't have frightened her so. May I visit her?"

"That won't be possible," the veteran replied uneasily and he noted the disappointment in the Danaan's eyes. "She needs rest. Best she isn't disturbed."

"Then please offer her my apology for the pain she must be suffering."

"I will pass on your thoughts to her," Fergus promised.

"There is an example of true nobility." Riona pointed to Mahon. "Your father must be an honorable man to have taught you to inquire after your enemies as if they were your greatest friends. I'm sure you can see why I don't blame my sons for their foolishness. The guiding hand of a good father is more valuable than anything in this life. The lack of it will bring dishonor and misery."

Fergus put a hand on the king's shoulder, hoping to interrupt before Brocan had a chance to retaliate.

"Lochie the Bard has returned to us. And he has brought his wife Isleen with him."

"His wife?" Mahon exclaimed. "Isleen? I had no idea Isleen was married."

"Where is she then?" Brocan inquired.

"She is sitting with your daughter, my lord," the Bard answered, stepping out of the shadows.

"Bring her to the fire then," Brocan ordered. "I'll meet this woman you have told us so much about."

Lochie bowed and turned to summon his companion. "Isleen!" he called sweetly with obvious delight in his voice. "The King of the Fir-Bolg would like to meet you. And he has a guest. I believe you know Mahon mac Cecht quite well."

After a long silent pause she poked her head out of the door and nodded a greeting to everyone.

"Come out and let's see you," Brocan demanded good-naturedly. "I've been looking forward to meeting Lochie's wife for some time."

As Isleen brushed past her companion she leaned in close to whisper venomously, "You should have mentioned this to me!"

Lochie shrugged his shoulders boyishly.

"How long have you been planning to introduce 'your wife' to these folk?"

Her companion rolled his eyes and turned up the palms of his hands to indicate this was not the time to enter into such a discussion.

"Remind me to have a quiet word with you later," Isleen hissed.

"This is my devoted wife, Isleen," Lochie announced, ignoring her tone. "She's a Druid-Seer of some renown."

Brocan took Isleen's hand. Mahon smiled sweetly to her when she acknowledged him.

"I know you have told me the story," Lochie cut in, "but the details seem to have slipped my mind. Where did you two meet?"

"At my father's court," Mahon answered for her.

"I'll wager you had no idea her husband was a famous Bard such as myself."

"I didn't know Isleen was married," the young man replied.

Riona smiled broadly, understanding exactly what the Bard was doing.

"Isleen," Lochie went on, "this is Riona ni Eriu, Queen of the Fir-Bolg of the Burren."

The Druid-Seer took Riona's hand and lowered her head in a respectful bow.

"Have you spent long at the Danaan court?" the queen inquired pleasantly. "Perhaps you can tell us something of the Danaan king. I find I have growing fascination with Cecht."

"I would be happy to speak with you privately later in the evening." The Seer smiled. "I can tell you the winter may be bitterly cold but it is never long enough when spent in the company of the Danaan king."

Brocan grunted. Riona sighed with contentment to know she had slipped her attack under his guard. And Isleen was impressed with the queen's ability to manipulate conversation to her will.

"Now if you don't mind," the Seer excused herself, bowing again, "I would like to return to sit with your daughter. Aoife needs the nurturing of a woman to calm the shock she has suffered."

"My wife will sit with her," Brocan interrupted. "With her mother to fuss over her the girl will soon recover. So you, Isleen, should stay with us and feast."

Riona flashed a glance at the other woman which clearly expressed her thoughts on the matter.

"A queen should be at the fireside with her guests and her husband," the Seer pointed out, intrigued by the little sparks flying among everyone at the fireside. "The girl has a slight fever and I am well versed in the treatment of that condition as I come from the north. I'll join you when I am sure your daughter is sleeping peacefully." Then Isleen nodded politely to everyone and withdrew silently to the hut.

"Lochie, will you give us a tale after dinner?" Brocan begged. "In honor of our Danaan guest."

"What tale would you have?"

"I would dearly love to hear the eulogy you composed for Fearna, Mahon's brother," the king replied without hesitation. "It was a beautiful song which did great honor to his father and people."

"Not tonight, my lord," Fergus suggested under his breath. "After all, it was his death which brought us here to the battleground. And this is his brother who will sit with us."

"All the more reason," Brocan argued, annoyed that nothing seemed to be going as he wanted.

"Please, my lord, listen to my advice," the veteran urged.

"Very well then," the king snapped. "What tale would you like to hear, my dear brother Fergus?"

"A tale to inspire the warriors in their fight tomorrow. Perhaps we should ask the opinion of our guest."

"With your indulgence I'd rather return immediately to my father," Mahon answered, once again making to rise. "Your offer is very gracious and I don't wish to insult your welcoming. But you know I wouldn't ask to be excused under normal circumstances."

Brocan gave a weak smile which revealed nothing of his thoughts on the matter. He knew the young Danaan was anxious to report on all he had seen in the Fir-Bolg camp, but he could not refuse to let the lad go back to his own people.

"You are not a prisoner," he replied reassuringly. "You are a guest. And you may leave when it suits you without the slightest risk of insult to anyone."

"Thank you, lord," Mahon said as he bowed. "I would prefer to leave immediately if you don't mind."

"I'll have two warriors escort you," the king promised. "I'm sorry your visit was so brief."

"I'll see you all on the battleground tomorrow," the Danaan replied stiffly.

"I pray we do not meet," Fergus cut in. "I would be sorry to have to cut down such a fine young man as yourself."

"Believe me, you won't have the opportunity," Mahon shot back. "Be warned, I'll slay you on the field if our paths cross." And with that the Danaan prince left, two Fir-Bolg warriors beside him to guide him back to his own territory.

As soon as the young warrior was gone beyond the watchtree King Brocan called for a seat. A wooden bench was brought for him, and there the Fir-Bolg king sat, staring silently into the fire until the roast boar was ready to be served. No one in the war party dared disturb him. Even Riona was silent, though it was because she was saving her words until she was alone with her husband.

Having decided the king and queen held no more entertainment for him, Lochie slipped away to Brocan's hut. Isleen was seated at the fire when he went in, so he picked up a three-legged stool and joined her.

She sighed deeply as he touched her on the shoulder. Aoife was asleep, though lines of sweat on her face revealed she was not resting peacefully. Isleen offered her companion a cup of mead that had warmed by the coals.

The Bard took the drink from her gratefully, savoring the liquor. "Mahon has gone back to his father," he told her after a moment. "It's safe for you to come out now. King Brocan and Queen Riona would like to sit and talk with you."

"Are you sure Mahon has gone?"

"Yes."

Her relief was obvious.

"Are you still angry with me?" Lochie ventured.

"I am. But I find I can't stay annoyed with you for long. This is a far more interesting court than King Cecht's. So much seems to be going on. The queen sparring with the king, the king's foster-brother caught in between. Three royal children who are full of mischief. And the tragic death of Fearna, the truth of which has yet to come out. Anguish, shame, dishonor, fear and bitterness all hang over these folk.

Little wonder you've been spending so much time with them. It's all quite intriguing. And I can see endless possibilities for the kind of sport you excel in."

"I knew you'd enjoy my game if you got a glimpse of it."

"But you haven't explained what your little game is," Isleen noted. "I don't understand what you hope to achieve by stirring the pot with these people."

"I'll let you know all that in good time," Lochie assured her.

"Well, be more careful in future. It wouldn't take much for Mahon to realize that I am not all I seem to be."

"That young man has other things on his mind."

"What other things?" Isleen demanded.

"I've a notion Aoife will end up marrying the last surviving son of the Danaan king," Lochie confided.

"She'd never be happy with one such as he," Isleen scoffed. "He can't sustain a decent conversation on any subject other than war and hunting. And you know what happens to a relationship when the conversation dies."

"Indeed." Lochie nodded. "You and I are very lucky we both love nothing better than to talk the days away. I'd have lost my reason long ago without all that idle chatter."

There was a hint of mockery in his voice which caught Isleen's attention. "You're plotting something interesting, aren't you?" She grinned.

"Maybe. But tell me true. Mahon seems to have

held your attention for quite a while despite his lack of conversation."

"He did so for a short time," she admitted. "But I was soon bored with him."

"I'm willing to wager Aofie falls in love with the Danaan prince," Lochie teased.

The injured young woman stirred in her sleep as her name was spoken. Isleen touched Aoife's forehead with a soothing hand.

"You'd be wasting a good wager," his companion said when she was sure the young woman had not overheard them. "This one is more fickle than most and far too intelligent to fall for a warrior like Mahon. She would have a Druid, a Brehon or a Bard; perhaps even a Faidh-Seer."

"What would you be willing to wager on?"

"If I'm right," Isleen told him, "and she doesn't marry the Danaan, I will have the right to ask one wish from you."

"That's a fine bet!" Lochie hummed with excitement. "And if she does marry him you must grant me one wish."

"Agreed!" she cried. "I do hope your plans don't rely on this marriage taking place."

"Not at all. But it will certainly make the outcome rather more interesting. You have no objection to me interfering in order to win, do you?"

"No objection at all," Isleen laughed. "As long as you don't object to my interference."

Lochie stood up and went to the doorway where

he held the flap of cowhide open for his companion. "I'm so happy we have managed to sort out our little differences," he whispered as he waited.

"So am I," Isleen sighed. She banked a lump of turf against the coals so it would burn slowly through the night.

"I have a feeling we are going to enjoy this little game," she added as she followed her companion out to sit with the King and Queen of the Fir-Bolg.

Chapter 7

JUST AS LOCHIE AND ISLEEN SAT DOWN THE KING RE-
turned, followed by two young men with long faces
and sullen expressions. It was obvious harsh words
had been spoken between Brocan and his sons. Sárán's
face was red with suppressed anger. Lom was unusually quiet and hung his head low. Very little besides
empty niceties passed around the gathering with the
roast pork.

It was not until the mead cups arrived that Fergus
coughed loudly to get everyone's attention. The king
looked up from his food and smiled warmly at his
foster-brother.

"A blessing on our king and queen," the veteran declared. "May Danu watch over our efforts tomorrow
as she has done so many times before." Then he
swallowed a cupful of liquor and the rest of the gathering followed suit.

When the first round of mead was finished Fergus

leaned toward his lord. When he spoke it was in barely a whisper, but it was enough to break the uneasy quiet around the cooking pit.

"My lord," the veteran began, "when you have finished your meal I have some urgent news to impart to you."

"What is it?" Brocan grunted, wishing he could brush aside the troubles of the day just for a little while.

"I would rather speak to you privately on the matter, my lord," Fergus stammered self-consciously, feeling all eyes around the fire upon him.

"Is it important?"

"Very important."

Brocan looked up from the flames and sighed. "Very well. But I have a few other matters to deal with first. None of us can afford the luxury of sleep tonight. Mahon will be going straight back to his father to report on how many warriors we have, where our lookouts are positioned and, most worrying of all, where we are camped.

"Surely the Danaans know our strength," Sárán protested.

"The battle may have been arranged in advance," his father retorted, "but we will not know how many warriors he has gathered until the fight has begun. And if he knows the whereabouts of our camp he could set sentries to scout behind us tomorrow. If we are outflanked by his force we have no chance of victory."

"What manner of king lets the enemy sit at his hearth on the night before a battle?" Riona derided.

"It was your son Sárán who brought the Danaan here," Brocan snapped.

"Lom and Aoife were with me," the young man protested. "I didn't act entirely alone."

"You are a troublemaker," Brocan hissed. "Your brother doesn't have the guile to embark on these little misadventures without some encouragement." The king didn't add that he knew perfectly well that Aoife was the instigator of this piece of mischief.

"This was none of my doing," Sárán cried. "Mahon attacked us! Lom and I were merely defending ourselves."

"Whatever the truth," Brocan dismissed, "I'm left to deal with the consequences of your actions. It must be the trickle of Danaan blood in your veins that compels you to behave with such disregard for decency."

"My mother is Eriu," Riona cut in, rising to the insult. "She is a queen of the Danaan folk, it is true, but she comes of an honored, ancient line."

"At least we can be thankful your father was a Fir-Bolg," the king replied caustically. "Eriu is only half Danaan so that diminishes the taint to your children."

"You ignorant savage!" the queen spat. "You think so highly of yourself, King Brocan. But in truth you are the petty chieftain of a province where the soil is barren, the rains unceasing and the royal talent for insult legendary. I'd strike you across the face for your insolence if it were not for the fact you reek of sea-weed and rotten fish."

"You managed to hold your breath long enough for us to conceive three children," Brocan laughed.

"How do you know they're yours?" she shot back.

The king's face turned bright red with fury.

"It is not only kings who behave so," Isleen intervened. "Every man thinks highly of himself. It is in their nature."

"There, we have the word of a wise Druid-Seer on the subject," the queen declared. "Why have we not seen you before at Dun Burren?"

"These last three winters I lodged with the Danaan king at Dun Gur as his guest," Isleen replied.

"But you are a Fir-Bolg!"

"The king does not hold any hatred for our people," the Seer replied, playing her part so well that Lochie could only smile in admiration of her performance. "He is a chieftain who values the contributions of all people."

"Tell us more," Riona hummed, certain any discussion of Cecht would annoy her husband.

"In appearance he is much the same as his son Mahon, though his hair is graying and he has an air of wisdom about him. He is generous and well loved by his people. And his children honor him as a good father and friend."

"Are you listening well, King Brocan?" Riona asked as an aside.

"I am a Fir-Bolg!" the king declared. "There is no

place for Danaan ways among my folk. Cecht has demanded an unjust honor price for the loss of his son Fearna. I have a right to object."

"And to risk the lives of your kinfolk in preserving your pride?" the queen spat.

"I've heard enough!" Brocan raged. "If you do not have anything productive to add to this discussion, kindly be quiet. The fact is the Danaan king's son has been in our camp this evening and will surely report our whereabouts and weaknesses to his father within the hour. I'm charged with the safety of my warriors and kin. I would prefer to concentrate on that problem first and listen to tales of the Danaan court later."

"We should move the camp," Sárán suggested, daring to speak up for the first time.

"By the time we have done that and set sentries again, we might as well have been awake all night," the king bellowed. We would need to work by torchlight, which would give our position away to the enemy. Moving would be a complete and utter waste of time."

The king spat a mouthful of mead into the fire. The liquor flared up as the flames caught it.

"So much valuable energy and effort was wasted today!" he went on, face reddening again. For a moment he stopped speaking, clearly trying to bring his temper under control. He poured another cup of mead from the bronze jug and sipped it before continuing.

"After midnight we'll keep a constant watch until dawn. The Danaans may plan to attack us by stealth in the night, but I am determined we will fight them face to face on the field tomorrow. In open, honorable battle."

"Cecht is an honorable man," Isleen protested. "He would never stoop to such a tactic."

"I have only your word on that!" Brocan grunted, dismissing the Seer's opinion out of hand.

"I must speak with you," Fergus hissed urgently, leaning close to the king's ear.

"Not now, brother. Can't you see the peril we are in? If we don't prepare our defenses, the Danaans will have the advantage. I want you to organize the watchmen for the night. Double the sentries and send out small patrols to ensure the enemy doesn't come upon us unawares."

"My lord," the veteran pleaded, "listen to me."

"No," Brocan cut in, holding the veteran by the sleeve, "you listen to me. I have an important announcement to make."

Fergus sighed, shaking his head.

"If I fall tomorrow," the king decreed for all to hear, "I nominate Fergus mac Fianan to rule as king in my place until the chieftains decide on a satisfactory candidate. I declare Queen Riona ineligible to rule in my place by virtue of her Danaan blood. And my sons are certainly not capable of taking the reins."

Fergus bowed humbly in formal acceptance of the great honor. And when he raised his eyes he could see admiration in every face except the queen's. Riona scowled at him in distaste.

"I will fight your decree through the Brehon courts," she declared coldly.

The veteran realized this would not be a good time to pass on his news about Aoife's confession. The queen could well use the revelation to fuel her attack on Brocan, and then the situation would truly become unbearable. He would have to speak with the king later in private. With that thought he left to go about his duties.

"Now there is one other matter I wish to deal with," Brocan hissed. "My three children." The king sat back in his low chair as a jug of water was passed to him. He took a long cooling drink then placed the vessel at his feet. "Aoife is sleeping?" he asked the Seer.

"She is resting peacefully, lord," Isleen answered.

"She has already been punished for her part in this escapade," the king decided. "Her arm will cause her considerable pain. She won't forget this episode in a hurry. But Sárán and Lom are another matter."

"Lom was not involved in our plans," Sárán cut in. "It was Aoife and I alone who decided to come to the battleground against your wishes."

"How did your brother know where to find you?" Brocan snapped, casting a suspicious glance at his wife. "Did your mother know anything about all this?"

"No," Sárán declared. "Mother knew nothing of our decision to follow you."

"I overheard the two of them planning everything," Lom admitted. "Aoife and Sárán are not discreet when it comes to plotting their adventures."

"You knew two of my subjects were going to disobey a command from their king and father," Brocan bellowed, "and you failed to report it to me?"

"I thought it best not to bother you. You were so busy with preparations for the battle."

"But you did not hesitate to go to your mother with the news?"

"Mother advised me to say nothing," Lom blurted before he realized he had been tricked.

The king turned to his wife with a self-satisfied smile. "It seems there's been some disloyalty among my kin," he stated, clearly pleased he had discovered the queen's indiscretion. "Why did you not send word to me when your son Lom gave you this information?"

"I tried to speak with you," Riona explained coolly. "But you had no time to listen. You were off planning your own adventure. Perhaps if you had discussed matters with me this might never have happened. Don't you see, your children were just seeking some attention from their father?"

Brocan frowned. He had heard this argument before. It did not impress him. "I am the king," he explained slowly, as if speaking to a child. "I have far-reaching responsibilities which demand my complete attention."

Brocan turned to Lom. "Do you see what trouble you have brought on us all by remaining silent? You are the only sensible one among my three children. Compared to you, Sárán and Aoife are nothing more than fools. That's why I am most annoyed at you. You should have told me!"

"Yes, Father."

"What else have you kept from me?" Brocan sighed. "What other surprises have these two got in store for me?"

Lom looked down at the ground, trying not to show how upset he really was. The young man was suddenly overcome with a desire to tell his father all that Sárán had told him about Fearna's death in the snow.

He turned his eyes into the fire so he would not have to face his father. The coals glowed orange with a thousand twisting shapes and shadows, but all the young man saw was Fearna's cold corpse.

"It is not Lom's fault," Sárán pleaded. "He had nothing to do with all this. If it had not been for him, both Aoife and I would have been killed. He saved our lives."

Lom looked up at his twin brother and gave a quick smile of gratitude.

"Tomorrow we fight a battle against an ancient enemy," the king sighed. "And in my opinion we stand a very good chance of losing the day. I will not place a punishment upon my sons tonight. If we are defeated I will almost certainly not be returning home. In which case the new king will decide such matters."

Brocan grinned with determination. "If by the graces of the Goddess Danu I live beyond tomorrow, my boys will know what wrath is," he promised. "For now, you are not to stray out of my sight for an instant. Not for any reason. Not to sleep. Not even to empty your bladder. Do you understand?"

"Does that mean we will accompany you to the battleground tomorrow?" Sárán asked with excitement.

"You will," Brocan confirmed. "And you will go unarmed."

"Unarmed?"

"Pray that we gain the day." The king chortled as he saw the black humor in what he was about to say. "Or by this time tomorrow you may find yourself a prisoner of that fine Danaan prince you wrestled to the ground and treated so poorly this morning."

"So the great circle comes around again," Lochie the Bard cut in. "I know a few fine tales along that theme," he offered.

"Not tonight, Bard of the North," the king replied, rubbing the heel of his hand across his forehead to soothe his headache. "Nothing portentous if you don't mind."

"What about the tale of Balor of the Evil Eye?" Isleen suggested and watched the color drain from her companion's face. She gently put an arm around his shoulders. "That is one of the best tales he tells," she informed everyone with a smug smile. "I never tire of hearing it."

"No," Brocan countered.

The Bard breathed easily and gave a relieved smile.

"That is where this whole business began. All our

differences with the Danaans can be traced back to those days," the king reminded them all.

"For there must be conflict in the world," Lochie stated in his clear storyteller's voice.

No one else but Isleen knew these had been Balor's very words to the Watchers before they were dispatched to do their work.

"Without conflict, pain, struggle, fear, and tragedy," went on Lochie, "the lessons of this world and the next would be worthless. Joy is the goal of all but it is bought dearly in this world."

"The laws pertaining to battle are what I would hear," Brocan decided suddenly. He did not wish to hear talk of fear or tragedy tonight.

"This should be very interesting," Isleen whispered to her companion. "The rules of battle explained by one who never shies away from cheating at every opportunity."

The Bard bowed slightly to acknowledge her quip but he did not let her know just how happy her comments made him.

"I was sure you would enjoy this game," he whispered to himself with delight.

Chapter 8

SÁRÁN WAS TOO RESTLESS TO STAY SEATED AT THE FIRE all night listening to Bardic recitations. His heart was wounded by his father's harsh rebuke. No harm had been done, he told himself. The little adventure he and his sister had indulged themselves in had caused some embarrassment but no one had been hurt.

But more than this, King Brocan had treated Mahon, the son of his enemy, with greater dignity and respect than he ever offered his children, just as he had treated Fearna with unfair favoritism. Sárán glanced across at his twin brother and wondered if Lom was having the same thoughts. But it was unlikely his brother would nurture resentment in his heart. Lom looked up to their father in a way Sárán had never understood.

After enduring the critical gaze of the warriors for a long while Sárán managed to slip away into the shadows to look in on his sister. No one noticed him leave the gathering, or if they did they thought better of interfering in the affairs of King Brocan's children.

When he reached her bedside Aoife seemed to be breathing lowly so he didn't stay long, instead he left the hut to wander off aimlessly for a while. Before long he found himself standing where he could observe the main fire without being seen. In the shadows he could overhear Lochie's recitation of the rules of war. Sárán leaned against a tree to listen, beginning to admit the foolishness of Aoife's adventure.

"You shouldn't blame yourself for what happened on the hilltop," a warm feminine voice soothed, and the young man spun around startled to see who had spoken. "Aoife led you into that terrible situation. You behaved honorably in defending her."

A trail of orange sparks glittered in the sea of Isleen's gorgeous green eyes. Something about her sweet comforting tone and her compassionate expression relaxed Sárán completely. The young man sighed as he turned to look toward the fire again.

"If only my father agreed with you," he replied. "King Cecht's sons are better treated in the Fir-Bolg court than Brocan's own."

"One day your father will be proud of you," Isleen assured him, putting a gentle hand on his shoulder. Now her voice was breathy and deep. "Pride is the only language the King of the Fir-Bolg understands. His respect is hard won."

The Seer moved closer and placed an arm around the young man. "You've made mistakes, it's true," she conceded, her face close to his. "I know about the circumstances surrounding the death of Fearna."

Sárán suddenly pulled away to look into her eyes. "What do you know?" he whispered, eyes darting this way and that, fearing their conversation would be overheard.

"I know it was not murder," the Seer replied, taking one of his hands in hers. "It was misadventure. Though you were a party to the young Danaan's drunkenness, it does not necessarily follow you were responsible for his death."

"I should have seen the danger."

"Fearna was hopelessly in love with your sister. The poor besotted fool would have done anything she asked of him. Don't blame yourself. It's Aoife who must answer for the crime. You were merely following after her to make sure no one was harmed."

"If that's true, then I failed miserably," Sárán said, biting his lip.

Isleen drew him closer to comfort him and Sárán caught the calming scent of lavender about her.

"You misjudged the situation," she purred. "We're all capable of such mistakes now and then. There is no sense in blaming yourself."

"If my father discovered Aoife and I were involved in the death of Fearna, he would never forgive us."

"He might," Isleen smiled, touching a finger to his chin as if she were talking to a child, "if I spoke to him about it."

Sárán frowned. "Why would you intervene on my behalf?"

"You'll make a fine Druid one day. If you have a mind to follow the sacred path of the Ollamh-Dreamers, I would like to take you on as a student."

"I've always thought of myself as a warrior." He shrugged.

"You'd do well to consider my offer. I have been searching for a suitable student for some time. I believe you would do perfectly."

Sárán suddenly felt very uncomfortable. He moved away from her slightly as the scent of lavender filled his senses, overwhelming him.

"You're a very clever young man," Isleen continued. "One day you'll be the Chief Bard of your kinfolk and perhaps your brother Lom will be King of the Fir-Bolg of the Burren."

She reached over and touched a finger to Sárán's cheek. "You are much more handsome than your father. I'll wager the young women follow after you like lost calves."

The young man blushed and shook his head meekly.

Isleen laughed a little to herself. "Then perhaps it's time you found yourself a woman to teach you something of such matters. A Druid-Seer must be skilled in the arts of music, poetry and dreaming, but if he is also a master of the arts of love, his name will be remembered down the generations."

"Wh-what do you mean?" Sárán stuttered nervously.

"We'll have to find you a good teacher," Isleen hummed, "if you are to fulfill your destiny as a great Ollamh-Dreamer."

"My father doesn't share your high opinion of me."

"Your father is an old fool," the Seer whispered. "He's too proud to make peace with the Danaans and too stupid to see his own kinfolk are tired of war. He's never won a decisive victory against King Cecht. Your father is weak-willed and prone to fits of temper which don't serve him when it comes to gaining the upper hand in negotiations."

"He'll not listen to any advice offered him," Sárán agreed. "Unless it comes from old Uncle Fergus."

"The veteran is a good-hearted man," Isleen noted. "But he is blinded by his love and devotion to your father. Between them they've crippled the Fir-Bolg of the Burren with their short-sighted strategies and their inept direction of the wars. Your clanspeople need a strong leader who's not afraid to take hard measures to gain victory. They need a man who'll lead the charge and win the battle once and for all."

"I should be king," the young man cut in gruffly.

Isleen started to laugh again.

"I'd be a good leader!" he snapped back.

"A king is nothing compared to a Druid. Kings only believe they wield power. But it is the Druid class who truly hold the reins. Brithemi create and enforce the law. The Ollamh-Dreamers, the Fathi, advise all rulers on all important matters. The Filidh-Bards keep history and cite precedent. The Poets among them preserve the memory of great events in their compositions. The Ceoltóiri Harpers travel the Otherworld and the future."

"But it's kings who go to war," the young man objected. "The warrior class protects the king and the king leads the warriors."

"Any strong-arm may train as a warrior," Isleen pressed. "It doesn't take any muscle between the ears to lift up a sword, but it takes wisdom to persuade warriors to lay down their weapons. Far easier to start a war than to stop one."

Sárán looked away.

"Why are you drawn so to power?" she inquired sharply.

"I'm not!" the lad quickly responded. "But I don't want to spend my days hauling nets, gathering seaweed for the gardens, or tending cows. I was bred for better things."

The young man looked into the Seer's eyes. "No one remembers the name of a fisherman, no matter how learned he was in his skill. I want my name to be spoken with respect and awe. No king's counselor will be recalled with such honor. And one day the Fir-Bolg will again rule the west from the Island of the Towers to the great rocks of Skellig."

"Ah, but with your brother Lom as King of the Fir-Bolg and you advising him," Isleen countered, "I have no doubt which of you would be the true ruler of your people."

"Lom's soul is too pure," Sárán conceded, "his ideas

too high-minded. Our father recognized that when we were quite young. I was always the more determined of us both. The chieftainship of the kindred clans of the Fir-Bolg will fall to me. But if I'm the power which supports the kingship of Lom," he reasoned, "he'll be praised for my actions should they succeed, but blamed should they fail."

"Bide the days patiently," Isleen crooned, stroking his forearm softly. "Let's await the outcome of the fight tomorrow. Whatever happens, your life is about to change forever. Better you have some part in deciding your path than simply leaving it up to others to plot it out for you."

"The Fir-Bolg are outnumbered," the young man sighed. "We can't hope to beat the enemy on the battleground."

"Even the warlike Danaans may be defeated by a stern eye, a stout heart, and a quick wit. If your father had the courage to charge at them without thought for his own safety or the consequences, even the Danaans would fall back in disarray. Cecht recognizes a determined attack when he sees one, and I don't believe he would stand against a warrior who seemed to throw aside all fear."

"My father is frightened?"

"He's scared out of his wits," Isleen chortled as if it were obvious. "Haven't you considered what's at stake? If the enemy win the fight tomorrow it will be the end of Brocan's reign and the beginning of a new era. The Fir-Bolg people will likely become an insignificant source of tribute to the greater Danaan kingdoms."

"There's nothing I can do about that," Sárán replied in frustration. "Matters have gone too far. It's out of my hands. If I had not been forbidden to carry weapons tomorrow—"

"Don't give up hope, my dear young man," Isleen interrupted. "There may yet be an opportunity for you to play your part in the fight. If not, then you must watch what happens carefully. The lessons you learn will be extremely valuable in the future."

She took his chin in her hand and forcibly turned his face to hers. "Whatever you do, remember you are descended from a race of Poets and Seers. You have the elixir of music in your veins, and the wisdom of the Brehons guides your spirit. Through your mother's people you have Danaan blood. Her kin are famed for their Druid ancestry. Take the path of the Ollamh-Dreamers. That road will lead to a life of high office."

"I'll consider your advice," the young man promised, unable to raise any further protest when looking into those beguiling green eyes.

"It'll be a sad day if the Fir-Bolg are dissolved among the Danaans." Isleen shook her head. "If your father can't pay the fine, you and your siblings will be ordered to marry into his people. That will be the end of our folk within a generation."

"I detest the Danaans!" Sárán replied in disgust. "I could never agree to such a marriage."

"Your sister Aoife will likely be forced to wed first. A child born of the Danaan and Fir-Bolg royal houses would command the allegiance of both peoples. Such a child would mark the merging of two old enemies and an end to conflict forever. But such a birth would also be the first of many."

"Aoife would never agree to wed a Danaan," Sárán laughed. "She despises them almost as much as I do."

"Do not judge all Danaans by your experience of one weak-willed and feeble-minded boy," Isleen warned him. "Fearna was not fit to rule. That was the only reason he was sent as a hostage to your people. He was of no value to his own. I have heard this discussed in the hall of King Cecht. The Danaans mean to marry Mahon to your sister to bring the wars to an end."

"I will not allow it!" Sárán spat.

"I knew I could rely on you to stand up for our people," she told him, patting him on the shoulder.

She smiled to think of her wager with Lochie. Then she leaned close to kiss Sárán lightly on the cheek. "When the time comes and you are looking for a teacher, I would be honored to tutor you. I am no expert on the subject of law—that is my husband's talent—but I am an authority on matters of love and dreaming. I have trained as a Seer," she added. "I know something of the future. Yours is bright as long as you make the correct decisions now. Follow your heart, not your head, and you may be surprised at the gifts which shower down upon you."

With that the Seer turned and walked back to the fire.

"Isleen is a Seer," Sárán said to himself, the last of his doubts washed away. "She has witnessed the future. If I ignore her advice I am fighting my own destiny. She told me to follow my heart. And so I shall."

Then he sat down in the shadows, leaning against the side of a tree.

"Be patient," he told himself. "Endure the troubles of today. In the morning the world will be turned upside down. And then my time will be at hand."

Chapter 9

Brocan wiped the sweat from his brow and squatted briefly by a sapling birch. Sword drawn, arrayed in full fighting gear, he steeled himself for battle and prayed to Danu that the victory would fall to him. At his side and all around him grouped tight as acorns on the oak were his band of warriors, kinfolk all.

Slow steady-handed veterans crouched beside young untried fighters. The healer Fineen, though Danaan by birth, was there as well to lend his skill if need should summon him. And relegated to the rear were the twins, Sárán and Lom, for Brocan did not trust them out of his sight.

No sound rose from this determined company. Faces were grim and hard, senses sharpened for any evidence of the foe. Step by careful step the warrior band crept toward the precincts of the battleground.

There was no sign of the enemy; no Danaan scouts had ventured out this far. The creatures of the forest ignored them. Soon enough sword arms would have work aplenty. So Brocan decided they should rest to catch their breath. At the ring of ash trees which marked the outer edge of a broad central courtyard they waited, keeping cover.

Every man and woman among the warriors fixed their concentration on the cleared space before them. For it was held sacred by the Fir-Bolg. It was an ancient meeting place named Óenach Samhain, the Samhain Assembly. On this open ground each turning of the seasons, on the eve of the first day of the new cycle, Druid kind and all the Burren folk would gather.

Samhain is the night which marks the beginning of the cold days of cattle slaughter. Next morning the breeding stock is separated from those animals destined to feed the clan through winter. But Samhain Eve is also the time of Draoi-Songs, the prayers of thanks, spells of creation, musical expressions of the seasons turning on the great wheel of eternity. These sacred songs had been celebrated since before the Fir-Bolg gave themselves that name.

Such holy incantations call on all the elements to rally. Winter cannot be allowed to triumph over life. Fire, water, earth and air must be summoned to bestow their influence evenly on the whole of Innisfail. To neglect the Draoi is to risk an eternal night, a frozen future. That is how it was in the days before the Islands of the West were flooded. Ice gripped the oceans, snow stifled growth, a frozen wasteland spread across the earth. But Draoi-Songs drove away the cold.

Life was harder then when the ice-rivers ran. The survival of the clans depended on the Draoi-Craft and the wisdom of the Druid kind as much as on the experience and good sense of the king. So every Samhain Eve the chieftains and Druids faced a test of their skills.

The test was named Tarbhfeis, the bull feast.

A Seer of the Faidh class who had earned the title Ollamh fasted three winters without meat or fish. Then on Samhain Eve, after ritual preparation, this Druid feasted on flesh and blood taken from a newly slain bull and retreated into a darkened cave or sacred mound where light and sound were strangers. And if all went well the Seer, imbued with the soul-force of the bull and the vitality of its blood, stepped into the Otherworld to glimpse the coming winter. Spirit journeys are seldom simple matters, but they yield vital clues which guide the learned sage along the way.

All the while the king must play Brandubh against the highest Druid in the land, or against his emissary. In this manner kings were vetoed from their office or confirmed in good judgment for another passing cycle of the seasons. This tradition continued long after the ice-rivers had thawed, even into the time of Brocan, King of the Fir-Bolg.

Mopping his sweating forehead with the sleeve of his saffron shirt, King Brocan thought back to the previous Samhain Eve. The Seer had been a gifted woman of the Bretani people who had their dwelling in the northeast. Her accent had been thick and her pronouncements colored by the strangeness of her speech, but Brocan reassured himself that all would be well. The Druids would not have confirmed him in the kingship if they had perceived any hint of trouble in the future. Yet the holy ones had not foreseen young Fearna's death, nor the dispute which brought his people to this field. Suddenly Brocan began to have doubts.

Nearby the bushes shuffled, startling him. The king cocked his head and squinted. "What was that?" he hissed, spreading his arms out to silence those around him. But his signal had the opposite effect. Each warrior quickly expressed an opinion under his breath.

"Be quiet!" the king commanded.

As they waited for any further noises, a slim young man stood up. His hair was as black as the underside of a cauldron. And he pushed his way roughly past any who stood between himself and the king.

"What is it now?" Sárán spat impatiently. "What's the delay?"

"Your father heard a noise," Fineen replied and in that instant a great shout rose up somewhere across the little valley. It was the war cry of the Danaans.

"We must make for higher ground!" the king decided. "If we can't see them, we can't fight them."

"I'll lead some warriors to scout that hill," Sárán declared. "We've been creeping around on our hands and knees since before dawn. How can we fight the Danaans if we don't know where to find them?"

"You'll do as you are told!" the king countered. "Fergus will lead the scouting party. You'll go with him, obey his commands, and learn from one who knows something of warfare."

"Very well, Father," Sárán answered, forcing a smile so everyone would see he was ready to serve the king. "I'll do as you command me!"

"No one is to attack unless the order comes from my own mouth," Brocan added, looking at Fergus.

The old veteran silently nodded his assurance.

"If we are set upon by the enemy I am sure we will give a good account of ourselves," Sárán cut in.

"You're only here because you deceived me," Brocan bellowed, realizing too late his raised voice would probably attract the attention of the enemy.

"I want your brother and yourself where my warriors can keep a watch on you," the king went on, lowering his voice again to a hoarse whisper. "I can't trust you to stay out of trouble. Just be glad I don't send you back to camp to sit with your mother. She'd surely keep you busy helping with the spinning."

"Mother wouldn't force me to do anything I didn't wish to do," the young man retorted.

"Riona is a troublemaker. I wish she were not your mother."

"Why isn't she here on the field to witness the fight?" Sárán asked.

"Because I trust her even less than I trust you and

Lom," Brocan spat back. "Now do as you are commanded or I'll not be answerable for what becomes of you."

"Lom and I captured an enemy warrior yesterday," Sárán protested. "Let us carry weapons."

Brocan laughed.

"Have you never any good words to say for us?" the young man shot back.

"None," the king said. "I've done my best to toughen you both up in preparation for life. For it is almost certain one of you will become king after me. Lom at least shows some promise. He has a good head on his shoulders and knows how to follow orders. But you, Sárán? If it weren't for the fact that you and your brother are twins, I would question my parentage of you."

"I'm not all that happy to call you my father either."

"Be careful. I could easily disown you."

"Do as our father asks you," Lom cut in. He had made his way forward when he heard the king's voice raised. "We're not warriors yet. Father has been fighting the Danaans all his life."

"That's part of the problem," Sárán replied angrily. "The king has grown stale and timid. I have no wish to be a warrior if I am required to demean myself as he does."

The two young men faced each other and to all who saw them they were each reflections in a polished bronze mirror. Black-haired, long-faced and wiry, with paling skins they were. And both had dark eyes as fathomless as the depths of the ocean.

Another great shout arose from across the battle-ground, shattering the unspoken tension between the twins.

"Lom," the king ordered quickly, "see that your brother doesn't come to harm. You pair are a danger to my other warriors. Sárán will watch over you in your first battle and you will keep an eye on him. That way at least one of you may return home safely this evening."

"Yes, Father," the pair answered, though Sárán's voice lacked conviction.

"Now go," Brocan told them sternly. "And don't cause me any further anguish. I'm already paying for the misdeeds of others. I'm compelled to fight this battle to clear a debt from my name. Don't compound the problem for me."

Fineen watched the two young men smile at each other. Their hair fell in the same way across their faces. Their voices usually accented the same words; they laughed in precisely the same manner and often at the same time. Few folk could tell Lom and Sárán apart. But the physician decided a skilled reader of souls might perceive some differences.

"Come along, lads," Fergus ordered. "We'd best get this job done."

The pair nodded then followed after the veteran. But as soon as they were out of earshot of the king Fergus stopped and beckoned the lads over to him.

"I saw your sister yesterday after her accident," he told them.

"I heard she suffered great pain," Lom replied.

"Not as much as you will suffer if you endanger my life or those of my warriors," Fergus replied with a cold threat. "Do you understand me? I know more about you lads than you might think, and if I were king you'd pay for your wrongdoing."

"I've done no wrong," Sárán scoffed.

Fergus leaned in close. "Aoife tells a different story," he hissed. "I know all about Fearna and I intend to tell your father before this battle becomes a needless slaughter."

The young man's face paled for a moment but then he objected defiantly, "I am the king's son Sárán, you cannot speak to me in that tone."

"I'm your uncle. I'll speak to you in whatever manner I see fit. Would you dare stand up to me?"

"Gladly," Sárán taunted. "Give me a sword."

"No!" Lom begged. "Calm yourselves."

"Give me a sword," his brother insisted.

"Sárán," Lom interrupted. "This is not a game. We've caused enough trouble already."

"I want a blade."

"Do you think I carry spare weapons around in case some young boy wants to take his first blooding in battle?" Fergus mocked. "If you want to carry a sword you'll have to return to camp and get one. I'll not restrain you. Go with my blessing."

"By the time I go back to fetch a sword the battle will be over," Sárán answered in outrage.

"Very likely." Fergus nodded.

"You call yourself a warrior?" Sárán spat. "Be good to your word and give me a blade!"

"Be quiet!" the veteran told him firmly. "Fineen is a master at setting broken bones. I've witnessed his work. I don't wish to see any more for a while but that won't stop me giving you a beating you'll never forget. So do as I tell you."

Fergus quickly passed instructions to the other three warriors in the scouting party, who set off up the hill, then ordered Lom and Sárán to follow him. They'd not gone far up the slope when the word came that the hilltop was deserted. Disappointed, Sárán followed Fergus back to the king without once sighting their opponents.

Not long afterward the entire war band reached the hill summit, still crouched low in case the Danaans should see them. They could hear shouts and taunts coming from across the valley but there was no visible sign of the enemy.

Brocan stared down toward the flat cleared space at the bottom of the hill. His eyes strained as he watched the opposite hilltop where Aoife and her brothers had encountered the enemy the previous day. But by the time the sun was three hands above the horizon he was no wiser of the Danaans' whereabouts. The king could feel himself becoming very tense, expecting an attack at any moment.

"This could be a vicious fight," Fergus began, knowing this might be his last chance to speak his news. Yet still he was unwilling for he and Brocan had been together since they were babes in arms. Fergus didn't want to bear any tidings which could break his brother's heart.

"I have never known the Danaans to withhold an attack in this manner unless their intention was a terrible slaughter," he continued hesitantly.

Brocan grunted agreement.

"Let us walk away from this quarrel and make a settlement."

The king turned his head sharply to his foster-brother. "It's too late for that!" he spat. "My honor would never—"

"My lord," Fergus interrupted, "there is something I must tell you."

"Not now, brother. Perhaps if we survive this battle we'll have time to talk."

"I've foolishly tarried in bringing this to your attention," the veteran went on, ignoring Brocan's reply. "This is not an easy subject to broach. But it'll be too late to speak to you after the fight."

At that moment the king stood up and stared at the opposite hill. "They're coming!" he announced loudly, taking no notice of the veteran. No sooner had he spoken than a hundred naked Danaans ran to the top of the hill across the little valley. There they stood in three long ranks, spears thrust toward the heavens, shields laid flat at their feet.

"There are so many of them," Brocan noted with quiet dismay.

A tall gray-bearded warrior stepped out from the

ranks of Danaan men and women to raise a sword above his head. As he let the weapon fall to his side the Danaans began chanting. It was a slow, steady song. The men thrummed a deep haunting chorus as the women's voices danced a lively melody around it.

Lom stood up beside his father to have a closer look. "They're wild people," he whispered in awe.

"They're savages," the king corrected.

"They're my people," Fineen added indignantly. "Try not to forget that when I'm tending your wounded warriors later in the day."

Brocan ignored him, staring transfixed by the enemy, despite having faced them many times before. The Danaans were painted head to foot in blue-green patterns similar to those they chiseled out on their standing stones. Spirals swirled about the faces, zig-zags snaked down their arms and legs. The hair of every one of them was caked with white clay so it stood up like the spiked grasses of the plains. The men were mostly clean-shaven. The women wild-eyed.

Brocan felt his stomach begin to turn. He had a sense some disaster was about to befall his people. Fergus was right, this would be a terrible fight.

Just then the warrior who had stepped out of the ranks put down his sword in front of him and the rhythmic chanting ceased instantly.

"I am Cecht," the warrior declared in a strong, commanding voice. "Who are you to come to the Óenach Samhain on a day when my people would quarrel with the Fir-Bolg of Burren?"

Brocan took half a dozen paces forward so he could be seen clearly. "I am the King of the Fir-Bolg of Burren," he declared. "I am called Brocan. I will answer your summons to fight."

"So be it!" Cecht replied. "Only full battle will atone for the loss of my youngest son to your cowardly, irresponsible stewards."

"Your son fell from his horse because he was not careful enough," Brocan protested. "His death was not the doing of any of my people."

Cecht did not speak another word. He knelt down quickly to pick up his sword from the grass and as he did so all his warriors knelt down also. When the Danaans rose to their feet again they had their shields in their hands. This polished wall of bronze caught the rays of the morning sun and dazzled the faces of the waiting Fir-Bolg. Brocan felt the hearts of his warriors waver.

"So that's why they chose that particular hill," Fergus mused, "to catch the morning sun."

"It is quite an impressive show," Brocan agreed. "But it'll take more than reflected sunlight to stop my people."

"We are forty," Fergus reminded his king urgently. "They are one hundred. I trust you don't imagine we can defeat them. We might wound their pride or ruffle their self-esteem, but they'll surely have the day. You can stop this now with a simple gesture of peace."

"In my heart of hearts I don't wish to fight," Brocan sighed. "I'm weary of warfare. But I've no choice. You know as well as I do Fearna was drunk when he fell from that horse. He was a guest in our house. I admit I should have been more vigilant, but I'll not be blamed for his death. I won't pay compensation."

"The lad was goaded on by your children," Fergus blurted.

"What?"

"Aoife told me last night," the veteran explained. "She and Sárán dared the boy to outdo them at drinking. It was all just light-hearted fun until the Danaan lad decided to take a midnight ride."

"That's not the story I heard," Brocan fumed. "I was told he had taken a bad temper, swallowed a jug of fine mead, then stolen a horse. Why didn't you tell me this earlier?"

"I have been trying, my lord. You wouldn't listen."

From the other hill King Cecht bellowed out another challenge. "Have you lost your courage, Brocan? Come and meet my folk on the holy ground between us. Or have the Fir-Bolg lost their stomach for battle?"

Brocan felt each word strike at him like a spear point. He turned around to avoid looking across at his enemy. "Sárán!" he grunted. "Come here."

"I am here," the young man answered as he stepped forward.

"You and your sister enticed the Danaan prince to drink heavily?"

"We did, Father," Sárán admitted without remorse. "I am not ashamed to admit Fearna would still be alive if he'd been sober. And it's true, Aoife and myself persuaded him to take a ride."

"Not ashamed?"

"He was a Danaan," Sárán said belligerently. "An enemy. He had captured your attention and he would have taken Aoife's also if he'd had the chance."

The king said nothing. His face was reddened with a mix of rage and embarrassment.

"It's not too late to save some lives," Brocan realized with defeat as he quickly reassessed the situation. "I'll pay the eric-fine for the Danaan prince and maybe all this can be forgotten."

"One hundred red cows," Fergus reminded him. "Maybe even more since we let the matter come as far as the battleground before we took action to settle damages."

"Where will I find one hundred cows?" Brocan asked in despair. "My people will likely go hungry this year and I will have to bear the shame of it all. This'll be the end of my kingship. The chieftains of the Fir-Bolg won't elect me again after this debacle."

The king closed his eyes a moment. When he opened them there was determination on his face once more. Without hesitation he strode directly toward the hilltop where the enemy could see him. Then Brocan held his arms wide, his sword in the air.

"I am Brocan, King of the Fir-Bolg of Burren," he shouted. "I have no wish for blood to be spilled over this matter. I would speak with King Cecht under a truce."

"You mustn't back down to them!" Sárán hissed, recalling Isleen's words of the night before. "You can't mean to just give in! No wonder folk are saying your kingship is ended." Sárán's eyes were two black coals lit with passionate anger.

Brocan's face emptied of emotion.

"This is your handiwork," Fergus growled. "Do not interfere."

Cecht was already making his way down to the cleared space between the hills, escorted by two of his warriors. The three Danaans were unarmed but in their battle paint they still seemed fierce and battle-ready.

"Take this, Sárán," Brocan ordered, handing the young man his sword with contempt. "You wanted to bear a blade in battle. Now you shall carry my weapon for the rest of the day. I'll not be in need of it." He turned to the old veteran. "Come with me, will you Fergus?"

"The Danaan king has two warriors for escort," Fergus cautioned.

"You're worth two Danaans," Brocan shot back. But when Fergus did not smile the king held a hand up to show he would take his friend's advice. "Fineen will come with us also."

"I hope we won't stand in need of his skill at setting bones," the veteran breathed solemnly.

Fergus handed his blade to Lom with an unspoken command to take good care of it. With that the three men started off down the hill toward the flat cleared place known as Óenach Samhain.

They'd not gone far when the ranks of Danaans began to jeer and shout insults at them. Brocan took it well, holding his head high as he walked, as if the taunts gave him all the more strength of purpose. Fergus shut the noise out of his mind completely, and Fineen was already composing a poem about the famous King Brocan of the Fir-Bolg who was the most honorable ruler in the land.

Near the edge of the battleground closest to the Fir-Bolg hill there was a flattened stone ten paces from the circle of trees. It was long and wide enough for two men to stand up above the heads of any listeners. This rock was used as a platform by the Brehons to pronounce the victors in any test of arms.

There at the Victory Stone Cecht and his two warriors waited for Brocan to arrive. All three Danaans nervously looked about them, expecting treachery at any moment. At the top of the Fir-Bolg hill Sárán muttered under his breath, cursing quietly as he watched the scene unfold.

"Father spoke of his reputation," the young man whispered to himself. "How will his good name live after this?"

"He has no choice in the matter," Lom cut in as if his brother had been addressing him.

"We can't stand by and let the King of the Fir-Bolg humble himself and his people before the Danaans," Sárán replied indignantly.

"There's nothing we can do," his brother answered. "If you'd told the truth about Fearna's death in the first place perhaps the situation might have been different."

Sárán accepted his brother's rebuke but in his mind he heard Isleen goading him on to act. She had foretold he would play an important part in the outcome of this battle, and she was a Seer who had obviously glimpsed the future. In a flash the young man knew what he must do.

"I must make amends. Father is right. This terrible shame is all my doing," Sárán whispered. "If he agrees to pay the eric-fine our people will go hungry. This could tear our clans apart."

"What can we possibly do now it has come to this?" Lom asked with resignation in his voice.

"There's only one thing to do," his twin told him coldly as he held up their father's sword.

Lom felt his blood turning to ice.

"What madness has come over you, brother?" he stuttered.

Sárán smiled as he raised his father's weapon to the sky, watching with awe as the highly polished bronze shone in the morning sun. Distorted, twisted shapes reflected on the surface of the blade. The young man stared at them and saw a bright future. He stepped forward so the Danaan warriors could see him.

Lom reached out in horror to grab his brother by the sleeve. But Sárán was already gone, racing recklessly down the slope toward the Victory Stone. Without a thought for the danger Lom hurled himself headlong after his twin, frantic to halt him before it was too late.

He waved his uncle's blade wildly to keep his balance on the rough ground as he shouted his brother's name to the four winds. But Sárán had a good lead on him and he was not making a sound as he ran. So it was Lom's shouting that first attracted Brocan's attention. The king had just spoken a greeting to Cecht when he heard his son's voice. He turned to see what all the commotion was about and was faced with the sight of Lom running furiously down toward him bearing a weapon. Perhaps because his brother was yelling at the top of his lungs, no one noticed Sárán.

Cecht stepped back as his two warriors instinctively shielded him with their bodies. The Danaans and the Fir-Bolg on opposite hills fell silent, shocked at this unbelievable breach of tradition.

It was Fineen who first noticed Sárán running toward them through the trees. The healer stepped away from Brocan and Fergus with his arms held out wide so the young man would plainly see he offered no threat.

"What are you doing?" Fineen demanded loudly.

Sárán had his eyes fixed on the Danaan king. He hardly even glanced at the healer. Fineen felt the blood drain from his face.

"You've come far enough," the healer declared, holding his hands high and placing himself directly in front of the young man. "Stop here or there'll be a terrible price to pay."

"Out of my way, Danaan!" Sárán cried venomously. "Or you'll be the first of your people to fall."

Sárán held out the sword level in front of him. Then he slashed at the air believing Fineen would step back out of the way to avoid the blow. But the healer had never dodged a blade in his life, much less trained for war. No one had ever raised as much as a hand to him. He had no idea what to do if attacked.

The physician held up a hand to shield his face and the blade struck his forearm. This weapon was not one of the sharp-edged cutting swords the Danaans often carried. It was a short stabbing instrument meant for fighting at very close quarters. The blade drew blood but it wasn't sharp enough to injure Fineen badly.

The shock of the blow passed quickly. The healer stared straight at Sárán who had ceased his charge and was standing panting with excitement and exertion. Suddenly Fineen forgot his pain, grabbed the blade and held it tight.

"Put the weapon down," he demanded. "Your actions will only bring grief. Lay the sword aside and return to the hilltop."

Sárán's face turned red. In a rage he wrenched the blade from the healer. And before anyone could come to Fineen's aid, Sárán stabbed the point of the weapon hard into the healer's chest.

At that moment Lom arrived, still screaming his

brother's name with all the force he could muster. Fergus was shocked out of inaction and he strode forward to punch Lom effortlessly to the ground. Then he swung around to deal with Sárán.

But before Fergus could lay a hand on the young man a great shout of outrage rose up from the Danaan ranks. The veteran looked up to see the enemy charging in an angered mass down the hill. There was fire in their eyes and hatred in their voices.

Cecht and his escort were gone. They had already retreated to safe ground to retrieve their weapons. Battle was now unavoidable. Fergus swallowed hard and not for the first time wondered if he was about to lose his life.

While the veteran was distracted Sárán thrust the sword point at the healer three more times. Fineen fell as his knees buckled under him and pain overcame his senses.

Fergus let his own fury wash over him. In a flash he caught Sárán by the back of the neck with one hand and disarmed him with the other. Then he pounded the lad with his fists, blinded by anger and shock. The veteran didn't stop until he felt Brocan dragging him away.

"Hurry!" the king cried, retrieving their two swords. "If you don't get a move on they'll be on us. Now we've no choice but to fight. What of Fineen?"

The veteran dropped Sárán who slumped on the ground, rendered senseless by his beating. Fergus quickly examined the healer and with the instinct of a battle-hardened warrior knew immediately that if Fineen wasn't dead he was close to it.

"There's nothing we can do to soothe him," he reported.

Fergus raised his eyes toward the approaching Danaans, then looked over his shoulder toward the Fir-Bolg ranks. King Brocan's warriors were charging down to aid their ruler but it was clear they would not reach the battleground in time.

"Retreat back up the hill!" Brocan bellowed. "You carry Lom. I'll take Sárán."

"Let them both rot!" Fergus cried angrily.

"They're my sons," Brocan protested.

Fergus grumbled but he didn't argue. He settled the unconscious body across his shoulders and made his way back up the hill. The charging Fir-Bolg spilled down the slope through the trees toward them.

Brocan was just behind Fergus as their warriors met them. The twins were dumped unceremoniously between two oaks and instantly forgotten. In the next second Brocan and Fergus raised their blades to join the tightly packed throng, all the warriors screaming wildly as they charged toward their doom.

At the foot of the Victory Stone the two war parties met with a great clash. There in that place the first blood was spilled between Fir-Bolg and Danaan. Brocan, overcome with shame, led the attack, daring death to strike him down, not caring if he lived another day. Fergus stayed close to his lord, loyally protecting him from unexpected assailants.

Three Fir-Bolg fell defending their king who pressed relentlessly forward toward Cecht, hoping to settle swiftly between them and keep the slaughter to a minimum. But the King of the Danaans kept falling back as his two bodyguards fended off all comers.

"Stand and fight me!" Brocan shouted in frustration. "This is between us. No need to waste other precious lives. Come and do battle!"

"If I can't trust you in peace, I'll not tempt your hand in war," Cecht shot back.

This only hardened Brocan's resolve and he pushed his way closer to the enemy leader. The cries of the injured he didn't hear. The entreaties of Fergus meant nothing to him. The thudding clash of bronze sword against shield was not worthy of his attention. His goal was clear. To save lives by surrendering his own.

The disgrace and infamy of his sons' actions overwhelmed Brocan. He did not wish to continue living for he knew he'd never be able to bear the humiliation. If he fell the battle would be ended since he had commanded his warriors to yield in the event of his death.

Suddenly he was struck across the side of the head with the flat of a blade and he fell onto one knee. Fergus was at his side in an instant to fend off the attack but Cecht's two bodyguards kept him busy. The king was dazed by the blow and fumbled around in the dirt for his sword. He had just found it when he received a heavy kick to his rib cage which sent him crashing full onto his side.

When he looked up the Danaan king was standing over him, the point of his weapon aimed down at Brocan's chest. Fergus was gone. There was no one to help the King of the Fir-Bolg.

"Do it!" Brocan whispered hoarsely. "Get it over with quickly so no more of our people need die in this stupid fight. My son has shamed me and you'd be doing me a great service to end my life now."

Cecht hesitated, realizing the attack on Fineen was none of Brocan's doing, that the offer of truce had been genuine.

"Get it over with," Brocan screamed, "or you'll have the senseless murder of more men on your hands." The King of the Fir-Bolg tore open his saffron shirt to bare his chest, daring his enemy to strike. His eyes radiated pain and resignation but there was a deep hatred there also.

And that woke Cecht from his pity. He knew it was his duty to kill this old adversary.

As Cecht raised his blade to plunge it down into his opponent's heart, Brocan shut his eyes to await the blow. But none came. Then he realized all was perfectly still around him. He knew without looking that all his warriors were about to witness his pitiful death, the price of his arrogance. He breathed deep, taking one last taste of the sweet air, expecting at any moment to hear the short sharp whistle of Cecht's sword as it bore down on his body.

But the sound that came to his ears was much more remarkable. A gorgeous high-pitched tinkling filled his consciousness. It was like the ringing of a bright new bronze harness, yet at the same time quite different. Try as he might he couldn't put a name to the source of this melodic cascade. The enchanting sound brought to mind Tir-Nan-Og, the Land of the Ever-Young, where harpers welcomed home the souls of the departed.

Brocan breathed out in relief and resignation. His life had ended. He was standing at the threshold of the lands beyond life.

Chapter 10

DALAN HAD MARCHED ALL NIGHT, FORCING HIS FEET to go on when his weary body would have surrendered to exhaustion. His vision at the pool had drained every last measure of energy from him, and it was only his discipline and sense of duty which drove him on.

It was long after sunrise when he had come at last, foot-sore and soul-tired, to the valley which ran down between two hills to the field of the Óenach Samhain. The Brehon had prayed with every step to Danu that no sword had yet been drawn.

The Druid knew this ground well enough. He had taken part in the rituals of Samhain Eve here in boyhood, though for the last ten winters he had dwelled in the east. He knew the battleground was not far off. The wooded hillsides restricted his view but his heart had been lightened when he couldn't see any warriors about.

At a place where the trees thinned a little the spur of one hill met with the foot of another and the path lay around the landscape like a twisted rope. The going had been hard here, for despite the even ground the track was sheltered from the sun so it was muddy from the previous day's rain.

Dalan knew the Victory Stone lay just beyond this path. He judged he had a mere fifty paces to walk before he caught sight of the monument. So, putting aside his urge to sit down, catch his breath and rest his aching back, he had trudged on through the mud.

Near the end of the path he had slipped his footing and fallen but in a few seconds had managed to get to his feet again. For the first time in many seasons Dalan thought he might have pushed himself too hard. His heart was beating wildly, his chest hurt and head ached with a pounding that kept pace with his pulse.

So it was with immense relief he found himself on open ground at the edge of the ring of ash trees. He looked out across the Óenach toward the Victory Stone and there he saw a group of warriors standing passively facing each other.

Dalan quickly realized there was a parley going on. None of these warriors was armed and their attitudes were calm. The Druid laid his harp case down by the nearest tree then carefully took his pack off his back and placed it on the grass. Finally his weary legs gave way and he sat down to rummage through the pack in search of his water bottle. When he had found the leather vessel he drank deeply then replaced the stopper. And in that instant the Brehon glimpsed a flash of red metal on the other side of the Oenach.

Without another thought Dalan leapt to his feet. Now his heart was pounding for fear not from exertion. He hadn't taken two steps before he witnessed a young man stabbing at a Druid dressed in an undyed cloak which marked him as a healer.

"Fineen!" the Brehon exclaimed.

He tore the leather cover from his harp, breaking a pair of straps in his haste. He had arrived at a crucial moment but he was still a long way from the Victory Stone. He offered a silent prayer to the Goddess Danu in the desperate hope he was not too late.

Before the Brehon knew what he was doing there was renewed strength in his limbs. His feet were running as they had never done before; his lungs were fit to burst. His shoulder would have shrieked in agony had it a voice, for the harp was heavy and it was not an instrument to hurry with.

A tenth of the distance between the trees and the Victory Stone lay behind the Druid when he saw the Danaans charging down from the heights above. Their nakedness declared their loyalty to Cecht, a king who held to the venerable tradition among his people of making war without armor.

Dalan almost dropped to his knees in despair when he heard the battle cry of the Fir-Bolg warriors as they flew down to the fight. Somehow the Brehon managed to keep moving forward but a good distance still separated him from the thick of battle when the first clash of arms fell on his ears.

By the time he had reached the Victory Stone, panting heavily, he hadn't even been sure whether he had the energy to climb up on it. But he had known he must if he was to have any hope of halting the slaughter. On the flat of the rock he had placed his harp, managing to drag his sore body up alongside. In moments his hands had been on the harp, though his fingers had been swollen and unwilling to do his bidding. With a supreme effort Dalan had touched the wires of his instrument and a favorite old tune unfolded at his command.

If he had been concerned no one would heed his music, the Druid need not have been. He had hardly reached the end of the first phrase when he had been noticed. By the time he had played through his tune once, most warriors were prostrating themselves at the base of the Victory Stone.

So Dalan played on, putting all his heart and spirit into the melody, conjuring an air of peace with which to enfold all present.

Brocan had ceased to question what was happening to him as his thoughts began to drift along with the music. He was completely enthralled and thoroughly defeated. For a long time the Fir-Bolg king conserved his breath and kept his eyes firmly shut. He could hear a tune he knew well. It was an air often played in his youth but seldom heard these days.

Under the high-pitched Fir-Bolg tune he discerned

a strident droning hum reminiscent of a Danaan warrior chant. And it was close by. In confusion the king dared to tentatively open his eyes. The scene that confronted him was dreamlike and uncanny.

Every warrior before him was laid on his stomach, flat on the ground. No one stirred. Brocan would have thought them all dead but for the fact that every pair of eyes seemed to be staring at him. Directly and fixedly on him. The Fir-Bolg king turned his gaze up to look questioningly at Cecht and his mouth dropped open in surprise.

Even the King of the Danaans had laid aside his weapon and was stretched out on the ground, gazing up. But Cecht was not staring at Brocan. His eyes were focused on a point behind the Fir-Bolg leader.

Brocan frowned. Perhaps this was how Death heralds his arrival, with the sweet music of the Otherworld to accompany him.

Soothing song to send the soul to its rest in the Halls of Waiting.

And then Brocan realized the melody he heard was a tune of the kind known as sleep music. This form of traditional lullaby was used by the healer Druids to bring a deep rest to those who were ill. When it was played on the battleground it was the signal for all hostilities to cease immediately. He was still alive! This was no music of the Otherworld.

The king half sat up. He knew he was defying the laws of the battleground by failing to lay himself flat on the ground in submission. But he had to know. He made out the shape of a man kneeling on the top of the Victory Stone and he gasped in awe. The stranger was dressed in a long coat made from what seemed to be countless black feathers. In front of this Druid a simple harp sat. It was an ordinary-looking instrument, much like any which the Bards usually carried. But this harp sparkled with energetic force. That magic which the Druids named the Draoi.

The harp strings did not have the dull green sheen of wires. These strings were a shining yellow reminiscent of gold. And the lilting, swaying, enticing melody went on until the King of the Fir-Bolg could no longer resist the urge to fall on his face and let himself be enveloped in the music.

Brocan had no sooner laid his head on the ground than the music ceased and he heard an unfamiliar voice.

"I am the Ollamh Dalan. I am a Brehon judge. I have come to this place to stop this stupid slaughter and to bring tidings which were revealed to the Gathering of Harpers in the east. I come with the blessing of the Dagda and in his name I command you to lay down your arms."

"This is none of your affair," Brocan managed to protest weakly without lifting his eyes.

"It's my business to announce and enforce the judgments of the Druid Assembly," was the sharp reply.

The king narrowed his eyes, regarding the Ollamh with closer scrutiny. This Brehon was not a Danaan, as almost all tended to be in these times. He was a brown-haired Fir-Bolg who might have stepped out of the old tales. The Raven-feather cloak he wore shone with a thousand shifting rainbows shimmering on a field of black. Then the king recognized the Druid. He had not been seen in these parts since he had been chosen as a boy to pursue the path of learning.

"It is the wisdom of the Druid Assembly that this trial by battle should cease immediately," the Brehon went on. "There'll be no more fighting today. The Dagda has decreed there will be no more war between the folk of the Fir-Bolg and their ancient enemies the Danaan. From the time of the last full moon two days ago an eternal alliance has been bound by each side."

"I heard nothing of that decision," Cecht protested. "Why was I not informed?"

"Your fellow Danaan kings sent messengers to you but you turned them away saying you would hear them after the battle. A decision had to be made in your absence."

"I should have been summoned!" Cecht insisted. "And so should Brocan for that matter."

"It was necessary to move quickly."

"What do you mean?" demanded Brocan.

"A terrible disaster has come upon us, but I will not speak of it until the injured and dead are tended," Dalan told them sternly. "Tonight there'll be a feast in honor of the peace. I'll speak then of my tidings, when all are rested and the battle fury has passed from your eyes. And then I will pass judgment on all that has happened this day."

"I bow to your wisdom," Brocan assured him, still shocked that he was alive.

"Then go about the task I've set you!" the Ollamh ordered. "You will set the fire pit only an axe throw from here and I'll stand upon the Victory Stone to address you. Now hurry to help the wounded."

"There is a brother Druid here who has been injured," Fergus called to the harper from amidst the rising warriors.

The Brehon followed after the veteran to where Fineen lay, his upper body drenched in blood. Dalan immediately sat down at his friend's side and touched the skin of the wounded man's cheek with the tip of his finger.

Fergus watched as the Brehon dragged the skin down a little to expose the white of one of Fineen's eyes. Abruptly Dalan turned to the veteran and there was a fearful expression on his face.

"This man has lost a great deal of blood. He will not live unless he is tended properly."

Fergus gasped and shook his head in disbelief. "I thought he must surely be dead," he stammered.

"He's lucky. The stabs didn't touch his internal organs. His rib cage was not breached. But he is weak. Pick him up and carry him to the camp," Dalan commanded. "If we're quick we may save him. And send someone to retrieve my pack. I left it over there at the edge of the trees."

The veteran carried Fineen carefully but securely in his arms up the hill toward the Fir-Bolg camp. Dalan followed with his harp until they came to where Lom and the still unconscious Sárán lay.

"How did these two come to be here?" the Brehon inquired. "They're not warriors, yet they're both injured." Lom had no chance to answer on his own behalf.

"I'll tell you the tale while you tend Fineen," Fergus cut in. "Though I am ashamed to relate this terrible business."

"What terrible business?" Dalan asked. "Were these two involved in the battle? That would be a serious break with custom."

"There's a lot more to the story than first meets the eye," Fergus began as he passed on up the hill out of Lom's hearing.

After the Brehon and the veteran had gone Lom lowered himself onto his back. His head was still spinning from the blow that had knocked him out. He glanced at his brother's body. Sárán was breathing steadily but his face was covered in blood and bruises.

Lom rolled on his side to cough the dust from his air passage. Then, as he stared at the broken face of his twin, he lapsed once more into a painful dreamy blackness.

Chapter 11

A RAVEN HAS NO HEARTH TO CALL HIS OWN. MY KIND may settle on rooftop or tree for a while but soon move on. Even our nests are abandoned the instant the last fledgling departs. We have our gathering places where the tribes congregate but the ways of your kind, with your filthy smoke-filled houses, are enough to turn a raven's stomach.

Among your people there are many of the same mind. Some are filled with the traveling spirit by tales told at a cozy hearth. Others through necessity or hardship find themselves walking the earth, drifting from one land to another, eternally searching. A few peoples have preserved the timeless traditions of the nomad. For these clans traveling is their life and life is their journey.

You Gaedhals are another breed altogether. Your ancestors lived and loved in the Islands of the West before the flood. No storyteller now lives who could give a reason why they departed that sacred land seeking new pastures to the east. The details have been lost with the passing of time.

Your own legends speak of an arduous voyage which took your ancestors first to Lochlann, home of the fierce Northmen. From there they made their way down a mighty waterway toward the Middle Sea. They named this great river after the deity who had always guided them. Her name was Danu. She was known as the Goddess of the Flowing Waters, Starlight on the Sea, Moon on the Lake, Queen of Women, Princess of the Crescent Horns.

The River Danu led them eventually by a long route to the lands of the Hibiri, the Judah and the Parsi. This was the start of their wandering. Their voyages were the subject of many songs. They were held in awe as fine warriors by all the folk they met. And they were richly honored for their skills in battle.

It was in the country of the Maat, a desert people, that the Gaedhals at last took their rest. The Maat were a warlike folk, custodians of three enormous man-made mountains constructed of hand-cut stone. They took the Gaedhals into service as mercenaries. And their priests taught the newcomers all the secrets of smelting the black metal and the white metal.

Three generations were born and passed away while the Gaedhals served the Pharaoh of Maat. But in time a new priest-king came to the throne and he was a peaceful man. He had no use for a large retinue of professional warriors. So the Pharaoh married his daughter Scota to Gall, the King of the Gaedhals. For the wedding dowry he gave ships, gold, cattle, and provisions. And then the Priest-King of Maat sent them off across the Middle Sea in search of new lands.

A small group of Hibiri tribespeople who had also served the Pharaoh went with them. And they were given a gift of gratitude from the priests—a piece of one of the three pointed mountains. The Gaedhals named it the Stone of Destiny. And it soon became their own version of the mystical Lia Fail which had been venerated by their ancestors in the Islands of the West.

Sacred knowledge bestowed by the priests on Scota and the Hibiri guided the travelers westward to a fabled land where the grass was thick and lush. And before many days had passed the Gaedhals landed their ships at the far edge of the Middle Sea, near where it pours through into the wide ocean.

They found open plains stretching away to the north. And once they crossed those desolate parts of the land they came to a fertile country. In honor of the Hibiri who had shared their knowledge of this place the Gaedhals named their new homeland Iber.

Scota proved to be an able queen who continued to rule long after her husband's death. And so every female leader of the Gaedhals ever after took the name in honor of her reputed courage, wisdom and strength.

The land of Iber was their home for many generations before an overwhelming incursion of merciless raiders from the south-land came to threaten their cattle, their crops and their livelihood. The Gaedhals, though expert in the art of war, were heavily outnumbered and gradually began to lose ground to the strangers. Within a dozen seasons of the first foreign incursions the rains became heavier than ever, destroying the harvests time after time. Then a disaster fell upon the Gaedhals which truly tested them to the limit of their endurance.

In a massive raid the southern barbarians slew more than half the able-bodied warriors of the Gaedhal. Not only were their defenses depleted but their herds of cattle went untended and the crops rotted in the field. At the height of these troubles their king, Míl, passed away suddenly, leaving his queen to deal with these catastrophes.

It was then that the last Queen Scota of Iber decided to continue the ancient journey of her folk. The Gaedhals had once prospered in this country but those days were ended. It was time to move on.

Scota sent her brothers out in small ships to search the seas for a place where the Gaedhals would be safe from attack and their cattle could be well provided for. The brothers returned with reports of a fertile land to the north, an island bounded by rough seas and treacherous rocks. Green rich pastures were common in this country; immense silent forests waited to be cleared for timber. Lakes and rivers abounded and there was plentiful game in the mountains and woodlands. And Scota heard tell that the inhabitants were gentle folk who lived simple lives. These natives were given to war when pressed but they preferred a peaceful existence.

What persuaded the queen to attempt to conquer this island, however, was the fact that the natives had never learned the secret of iron and steel. Their weapons were crude bronze artifacts from a bygone age. Pitted against the Gaedhals who had been renowned warriors for generations, these poor folk were defenseless.

Nine moons after her husband Míl's passing, Scota suffered a dream, the first of many. The land of Eriu beckoned her. And she answered the summons, certain this would be the final homeland of her people.

Seasons flew by while preparations were made for the epic voyage to Eriu. Ten winters after her brothers returned, the Queen of the Gaedhals stepped on board a ship and in a mighty fleet her people set out on the next part of their remarkable journey.

And thus brewed the terrible conflict I witnessed in my youth. Greed fermented into conquest and your people drank their fill of war.

Ravens have long memories. And though I had not the wisdom of the feathered kind in those days, even so I sensed some change upon the wind. Before the enchanter sang me into this shape, before I was called Lom-dubh, the land of Innisfail was turned into a battlefield.

* * *

Heavy sparse droplets pelted down onto the young woman's bare skin. She tentatively touched three fingers to her cheek as the rain ran over her. When she looked at her hand it was smeared red. All around her the other warriors of her kin stood silent, patiently waiting for the downpour to cease.

Bright ochre war paint daubed on their faces and in their hair streamed down over arms and legs so each man and woman among them seemed to have been bathed in blood. To the young woman this seemed a frightening portent.

You've fought many battles, Scota, she reassured herself. This is just another one. You're young yet and strong. You've nothing to fear. But the conviction in these words was not matched in the depths of her being.

Her inner voice spoke clearly to her and the message hit her as hard as a slap in the face. You're dreaming!

Scota felt her whole body shiver. If this was a dream, it was uncannily real. She banished the voice and struggled to concentrate on the task at hand. Now more than ever before she knew she had to hold her nerve. This fight would decide the destiny of her people. There could be no turning to retreat. There was nowhere to run but back into the sea from whence her warriors had come.

"I'm the Queen of the Gaels!" she cried, emptying her lungs with a mighty shout. "I'm the Sovereign Lady of the South!"

The heavens answered her boast with a brilliant shaft of purple lightning which tore open the sky to strike the foot of the hill before her. The blast of its bellowing voice was defiant and unwavering. An unexpected tempest howled around her warriors as if choosing to side with the enemy in this conflict.

Courageous warriors who had battled the bloodthirsty invaders of southern Iber fell back before the elements. The bravest few held their ground wide-eyed with awe and shock. But high on the hill before her the hosts of the Tuatha De Danaan and the Fir-Bolg stood shoulder to shoulder, unmoved by the spectacle before them.

The air became biting cold and the rain intensified. It stung against Scota's arms as it fell, striking her finely wrought scale armor in a deafening chorus. Mud flew up around her knees, churned up by the force of the squall.

Then, just as suddenly as it had begun, the downpour ceased and the battlefield fell silent. Scota shuddered with anxious anticipation. The unearthly quiet unnerved her after the quick-tempered storm, and she wondered if enemy Druids had summoned the elements to their cause.

Another flash in the sky lent its sickly light to the scene. It was immediately chased along by a shuddering clap of thunder that set the chariot horses screaming. The clouds rolled in and the hill was snatched from sight.

Scota was sure her heart would burst from her rib

cage with fear but she determined not to flinch. Her sword, bright and silver, was crying out for war. Numb fingers gripped the cold hilt and the queen summoned all her will to rally the warriors of the Gaedhal.

"Now!" she screamed. "Now this land will be ours forever!"

She forced her feet one after the other forward toward the hill. To her relief a throng of red ochre warriors faithfully swarmed around her. She was sure they'd have followed her to the very gates of the Otherworld if she had commanded it.

As the black clouds retreated again the hilltop was gradually revealed. Three banners had appeared, each at least as tall and broad as an oak. The enemy gathered around these banners, well armored for the fight. The queen wondered how her warriors would ever break that steadfast line.

Halfway up the hill Scota stopped to touch the earth and catch her breath. Over her head the deadly arrows of her tribesmen sailed toward their helpless targets. A few of the enemy fell. But wherever one foreign warrior was struck, another took his place.

Now Scota was feeling hot from the climb. Sweat and rainwater mixed with red war paint ran into her eyes. She tasted salt and earth in her mouth and breathed in the heady aroma of sodden soil. Unceremoniously she dropped her shield. It had become suddenly cumbersome, too weighty and unwieldy to be of any use. Her own folk passed her by as she loosed the straps of her scale armor. The garment fashioned from tiny steel plates fell to the ground with a clatter.

Relieved of these burdens Scota breathed more easily. Now she was ready to finish the climb. Before she had walked another five steps a war cry shook the earth. A savage bowel-trembling shout arose from the top of the hill as the enemy poured forth in a torrent of righteous rage. Down the steep slope they careened, spears at the ready, axes poised to strike, swords raised. Some among their number were completely naked but for the blue-green designs painted upon their flesh. Their hair was white as snow, every one of them.

The queen's resolve faded. She could not will her feet to move another step. And while she struggled with herself to keep advancing, the enemy fell upon the leading ranks of her warriors with a resounding crash of weapons. Many Gaedhals wavered in that moment and some retreated in dismay.

Before Scota realized her own peril a naked stranger armed with a broadaxe fell upon her in an untamed fury. Scota lifted her blade to dispatch him but her hands were weakened and she could not strike.

"I'm not afraid of you!" she bellowed as she managed to parry his blow.

But the force of his attack was overwhelming. Scota slipped back in the mud, clutching at the hilt of her sword with both hands as he raised his axe to strike. Instinct commanded her to act but her limbs refused to move. All the queen could do was watch this stranger in his fierce battle paint prepare to put an end to her.

"I won't let you murder me!" she cried and at that very instant an arrow fell from the sky. It struck the stranger near to the collarbone. The axe dropped from his hand onto the muddy earth at Scota's side.

Before the stranger had managed to fall back out of the way the queen regained her feet. Then, like sunlight spilling into a dark room, all weakness passed out of her body. With another fierce cry she drove her weapon deep into the enemy warrior's chest.

His eyes widened in agony and surprise as Scota deftly pulled the weapon out again. The stranger was bathed in his own blood but he did not fall. He stood proud and defiant. And when he caught the queen's eye he smiled.

"I am Scota, Queen of the Gaels," she told him.

"I am Mahon, son of King Cecht of the Tuatha De Danaan," he replied.

As he spoke he plucked the arrow from his shoulder and threw it down upon the ground contemptuously. "You'll not defeat us so easily," he cried, holding the wound where her sword had stabbed him.

Scota raised her blade to strike at him again but was distracted before the blow could fall. To her bafflement the warrior's injury swiftly festered, dried out and began to heal. The queen looked down at the stab wound in his chest and it too was slowly covering with fresh skin as if it had never been.

To her astonishment the stranger calmly bent over to retrieve his axe. All around her the battle still raged fiercely. Scota shivered. The sword dropped from her hand. She couldn't speak.

Her helm was knocked off her head by another assailant before she knew what had happened. Then she was lying on her back in the mud again. The point of a spear was pressed into her belly and a wild-looking woman gripped the shaft. This warrior was dressed for battle in bronze-ringed armor. Her helm was polished to a coppery red that almost matched the color of her hair. A strip of blue pigment three fingers wide crossed her face from ear to ear. The whites of her eyes stood out amid the blue, making her seem all the more fierce.

"I'm Riona, daughter of Eriu!" the woman declared.

"I'm the Queen of the South!" Scota shot back. "My people have won this land from you."

"The country of Innisfail will belong to your sons and daughters forever," the woman told her, "but they have paid for it with your blood, Scota."

Then the strange woman pressed the spear point hard into the queen's body. Scota felt her flesh tearing under the weapon. With strained breath she gasped a vain cry for help. No one answered. No warrior came to her aid.

"Where are my sons?" she begged.

Already the world about her was darkening. Her vision was fading away with each breath.

"Your boys have won a great victory," Riona assured her.

"The struggle is ended?" the dying queen asked.

"It is ended."

Then Scota, Queen of the Gaels, prepared to surrender her spirit. The smell of battle and blood was all about her. Smoke caught in her throat.

"Mother?" a familiar voice begged.

Scota did not have the energy to open her eyes but she knew it was Míl's youngest son who cradled her head in his arms.

"Eber," she whispered. "Don't leave me."

These three words spent the last of her strength. Then the queen's soul departed and Scota was at peace.

Gentle lapping waves washed against the side of the ship. It was a lulling and beautiful sound, the kind of soft music Poets speak of. It was like the soothing voice of a lover. The vessel's slow, almost unnoticeable rocking had a calming effect on all her passengers. Even the three men who were gathered around Scota's bed waiting for her to wake.

"I heard her cry out in the middle of the night," the youngest stated. "I came to comfort her but she was talking nonsense again. Something about the struggle being ended. She begged me to stay at her side."

His dark brown hair was braided carefully into long strands which were secured behind the crown of his head. As a gesture of frustration he loosed them and the plaits fell about his shoulders.

"Three times this month the sickness has come upon her," he went on. "And on each occasion she's fallen deathly ill afterward. When she could speak all she talked about was this land across the ocean where she says our people will find peace. My brothers, I am worried for her."

The eldest of the three nodded sympathetically. "I understand your concern, Eber," Amergin said softly, running his hand through his graying brown beard.

"She's dying, isn't she?" the last of the three inquired, voicing the thought that had been haunting Eber.

"No, Éremon," Amergin stated confidently, smiling at his fair-haired brother. "She's suffering. But she'll not die yet. It's not her time."

"The visions are driving her to distraction," Eber cut in. "If this goes on she'll surely not survive the winter. You're a Poet, Amergin. You've knowledge of such matters. What's causing these dreams?"

"Our father's death was a contributing factor. Mother has taken on all the responsibilities of kingship and this burden has been hard to bear. She's ruled wisely while twelve winters passed by. And she's had to put aside her own grief for the good of her people."

"She's no longer fit to rule," Éremon declared. His blue eyes flashed as he gave voice to a view he had long suppressed. "One of us should assume the kingship."

"It's too early to say that!" the Poet snapped. "And

it's not for one such as yourself to make such state-
ments publicly. You may be the son of Míl but so are
Eber and myself. Don't be too hasty in your wish to
walk in our father's shoes. You may find they blister
your feet."

Éremon stood up. "Amergin," he stated coldly,
"you and I are sons of Míl by Scota. Eber may resem-
ble her in many ways but he is only our half-brother.
His mother's family are not of noble birth. He'll
never be considered for the kingship."

Eber looked away and bit his tongue. He knew it was
best to stay silent when Éremon was in this mood.

"I may be a Druid," the Poet replied, "but I'm just as
entitled to rule as you are. Have you forgotten it is the
responsibility of the Druid Council of the Northern
Iber to decide this matter? You're a fine warrior but it
will take more than a well-meaning strongman to save
our people from the coming troubles and strife."

"I'm going to fetch some mead," Éremon spat as if
he had heard nothing his older brother had said. "My
views are obviously not welcome here."

"Bring some meat with you when you return. And
some wine," Amergin told him, ignoring his brother's
fit of pique. "Mother will need to take food when she
wakes."

Éremon grunted in reply as he climbed a ladder up
to the ship's deck and was gone.

"Don't take anything he says to heart," Amergin advised his younger brother after Éremon had gone.

"She's always treated me as if I were her own,"

Eber protested. "My birth marked the passing of my natural mother from this life. Scota took her place long ago."

"You've been a better son to her than some," the Poet nodded, touching the young warrior on the shoulder in reassurance.

"What has she told you of these dreams?" Eber whispered.

"She reckons the spirits of that place sing to her in her sleep."

"I believe her," the younger man breathed as he brushed his fingers tenderly through Scota's hair.

"And I believe her dreams are true visions of the future, of all that will be."

As Amergin spoke the woman under the bedcovers began to stir from her long sleep.

"Mother?" Eber whispered as he cradled her head gently in his arms. "Are you awake?"

She opened her eyes and stared up at her son. "Water," she wheezed painfully through a dry throat.

Amergin was already handing a cupful to his brother. Eber placed the vessel carefully to Scota's lips. She drank deep before she lay back again to breathe peacefully. But when Scota had rested for a few short breaths her eyes shot open again. And she stared directly at her eldest son, the Poet.

"How's the breeze?" she demanded.

"Nothing to speak of," he replied. "We're still becalmed and sitting beyond the ninth wave as we agreed."

"I don't trust those natives," she hissed. "They're setting a trap for us. I can smell it."

"Rest now," Eber soothed. "We'll talk of these matters when you're well again."

"Have you witnessed more of the future in your dreams?" Amergin asked.

"I have," she affirmed. "Each vision is clearer than the last. And with every one I'm granted a new glimpse of the days to come."

"You must rest," her youngest son insisted. "The grief of our father's death has not washed from you yet." Eber placed a firm hand on his mother's shoulder but she shrugged it away.

"What do you know of my grief?" she retorted and immediately regretted the sharpness of her tone.

Eber grabbed her hand but she shook his grip until he let go.

"I am Scota, Queen of the Gaels," she declared sternly. "I'm not an invalid."

"Yes, Mother," the young man replied, bowing his head.

"Is it morning?" she asked.

"It is," Eber replied. "Three hours after the dawn."

"I must prepare to meet with one of the daughters of Eriu," Scota stated. "And she'll not wait for me."

"Is that the name of this land?" Eber asked. "Eriu?"

"The natives call it Innisfail," she told him.

"That's a word from the old language of our ancestors," Amergin breathed. "It means the Island of Destiny. It will truly be the island of our destiny."

The queen frowned as she touched a hand to her cheek. When she examined her fingers she was relieved to find they did not run red. "I dreamed I was a girl again," she sighed, staring off into a dark corner. "I imagined I was a young warrior with strength and vigor in my arms. But in truth I'm old. My days are nearing their end and my people have no home."

Then Scota looked her youngest son squarely in the eyes. "Eber," she said softly. "I don't want you arguing with your brother Éremon over the kingship after I'm gone. I have a solution to the problem which will satisfy everyone."

"What?" Amergin inquired.

"Eber will be King of the South. And Éremon will be King of the North."

"And what of me?" the Poet cut in.

"You'll be adviser to both," the queen replied. "And you'll be honored as an equal by them."

"Éremon will object," Eber noted. "He wishes to be king over all the Gaedhals."

"We'll leave him to conquer the northern parts of the island," Scota decided. "If he's kept busy he won't have time to argue. For now Amergin will act as his counselor and I will take the role of your teacher, Eber. Fear not. I'll guide you well. For my spirit has already walked the hills of Innisfail. I know the nature of its people. My own destiny is to one day die on a hillside there in a beautiful place shrouded by a misty fall of rain."

"Don't talk of your own death, Mother," the Poet

advised gently. "You've many seasons yet amongst us."

"Can't you see how old I've become?" She smiled. "I've worked myself to exhaustion with the duties of a queen." Scota dragged herself up off the bed and swung her feet down onto the floor. Then she took Amergin's hand. "We must prepare now for the future," she sighed. "I'll be gone soon enough and then you'll be left to carry on without me."

"You have many seasons ahead of you," Amergin insisted. "It's dangerous to interpret a vision without training in the art of the Seer."

The queen laughed at her eldest son, surprised that one who had spent so much time studying the ways of wisdom could be so blind to the truth.

"In the land of Eriu I'll reclaim my youth," Scota told him. "I'll dance again like I did as a girl. And you, Eber, will be by my side."

Chapter 12

IT WAS JUST COMING TO LATE AFTERNOON WHEN LOCHIE the Watcher stuck his head in through the door of the king's hut. In a mischievous mood he had taken on his old comfortable form, all bald head, gnarled fingers and glowing eyes. It amused him to observe the reactions of mortals to this shape.

Aoife stirred from her troubled sleep, thinking a bad dream had woken her. Then she noticed a shadow in the doorway.

"Who are you?" she gasped, surprised at the dryness in her throat.

There was a faint scent of lavender in the air. The fragrance was so pure and clean the sweetness of it seemed to cling to her lungs.

"I am a friend," came the reply.

The young woman started to rise in panic when she didn't recognize the voice.

"Would you like some water?" the Watcher asked her softly.

Aoife was so touched by the gentleness of his tone she immediately relaxed. With a loud sigh she lay back among the bedclothes, surprised at her own skittishness. This fellow must be a healer or a Druid come to check on her.

"Yes, please. Some water."

"I'll fetch you some.

Lochie departed. Shortly he returned with a skin full of cool spring water. He helped the young woman sit up so she could drink deeply from the neck of the vessel. When the dryness in her throat was at last abated she hummed to let him know she'd had enough.

"Are you a Druid?" the young woman asked, noticing the dark cloak he wore.

"Yes. That's what I am," the Watcher replied as if he had just realized it himself.

Lochie shoved the cork into the neck of the skin and placed the vessel down beside the furs. "Now you'll have water whenever you wish it. It's here by the bed."

"I wish only for sleep," Aoife whispered. "If I could rest peacefully I'd be content."

"You shall have your wish," the Watcher promised and his eyes lit with a passion he hadn't felt in generations.

"If only you could grant it," the young woman

replied in despair. "But I have a heavy heart that won't release me from a weight of guilt."

Lochie closed his eyes to savor the moment. A wish freely asked, he told himself, was the sweetest favor a mortal could bestow. From the simplest desires a thousand fears could blossom. And fear was nourishment for the Watcher kind.

"I assure you I can grant you whatever you hope for," he told her softly.

With those words Aoife closed her eyes and fell into a sound, healing sleep. Lochie smiled then leaned closer to her face so he could observe her.

"You're a pretty one, aren't you, my dear girl?" he whispered. "I wonder what it'd take to convince you to wed young Mahon? What dreams shall I send you? Would you like to imagine the lad saving you from a band of renegade Gaedhals?" The Watcher reached out a finger to stroke her cheek tenderly. "Or would you like to dream of him building you a house? Or the faces of your unborn children? Or would you like some more dancing?"

Suddenly Lochie froze, every sense on alert.

"Is she sleeping?" a deep confident voice inquired quietly.

The Watcher spun around. Before him stood King Brocan, frowning to see a stranger tending his daughter.

"Who are you?" Brocan demanded. "What are you doing in my hut?"

Lochie took three slow measured steps toward the king. And as the Watcher glided forward his face passed through the firelight and miraculously changed before Brocan's eyes. Where there had been what seemed to be hairless skin on top of his head there were now short cropped black strands. And where there had appeared to have been a strange glow there were now two moist gentle eyes peering back full of compassion.

"I am Lochie," he declared in a firm, clear voice.

Brocan squinted and suddenly the man was no longer a stranger. "So you are," the king exclaimed, still not quite believing what he saw. "It must have been the shadows that confused me."

"Indeed."

Brocan swallowed hard. An urgent desire to turn and run came over him. Then, just as abruptly, the sensation disappeared and he breathed easily again. In moments he was laughing at his own foolishness.

The Bard touched the king's arm to reassure him. Then he laughed too, convivially sharing Brocan's embarrassment.

"I've been a warrior too long," the king confided, slapping the Bard on the back. "I see enemies behind every bush and traitors at every table. I'm too old for this."

"You mustn't imagine your work is done!" the Bard retorted in alarm. "You've only just begun the long journey of your life."

"I'm forty-eight summers on this earth," the king

said solemnly. "All my childhood friends are gone except for Fergus. I've lived beyond the span of seasons allocated to most warriors."

"That doesn't give you good cause for regret," the Druid pointed out.

"I was defeated today in both war and diplomacy," Brocan noted bitterly. "Perhaps the days of my leadership are done."

"But the trials of your kingship have just begun," Lochie confided in a low voice. "Dalan bears tidings of invaders from over the sea, but their quarrel is with the Danaans. They'll not venture to the west where the land is near barren. The Brehon has come to ensure your alliance with King Cecht, but it's a Danaan trick."

"Dalan is a Fir-Bolg," Brocan scoffed. "He wouldn't betray his own people."

"He is one of our people by birth," Lochie whispered. "But he's a Danaan by habit, as most Druids tend to be in these times. It's safer to accept the dominance of the old enemy than to openly oppose it."

"What are you saying?" Brocan demanded, hardly believing his ears.

"You're the last independent king of the Fir-Bolg. Even King Lianan of the Cairige pays tribute to the Danaans and accepts their overlordship."

"It's true," Brocan sighed. "No one has the will to resist them any longer. Their ways are intoxicating to our folk."

"Many still resist their charms, even if they don't

do so openly. In the company of the Druids there are some, myself and my wife Isleen among them, who'll never bow down to the Danaans. And as long as our people have kings such as yourself, we retain strong hopes that Innisfail, the ancient homeland, will be ours to rule again."

"Yes," the king muttered, overwhelmed that in this darkest of hours there were others who understood his concerns. Perhaps, he told himself, there was hope for his people and his dignity.

"Hope," Lochie echoed and Brocan was startled that the Bard seemed to have heard his thoughts.

"You are our hope," the Bard whispered in a soft warm tone. "Don't ever give in. Placate the Danaans, yes. Accept their hard judgments against you, certainly. But most of all be patient. The day will come when the Fir-Bolg rise again. You must never endanger that prospect by foolishly entering into an alliance."

"Thank you, Bard," Brocan said quietly.

"Remember, my lord," Lochie added as he moved toward the door, "you may call on my advice at any time of the day or night. I'll serve you faithfully. For you serve our people."

With that the Bard bowed his head, put a hand to his breast, and left the king alone in the firelight to decide his next move.

Dalan, wrapped in his Raven-feather cloak, sat on the Victory Stone as the sky began to darken. No one disturbed him. Danaan and Fir-Bolg alike recognized he was searching for the inspiration to pass a judgment. Such responsibilities were left to the Brehons because they were trained to walk the roads of the Other-world and the paths of the legends, where all questions could be answered.

In seeking a solution to this difficult matter Dalan knew he would have to draw on all his internal strength, to enter a state of being where the material world and its trials became simple matters easily resolved. The first step to that stillness was a condition often likened to hibernation. Once achieved the senses lost importance, overruled by the imagination. And if approached with care, the beings who served the races of the earth as guides from the beyond were said to give freely of their advice.

Dalan the Brehon began his slow breathing. His body started to relax; his mind emptied of trivial thoughts. He made a hissing noise as he exhaled air through his mouth. This was a sound which would guide him back to his body from the other side when the time came and announce clearly to passers-by that he was not to be disturbed.

However, Dalan found he couldn't concentrate on his task. The memory of his strange vision by the stream was starkly fresh in his awareness. The details of the dream still haunted him. After struggling unsuccessfully with his consciousness the Brehon opened his eyes, and at the same time ceased his steady breath control.

Dalan found it hard to believe that two of the Watchers of old could have survived the long generations since the time of Balor as Cuimhne had told him. Why had they not made their presence felt? He was sure the Druid Assembly would have recognized their dabbling in the affairs of Danaan and Fir-Bolg. Yet the message of his dream had been so clear. The Watchers must surely be abroad in the land, and he resolved to be wary of their meddling. Eventually, in the stillness of the deserted battleground, he was able to clear all worries from his consciousness and he felt himself drifting off into a strange half-sleep.

It seemed to Dalan he had only just closed his eyes when he heard his name called out. The Brehon sat up straight and uncrossed his numb legs. There was no one about in the evening light so he decided to get to his feet. He threw the feather cloak off him as he rose and it fell to the ground in an untidy pile.

"Is it time for the judgment yet?" he called out.

"Soon enough," came the answer.

Dalan noticed the air was unusually warm, and knew a dream trance had come on him again. It seemed he was alone in the hillfort of Dun Burren. In the gathering mists of dusk he could not see very far but he recognized his old home well enough. Dalan had spent part of his boyhood in this place. He loved every stone in the wall and every house the defenses encircled. He was overjoyed to be in familiar territory. His visions usually took him to places shrouded in anguish and portent.

His kindred no longer dwelled here. They had gone south soon after he had taken his vows and his family now called the lands of the Cairige home.

As the mist lifted unexpectedly the Brehon swallowed hard in shock at what he saw. It was a scene that would haunt him for the rest of his days. And ever after he'd be unable to look on his old home again without sadness.

The stone walls of the hillfort seemed to have fallen and they were covered in unruly grasses. The houses he knew so well were all gone. Where the courtyard had once been, wild goats grazed quietly in the fading light. It was as if a thousand seasons had passed by, leaving him alone untouched by time.

"Where am I?" the Brehon asked, and he was surprised at the hoarse rattle of his words.

"You've come to the hillfort of the King of the Fir-Bolg of the Burren," a strange, disembodied voice replied. "Do you not know this place? You've spent many nights here."

"It's not as I remember it."

"It would've been better if you'd asked when rather than where," the stranger teased.

"What do you mean?"

"You're looking on the future."

"Who are you?" Dalan gasped.

"Can you not think of a more imaginative question?" the stranger sighed in a mocking tone.

As Dalan turned to face the speaker a kneeling figure slowly took shape amongst a pile of broken rocks.

The man stood up, shook the dust off his clothes and approached, removing the hood which concealed his face.

The stranger was completely bald and his eyes burned with a bright green unearthly fire. His skin was a waxy white, his fingers long and bony.

"Good morning to you, Brehon," the man offered warmly. "I trust you're not too distressed by my sudden appearance."

"What in Danu's name are you?"

"At last a question worthy of your profession!" the stranger exclaimed.

"Give me an answer."

"I am the second-last of my kind," the man replied. "Can you answer the riddle of my being?"

"Watcher," Dalan muttered without hesitation.

"You are to be congratulated. Your knowledge of the legends is impressive."

The stranger held a palm up and a little fire near Dalan flared into a large blaze. The Brehon stepped back startled, covering his eyes from the intense brightness of it. Then he smelled roast pork and saw that a pig's carcass was cooking on a long metal spit over the fire.

"Iron is not only excellent for making weapons," the Watcher noted, pointing to the fire pit. "It's perfect for fashioning cooking utensils. Especially roasting spits."

"What do you want of me?" Dalan asked cautiously.

"I thought we might make a little trivial conversation before we settle down to discuss business. But since you seem to be in a hurry, I'll come to the point."

Quick as a flash of lightning the stranger was sitting by the fire. By the time the Brehon caught up with him he was carving into the roast with a large knife. He carefully placed the thick slices in a wooden bowl.

"Are you truly one of Balor's breed?"

"Of course I am!"

"How did you come to enter my meditations?"

"Make no mistake," the Watcher declared as he skillfully worked the meat knife. "What you see around you is not your world, nor has it sprung from your imagination or meditation. I've made it and have lordship over it all. I advise you to bear that in mind while you're here."

"Why have you brought me to this place?"

"Because I respect your wisdom." The Watcher shrugged. "I appreciate a worthy opponent. And because you are the only one of your people who even suspects my ancient companion and myself to be of Balor's making."

"Balor is gone. You have nothing left to fight for."

The Watcher held up his hand. "I've already heard that argument," he protested. "If you'll forgive me pointing out the obvious flaw in your reasoning, I still exist. Balor is no more, it's true, but the cause to which my companion and I were sworn is very much alive as much as we are."

The stranger held out a wooden bowl piled with steaming cuts of choicest meat. "Though I must admit I don't have the enthusiasm I once had. Will you take some food with me?"

Dalan shook his head.

"I don't often have an opportunity to express generosity," the Watcher insisted. "I'd consider it an honor if you accept my humble hospitality."

The Brehon bowed his head, remembering that even in the house of an enemy, tradition demanded humility of a Druid. He held out his hand to take the bowl.

"You've no idea how much I appreciate your gesture." His host smiled. "Is the evening too warm?"

Dalan shook his head.

"If it becomes so, please let me know. As I told you, I'm lord of this place. I may grant you whatever weather your heart desires."

The Brehon tentatively tasted the roast pork. It was sweet and strong, basted in honey, the way he loved it.

"I've not eaten meat as sweet as this since I was a child." The Brehon hummed as he ate.

"Thank you." The stranger bowed.

As Dalan sucked the juice off his fingers he noticed there was a silver mead cup in the Watcher's hand.

"Sample this," the stranger offered. "It's brewed to

an old Fomorian recipe with ground hazelnuts and the subtle flavors of wild herbs."

Dalan took the cup and put it to his mouth.

"It's a very fine brew," the Brehon congratulated his host.

"The Fomor were skilled cooks and brewers. Our craftsmen were renowned also. As were our Poets and musicians. They're all gone now."

The Brehon chewed his meat slowly as he listened.

"Of course you've been educated to think of us as evil." The Watcher laughed. "But you, my friend, know better than that. The world is not so simple a place. And you're doubtless aware the tales of your ancestors are tinged with hatred born of warfare, famine and hardship. Not everything you've been told about us is true."

"I'm a Brehon," Dalan said. "I'm sworn to truth."

"And how do you know what truth is?"

The Druid thought for a moment. "Truth is the essence of all things," he replied eventually. "It is all things."

"Is there no such thing as untruth?"

"Untruth is merely truth in disguise. Truth can't be hidden. It doesn't wither in the presence of untruth. Lies can't live unless they're grafted onto the truth."

"You're very wise." The Watcher nodded. "But what I consider to be truth may be quite different from what you consider it to be."

"Truth transcends the viewpoint of the individual,"

Dalan ventured. "It's not merely opinion or specula-
tion. Truth can be proved to exist."

"Perhaps you've more to learn than you realize."
The Watcher smiled. "May I ask you a question?"

The Brehon nodded.

"Do you consider me and my kind to be evil?"

"Your skill is in making others believe your version
of the truth," Dalan reasoned. "I've heard the tales of
how you courted King Bres of the Danaans and convinced him to desert his own people for Balor."

"Bres thought highly of himself," the Watcher reminisced. "It was a simple thing to present a convincing
argument to him."

"You incited him to make war on his own folk."

"But does that make me evil?" the stranger countered. "Certainly not in the eyes of my own folk who
were threatened with extinction by the Danaans."

The Brehon sighed as he considered the argument.
"I suppose you're right," he answered slowly. "I per-
sonally believe there's no such thing as evil. There's
only the darker side of this world, which simple folk
explain away as a demonic force. The truth is always
much more complicated than that."

"You are a little wise. Small wonder you've been
spoken of as the next Dagda."

Dalan smiled, realizing the Watcher wanted him to
ask about his own future. However, the Brehon was
not distracted by this temptation. "Your words and
deeds brought suffering to many," he stated. "You
must be aware of the consequences of your actions. It

follows that you don't respect your fellow beings. That's a crime under the Brehon laws."

"Am I an outlaw then?"

Dalan shrugged. "You're an outlaw who's obviously capable of great achievements for you're clearly very talented. This illusion alone is very impressive. The flavors, the aromas, the sights and sounds are incredibly convincing but of course I know the dream will not endure."

"The invaders have come here because I inspired their queen with dreams like this one," the stranger informed his guest.

"To what end?"

"My companion and I are nourished by the fear others experience. Anguish is like honey wine to us. We crave the terror of those who walk as mortals. When I smell fright on the wind it sets my stomach to growling in the same way the aroma of roast pork reminds you of your hunger. I can't say this state of being is entirely pleasant, but this was Balor's legacy to us. It is our nature."

"But why draw the invaders to this shore?" Dalan insisted. "Have you no feeling for the suffering that will surely result?"

"I was a Brehon once," the Watcher went on uninterrupted. "All of our kind were students of the Druid path just like yourself. I was dedicated to truth, to justice, to healing and to the laws of my people. When Balor offered me the opportunity to take the form I now possess I really believed the transformation would empower me to perform great good for my people. Balor was a clever manipulator. He didn't tell us we'd merely be the playing pieces in his great game."

"You were a Druid?" Dalan stammered. "And yet you betrayed your vows as a Guardian of the Spirit?"

"I didn't betray anything or anyone!" the Watcher snapped. "I was betrayed. Balor lied to us. He twisted the truth and had us believe we'd bring about a new age of peace in Innisfail. He made us think we'd be the keepers of wisdom and the silent judges of the unjust."

The stranger took a piece of meat. He chewed it vigorously to keep his temper in check. After a moment the Watcher took a mouthful of liquor and went on.

"In fact it was our fate to interfere in the lives of the Fir-Bolg and the Danaan. Balor never explained to any of us we'd suffer a hunger for fear."

"What happened to the others?" Dalan interrupted.

The stranger's eyes glowed brightly green as he shook his head. "I believe the answer to that question has already been revealed to you."

As the Watcher spoke the rising moon appeared in the sky, the light of the fire died down and the wind blew into a buffeting gale that tore at Dalan's cloak. The Brehon looked to the sky to get his bearings and saw the familiar stars arrayed before him.

In the northern part of the heavens long streaming luminescent streaks danced about, filling the dark blue sky with rainbow colors.

"The Northern Lights?" he gasped.

"I see you know something of the stars and the movement of the heavens," the Watcher breathed, his own voice full of awe. "This wonder was first shown to me by Balor."

"Does this place lie within the bounds of Innisfail?" Dalan inquired.

"It does."

"And this is where your companions dwell?"

The stranger turned to the Druid and touched his shoulder. "They're beyond even this excuse for existence I endure," he explained. "The seven are standing about us now silent and immortal, though they don't breathe and they no longer have any care for the world."

Dalan looked about him. He noticed they were standing in the middle of a grassy patch almost completely encircled by standing stones of blue granite. This place was not quite the same as the hill in his earlier dream.

"I've seen them before," the Brehon admitted. "But Cuimhne showed them standing on a higher hill."

"Everything is as I will it," the stranger reminded him. Then he took the Brehon by the arm and led him closer to the stones. "There are two spaces left. Two places reserved for my companion and myself when we're ready to relinquish our current existence. I'm sure my old friend Cuimhne explained that to you when she issued her warning."

"Who is Cuimhne?"

"She guards us. And she has a connection with you. But you have bathed in the Well of Forgetfulness. I don't expect you to remember the past. Perhaps you'll find each other in the future again."

"You're not making sense."

"You're not listening. You have no memory of her for the time being. You'd best leave it at that."

Dalan frowned.

"Unless we find a way to postpone our decline until the bonds of Balor may be broken," the Watcher continued, "my companion and I are doomed to a terrible fate."

"To continue as your master intended, feeding on the fear of mortals until your soul won't accept any more."

The stranger shrugged. "You've judged us harshly, Druid. And Cuimhne hasn't given you the full tale. But tell me true. Would you submit to such a fate without searching for another way?"

The Brehon dropped his gaze so he would not have to meet the Watcher's eyes. "I wouldn't be able to justify my continued existence," he replied, "if I relied on the suffering of others for my nourishment."

"But mortals will suffer whether the Watchers walk or not. We merely profit by fear. In some respects it could be argued we take anguish and turn it into a nurturing and life-giving force."

"Why have you brought me here?" the Brehon asked again.

"To reason with you. To ask you to let us be. If we interfere in the affairs of mortals it's only to bring matters to a swifter conclusion. We don't create the conflicts, not entirely anyway. We take advantage of them. We feed from them. And we need to build our strength if we're going to escape our bonds."

"Do you know of the Druid Assembly's plan to withdraw the Danaans and the Fir-Bolg into the Otherworld?" Dalan asked.

"I know something of it," the Watcher admitted. "And I condemn the Druid Assembly for their foolishness. They've no idea what a burden immortality will become. I was a good-hearted Brehon once. I had high ideals and dreams of making this land a peaceful place. But look at me now. This world changes slowly so that in one allotted lifetime it may seem as if nothing has altered. The body dies, the spirit passes on to new beginnings and the soul drinks from the Well of Forgetfulness when it returns home to the sun." The stranger squeezed his fingers into Dalan's shoulder to emphasize his point.

"That's the way of nature. The spirit must be cleansed after a time on this earth. Otherwise it becomes tainted and disturbed. My soul is not what it once was. It craves what it formerly reviled. In my depths untouched for long ages, I'm a soul not unlike yourself."

"You speak of the fear of others," Dalan noted.

"You speak of how you feed on that fear. And yet it's your own dread that keeps you fighting against fate."

"If I don't find a way to cheat Balor I'm destined to take one of those two empty places in the circle. I'll discover a way one day, but until then I must accept my nature and live on until I can be healed."

Dalan frowned, swayed by the Watcher's argument.

"You're a judge," the stranger appealed, picking up on the Brehon's thoughts. "How would you try me? What penalty would you impose if my case came before you? Would you find me guilty of wrongdoing?"

"It's not your circumstances that condemn you," Dalan replied. "You've been dealt with unjustly and I wouldn't wish your fate on anyone. It's your lack of compassion for others which is the crime. If you possessed any respect for the mortal kind you wouldn't involve yourself in their affairs. You profit by the misfortune of your fellow beings. If you were a mortal you would be subject to a fine for every life you have interfered with."

"I have compassion," the Watcher protested. "I suffer in my spirit for that luxury every day. I have great respect for the mortal kind. For I desire a gift which they may experience at any time but which is denied to me: the peace of a sleeping soul."

"If I promise to search for a way to help you," Dalan relented, "will you guarantee that you'll cease to be involved in the affairs of mortals? The treaty between the Fir-Bolg and the Danaans must be negotiated so both parties can face the invaders with strength of purpose."

"I can't promise you anything since it's in my nature to take advantage of conflict."

"You're making excuses," Dalan sighed.

"I'd welcome a resolution to my soul's imprisonment," the stranger grunted, "and I'd submit to anything in order to avoid the same end as my friends over there." The Watcher gestured toward the standing stones.

"How did Balor convince you to take this path?" the Brehon asked curiously.

"I was younger. I thought myself wise enough to be able to weather the seasons. What's missing from one's life is often more powerful than that which one holds. Always remember that, my dear Brehon, and you'll have compassion for me."

"The tales say you were offered great riches and power in exchange for your souls."

The Watcher laughed aloud, obviously amused by this. "The truth is we were all granted a single wish. Yes, some of my brothers and sisters chose wealth or influence, things which only have meaning in the mortal world. Those who did were very shortsighted. I'm fortunate my wish wasn't easily satisfied. This is one reason I've not withdrawn from the world in defeat and utter boredom. My desire has not yet been sated."

"What did you wish for?"

"Unquenchable passion," the Watcher replied with

a wry smile. And then he quoted from an ancient Fomorian ballad. " 'Passion ripens to hunger and the fruit thereof is sweet. The liquor of the fruit cures all weariness, refreshes, replenishes, renews. There is no sorrow, no regret, nor enduring sickness where Passion dwells. Don't tell me your soul is weary. Embrace your life. Drink from the Well of Passion.' "

Dalan felt an aching in his forehead and he touched his fingers to his brow.

"I must leave you now," the stranger told him. "I've work to do and it will not wait. Consider my words. And if you should solve my problem, remember I'll reward you well for your help."

"I only wish you to cease your interference in the ways of mortals," the Brehon replied through the pain of his headache. "I don't seek rewards."

"That's what makes you all the more worthy of a prize. And it's why I have confidence you'll be able to help my companion and myself."

"Where should I begin searching for an answer?"

"It'll come to you I'm certain for I've traveled to the dark place. I've seen what was and is. And I've been shown what will be. I know you're the one I've been searching for through the generations. And I'm sure you'll have the skill to wield the power when it's in your hands."

"What power?" Dalan pleaded.

But the Watcher was gone. The vision had faded. The Brehon was alone, once more seated on the Victory Stone. The sun was low in the sky now and Dalan decided he couldn't waste any more time deliberating. There were folk waiting on his wisdom. He hadn't come to a solution to the problem he'd set out to solve. He'd have to trust to his instincts. For now it was time to go to meet the two rival kings of the Danaan and Fir-Bolg.

Chapter 13

WHEN LOM AWOKE HE FELT REFRESHED AND WELL. The king's dry-stone hut was dark and there was a lot of smoke in the room. In the meager glow of the firelight he could just make out the shapes of three others wrapped in furs sleeping nearby.

As he lay half awake the hut was suddenly filled with bright light as the cowhide flap covering the door was pulled aside. Lom held his hands over his eyes, but squinting through the gaps in his fingers he glimpsed two figures. One of the men held a torch just outside the door.

"Fineen is too gravely ill to leave his bed for a few days," one man's voice stated as Lom pretended to be asleep. "But your three children will attend the fire at the Victory Stone later this evening close to midnight. I have a role for each of them in my judgment."

"Very well, Dalan," King Brocan promised. "They'll

attend if I have to carry them down to the stone my-self."

"I understand how you must be feeling," the Bre-hon soothed. "The tale I've heard so far is very sad. But tonight there'll be no secrets between Danaan and Fir-Bolg. You must make an effort to be perfectly honest with Cecht. As I have told you, there's a great deal at stake here for all our peoples."

"We will drive the invaders away from these shores," Brocan stated confidently.

"I fear you're wrong," Dalan replied. "They have a weapon which scatters all before it. It is so devastat-ing the Druid Assembly is considering calling a Draoi-Song down upon the foreigners."

"That's not been done for generations," the king remarked skeptically. "Is there anyone alive who knows how to do it?"

"The Druids are keepers of the law and protectors of the lore. We have remembered much that others have forgotten. But these new folk are like no other invaders who have come before. We will succumb to them unless we use the knowledge that originated in the long-ago."

"What is this weapon which causes you so much concern?"

"I'll tell you at the Victory Stone," Dalan assured the king. "Now we'll meet with Cecht, you and I. It will be necessary to have peace between you both be-fore we meet in public tonight. Once we have secured an alliance between you, it will be time to plan for war."

"I don't understand." The king frowned. "I have no quarrel with these invaders. They are hardly likely to take the barren lands of the west from my people. This part of the country barely supports the Fir-Bolg and we are few in number. Perhaps you've spent too long among the Danaans." The king had not forgotten Lochie's advice. "You'll have to present a convincing argument if you want me to commit my people to any such alliance."

"The invaders want this whole country for themselves," Dalan sighed. "These warriors who have come are but a small advance party whose duty is to deal with any opposition to their conquest. The bulk of their people, and they have many kinfolk, are waiting in the Iberi lands for news of victory. Once they have secured this island they will send for their families. Then we will be hard pressed to resist their coming. And they will want every bit of land they can lay claim to."

"I could negotiate a separate peace with the foreigners," Brocan suggested.

"The Danaans and the Fir-Bolg are the guardians of this land," the Brehon reminded him. "When you took your oath of office you promised to defend this island to the last drop of your blood. And believe me, you will have to fight if the Draoi-Craft of the Ollamh-Dreamers does not prove effective against them."

"I would prefer to examine the possibility of a treaty," Brocan repeated.

"These newcomers come from the same stock as our ancestors but they are an uncivilized folk who do not recognize the Druid laws as we do."

"They would surely honor a treaty sworn in good faith."

"I do not know if they hold such oath-taking to be valid," Dalan sighed. "Certainly their laws differ from ours in many ways. For example, they set the penalty for the killing of a kinsman at death."

"A life for a life!" the king gasped, truly horrified. "That serves no purpose but to rid the land of the murderer. What of the killer's soul? Is there no path to redemption through recompense?"

"It is a barbaric practice. And it makes it all the more difficult to imagine they are descended from our common ancestors."

"Let us go then." Brocan nodded. "I will throw off my pride to do what I can to make amends. For the moment I will accept your advice. But if I can find an opportunity to avoid war, I will take it, even if that means abandoning the Danaans to their fate."

"I am afraid you have been placed in a position where that is highly unlikely," Dalan told him. "Do not expect my judgment upon you will be an easy one. You owe a great debt to King Cecht and there will be no avoiding it."

"I will pay my debts. I always do."

"This may be more than your people can afford."

"Will you bring a fine against me for Fineen's injuries?"

"Of course."

"I beg you to consider an alternative," Brocan ventured. "My people will be crippled by all the fines imposed on us."

"What did you have in mind?"

"The Druid Path," the king replied.

Dalan sighed. "I'll consider it." He nodded.

"Such a judgment would be very welcome to all my folk, I'm sure. The lad has been nothing but trouble."

"I will require assurances," the Brehon informed him.

With that the orange torchlight withdrew and the flap dropped back into place, returning the hut to darkness once more. Lom lay on his back for a long while, knowing the Brehon would not let the Fir-Bolg off lightly. He closed his eyes, thinking of invaders coming across the sea, and before long he had drifted off again. Suddenly someone was gently shaking him. Then he saw Dalan's face before him.

"Are you well enough to rise?"

"I am," he muttered.

The Druid passed on to Aoife. She woke quickly and he helped her to sit up.

Lom reached over to pull the blankets away from Sárán and as he did so he felt a sharp pain in the back of his head. He soon forgot his own troubles though when he saw the bandages covering his brother's face. "What have they done to you?" Lom exclaimed.

"It looks much worse than it is," Dalan stated. "Help him up, will you, while I attend to Aoife. You must all be dressed up for a feast tonight."

"I would rather stay in bed," Aoife complained. Her head was pounding and her vision blurred. "My arm is burning with pain."

"Nevertheless you will get dressed to go to the feast. I am to pass my judgment upon you publicly at the Victory Stone."

Aoife nodded, though she did not fully understand what was being said to her. Her mind was in confusion. She had no idea whether it was day or night and she was only vaguely aware of the people around her.

When the three of them were finally ready Brocan carried Aoife while Fergus cradled Sárán in his arms. Lom followed after, head bowed, leaning against Dalan. By the time they reached the fireplace on the battleground the stars were shining brightly in the dark blue heavens and the faces of the assembled warriors were lit by orange firelight.

Sárán was wide awake, though he was quite groggy, by the time the veteran set him down next to Aoife on furs laid out in front of the stone. Torches had been arranged around the rock where Dalan was to deliver his judgment. Lom watched his stern-faced father bow before the Danaan king and his son Mahon before moving to his place in the assembly.

Directly opposite the Danaans stood Lom's mother, Riona, Queen of the Fir-Bolg. She was dressed in a dark green tunic of fine wool which fell to her ankles.

Her hair was braided into many intricate knots held in place by polished bronze pins. Her dark rust-colored cloak was held at the left shoulder by a brooch decorated with yellow enamel work. Beside her stood Isleen wrapped in dark blue. These two red-haired women attracted all eyes to them with their quiet confidence and strength. And their expressions mirrored each other so that many wondered if they might be sisters.

Riona didn't acknowledge her husband's arrival. She didn't so much as twitch as Brocan took his position beside her. The Fir-Bolg queen had already managed to catch Cecht's attention. The Danaan king smiled at her through the long locks of golden hair which framed his face. And his eyes were drawn back to her and her companion Isleen again and again as he scanned the gathering.

Lochie the Bard took a place among the warriors where he could observe proceedings without attracting too much attention. There were a few folk he wanted to watch, to size up their reactions for future reference.

When all the warriors of both camps were waiting in silence, Dalan walked off into the darkness and disappeared completely. Each man looked at his neighbor, puzzling over such behavior. But their silent questions were answered when Dalan returned a short while later carrying his harp.

The Brehon climbed up onto the Victory Stone where everyone could see him. Then he knelt down

with his instrument tucked in close beside him. When
he was comfortable he ran his long, gnarled fingers
over the strings to make sure the harp had kept its tuning. One wire needed a little adjustment but the waiting warriors did not show any signs of impatience.

With a touch of the tuning key Dalan's instrument
was singing in harmony again. The melody was a slow
grieving lament. Some of the Danaans began humming lowly in accompaniment as they recognized the
music. Everyone bowed his head in silent respect for
the dead. Three Danaans and three Fir-Bolg had fallen
in the fight that morning and a further twenty warriors had been injured.

"These strings are remarkable, aren't they?" the
Brehon sighed when he had finished, placing the instrument tenderly down on the stone beside him.
"They were a gift from a Bard of the Milesian people,"
he informed everyone.

"Who are the Milesians?" Brocan asked, ritually
inviting the Brehon to present his tale. Dalan had chosen the king to ask this question since he had already
heard these tidings.

"The newcomers call themselves the sons and
daughters of King Míl of the Iberi lands. They also go
by the name Gaedhals after one of their ancestors.
Their fleet has sailed from the southern shore seeking
a new homeland for their folk and fresh pastures for
their cattle."

"Do they intend war?" the Fir-Bolg king cut in, just
as the Brehon had instructed.

"Their Chief Bard was sent to the court of the Dagda with a message," Dalan explained. "They have offered us a choice. Either we enter into a treaty to share this island which we call Innisfail, or they will bring war to us. No matter which choice we make they intend to rule over our peoples."

Every warrior suddenly began speaking at once, protesting the arrogance of such a threat.

Dalan held up his hand to calm the crowd. "I believe they are capable of defeating us," he told them. "Even if we band together, Fir-Bolg and Danaan, in the strongest alliance since the days of Balor, it's plain to me we can't win against these folk."

"How many are there?" Cecht inquired.

"No more than three thousand."

"Forgive me, Brehon," the Danaan king laughed, "I mean no disrespect, but we could raise five thousand within one moon."

"Numbers will not win the day," Dalan stated. "These folk have a weapon which we cannot match."

"What weapon is that?" Brocan scoffed. "If we outnumber them nearly two to one, they will not prevail. And surely the Druid Assembly has some surprises in store."

"Naturally we have a few remaining courses of action which could be pursued." Dalan nodded.

"Then why this sudden panic? We have faced off invaders before and we will do so again."

"They speak our language and hold laws somewhat similar to the Druid doctrines we observe," the Brehon continued. "I told you earlier the Milesian Bard gave me a gift of harp strings. These wires are unlike any I have ever known. There is gold and bronze in their making, though I don't know the secret of it. The Gaedhals have mastered the mystery of the dark metal and the bright metal. This wire is not only sweet-sounding, it's strong."

"Harp strings don't win battles," Fergus declared confidently.

"This harp ended a fight today," Dalan answered sharply. "But it's not the Milesians' knowledge of music wire which will prove the greatest threat to us. Their Chief Bard gave me another gift."

With that the Brehon raised his hand to beckon an attendant. The servant ran to him carrying a long narrow object wrapped in a thick blue woolen cloak.

"I see they are fine weavers also," the veteran observed and many of the company laughed. "Perhaps they'll try to suffocate us in our beds during the night!"

Dalan didn't take any notice of the jibe. He pulled the cloak away to reveal a strange bright sword that shone silver in the moonlight. All the assembled warriors sighed as one at the beauty of the weapon.

"This blade is fashioned from a metal stronger than anything our smiths can create. The edge is sharper and easier to repair. These swords will defeat us."

"Nonsense!" Fergus huffed. "It will take a well-trained warrior to better me in a fight."

"Brocan," Dalan cried, "take this blade. See if Fergus can strike you with his sword."

The Brehon handed the weapon down to the King of the Fir-Bolg who immediately weighed it in his hand.

"It's well balanced," Brocan noted immediately.

"Spar with your king," the Brehon told Fergus.

The veteran took up a sword from those discarded at the edge of the field then walked calmly over to his king. Brocan waited patiently for Fergus to make the first move. When he did so the king easily blocked the stab.

"It is a fine weapon," Brocan commented.

Fergus swung his sword over his head to give his king plenty of time to react and then brought it down so that Brocan could block it. When the two blades met there was a loud crack as the veteran's blade of bronze shattered in his hand.

King Brocan stepped back. And the entire crowd of warriors held their breath as he examined the Milesian sword.

"There is hardly a scratch on it," Brocan stuttered in disbelief.

"We cannot make these swords," Dalan continued. "Our smiths know nothing of the metal. They are ignorant of the process involved in producing it. These weapons are not created from a casting, they are hammered out flat many times and folded over to toughen the edges. Then the iron is plunged into the forge and tempered in water. Such skills are exacting and a lifetime in the learning."

"What can we do against such weaponry?" Brocan exclaimed as he handed the blade to Cecht.

The Danaan king swung the sword around his head and sliced it through the air. "It's magnificent!" he declared.

The Danaan king caught Riona's admiring glance, her eyes sparkling in the firelight. He smiled in her direction, but the queen turned her head away demurely, though Isleen nodded to him. Cecht bowed slightly to acknowledge the Seer and she smiled broadly.

"I don't believe we can defeat the Milesians in war," the Brehon repeated. "Nevertheless the Druid Assembly has decided we must do everything in our power to prevent the foreigners landing on our shores. Nine Ollamh-Harpers are about to commence conjuring a tempest the like of which has never been seen before over Innisfail. It is our hope the storm will sweep the strangers' ships away from our shores, if it doesn't destroy them."

"Such a storm-calling has not been attempted since the ancient days," Cecht cut in. "It takes great expertise. Even Balor of the Evil Eye didn't dare make use of this knowledge. Remember the old tales? Do you recall what became of the Islands of the West when the ancient Druids called on the forces of wind and water?"

"It is true that Druids of the Blessed Isles abused their talents," Dalan countered. "That is why the old homeland was destroyed by the sea. But those who survived the upheavals learned much from these mistakes. The Draoi-Craft has been passed down to us. And the Ollamh-Harpers will not let the storms get out of their control."

"You Druids can use the harp to bring a tempest into being?" Fergus inquired.

"That is true."

"Then why was this Draoi-Craft not used to drive Balor out of his island fortress in the days of our forefathers?"

"The resulting tumult is so terrible and so devastating that if it were not strictly kept in check it could sweep Innisfail away forever," the Brehon explained. "You must also remember that Balor was very powerful. His eyes were everywhere. And he had the nine Watchers to do his bidding."

At the mention of the Watchers everyone hummed, hoping to hear the tale. Lochie caught Isleen's eye and they shared a private moment of amusement. King Cecht, noticing the Seer looking intensely into the crowd, followed her gaze. He saw Lochie sitting among the warriors and realized this man was her husband. He'd heard a rumor she was married. Now he saw the man he found himself disappointed. The Bard didn't seem to be remarkable in any way. Indeed he was an ordinary-looking man who might easily be lost in a crowd.

"So we can only wait to witness the outcome of this tempest?" Brocan was asking.

"We must all work together," the Brehon declared. "Danaan and Fir-Bolg must prepare for the great storm to come which will certainly flood parts of the country, mostly the east. But the tempest could do great damage to life and property. And if it does not drive the invaders away, we must be ready for war. In the case of that eventuality the Druid Assembly has proposed another solution which will keep war at bay. But I am not permitted to speak of it yet."

"What other news is there?" the Danaan king inquired. "You did not travel from the other side of the island just to present these tidings. You are an important Brehon who may one day hold the office of Dagda. Any messenger could have brought this news."

"The Druid Assembly has commanded me to deliver a valuable prize," Dalan stated. For the first time in many seasons the Brehon felt his voice weaken with apprehension. He coughed to clear his throat, then signaled to the servant. The man nodded and disappeared into the darkness.

"What prize?" Cecht demanded to know.

"I bear an honor boon which accompanies a command to cease the trial by contest between your peoples," the Brehon explained. "Unfortunately I did not arrive in time to prevent blood from being spilled. But acceptance of the prize is to be taken as a sign that all hostilities between Brocan and Cecht will cease immediately."

The servant returned carrying a great bronze cauldron which he set on the Victory Stone for all to see. The vessel was a beautifully cast piece of work covered in designs depicting the animals of the forest and the fish of the rivers and seas. In the center of these creatures sat a man with the horns of a stag and the eyes of a fox.

Everyone knew what it was without the need for explanation. A Cauldron of Plenty was only bestowed as a personal gift from the Dagda in recognition of the wise rule of a generous leader. These vessels were exact copies of the original cauldron which had been fashioned in the Islands of the West in ancient days. The Dagda now held that vessel in his keeping and it was said to have several properties about it. First, any food the owner could imagine would be instantly produced by the cauldron. Second, it never ran out of food, so a host could be fed from it easily. Third, any corpse dipped into the sacred vessel would be miraculously restored to life for a period.

This vessel had none of these properties. But it inferred a reputation for open-handedness, skilled husbandry of resources and hence the respect of the Druid Assembly.

"I present to this gathering," Dalan announced, "the Cauldron of Plenty."

There was a sigh of wonder from every soul gathered there by the fire. Even Lochie sat forward to have a better look at the precious vessel.

"It's a gift of friendship and honor," the Brehon explained.

"Which of us is to receive it?" the Danaan king asked with suspicion.

"The Dagda awards this vessel to Brocan, King of the Fir-Bolg of the Burren," Dalan declared, disguising his trepidation. "And with it goes a dowry of forty cows. These animals remain in the trust of the Dagda but all their offspring will be delivered to Dun Burren as they become old enough."

"Treachery walked on this field today!" Cecht bellowed, losing his temper. "Brocan's own sons would have attempted to kill me while their father was speaking of peace."

"I have heard several reports of the fight this morning," Dalan cut in. "I don't believe there was ever any risk of you being struck down by either of those unblooded youths. Your personal guards were at your side throughout. But I don't begrudge you your outrage. Sárán and Lom acted with no regard for the law."

"And this is how that treachery is to be rewarded?" Cecht spat. "With a high honor, calves and praise from the Dagda no less."

"This gifting was decided before the events of this morning unfolded," the Brehon noted dryly. "I don't have the authority to disobey the Dagda's instructions. He commanded me to bring the cauldron here and present it to Brocan as a peace offering. I had no idea the peace would already be broken before I arrived."

"You may not be able to remedy the injustice done on this field today," Cecht retorted. "But you must render your judgment now before all this assembly. The sons of Brocan attempted to murder me during a negotiation for peace. I demand a verdict against them to recompense my honor."

"Fergus and myself stopped the boys before they were close enough to do you any harm," Brocan cut in. "Those two headstrong lads could not have reached you unless I had wished it."

"How do I know you did not wish it?" the Danaan king shot back.

"Because I gave you my word we would speak under truce."

"The word of a Fir-Bolg! I'd rather trust my soul into the hands of the Watchers!" Cecht scoffed, then noticed Isleen smiling broadly at some private joke shared with her husband.

"It is time I ended this dispute," Dalan rebuked them both. "Before either of you speak words you will regret you must accept that the old feud must end."

The Brehon pointed to Brocan's children.

"Those young ones acted the way they did because they did not know or understand the law," Dalan declared. "The duty to teach them such customs and regulations is their father's. But Brocan has not had time to educate his offspring. The King of the Fir-Bolg has been obsessed all his life with defending his lands against his traditional enemies, the Danaans."

"The incident was a mistake, a misunderstanding,"

Brocan sighed with a wave of his hand. "There is no use in me contesting guilt. It is true I should have kept a closer eye on my children. I submit to be fined and I will accept your verdict, Dalan. And with my submission I accept the Cauldron of Plenty and an end to the war between our peoples."

"I tried to reason with my husband," Riona interrupted, "but he would not listen to me. Contrary to custom he does not regard my opinion as important."

"Those are unworthy words," Brocan spat. "Whenever I make a decision you take the opposite standpoint. And often you berate me in front of the chieftains of our people. I know you only wish to see me embarrassed. You think that will sway me to your views. When I stand firm against your tricks it only aggravates your anger."

"I am your equal!" she replied. "You have not listened to a word I've said since young Fearna was found in the snow. The chieftains mutter behind your back, the warriors talk openly of treachery in your hall, and the women marvel that I ever consented to be your queen."

"I have heard enough from you!" the king retorted. "I am the one who will bear the brunt of this lawsuit. I will have to find a way to pay the fine for Fearna. You do not need to worry yourself about such matters. You should be grateful I have relieved you of the responsibility."

"You are speaking over the top of your betters again. Dalan was about to deliver his verdict."

"Hear my judgment!" the Brehon exclaimed, hoping to quiet both of them. "In the old days, in the time of Balor, the Danaans and the Fir-Bolg formed an alliance to defeat the Evil Eye. They forged this pact out of desperation and guaranteed it with hostages."

The Danaan king's jaw dropped open in surprise as he guessed what Dalan was about to say. "No child of mine is ever going to live among these vicious folk again!" he declared. "I've lost one boy to that savage. I won't sacrifice another."

"You will accept my judgment. I'm a Brehon empowered by the Druid Assembly to bring peace between you both. You are the last of your peoples to maintain hostility toward one another."

Dalan breathed deeply, filling his lungs to settle his nerves a little before going on.

"Since the lack of a proper education in law caused this strife, two of Brocan's children will take holy orders. Sárán and Aoife are bound from this day to the Druid Path. Since it would be unjust to take all three children from their father, Lom will stay at Dun Burren. He will train to become a warrior so that he may one day rule the Fir-Bolg with wisdom."

All three children looked stunned by the harshness of the decision, but none of them dared speak lest Dalan impose a further penalty on them.

"It seems to me that Aoife and Sárán are particularly at fault in that they spurred each other on to foolish acts. Lom, I believe, was simply caught up in the repercussions. For that reason I have decided he is only in need of guidance. That I leave to his father to provide."

"May he find the wisdom to perform that duty well, even if he can't fulfill any of his other obligations," Riona quipped.

The Brehon paused until she had finished. He wanted to make sure everyone present was listening. "Aoife will remain with Lom in the house of their father until she recovers from her injury. Then she will become my personal student. Sárán will travel to the court of the Danaan king with Fineen when the healer has regained his strength."

Sárán's face paled. He held his hands over his eyes as the full meaning of the sentence dawned on him.

"Since Fineen very nearly perished at your hand," the Brehon concluded, "it is only just that you serve him as his student and learn everything he can teach you. From this day Sárán will be a son to King Cecht. Mahon mac Cecht will go to the court of King Brocan and be as a son to him. This way each will have his own blood in the court of the other ruler. It may give you both a fresh view of the differences which have arisen in the past."

"You are not serious!" the Danaan king protested. "Sárán would have murdered me and you want me to foster him?"

"He will learn to respect you and so will think twice about taking issue with you in the future. In time the young man will realize he owes you a debt of gratitude. He will be loyal to you if he is taught honor."

"Honor I can teach him. Gratitude can be bought. But respect is another thing. Respect is more difficult. That I cannot bestow upon him. That should have been learned at his father's knee."

"Let that be your challenge then." Dalan smiled. "Now you have a son to raise in place of Fearna who died so prematurely."

"The last son I gave into Brocan's care died a terrible death alone in the snow," Cecht hissed. "All because of Brocan's neglect. How many sons must I give up to the Fir-Bolg before they offer the hand of peace with sincerity?"

"Mahon is older," the Brehon noted, "and somewhat wiser. He will flourish in the Fir-Bolg court. Sárán is your son now. You must learn to forgive him as you would your own flesh and blood. Think of him not as taking Fearna's place, but as walking hand in hand with the spirit of your youngest son."

"Fearna would have liked that, I think," Mahon observed. "He was a great friend of Sárán, I believe."

"If only that were true," Brocan cut in and then felt all eyes upon him. "The facts of the matter are difficult to believe, and harder still for me to relate. But now it is time for the truth."

"What truth?" Cecht hissed, searching the other man's eyes.

"Fearna drank heavily on the night of his death because my son Sárán and my daughter Aoife goaded him on to it. Then when he was completely lost to reason they enticed him onto a horse. This they perhaps considered quite entertaining. I am sure they had no idea of the dangers."

"Your children led my son to his death?" the Danaan shrieked, barely able to withhold his rage and shock.

"And most shameful of all, after he was thrown to his death they left his body unguarded in the winter forest and spoke nothing of their part in the misadventure."

Cecht stared intently at the son of the Fir-Bolg king as if he were searching the man's soul. Then tears began to well up in the Danaan's eyes. "You, Sárán?" the King of the Danaans whispered, lost for words to express his grief and despair. "You murdered my son?"

Sárán did not move but the guilt on his face was clear to everyone. Cecht turned to Aoife. She was already nodding with her eyes shut tight, trying not to sob.

"I am to raise this youth as if he were my own blood?" Cecht asked again incredulously. "As my own dearest offspring? You cannot be serious."

"I am. That is my judgment." Dalan nodded. "You may not think my verdict very wise. You might consider the penalty against the lad unjust to yourself. But you must accept my decision."

"I accept it," the Danaan hastened, not wishing to seem to be defying the Brehon. "Just don't expect me to be dancing around the fire for joy. And what about

the eric-fine for Fearna? Considering the circumstances, I believe the claim against Brocan should
surely increase."

"I agree with you," Dalan assured him. "I have already had time to consider this because Brocan came
to me this afternoon with the full tale. In all fairness
he only learned the truth himself this morning. That
was why he asked for a truce with you on the field."

The Danaan king frowned.

"The fine was originally set at one hundred cows,"
Dalan went on. "That is obviously not enough considering the involvement of Brocan's son and daughter."

The King of the Fir-Bolg held his head high as he
silently prayed to his ancestors that the penalty would
not be too great.

"I don't want to cause hardship to the Fir-Bolg but
I cannot appear too lenient either," the Brehon informed his listeners. "This has been a difficult settlement to judge."

He paused as everyone fell perfectly quiet.

"Three hundred and ninety cows," Dalan announced sternly.

"Three hundred and ninety!" Brocan coughed with
disbelief. "My kinfolk will starve!"

"To be paid in installments," the Brehon went on.
"Ten cows per cycle of the seasons for the next thirty-
nine cycles. Until all the cows plus their subsequent
offspring total three hundred and ninety."

Brocan's gloom lifted a little. He realized Dalan
was suggesting the cows should be in calving when

handed over to the Danaans. This would mean a cross-breeding of the Fir-Bolg stock with Danaan cattle. The Fir-Bolg possessed a breed that were long-haired, stocky, red-brown and fierce. Danaan cattle were wet-eyed and gentle, large and slow. Dalan's mean careful and patient ~~~ A successful crossbreeding would ~~~ guaranteeing survival of the bloodstock. Each side would certainly benefit from the help of the other. Such cooperation would help create and seal new friendship.

"The difference between the Fir-Bolg cattle," Dalan began, "and the Danaan breed is the only major distinction between our peoples. Since the defeat of Balor and the Fomorian hordes the two races have come closer to each other. We share a common language, a common music, a common law and lore. If it were not for the obvious evidence of the cows, a stranger might not be able to say who was Danaan or who was not."

Brocan smiled.

"We are the only two kings still fighting with each other," Cecht conceded. "All the others began working together generations ago."

"It is time we put an end to the quarrel," Brocan agreed reluctantly, seeing he had no real choice in the matter. "Adding the offspring of the cows to the tally will ease the burden, but three hundred and ninety cows is a high price to pay for peace."

"As high as the cost of the loss of my son was to me?" Cecht asked. "And the cost to my pride if I must treat Sárán of the Treacherous Intent as my son?"

"The judgment is fair," the Fir-Bolg king admitted.

Cecht turned to Dalan. "I have my reservations but it seems we both agree with the spirit of your wisdom."

"Then let us feast," the Brehon declared, relieved matters had been settled so easily. "Now we must begin to plan the defense of this menace from across the seas. While we celebrate this new alliance with food and drink I will tell the story of the Milesians in full for I had it from their Chief Bard and it is a good tale."

Chapter 14

AFTER ALL THE WARRIORS, MEN AND WOMEN WERE seated on the ground with their meal Dalan settled on the top of the stone to tell the tale of the invaders, the folk who called themselves the Milesians. Cecht noticed that Isleen and Lochie did not stay for the meal. They had disappeared together into the darkness when Dalan called the feast.

"The Gaedhals are kinfolk to our people," the Brehon began. "Though they traveled a different path to reach Innisfail. Their last king was called Míl and he lived in the land of the Iberi to the south over the ocean. His ancestors came from Falias, one of the ancient cities of our own forebears on the Islands of the West." The Brehon coughed to clear his throat. "The Fir-Bolg and the Tuatha De Danaan were one people with the Gaedhals in those days."

"Are they truly kin to us?" Brocan cut in.

"Strictly speaking they are," Dalan replied cautiously. "Though their ways are somewhat barbarous. King Gaedhal was a renegade, a raider, a pirate and at one time an outcast. His descendants have inherited his disdain for the law. But Míl, their last king, was famed as a just man. Therefore they prefer to be known by his name rather than by that which our ancestors knew them, the Gaedhals."

"Why should we go to war with our cousins?" Cecht asked and Brocan smiled to think that a close blood tie had never before stopped the Danaans from engaging in battle.

"You and I aren't such distant kinfolk," the King of the Fir-Bolg pointed out. "And yet we've been at war for generations."

"Our kinship is close," Cecht admitted. "We fought against your folk because your ancestors wouldn't yield a portion of the land to us."

"You'd no right to demand it."

"Right of conquest," the Danaan king countered. "That's our claim on this land. We defeated your people at the battle of Mag Tuireadh. A treaty was agreed and we should have lived in peace after it."

"But your warriors didn't honor the treaty," Brocan reminded him. "They entered the holy places without leave from our Druids. They cut down the oak groves and planted their own trees."

"Then your kings made a treacherous pact with the Fomor," Cecht countered.

"What choice did they have but to seek help from beyond the shores of Innisfail?"

"Balor, King of the Fomorians, was our common enemy," King Cecht reminded him. "His sea-raiders murdered Fir-Bolg and Danaan alike. And they were strangers. They were not people of Danu as we are. The Fomor came from the frozen north."

"The Fir-Bolg had driven out the Fomorians long before your folk sailed to these shores. Balor offered us freedom from Danaan rule if we followed him."

"You were betrayed by him," the Danaan king scoffed.

"We weren't to know of the weapon he'd created," Brocan protested. "We weren't to know he'd use the Evil Eye to attack our own folk once the host of the Danaan had been defeated. And we couldn't have even guessed he had created the Watchers. If these things had been known to us, and if the Danaans had listened to our grievances about their unjust rule of Innisfail, the war with Balor would never have happened the way it did."

"The western Fir-Bolg of the Burren were Balor's strongest supporters," Cecht hissed. "Your clan. Your kin."

"Be careful, my lord," Riona interrupted, "or my husband will end up fighting the Fomorian wars all over again with you. He can be very stubborn." Her lips moved in the faintest hint of a smile.

"You're both talking about times long past," Dalan agreed. "Mistakes were made on both sides. But often what ails us can also heal us, as Fineen would say. We must learn from our mistakes so we may stand united in the face of this new threat."

"It's plain to me the Danaans should fight their own battles and leave the Fir-Bolg to pursue our separate destiny," Brocan declared.

"The destiny of the Danaans and the Fir-Bolg is entwined whether you like it or not," the Brehon countered. "We've already become one people. The Druid Assembly is made up of men and women from both kin. The kings of the east and north refer to their subjects as Tuatha De Danaan. The People of the Goddess Danu. She's our common ancestor and she's watching over us as always."

"Is Danu the ancestor of the Milesians?" Cecht cut in. "You said they're our cousins."

"They claim to be of her bloodline," Dalan told him. "But they trace themselves from one of their early queens."

"Will we find ourselves threatened by the Milesian Draoi?" the Danaan pressed.

Dalan shrugged his shoulders. "We don't know much about their skills in the Draoi-Craft."

"Then we must call on the sacred treasures bequeathed to us by our ancestors," Cecht decided. "That would put paid to the power of their Druids. And it'd settle the problem of these invaders without the need for alliance with the Fir-Bolg."

There was a general murmur of approval from all the Danaans at this suggestion.

"Everywhere else in Innisfail there is already alliance," Dalan replied in frustration. "All the other kings have been at peace for more than three generations. Only you two keep the coals of the old quarrel glowing bright. Your fellow kings and chieftains need all your warriors to fight."

"What of the four treasures?" Brocan protested. "Cecht is right. The treasures would surely end any threat from the Milesians."

"The Druid Assembly is reluctant to bring the four treasures to bear. The sacred gifts of our ancestors have lain silent since the defeat of Balor. Even in those times the Druid Assembly was not happy to call on the awesome Draoi which the treasures can rise. And in these times there's not anyone living who has even witnessed the use of them. The secrets of their rituals are remembered but no one has practiced ceremonies for the four treasures since before the time of Balor."

"The Sword of Cleaving should be delivered to the warrior class," Cecht argued. "The Druid master, Uscias of Findias, created that blade for my people to use should the need arise."

"And the Spear of Flame should be given over also," Brocan added. "These weapons were merely given into the care of the Druids in the ancient days. It's time they were returned to the warriors who can wield them for the good of all."

Dalan smiled. "Esras of Gorias was a renowned and wise Druid. When he fashioned the Spear of Flame for your ancestors, Brocan, he understood he had given into their hands a weapon so devastating no warrior would be able to withstand the temptation to use it. Or to use it often if given the opportunity.

That's why the Ollamh-Dreamers hold that weapon in their keeping. Only the Dream-Seers can be trusted to preserve such an artifact without the temptation to employ it."

"What would Druids know of warfare?" the Fir-Bolg king scoffed.

"The Ollamh-Dreamers hold a strong connection with the Otherworld; matters which seem important to us are trivial to any who walk the paths of the lands beyond life. The Spear of Flame has been used with ill intent in the past. In war against the Fomor the Fir-Bolg directed the heat of the Spear toward the watch-towers of their enemies. The very stones of the fortresses melted before the power of that weapon. I need not explain to you what effect that Spear had on the Fomor themselves."

"The Fomorians were our enemies," Brocan protested.

"And if you had possessed the Spear of Flame, would you have directed it toward the Danaans?"

Brocan dropped his head and did not answer.

Dalan continued, "The Druid Assembly has agreed that the sacred treasures are beyond the skill of any living warrior to wield."

"Surely the warrior class should be allowed to make that decision," Cecht grunted. "We've trained all our lives to protect our people from outside threat. It's all we know."

"You've spent your adult lives squabbling," Riona laughed, cutting in again. "You've hurled everything from petty insults to war spears at each other. If the

Druid Assembly were to release the spear and the sword into your hands, I'm sure you would quickly dispatch the Milesians. But it wouldn't be long before you turned these two weapons against each other. Innisfail would be devastated."

Both kings looked to the ground together and fell silent at her rebuke.

"The four treasures of Innisfail," Dalan told them, "are to be kept from harm and harmful intent. You have only to walk the countryside around to see the damage the sword and the spear did when they were used. When the war with the Fomor was done, it was the warriors who gave the sacred treasures into the keeping of the Ollamh-Dreamers. Those kings who'd seen the devastation didn't want to witness such destruction again. Nor did they want to pass that power on to their children.

"The Cauldron of Plenty, the Stone of Destiny, the Sword of Cleaving and the Spear of Flame are at this moment being concealed deep within the earth in a place where only the Ollamh-Dreamers will be able to find them again. Those objects will stay beyond the reach of all until the danger of invasion has passed."

"The Druid Assembly has made this decision." Cecht was unconvinced. "And as always the Druids are serving their own ends. They don't tell us ordinary folk all we should know. They throw us scraps of information in the same way I cast fatty portions of meat to my dogs. We never see the choicest cuts of the roast."

"The Druid Assembly has a responsibility just as you do," the Brehon snapped. "Do you think we could avoid invasion forever? This land is rich and fertile. The seas all about are abundant with the fruits of the ocean. It was inevitable some adventurer from beyond the waves would come to our land one day, see the bounty we enjoy, then try to take it away from us."

Dalan turned to the gathered warriors, hoping to appeal to his listeners.

"The Druid Assembly has known about the coming of the Gaedhals for a long while. Their arrival was prophesied. And so the Dagda and his advisers have had many seasons to formulate their strategy. War is not the way of the holy orders. We don't rely on our skill at arms to perform our duties. It's the responsibility of the Druid class to ensure all other possibilities are exhausted before the warriors are called upon to do their duty. And you as warriors must realize you're our last line of defense."

"If the Fir-Bolg retain our sovereignty over western Innisfail," Brocan nodded, "I'll be satisfied. I don't wish to share this land with any more invaders."

"And the Danaan folk wish only for peace," Cecht agreed, grudgingly. "If these aims can be achieved without bloodshed, then I'll be happy. But if the Druid Assembly has judged poorly, each and every one of us here tonight will regret the day we placed our faith in unreliable Draoi tricks over the firm hand of the warriors."

"I pray it never comes to that," Dalan sighed. "May Danu protect us."

While the warriors of the Fir-Bolg and the Danaan were listening to Dalan's tales Isleen and Lochie had already departed the battleground to travel north. They covered great distances quickly for they were not bound to the material world as others were. Once they shed their skins they were free to go wherever they wished.

They hovered over the Island of the Tower, a bleak deserted mass of rock and ruins off the northern coast of Innisfail. No one lived there anymore. No fisherman or traveler ever visited. It was a barren, cold, lonely and haunting place. Only the two remaining Watchers ever stood upon its stony shore to look back on Innisfail with envy and vengeance.

Balor's fortress had long since been dismantled by the victorious Danaans. The beautifully hewn stones of its walls had been hurled into the ocean so they might never be used again. Just beneath the surface of the waves at low tide these blocks could still sometimes be glimpsed scattered haphazardly as if they had tumbled down to the shore in the destruction of the Tower of Balor.

"I remember best of all," Lochie began wistfully, "the polished surface of the stone which covered the tower."

"It was the same as fine glass," Isleen reminisced. "At dusk the whole structure glowed in a golden fire lit by the brilliance of the dying sun."

"And in the evening as the Northern Lights danced around the sky the tower mirrored their spectacle," Lochie added.

"Now this place is empty," Isleen said sadly. "Even the ghosts have long since departed. Only we return again and again."

"Are we not ghosts?"

"Ghosts!" Isleen gasped in shock. "I don't think of myself as a ghost. I'm a living being. I've retained my mental faculties. I choose where I go. I'm not bound to a particular place or person. And if I wish I can leave this world whenever I choose."

"As long as you have no fear of spending the rest of eternity trapped within a granite standing stone wishing every moment that the moments would wear down your prison into sand."

"I have fed on fear for so long," she admitted, "that I do not always recognize it in myself."

"We inspire fear," Lochie pointed out. "But not the fear a simple haunting might conjure. We are masters of dread and yet few folk feel uncomfortable in our presence."

"If only they knew!" she laughed.

"Dalan knows."

"What?"

"I've spoken with him," he stated baldly.

"Are you mad?" Isleen raged. "We're forbidden to make contact with anyone on that subject. It's strictly against the laws of Balor."

"Let him come and reprimand me," Lochie laughed.

Then he turned away from the ocean to look back at the island. "Balor!" he cried. "I've broken your laws. Come and deal out your justice and punishment. Do your worst. I don't fear you anymore."

His voice echoed over the rocks. There was no answer.

"There are no rules to bind us any longer," Lochie told Isleen. "No one can tell us what we may or may not do. If we choose to break convention, who'll berate us? Certainly not old Balor. He's gone."

Isleen frowned. "I know it's true but in the back of my mind I haven't been able to accept it. I've carried on all along as if nothing had changed since the defeat of our people."

"It is time we threw off any thoughts of revenge or victory against the Danaans. Our folk are long gone. The sea-raiders of the Fomor have passed away forever. We must look to our own future. I have a feeling that if we can overcome this terrible burden we carry, we will have achieved a great victory for our people."

"What did you tell the Brehon?"

"Everything," Lochie confessed. "Except that we are posing as two Druids from the north."

"Why him?" Isleen demanded.

"Dalan was given to the Ollamh-Dreamers when he began his training. As his talent was realized he was sent by his teachers to study law. He may one day be elected to the office of Dagda. If we can gain his sympathy and support he may be able to help us find the peace we are both so desperately seeking."

"Why would one such as he choose to help us? We are his enemies, sworn to bring havoc to his people at every opportunity."

"He is a good man. And I believe he has a gentle heart. Dalan cannot stand to see any soul in suffering. That is why he has been selected as a possible candidate for Dagda.

"Dalan has been researching the Draoi-Music," Lochie explained. "The Ollamh-Dreamers are compiling a collection of songs of power which were used in the ancient days to bring plenty or to curse the land as the singers wished. There may be a song in that collection which will free us from our bonds."

"Can you be certain?" she snapped, still unconvinced by his decision to reveal their presence to Dalan.

"No," Lochie admitted, "but I don't believe Balor would have created creatures such as us without also retaining the power to destroy us if necessary."

Isleen's eyes lit with hope. "You're right," she whispered, beginning to see his point. "Why didn't we think of it before?"

"Our loyalty to Balor blinded us. Until now it would have been unthinkable for us to consider betraying him, even though he's little more than a memory."

"Yet all along he'd planned to eradicate us when we'd outlived our usefulness to him," Isleen ruminated. "Is that what you're saying?"

"You knew him as well as I did," Lochie replied coldly. "What do you think he would have done with us if we'd become difficult? Or if we'd held him to ransom with our power? Balor took a great risk in creating beings more powerful than himself. He must have had a plan to deal with us if we ever challenged him."

"Why do you think the answer lies in the Draoi-Music?" Isleen pressed.

"Because Balor was fascinated with all things Danaan. And because the Danaans only used their songs to control the elements and the material world. They had no mastery over the spirit with their songs."

"Yet they knew the melodies for opening the door-way between the worlds," Isleen pointed out.

"They knew how to summon the physical doorway on this side," Lochie countered, "but they had no knowledge of what lay beyond. They still don't know very much about the spirit world really, do they?"

"You're right," she conceded. "But how do we convince Dalan to help us?"

"He is sympathetic. But more importantly he would dearly love to see us banished from the world to the Halls of Waiting because he sees us as a threat to the peace and stability of Innisfail."

"Have you asked him to help us?"

"I have," Lochie sighed. "But I fear he is distracted with this invasion. I now regret I ever drew the Gaedhals to this land for Dalan will have no time to help us until the invaders have been dealt with."

"Then we must give him good reason to want to help us," Isleen declared.

"What do you mean?"

"The Milesians are here now. We may as well use their presence to our advantage. If we openly cause havoc, perhaps Dalan will be inspired to work harder to find a way to release us."

"Do you mean we should reveal ourselves?" Lochie asked incredulously.

"Yes. What have we got to lose? They can't touch us."

Her companion smiled. "I believe you may be right. Throughout the generations we've stayed behind the scenes, never letting any mortal see through our many disguises. To do so now would inject a sense of urgency into proceedings. It'd give Dalan a real opponent to focus on.

"I'm tired," Lochie continued, "I'm ready for the release of death. Let this be our last campaign."

"So be it," Isleen agreed. "One way or another we can't continue this existence much longer. Going out among the mortals again has made me realize how bored I am. Let's make one last effort and then we'll retire."

"One last effort," Lochie echoed. "And for the first time we'll fight our true enemy. The one who set us on this path. Balor."

"There's only one other matter that will have to be settled," Isleen reminded him.

"What's that?"

"The business of our wager. I hope you haven't forgotten the little bet we made."

"I remember," Lochie laughed. "I hope you've been working hard at winning."

"I have," Isleen assured him. "I've given the matter a lot of thought. Aoife will not wed Mahon. Do you not recall the songs of our youth, when the Bards often sang of such hopeless love?"

He smiled at her, then answered with a love poem he had heard when he was a young mortal man. "Release your grip. Let go your desperate hold on the lesser things in life. Rush forward. No need to move your feet. Fly toward the infinite sky. Heart, fill yourself with joy. Each beat overflows with love. Risk everything. Ask for nothing."

Isleen brushed her hand over his as their eyes met. And there they sat in silence for a long while, each remembering the days of long ago.

Chapter 15

Now pay attention to me for I'll tell a tale you Gaedhals have almost forgotten. Ravens don't forget. And Lom-Dubh knows many stories from the ancient days.

Balor of the Evil Eye was an ancient, evil-minded king of the Fomor. His ancestors had tried to take Innisfail from the Fir-Bolg and failed. But he, a learned Druid of his people, had devised a plan to enslave the inhabitants of the island. And he was very nearly successful.

The Fomor were a disfigured race feared for their cruelty and callousness. When their fleet appeared on the horizon, the King of the Danaan people and the King of the Fir-Bolg called their warriors together, though the two peoples refused to cooperate. The kings of Innisfail imagined they would easily drive the Fomor away. But they reckoned without the ingenuity of Balor. He was a gifted war-leader. His warriors were trained in subterfuge and ambush. But when they came from the sea in their first attack they were driven back into their boats by the Fir-Bolg.

Balor demanded a share of Innisfail. The King of the Fir-Bolg granted him what he asked and gave to him the barren and rocky Island of the Tower, which lies to the north. In defeat Balor turned the Fir-Bolg's insult to his advantage. For now, instead of spending days sailing across the open sea from the Isles of the Bretani which were his homeland, he could land warriors quickly and easily on any part of the island.

Balor built a mighty tower on that island, making use of the tall cliffs and rocky landing places. The Fir-Bolg did not realize their mistake in giving him ground for two full turnings of the seasons. In that time the Fomor fortified their island so no ship could land unless it was on Balor's command. Not so much as a seal could bask on the rocks without his leave.

And Balor in his crafty way fashioned a weapon from the stones of the island and the skill of his wizardry. The Eye of Evil it was called. It was a stone some say, or a cauldron turned on its side. Only the King of the Fomor himself could truly tell you how it was constructed. But the nature of the weapon was that when the shields which covered it were removed, a terrible thing happened. A beam of red light swept across the land and burned all the Fir-Bolg warriors as surely as if they had been sitting in the middle of the fire. And Balor could direct this weapon wherever he willed.

So heavy were the shields placed in front of the Eye it took four warriors to lift them, like the lid of a giant eye. And so the fearsome weapon came to be known as the Eye of Evil. Truly no such thing has ever been seen since in Innisfail for the Druid Assembly outlawed all such creations in later days.

But the Evil Eye was only one of the many weapons in Balor's arsenal. At the same time as his craftsmen were constructing the great Eye, Balor selected nine from among his people to carry out a terrible duty. These men and women were amongst the most deformed of the Fomorians. They were known as the Watchers.

They were descended from folk who had served as sailors to the Sea-King in the Isles of the West before that land was torn apart by war and famine. It is said their ancestors suffered poisoning when the Sea-King sent a yellow fog to stop them leaving in the last days before the great flood. Ever after strange deformities were passed down through the generations among their kindred.

Each of these nine chosen ones was given a special responsibility and a unique gift. But service to their master involved a terrible price. They were to be cast into the Otherworld forever, their physical bodies stripped away. They became shape-shifting spirits who could take on any form they wished in the service of their king. It was their task to sow discontent and unrest among his enemies.

The Watchers spread their discord in subtle ways

so the Danaans and the Fir-Bolg could not resolve their differences and unite. This was the cornerstone of Balor's plan. He could defeat one without the intervention of the other, but if the two foes joined in an alliance he knew he would never prevail.

As it happened the Watchers were very successful. The Fir-Bolg and the Danaans soon came to distrust one another, so much so that when the Fomor launched their attack on the Danaan people the Fir-Bolg did not come to their aid. And as a result there was much animosity between the two folk.

At Mag Tuireadh, where generations before the Danaans had been victorious in their first battle against the defending Fir-Bolg, there was another terrible fight. The second battle of Mag Tuireadh was a narrow defeat for the Fomor but only because Balor's Eye had not been completed in time. Nuadu, King of the Danaans, lost an arm on the battlefield and afterward was forced by convention to relinquish his position as ruler.

No king who is unsound in spirit, body or soul may continue to perform his duties. He must step down. Diancecht, the famous Danaan healer, fashioned an arm of silver for Nuadu but Bres was elected king in his place. And the day of his ascension was a sad one for the Danaans. Bres was entirely under the influence of the Watchers. He did nothing without consulting them, thinking them to be wise Otherworld beings who cared for the future of his people.

He could not have been more wrong. The reign of

Bres was disastrous. And while he dithered with the defenses of this island and with petty wars against the Fir-Bolg, Balor came closer, day by day, to completing work on the Evil Eye.

By the time the Chief Druid of the Danaans had called a council to berate Bres, the damage was already done. In the meantime Cian, the son of Diancecht, fashioned an arm of flesh for Nuadu and Bres was immediately replaced when the council convened. Bres was so bitter at his dismissal and so completely wooed by the Watchers that he went directly to serve Balor. That was the darkest time Innisfail has ever known.

But eventually a savior came to the Danaans. That stranger was Lugh Samildanach and he was the grandson of Balor. It was Lugh who convinced the Dagda and King Nuadu to enter into an alliance with the Fir-Bolg. Together the two armies assaulted the Island of the Tower, though they lost many warriors to the deathly glare of the Evil Eye.

Lugh climbed the great tower while the Fomorians were fighting off their enemies. And there he found Balor. He killed his grandfather with a stone from his sling, cut the Fomor king's head off and turned the Evil Eye around to face Balor's own people. That is how they were destroyed once and forever after. And I, Lom-Dubh, can tell you humans with such brief memories, Innisfail has never known such a devastating war since.

* * *

Four seasons passed after the honor fight at Óenach Samhain. Summer's warmth gave way to the cold rains of leaf-fall. Winter's white vengeance buried the land, holding off the triumph of spring for as long as possible. At Dun Burren the revitalized sun spread its warm cloak across the landscape, and the countryside bloomed into countless colors.

Mahon stopped outside the small round dry-stone house where Aoife was taking her daily harp lesson. Enthralled by the music he waited there for a long while listening to the gentle rise and fall of the sparkling notes. And he let his thoughts drift off to other places.

Tinkling harmonies floated out the door to fill his head with visions of far-off mountains and the steady drums of war. Even though his people had been at war with the Milesian invaders for an entire cycle of the seasons, he had never seen one of their ships, much less met any of their warriors in battle.

Dalan's harp was renowned for its strong wires, a gift from the Milesian Bard Amergin. Mahon wondered if that was why the invaders filled his thoughts whenever he heard this instrument.

Aoife began to sing as she played. It was an old air but Mahon had never heard the words before.

"Your eyes are gold," she crooned softly as her fingers expertly touched the strings, bringing the harp to life in a way that Dalan for all his skill could not. "If I am the harp, you are the hands which caress the music from me. No melody is heard but the one we play together. Let me know your beauty. Show me the warmth within. And like a bee crossing the fields at dusk I will return to you each evening and share the honey of our love."

She finished singing but continued to play as Mahon drifted off into his own thoughts. The young warrior sat down on the grass, untied his long golden hair and ran his fingers through it. After a few minutes he lay on his back and closed his eyes to bathe in the tingling sunlight.

He felt trapped here in this backwater while the war raged on and the foreigners heaped defeat and humiliation upon his people. During the previous winter Mahon had decided he must leave the Burren, homeland to his foster-father the Fir-Bolg king Brocan, to return to his people and stand with them through this peril. But his heart would not let him leave.

"Your people are here," Dalan spoke up. "I know what you're thinking."

The Brehon was standing at the entrance to the house, waiting for Mahon to notice him. The music had ceased. The Danaan sat up, startled at the intrusion on his thoughts.

"You're the hostage of Brocan," Dalan went on. "He's your family now and his kinfolk are yours. Your duty is in Dun Burren."

"And what of my blood-kin? I can't just forget them."

"Your father can do without you. He has a good following of warriors."

"The Milesians haven't even been sighted on this side of the coast," Mahon complained. "We might never encounter them. What if they give up this invasion and sail away forever?"

"That would be the answer to all our prayers," the Brehon noted dryly.

"Yes, of course," the young warrior stuttered.

"Have you some business to discuss with me?" Dalan inquired tersely.

Mahon shook his head in embarrassment.

"Then go away. You're disturbing the lesson with your presence. How do you expect her to improve if you're always listening over her shoulder, distracting her?"

"I'm sorry," Mahon muttered and hurried off.

Dalan watched as the young warrior made off toward the king's hall. When Mahon had disappeared inside, the Brehon pulled down the cowhide door flap and returned to the central hearth. There he sat down beside his pupil amid the smoke from the fire.

Thoughtfully Dalan picked up a wooden cup and held it to his lips. He swallowed a mouthful of mead, then took a deep breath. "What are you going to do about him?" the Brehon demanded.

"What can I do?" Aoife laughed, with a blush. "Can I help it if he's gone completely mad?"

"I should have taken you back to the east far away from your home," the Brehon told her.

"The Dagda is relying on your wisdom in the west," Aoife pointed out. "You're the finest judge in all of Innisfail. My father needs your advice. We can't leave Dun Burren, not yet."

Dalan grunted his acknowledgment. "Well, we can't have that poor young fool wandering around with those big eyes looking like a lost calf. He tripped over a goat yesterday. The shock sent the animal into a wild fury of destruction. It was last seen chewing on a pair of my best walking boots."

Aoife covered her mouth to stifle a giggle.

"This is no laughing matter," the teacher rebuked her.

"No," she agreed, pursing her lips to control her laughter.

"The poor fellow's feeling so rejected by you he's talking about going off to fight the Milesians! You must do something about him before he gets himself in trouble."

"What do you want me to do?"

"Talk to him," the Druid advised. "Acknowledge his existence. Help him catch the goat. I don't know, you think of something."

"I'm quite happy with the nature of the situation at the moment, thank you," the young woman replied abruptly.

"Do you feel nothing for him that you torture him so?"

"On the contrary, I may have strong feelings for him," she replied. "I think he will be a fine husband and a good father to his children some day. But I'm not sure if I want to marry him yet. As soon as I've made a decision I'll let you know."

"Let him know too, won't you?" Dalan told her wryly. "Whatever you do, don't let it go on until the end of summer. No one likes to have their prize dangled in front of them for too long. You may find him traveling off to the east if his net drags up empty too often."

"I'll make up my mind soon enough," she snapped. "He's a Danaan in any case. Father would never allow us to be wedded."

"You're wrong." The Brehon smiled. "Such a marriage would seal the alliance with the Danaans. So in principle it would be endorsed and supported by the Druid Assembly. Cecht and Brocan would have to accept it."

"Would they?"

"They'd not dare reject such a proposal. The other kings would refuse to have honorable dealings with them ever again."

"Father would certainly fight against the idea." Dalan thought he caught a hint of disappointment in Aoife's voice. "He has no love for the Danaans."

"He'll have to get to like them," the Brehon told her. "Cecht will be arriving today to hear the latest news from the Druid Assembly. Fineen the healer is carrying word from the east and he's expected this evening."

"Sárán will be with him?"

"Yes. Your brother is progressing well with his studies I'm told."

"I haven't seen him since he and Fineen journeyed by here before the snows."

"The Milesians have sent many raiders out across the island these last four seasons. They were even out at mid-winter. That proves their barbarity and their desperation to feed their people. Little wonder it wasn't safe enough for Fineen and Sárán to return to us."

"This must be good news then!" Aoife declared.

"How do you come to that conclusion?"

"You said it has been unsafe for them to travel since mid-winter. But now they are returning. The danger must have abated."

"It may not be as simple as that," the Brehon sighed. "The message may be so important and the situation so desperate that risks had to be taken." As soon as Dalan heard his own words he knew they were true. There was no question. It was bad news Fineen was bearing. Good news could have waited until the threat had passed.

"Play me two more airs," he instructed his student. "Then I release you for the remainder of the day to think carefully on that young warrior you have beguiled. I don't know what petty love charm you have tried on him but I warn you to beware of such things. Whatever spell you sing comes back to you nine times. Calculate the cost carefully or you may find yourself tied to him beyond this life."

"I'm not sure I'd complain about that." She smiled.

"You would if you found out his feet had the odor of stale cider vinegar," Dalan noted dryly. "I nearly married a woman once. By the mercy of the goddess of our people I caught her removing her boots and of course from that moment marriage was out of the question."

The young woman frowned, not sure whether her teacher was being serious. "Thank you, master." She nodded politely. "If I notice any unexplained aromas in the air, I'll let you know. Perhaps I'll ask Mahon to dance with me this evening . . ."

"I know what your game is." The Brehon smiled. "I will be performing some dances this evening, as it happens. Brocan asked for them especially.

"Now, let's get back to work. You talk too much and you practice too little." Seeing Aoife's stricken face he softened. "But you're a fine harper and you have an enchanting voice, though your other studies are outstripped by your passion for music. Your arm has healed well and your fingers are nimble at the wires. You might be a competent musician one day."

"Thank you." Aoife smiled, taking the best of what he told her and ignoring the rest. Then she settled the harp against her shoulder and began once more to play.

Cecht and twenty of his Danaan warriors arrived at the fortified hill of Dun Burren at sunset. They had taken a long road because scouts had reported the presence of a Milesian ship aground in the bay. There had been no sightings of any of the invaders, though there were marks where a vessel had been dragged ashore through the wet sand. The enemy had arrived but managed to elude the Danaans.

"It was not a large ship," Cecht told the Fir-Bolg king as he took a Cup of Welcome from his host. "It may have had a crew of seven or eight warriors but no more than that. I guess they are scouting out good landing places in the west. The war has come to us at last."

"I have heard there is a shortage of food in the east," Brocan added. "The Milesians are moving on to more fertile ground."

Both kings looked at each other and shared a moment of foreboding.

"This is the most barren part of the coast." Cecht shook his head. Then he swallowed all the mead in the silver cup. "Things must be desperate in the east and south if the invaders are scouring these shores for food."

The Danaan king handed the drinking vessel back to Brocan with a slight bow of the head in thanks. "Has Fineen arrived?" he asked the Fir-Bolg king.

"We expect him at any moment. Go and dress in your finest for the feast. This may be good news or ill but there will be music and stories this evening nevertheless."

"I was hoping to speak with Mahon," Cecht retorted.

"On what matter?"

"He is my son."

"You are mistaken," Brocan added coldly. "He is a member of my household. You may meet and speak with him at the feast as befits his position within this community and your rank."

"I am told Sárán is proving to be a fine student," Cecht added, trying to be conciliatory.

"I will wait to hear what his teacher, Fineen, has to say on the matter," the Fir-Bolg king answered sharply.

Cecht rolled his eyes in frustration and sighed. With that Fergus the veteran led the Danaan king to his lodgings in Brocan's hall.

Aoife emerged from the little round house she shared with her brother Lom just as Cecht was entering the king's hall. She threw her long green cloak around her shoulders and secured it in the crook of her arm to keep it from dragging in the dust. Then she headed off toward the hall to stand beside her mother and father while they performed the formal ritual of welcoming. The night was chilly for the time of year and she looked forward to the warmth of her father's house.

Aoife was twenty paces away from the king's hall when she caught the odor of roast boar. Her stomach began to grumble with anticipation and she quickened her pace a little. She wondered if Mahon would consent to dance with her this night and she wished with all her willpower her father would not disapprove of their match.

These thoughts and many others flashed through the young woman's mind as she reached out to lift the leather cover which blocked the door to the king's hall. Suddenly another hand snatched hers and held it tight.

Aoife stopped, startled by the intrusion into her daydream. Her eyes darted to the gray sleeve covering the wrist and then to the face of her assailant. A warm flush passed through her as she looked into the blue mirthful eyes.

"Aoife?"

"Mahon," she whispered. "Are you coming in to greet your father?"

"I thought perhaps you might like to take a walk along the ramparts to watch the sun set over the western ocean."

The young woman smiled. "Not tonight. I have duties to fulfill."

The young Danaan was crestfallen but he did his best to hide his disappointment.

"But after the feast," Aoife went on, "perhaps we could go for a walk to look at the stars."

"The sunset wasn't going to be that wonderful anyway." Mahon grinned. "There's a storm front coming in from the ocean."

"Then we won't see any stars either."

"The walk will do us good."

"I'll see you after the dance then?" she offered, but even as she spoke the words she realized her mistake. "I mean the welcoming feast," she amended quickly.

Aoife didn't want the young warrior to think she was too eager.

Mahon's face brightened and he held the flap up for her to enter, following after. The air inside the hall was smoky and the light dim. From the door it was difficult to recognize the faces of folk milling about the fire. But Dalan caught Aoife almost as soon as she entered the room.

"Where's my harp?" he asked her.

"I don't know," she replied in confusion.

"If you want me to play your dance, you must go and fetch it. And you must do the tuning as well," the Brehon told her.

She nodded.

"And no chanting little love charms over it," Dalan warned only half seriously. "You don't know what trouble you could cause. Remember there are mischievous spirits in this world who hear our every thought. If you desire something too much, you may find the wish is granted."

"What would be wrong with that?"

"If Mahon's feet smell you will know soon enough what trouble ill-considered wishes may bring."

Aoife laughed at her teacher's gentle rebuke and in a moment was out crossing the courtyard, headed for the house reserved for Poets and Druids, which was just a smaller version of the king's hall. As the young woman went in she coughed. The air was stale and the fire smoldering.

She placed a slab of turf in the coals and built up the

glowing embers around it to help clear the air. Then she took up the harp which had been resting near Dalan's sleeping furs. It didn't take her long to tune the instrument, after which she wrapped it carefully in its leather case so that it did not lose its tuning.

Before she left she couldn't resist doing something her teacher had told her not to.

"I don't care for the consequences," she said confidently out loud. "I would want Mahon for my own even if his feet were to smell like a sulfur pit." Then she looked to the ceiling nervously. "I don't mean to say I want his feet to smell bad," she added hastily in case any spirits had overheard her.

Aoife reached into her cloak and withdrew a leather bag. She emptied the contents onto the floor in front of the fire. Nine dark red rosebuds tumbled out. She counted them quickly then lined them up in a row.

"There's nine rosebuds in a row. Six to make your fire grow." As Aoife spoke these words she tossed the first six buds into the coals where they slowly began to roast. "Two so you'll drink from my well," she went on, dropping another pair amidst the glowing turf. "And the last of all seals this spell."

Her incantation complete Aoife slung the harp case over her shoulder and stepped out into the deepening shades of evening. In the far distance she heard the muffled rumble of thunder. Storm clouds were indeed gathering as Mahon had predicted.

"Keep the rain off until tomorrow, I beg you," she

whispered under her breath in a private prayer to the Goddess Danu.

"Is that your wish?" a voice interrupted and the young woman jumped with surprise.

"Who's that?" she blurted as she turned to the speaker.

"Perhaps you don't remember me?" The stranger laughed. "You were suffering terribly from the pain when I last saw you. You had just broken your arm."

The young woman shook her head. She had no recollection of this fellow. Then a vague memory came to her and she felt a wave of coldness pass through her body.

"I am sorry," she began but didn't have the chance to continue.

"That's quite all right." The stranger laughed again. "My name is Lochie. I am a Bard."

Just then there was a flurry of movement nearby which distracted Aoife's attention. When she looked back at the Bard a red-headed woman had appeared as if she had been concealed deep within the folds of his cloak. The woman held out her hand to Aoife.

"I am Isleen," she announced. "I am a Seer."

"And she is my wife," Lochie reminded his companion, slapping her gently on the back of the hand.

Aoife's gaze was drawn immediately to the Bard's fingers. He had the shaped fingernails of a harper and they were the most exquisitely formed nails she had ever seen on a musician.

"I do know you," Aoife gasped with relief. "Lochie,

you are the Bard who composed that beautiful eulogy for Fearna."

"You do remember me." The Bard smiled.

Then he shook his head and his expression became solemn. "A sad thing it was the way that lad died."

"Yes," the young woman agreed uncomfortably, feeling as though the stranger's eyes were burning into her like the fabled Evil Eye of Balor.

"Have you been working hard to earn forgiveness?" Lochie inquired.

"I have."

"Then you may be a Bard yourself one day." Lochie smiled. "If it hadn't been for your part in his death, you might have become a warrior. That would have been a terrible waste. So it's all been for the best. Without a doubt it was your destiny to take the Druid orders as much as it was for Fearna to break his neck on a drunken ride."

Aoife nodded.

"You're very fortunate he hasn't returned to haunt you," Isleen cut in. "It's often the case when an innocent has been wronged."

"Are you going to attend the feast this night?" Aoife cut in quickly, changing the subject.

"We've just now arrived," Isleen replied. "We'll be in presently. I have spent some time at the Danaan court. I'm well known to King Cecht and I'm looking forward to meeting him again."

"You're acquainted with his son, Mahon, I believe," Lochie added mischievously.

"He has been dwelling here for four seasons."
Aoife shrugged. "How could I ignore him?"

"Indeed." Lochie smiled. "A fine young man he is."

"Though lacking a sharp wit," Isleen cut in. "And
his conversation is tedious."

"I don't mind that he doesn't speak much." Aoife
smiled. "I think he's a fine young man."

"You'd mind his dearth of witty speech if you were
locked away with him every day."

"You two would make a fine match," Lochie
hummed over the top of his companion. "Have you
thought about it?"

Aoife blushed a bright red that made the freckles
on her cheeks vanish.

"Husband, for a Bard you talk a lot of gibberish,"
Isleen snapped.

"I do think highly of Mahon," the young woman admitted.

"There you are," Lochie hummed. "A fine match
you'd both make." Then he leaned very close to whisper. "If you sit outside the music house, no one will
ask you to dance."

The young girl laughed nervously. "You're welcome in my father's hall," she assured them, pulling
back the cowhide entrance to the hall and beckoning
for them to go before her.

"Let us wash from the journey before we go in,"
Isleen begged.

"I'll present you to my father when you return,"
Aoife agreed with a bow.

The two Druids returned the gesture then went off to find fresh water for washing.

"Who were you talking to, daughter?" Brocan asked Aoife as soon as she was inside the hall.

"Lochie and his wife Isleen," she answered.

Dalan and Cecht struggled to suppress their amusement.

"What's the matter? What is going on?" she begged, confused.

"If you were speaking to those two you will make a great Druid," Dalan told her. "For you have the gift of the sight."

"What do you mean?"

"Lochie and Isleen have been aiding the Dagda with the war in the east," the Brehon explained. "They'll certainly not be returning here for several cycles of the moon."

Aoife frowned then shrugged, confident she would be proved right when the two Druids were washed and refreshed.

Cecht turned to King Brocan and spoke lowly so that no one else would hear what was said. "If those two Druids are here at Dun Burren they must surely walk in the Otherworld. I often bring Isleen so strongly to mind I would swear she was with me, though I know it to be impossible. Once or twice I was certain she spoke to me in my dreams."

"The spoons are already being laid out," Brocan interrupted.

"It's time for a dance before we take seats around the fire," declared Dalan.

Riona, her red locks streaked with gray in long braids, entered the building at that moment. Cecht's eyes lit with joy at seeing her.

"The Goddess Danu is walking among us!" he exclaimed.

"This is my wife." Brocan coughed, noticing that the Danaan king was staring at her. "You have met before."

"Yes, we have," Cecht answered without moving his eyes from the Fir-Bolg queen. "You are looking very well, Riona," he told her.

"Thank you, Cecht. You are looking rested and content."

"The more so for seeing you, my dear."

Dalan was already strumming the harp gently to check Aoife's tuning. That was quickly done and he nodded to her to acknowledge a job well done. As soon as he had got himself comfortable the Brehon struck a chord to bring everyone's attention to him.

Then, with a delicate run down the strings, Dalan launched into a lively dance. No one needed to be coaxed into joining the joyous rhythm of his fingers. In moments people were dancing merrily all around the room.

Aoife stayed to one side of the hall, swaying gently, eyes closed and hands held in front of her. Once in a while she'd open one eye and sneak a glance at Mahon who stood at the other side of the fire.

Riona went straight to Cecht and grabbed his hand. The two of them were soon swaying around the room, staring into each other's eyes as if they had known each other all their lives. Brocan danced too, but he scowled whenever he noticed his wife so close to the Danaan king.

A drummer entered the hall drawn by the music and he struck up a beat on his bodhran, which caused a few folk to call out in admiration at his skill. Then the older folk who had stayed near the fire joined the throng.

Fergus laughed aloud to see Brocan's old cousin kicking up his heels like a youngster. "An old pair of boots is best for a long night of dancing," he quipped as the hall erupted with laughter.

Aoife half-opened her eyes to take another glimpse at Mahon. But the young Danaan was gone. She searched the hall but to her disappointment he was nowhere to be seen. Then, just as her hopes were dashed, she felt a pair of strong hands move around her waist from behind.

"Will you lift your feet with me?" Mahon asked as he moved in close.

She laughed in surprise at his sudden appearance then wondered why she had doubted her spell would draw him in.

"Just don't be bruising my toes like last time," she warned him.

"It's your lips I'd be bruising," he answered quickly.

"Whisht with you. Show me how you dance and

maybe I'll let you kiss my bruises to make them better."

Mahon swung her around and the two of them stared intently into each other's eyes as the music picked up pace. Aoife's heart was beating in time with the bodhran as her feet flew on the hard-packed earthen floor. As she watched Mahon's face Aoife recalled her dancing vision.

"I dreamed about you," she murmured, leaning close so no one else would hear.

"I've been dreaming of you since the first moment we met," he replied.

Aoife threw her head back and laughed. "I'll wager you melt the hearts of those pretty Danaan girls with your witty lies."

Mahon frowned again but this time there was hurt in his expression. "I'm not lying to you," he protested and she saw that he wasn't.

Before Aoife could whisper to him that she was joking, the music ceased and the hall erupted in cheers at Dalan's skill. Then Mahon moved to his place at the other side of the hall without another word to her.

"That's enough for now!" the Brehon declared. "I'm a skilled judge but a poor musician."

"Then we'll take our lawsuits to the bodhran player and you can sit at the harp all night," Cecht complimented him.

The Danaan king led Riona to her seat at the fire while her husband's eyes followed them darkly.

"It's time we took our seats," Brocan insisted with a cough. "The food and drink will be served soon. I want to get the formalities out of the way before the messengers arrive."

Aoife caught Mahon's attention and he smiled at her from across the hall. She drank in the sparkling beauty of his eyes and knew he had forgiven her. Then the young woman was distracted by the sound of her mother's voice resounding through the hall.

"My lord," the queen began, addressing the highest ranking guest, "King Cecht of the Danaan people. Welcome to the home of Riona and Brocan. Treat this house as if it were your own. If you wish for anything it will be given to you. While you are here you will have the best there is."

There was a smile in Riona's eyes that did not go unnoticed by Aoife. The young woman recalled what Dalan had said to her earlier, that playing the harp every day opened the senses and sharpened the instincts.

She turned away to find Mahon seated right beside her. He had crossed the floor without her even noticing.

"Don't you think that my mother and your father seem to be captivated with each other?" she asked.

"As a Danaan I can understand the attraction," he whispered just loud enough for her to hear, "for you are certainly her daughter. If your mother were not wed to Brocan she would make a fine match for my father," Mahon added, seeing Riona and Cecht flirting across the table.

"But she is married and she is Queen of the Fir-Bolg," the young woman retorted sharply, shocked that her mother was behaving so in front of her father and family. "Cecht is encouraging her. Do you Danaans have no respect for the bonds of marriage?"

"Of course we do. But we have too much respect for any woman to expect her to always honor those bonds."

"What do you mean?"

"If your mother was content with Brocan she would not be making eyes at my father."

"What would you do if you were my father?"

"If I were Brocan," Mahon began, working his reply carefully, "I would never have let matters come to this. I would have made sure my queen had no reason to look elsewhere for her pleasure."

Aoife smiled but they were soon interrupted by someone tugging vigorously at Mahon's sleeve.

"Mahon!" Dalan bellowed. "Are you deaf?"

"He's blinded," King Cecht quipped. "And that kind of blindness always ends with deafness. I am not surprised he is enthralled with young Aoife. She is only a shadow of her mother's beauty yet she is breathtaking to behold."

Riona shook her head and laughed.

"Let them alone," Brocan snapped. "I know what you're up to!"

Riona stopped laughing. Cecht swallowed hard.

"What would we be up to?" the queen asked, derision in her voice.

"You are trying to convince me that Mahon and Aoife would make a good match."

Cecht coughed and Riona squinted to show she was thinking carefully about her next words.

"Don't you think they would be a good match?" the queen inquired.

"Of course they would!" the king grumbled. "That's not the point. You could have simply asked me my opinion."

"I might have done. What do they have to say about it?"

"They have not had a chance to think about it!" Riona snapped. "They certainly haven't had an opportunity to discuss it."

"Leave them alone, you interfering old nose," Brocan replied. "Let them make up their own minds about it in their own time."

"Then we'll still be here waiting for their word when the snow comes again," the queen sighed.

"What is the rush? You weren't that set on me that it couldn't wait till winter."

"I was a queen in my own right then," she reminded him. "You were still a warrior chieftain with high hopes. You are king because of me. Because my children were descended from the Fir-Bolg royal clans of old. And because my mother is Eriu."

"I am king because I was elected to the post by my fellow chieftains," Brocan spat, finally losing his temper. "But this is not the place for such quarrels," he added, hoping Cecht and Dalan were not offended.

The chieftains of the Fir-Bolg and their kin were already filling the hall by this time. Brocan called on them all to take their places around the fire. Then he called for the mead barrel.

"I would dearly love to hear a tale of the old days," Riona sighed, turning to the Brehon. "A tale of my ancestors."

"A story of betrayal, love and strength of purpose," Cecht added.

"A song to put away the fears of the world," Aoife cut in. "A poem to banish despair. A tale to end sorrow."

"You're learning very well, my friend," Dalan told her. "Soon enough you'll be ready to take your blue robes."

Mead was brought for the company in great earthenware jars, and wooden cups were distributed. Then the Danaan king ordered a box to be opened. Within were tightly packed many silver spoons for the broth. These wide flat eating utensils were little more than scoops for picking out pieces of meat from the soup, but they were ornately decorated. The spoon Aoife received was etched with spirals and zigzags in the same patterns worn by the Danaan warriors in battle.

King Cecht stood when the spoons had been distributed. "This is my gift of peace to the people of the Burren," he began. "I hope whenever you sit down to your broth you will think of my folk with friendship."

There was a general chorus of approval as Cecht resumed his seat and King Brocan rose to reply.

"Danaan and Fir-Bolg have been enemies since before our grandfathers were born," he began. "Tonight we will once more mend the rift that has kept us apart for so long and strengthen our bond. Whatever the news may be that is coming to us, we will never again resort to war in order to settle our differences. And our children's children will know nothing of the fighting we have experienced all our lives."

Brocan sat down with his son Lom behind him as befitted the son of a king. Then Dalan took his turn to speak as a Brehon judge and told them all he knew of Balor and the failed alliance between the Fir-Bolg and Danaan of old.

"We must not make the same mistakes," the Brehon ended. "Balor was a clever manipulator but he could have been easily defeated if our folk had banded together."

"A timely tale," Cecht congratulated Dalan. "For now the Milesians have replaced the Fomor as our deadly enemies and we must hold fast together against them."

"Indeed our peoples must unite without delay," Dalan agreed. "If we don't put the past aside, the land of Innisfail will fall to the invader and our peoples will be destroyed."

"So that's what this is all about?" Brocan fumed. "This gathering was requested by the Druid Assembly. I was told Fineen was to bring news of the war. But in truth it's an elaborate plan to convince me to send my warriors off to fight in a conflict that has not even touched my folk.

"Well, I will not fight an unnecessary war."

"You've given an assurance to aid the Danaans. Have you forgotten?" Dalan demanded.

"I'll not send men and women of the Burren away to die for the sake of the Danaans!" the Fir-Bolg king said emphatically. "If the Danaan kingdoms are threatened by these invaders, that's their difficulty. The people of the Burren will not be involved and that is an end to the matter."

"And what will you do when the Milesians have defeated the Danaan armies and murdered the Druid Assembly?" Cecht asked.

"We'll make a treaty with them."

"You don't know these folk," the Danaan scoffed. "They delight in war. They sing songs of their brave youths who are reckless in battle and who kill for the sake of it." Cecht sat forward to press home his next point. "In that at least you have a common thread."

"What do you mean?"

"The crime your children committed may have been adjudged by a Brehon," Cecht spat, "and the breach of tradition punished, but the foal learns to kick from the stallion. Your children were taught the rules of conduct by their father and king."

"How dare you insult me in my own hall?" Brocan shouted. "The debt is being paid."

"I'm merely speaking what is on the minds of most folk," the Danaan retorted.

"Savage!" the Fir-Bolg yelled. "What would you know of honor? You who charges into battle naked and then calls your enemy uncivilized when you're beaten."

"My warriors were never beaten by the Fir-Bolg of the Burren."

"Bring me my sword!" Brocan bellowed. "We'll go outside and settle this forever. Cecht and I will fight to the death and then we'll see if you've never been defeated."

The Danaan king stood up and threw his cup down upon the floor. "Such is the niggardly hospitality of Brocan," he said addressing the entire hall, "that he can't even wait until the broth comes around before he's goading his guests on to a fight."

"That's enough!" Dalan cried and his voice resounded through the king's hall. "The first one of you to move from your place will be under a Brehon interdict. And I'll advise the Druid Assembly to impose banishment on you both."

"This is my hall!" Brocan grunted. "And you're one of my own people. Would you stand with the enemy rather than the king of your kin?"

"The real enemy is not the Danaans," Dalan insisted. "The war between our folk should have ended before you and I were born. The real threat is from the Gaedhals. If we do not bury our past differences we will all be wiped away before the invaders like a bank of sand before the incoming tide."

"Dalan is right," Riona declared. "I may be your wife and the Queen of the Fir-Bolg, but I'll not stand by you if you take up the old fight again. It's time for us to join with the Danaans for the sake of our own survival. I'll divorce you if you don't fulfill your obligations under the treaty."

"Even you have turned against me!" Brocan sighed.

"I am not against you," Riona assured him. "But I will not see Fir-Bolg lives wasted in a stupid fight that would still expose us to a Milesian attack. Do you really believe we could defeat the Danaans or the Gaedhals in open battle? You're lying to yourself if you do. We are not the great people we once were. We've become a little folk, petty and quarrelsome. Your warring has done that."

She waited to hear his protest. When there was none she went on. "The Danaans of north, east, and south could unite to annihilate us whenever they wish."

"It wouldn't be easy," Brocan replied defiantly.

"No other Fir-Bolg chieftain would stand with you," Dalan told him. "They would side with the Danaans. The folk of King Cecht have been good to the other Fir-Bolg folk of the west. You would be isolated and vulnerable to attack from the Milesians."

"The Milesians won't come this far west."

"They're already here!" Cecht exclaimed. "One of their ships was seen in the Bay of Gaillimh and I myself saw the ruts one of their boats made in the sand. The war has come to you, Brocan, so you must join with me to rid the west of this menace. For the sake of your people's future."

"If my folk are swallowed up in the kingdoms of the Danaans they have no future. These Milesians are not the first invaders to have come to Innisfail, you know. The Danaans were considered the invaders once."

"You're speaking of a time that passed generations ago," Dalan reminded him. "The world changes as surely as the seasons. Since the battle four seasons ago when you promised to uphold my judgment you have not aided the Danaans even once in their defense of the coast."

"I promised nothing," Brocan protested. "It was my children who were judged, not me."

"He is the Bres of our age," Cecht commented.

"What do you mean?" Brocan shouted, his face bright red with rage. "Are you calling me a traitor?"

"Yes."

"I made no pact formally binding me to fight your wars for you. How can I be called traitor?"

"You are treacherous," Riona cut in. "For you will not side with anyone until you have decided who offers the best advantage, Danaan or Milesian."

The cowhide flap to the king's hall was pulled aside as she spoke and two weary travelers bent low to enter the room. No one noticed the pair of latecomers and they did not intervene in the argument. They just stood silent and patient in the shadows, waiting for the right moment to announce themselves.

"You must join with Cecht," Dalan pressed. "You have no choice in the matter. Your people wish to live in peace. Only you have this notion that the old fight should continue."

"If this is the message the Druid Assembly would have me answer," Brocan said with finality, "then Fineen is wasting his time in coming to the Burren. He might as well stay at home with his Danaan friends."

"I'm sorry to hear you say that," a voice interrupted and all heads turned toward the door.

"Fineen?" Dalan asked. "Is that you?"

The healer stepped forward into the light. Sárán was beside him in an instant.

"It is I," the healer confirmed. "Fineen the healer, messenger of the Druid Assembly."

"How long have you been standing there?" Brocan asked suspiciously.

"Long enough to understand there is some disagreement between yourself and Cecht," Fineen answered carefully. "But not long enough to know the details of the dispute."

"I will tell you," the Fir-Bolg king retorted. "I refuse to ally myself with the Danaans."

"That's it?" the healer inquired.

"That is all there is to it."

"Will you do me the courtesy of listening to my message before you make up your mind?"

"I have made my decision and I will not retreat from it."

"I will tell you my news in any case," Fineen stated

coldly, bristling at the manner in which he was being addressed. "If you will do me the honor of passing the Welcome Cup?"

Brocan blushed. He was angry but there was no excuse for failing to observe the rituals of hospitality. "Forgive me, healer," the king begged in a gentle tone. "I have allowed myself to become distraught."

"These are difficult times." Fineen nodded. "I will forgive you when my thirst is quenched."

Brocan took the silver cup reserved for honored guests and dipped it in a mead jar. Then he handed the vessel to Fineen with a bow. The healer took a sip, enough to indicate that the ritual had been observed, and then passed it on to his student.

"Welcome home, my son," Riona said tenderly.

"Thank you, Mother," the young man replied with a shy smile.

"Please take a seat by the fire," Brocan offered, his voice calmer.

"Thank you. I'll stand."

"Welcome, brother physician," Dalan added. "Will you not take some food and drink before you perform your duties?"

"There's no time for that," Fineen declared. "It seems I've arrived just in time to avert a terrible disaster."

"Come by the fire and speak," the Fir-Bolg king insisted.

Fineen walked slowly to the fireside and was handed a wooden bowl of mead. He sipped at it for a moment. Everyone in the hall was perfectly silent as they waited, even though they were hungry and the broth filled the house with an enticing aroma.

"I come from the Druid Assembly," the healer began. But they all knew that and so the hall was full of blank expressions. "I bring news and a message. I will tell you the news of the war first." He took a long draught of mead and then put the cup down by the fire to warm. "The Milesians are skilled warriors, and they have renowned Bards and Brehons among them. You are all aware that the wisest and most skilled of our own Druid musicians failed in their attempt to raise a mighty storm against the Milesian ships."

Fineen paused to look from Brocan to Cecht. "At first we all thought the spell had gone out of control and destroyed the harpers in its unimaginable ferocity. We now know what turned the tempest-making around. It was a song. And it was sung by Amergin, the Chief Bard of the Milesians."

The listeners gasped, unable to suppress their shock.

The healer cleared his throat. "It took great skill for the Danaan Druids to raise their storm against the Milesian ships. The power of their music rang long after through the whole land as the tale passed from mouth to ear at countless firesides," Fineen told them.

Now he was chanting in the fashion of the ancient storytellers who lived in the days before the Danaans came to Innisfail. And to all who listened it was as if he had stepped out from those days when the Isles of the West still sat above the ocean waves.

"Amergin is a rare Druid. And he proves the Milesians are truly an honorable race. When I met him he was very polite and agreeable, even though he carried hard word from his brother Éremon, their chieftain. His ultimatum, as you know, was simple: the Danaans, the Fir-Bolg and all the other smaller peoples of Innisfail were to relinquish the island to his folk or face war.

"The renowned Poet granted a turning of the moon for the three Danaan kings and the council of the Fir-Bolg to decide whether or not they would defend Innisfail. The Druid Assembly of the Tuatha De Danaan used this time to prepare the Music of the Tempest. As the Milesian fleet approached the shore a massive storm, conjured by the harpers, swept down upon them."

Fineen put out his hand for another cup of mead and no one so much as made a sound while they waited for him to continue. They had all heard parts of this tale from travelers and other wandering Bards, but Fineen was the first of such skill to know the whole story, past to present.

When he had taken a drink the healer coughed to indicate he was ready to continue. Then he launched into the tale afresh. "But the storm our harpers conjured was too violent. It soon became unpredictable and blew in toward the coast. The Druids who had created it were swept away in its brutality as it passed to the north. Amergin's song had added just enough weight to the tempest to make it unmanageable. When the storm was gone, most of the Milesian ships remained afloat and in good condition.

"The invaders landed soon after and the island of Innisfail sank into a war that has lasted an entire turning of the cycle of the seasons. The Gaedhals have had the upper hand from the beginning. Their weapons are superior. They do not have to worry about planting crops or seeing to herds, they feed themselves by plunder.

"And they are able to move on quickly when they have exhausted the pickings. Our warriors rarely arrive in time to catch them for we have no ships. Four seasons have passed of this conflict. Many fields have not been planted because the people are war-weakened. Cattle are left to wander and mills allowed to fall into disrepair. The Danaans and the Fir-Bolg are edging day by day into famine."

"What has this to do with me?" Brocan cut in, though he knew it was extremely impolite to interrupt.

"There are reports the Milesians have sent a fleet to the west," Fineen told him.

"I can confirm it," Cecht asserted.

"Then I fear we may already be on the brink of war in this part of the island," the healer said solemnly. "Do not underestimate the fighting prowess of the invaders. They do not fight pitched battles. Their tactic is to raid for food and livestock, to take hostages for ransom and to destroy as many of our fishing boats as possible."

"They'll not come here," the Fir-Bolg king retorted. "I have no quarrel with them."

"The Milesians do have a quarrel with you." Fineen smiled, impressed at Brocan's stubbornness. "And they will bring it here soon enough. The Circle of Seers convened last Samhain. And they have witnessed the future."

"What did they see?" Dalan asked excitedly.

"The Gaedhals will win this land from us. There's no doubt. And the time is not far off."

"I don't believe you," Brocan scoffed. "The Seers are mistaken."

"The Seers are never mistaken. Misguided sometimes but never mistaken. The Gaedhals have set their sights on this country and they will take it. Nothing is more certain. We can't stand against them. Your band of warriors, Brocan, won't be able to hold them at bay."

"We'll not fight."

"The future has been foretold." The healer shrugged. "So we must prepare for the great change which will soon overtake us all."

"It's hopeless then," Cecht sighed in defeat. "We might as well give in now and save ourselves any more bloodshed."

"We need not be so hasty in giving up hope."

"Is there a way to defeat them?" Cecht asked.

"We were presented with several courses of action

which could," Fineen replied. "The Druid Assembly has discussed them all and I will relate to you their conclusions."

Brocan sat back, stretched his feet to the fire and frowned. He was unmoved by all this talk and quietly outraged by Riona's threat of divorce.

"We could raise a war band and force the Milesians into a fair fight," the healer began. "But we cannot stand against their weapons. And we have no ships, so it's very difficult to transport our warriors quickly from one place to another. And the Seers assured the Druid Assembly all such efforts would be in vain. Indeed, if we go to war with a mind to win, we'll be scattered to the four winds."

"What else can we do?" Cecht shrugged. "Let them walk over us?"

"There may be another way," Fineen replied cautiously. "The Seers have presented a solution which is worth considering."

"What?" Dalan asked.

"A negotiated peace."

"Do you mean the Druids advocate relinquishing our claim over the land of Innisfail?" Brocan spat.

"In part," Fineen conceded. "The Druid Assembly has decided the best path for us to take is a combination of aggression and submission. We will engage the Milesians in a battle to decide who'll take Innisfail as their own. No one expects we'll be victorious, but we'll certainly make enough of an impression on the invaders that they'll accept our terms."

"What terms?" Brocan asked, full of suspicion.

"The Druid Assembly has decided it is time to make use of the doorway between the worlds," Fineen explained. "Once the ancient mystical doorway has been breached, our folk will withdraw into the Otherworld. But because we are tied to this island by ancestral longing we will bargain to remain free to travel back and forth to this world at will."

"No!" Brocan spat. "I'll not give up my land. The Otherworld may be real enough to you Druids, but it's a realm of fear for a warrior who knows little of the ways of the spirit. You speak of opening the mystical doorway as if it were nothing more than opening the door to this hall. I know that's not true. And I won't expose my folk to the potential dangers of such an exercise."

"Then you and all your people will perish."

"Rather that than give up our homes."

"A new life awaits us on the other side," Fineen reasoned. "A life free from any further threat of invasion. It is our last hope, for these Gaedhals won't be the last adventurers to come sailing around our coast with greed in their eyes."

"And what of this battle? How many will die putting up a good show?" the Fir-Bolg king snapped. "The cost will be high, I'll wager."

"No Danaan or Fir-Bolg will perish," the healer assured him. "The Council of Druid Physicians will provide a healing liquor made from the red berries of the first Quicken Tree which grew long ago in the Islands of the West. To any who drink of it no injury will be fatal, no wound will bleed. To the Gaedhals it will seem as if we are invincible."

"With such a liquor in our possession we would be invincible," Brocan pointed out. "A warrior who cannot be killed is a warrior who cannot be defeated. Why relinquish the land if we cannot lose the war?"

"We may drive the Gaedhals off at first, but they will return in time. There will be no end to the fighting until they get what they came for. Also it makes good sense for us to allow them to take over the responsibility for protecting this island. They have the weapons. We have the Draoi. In partnership we will never face a major threat again."

"But we must keep the secret of the Quicken Brew to ourselves," Dalan realized. "To share it with the Gaedhals could prove disastrous unless they develop a rule of law which is compatible with the Brehon code."

"Indeed," the healer agreed. "The Quicken Brew will only be received by Danaan and Fir-Bolg. In this way our folk will rule Innisfail while the Milesians believe the land to be theirs."

"Tell us more about the brew," Brocan interrupted.

"The liquor works quickly the first time it is administered," Fineen explained. "A deathly wound will heal immediately. After that the potion will prolong life but not necessarily heal all injuries. Those who drink of it in the winter will not begin to age until the next year. They will not become sick. They will not suffer from minor wounds."

"So the intention is to use this healing effect on the battlefield to impress the invaders?" Cecht asked.

"If they believe we are invincible they will quickly make terms with us and avoid further conflict." Fineen nodded. "They won't expect us to cede the country to them. So I believe they will accept our conditions readily."

"It is a good plan," the Danaan king agreed. "By these means we will have a place to live and our people will not suffer war any longer."

"Draoi-Craft!" Brocan grunted. "My people will lose their homes and their livelihoods with no guarantee this wild plan will work."

"They'll lose everything anyway," Riona rebuked him. "Are you so stupid you can't see that?"

"I can see through you," her husband laughed harshly. "You'd like nothing better than immortality. Well the Otherworld is not meant for mortals."

"Many of the old ones in the days of the Islands of the West took that path," she countered. "And they managed to survive the destruction of that land."

"This island is not about to sink beneath the waves! The Dagda is asking us to abandon our life and country to walk into the unknown."

"Coward!" she spat contemptuously.

"Innisfail will not vanish," Dalan cut in. "But it may as well. It will be beyond our reach unless we negotiate a peace and establish a safe haven for our people where no future invader can strike at us."

"The Milesians have fine weapons," Fineen continued. "Their Bards are master poets though not as accomplished as our own. And their musicians are among the most skilled I have ever heard. But they don't have the secret of healing which our people brought from the lands of the west. Nor do they know any more than the basics of the Draoi-Music. They will certainly be impressed by the revival of our warriors before their very eyes and the opening of the doorway to the Otherworld."

Riona stood up. "As Queen of the Fir-Bolg of the Burren I endorse this plan wholeheartedly. And I ask that Fineen present it to the Council of Chieftains to consider."

"I'll not take part in this underhanded trick," Brocan announced. "If there is to be a fight then let it be fair."

"What's wrong with you?" his wife growled in frustration. "I wish I'd known I was marrying a fool."

"I don't wish to live behind the veil of the Otherworld," Brocan told her flatly. "That place holds no appeal for me. I was born on the Burren and I'll die here. Death holds no terror for me. When the time comes I'll go to my fate without flinching, as my ancestors have done before me. I'll not be a party to Druid deceptions which are plainly dishonorable and dangerous."

"And what if you're attacked by the Milesians?" Cecht inquired. "Who will you turn to for help once the rest of your kinfolk have retreated behind the veil?"

"You are not my kin," the Fir-Bolg dismissed. "I couldn't rely on you in any case. If my people are attacked I'll raise the Fir-Bolg and defend the Burren. But in truth I don't believe the Milesians will come here. This is a harsh place. It takes great skill to work a living from this rocky land and the seashore around about. There's enough food for my people, but only just and that's hard won. If the invaders come here they'll not flourish."

"Your wife's right. You are a fool," Cecht stated flatly. "You'll perish and any of your people who remain with you will be forgotten."

"If you don't reconsider," Riona declared, "the Council of the Chieftains will overrule your decision."

"You would not dare call a council to oppose me!" Brocan shouted. "I was elected to lead the people of the Burren until the next Samhain Eve and I'll continue to make decisions on their behalf. If you wish to see me deposed you will have to wait until the start of winter when the elections are held again."

"This can't wait for the Samhain elections," his wife countered. "The war will be over by then and our people scattered to the winds. It must be decided immediately."

"I'll oppose you."

"I've already summoned the chieftains," Riona stated coldly. "I anticipated your hard-headed rebuff of an alliance with the Danaans. Several chieftains from distant duns are yet to arrive. All the leaders of

our people will be gathered here by noon tomorrow
and it'll be decided then. Fineen, Dalan and Cecht
will be invited to present their case and you will abide
by the wisdom of the council."

Brocan took a deep breath, appalled his queen had
taken such a step without consulting him. "I always
believed we were equals in our rule," he stuttered in
shock.

"If you don't retreat from your position," she told
him sternly, "I will relinquish my title, my duties and
my allegiance to you."

Brocan's eyes narrowed. "You have already given
up your loyalty to me," he observed archly. "The
Danaan king has that now, I can plainly see. But don't
imagine such a threat will convince me to change my
mind. I'm the king. I must put my duty to my people
above everything else. Go from this hall tonight to
your own house and I'll not speak with you again except in the Council of Chieftains."

"Very well."

"You've betrayed me and you've betrayed the Fir-
Bolg of the Burren. You would be better to go now
and dwell with the Danaans than to stay here where
you'll be despised as a traitor."

Riona rose from her seat without a word of reply,
bowed to Dalan, Fineen and last of all to Cecht. As
she bowed her head respectfully the Danaan king
spoke the words of farewell which were customary
among his people, but there was a deeper meaning
behind them now. And their eyes betrayed it to all

who saw them. "There's always mead in my house, for whenever a friend should visit. Love is also a golden liquor tasting of honey. I'll keep a good store of it in case you come by."

Riona smiled and turned away quickly. As she passed Sárán she touched his hand in greeting. She left the hall with all eyes on her and most of them were admiring.

The queen was so dignified and proud as she departed that Brocan began to regret his words immediately, realizing she was well loved by the people. In his heart he knew there was a strong possibility she was right. But their partnership had deteriorated to the point where his pride would not let him agree with her.

"I can see there's nothing more to be achieved here tonight," the Danaan king announced after Riona had departed. "I'll retire and await the decision of the council tomorrow."

As Cecht stood up Brocan addressed him. "It's only because I am hospitable that I allow you to remain here as my guest," the Fir-Bolg king told him. "You've poisoned my wife against me and seduced my people into fighting your war. But you've not deluded me. I can clearly see what you are after. If it is my queen, then take her, you are welcome to her. If it is my wealth and cattle, you will find some way to wrest them from my grasp in time. But you will never have my allegiance, no matter how clever your arguments or how many of my own kinfolk you win over."

"Good night," the Danaan king replied formally but Brocan sat in stony-faced silence until Cecht was gone.

"Dalan of the Deception you shall be called," the Fir-Bolg king hissed under his breath but still loud enough he could be heard by those close to the fire. "You've deserted your own folk for the ways of the Danaan Druids. Drink deep and eat your fill this night. You will not be welcome under this roof again."

"I hope by the morning you regret those words," the Brehon sighed. "If you have I will forgive you. I am not a traitor to my people. I am a Druid. I must follow the wisdom of the Dagda in all things." Dalan bowed, finished his mead and rose from his seat to leave.

"You go with him, Fineen," Brocan demanded. "I'll not have a Danaan at my fire again."

Then he looked at Sárán whose eyes were directed at the floor. "And take that worthless son of the half-breed Fir-Bolg queen with you. He too has become a Danaan and I'll not have him here."

Sárán looked up at his father and his eyes were full of hurt, but the king did not show any sign of remorse.

"Can't you see you are standing alone?" Sárán asked, glancing over at his brother now who was clearly taken aback by their father's bitterness.

"Get out!" the Fir-Bolg king yelled. "I would rather see this hall burned to the ground than suffer to have you sit under its roof again."

Sárán bowed his head in respect, though in that instant he felt none. By the time he reached the door the young man had resolved to do everything in his power to oppose his father.

Dalan and Fineen followed after. As soon as they were all gone Brocan stood up.

"Enjoy your meal, daughter," he told Aoife. "And the idle conversation of Mahon, son of Cecht. He'll be leaving tomorrow and will not be returning to this hillfort again. If you choose his company over mine you'll go with him."

"I follow my teacher, Dalan the Brehon," she answered sharply.

"That's your decision. Don't expect me to regard you as my offspring if you do."

Brocan tossed the last mouthful of his mead into the fire and it flared up to the rooftree with light and sparks. And then the King of the Fir-Bolg of the Burren was gone into the night.

Chapter 16

CECHT WAS WALKING TOWARD THE RAMPARTS OF THE hillfort when he noticed a commotion at the gate. He quickly looked around, hoping to find Riona, but there was no sign of her nearby. So he shrugged his shoulders and decided to find out what had attracted the sentries' attention.

The Danaan king had not walked more than ten paces when he heard a voice he recognized but one he had hardly expected to hear.

"My name is Isleen the Seer," the woman was insisting, "and this is my husband, Lochie. Surely you know us well enough. We have just been down to the spring to wash and were returning."

"The guard has just changed," one of the sentries explained. "I did not see you go out."

"And you were not expected," Cecht cut in as he approached the gate. "Indeed I am surprised to see you here. We did not believe Aoife when she said she had spoken with you."

"We have been following a Milesian scout," Lochie explained. "He joined his ship not far from here and they sailed south. My wife and I thought we had better report this to Brocan."

"You'll find him in his hall," the king told them. "But don't expect him to be in good humor. He has all but declared eternal war on the Danaan people and turned his own folk against him at the same time. He may not be king for long if he does not relent."

"It is good to see you again," Isleen greeted, a coldness in her voice which indicated she was merely being polite.

"There was a time when you spent a great deal of time at my fortress," Cecht said quietly to her. "Is Dun Gur not to your taste anymore?"

"I am a Seer. I go where the Druid Assembly sends me. What are you doing here?"

"At present I am looking for Riona, the Queen of the Fir-Bolg. She and her husband have had a falling-out and I would like to comfort her."

"I am sure you would." Isleen hummed. "The queen has gone down to the sea. We passed her on the way up here. She was not in a very welcoming mood."

"You must forgive her," Cecht begged. "She's had a very difficult time with Brocan."

"I hope she's not expecting you to heal her hurt," the Seer retorted.

The king looked to the ground, avoiding her eyes.

"I'd heard a rumor that you were married," he said, "though I have not had the opportunity to meet your husband properly."

"It was a very recent occurrence," Isleen informed him. Then she looked to her companion. "Lochie, this is Cecht, King of the Tuatha De Danaan of the south and west. Cecht, this is my husband Lochie. Now you've been introduced."

"Greetings," the Danaan replied. "It's a pleasure to meet you." He bowed.

"And you," Lochie answered cheerfully.

"Well, I won't keep you from delivering your news to Brocan," Cecht sighed. "If anyone is looking for me I'll be with Queen Riona."

And with that Cecht pushed past, acknowledged the sentries and was soon beyond the circle of torchlight and heading down to the seashore.

Lochie smiled at his companion as they made their way to the king's hall. "I'm so sorry for intruding," he began insincerely. "I had no idea you were setting the King of the Danaans in your sights. I was under the impression it was his son you were chasing."

"You should learn to keep your place," she hissed.

As she spoke they saw Brocan leaving his hall, his son Lom at his side.

"We have tidings for you!" Lochie called out. "Important news concerning the arrival of the Milesian fleet."

Reluctantly the Fir-Bolg king waited for them to approach, listened to their story and then begged to be excused. "My son and I are tired. He's off to bed and I wish to go somewhere warm and quiet to rest. There is a spare hut opposite the gate. Come to me after everyone else has gone to bed and we will talk then."

They waited until the king had gone and then Isleen spoke to her companion.

"So do you think Mahon will wed with Aoife? Her father doesn't seem too impressed with the Danaans at present."

"This is a temporary affliction he is suffering from," Lochie laughed. "I've no doubt that with or without her father's permission Aoife will find the young Danaan prince irresistible. Indeed he may become more alluring to her if her father disapproves."

"Perhaps," Isleen conceded, a wicked gleam in her eye. "But let us wait and see what the invaders bring."

"We have a busy night ahead of us," Lochie sighed.

At that moment Mahon emerged from the hall and made his way to the young warriors' hut where he slept. Lochie and Isleen were careful to slip into the shadows so he wouldn't see them. When the Danaan had disappeared Isleen observed under her breath, "He has gone to his bed alone this night."

"Shall we take some food and drink before we visit the Fir-Bolg king?" Lochie asked. "I would dearly love to sit with the Poets for a while."

His partner nodded and they went to the king's hall in search of the Druids. But when the pair arrived at the fireside there was no sign of Fineen or Dalan.

They were welcomed by Aoife into the hall and the Welcome Cup was passed into their hands.

"I knew it was you," exclaimed Aoife when they had been made comfortable. "I knew I wasn't dreaming."

Isleen raised an eyebrow at Lochie. "Where is Mahon tonight?" she asked the young woman, casually changing the subject.

"He was tired," she answered with disappointment in her voice. "There was a disagreement between my father and his. He thought it best to retire."

"Perhaps you should seek him out," Lochie suggested. "He's probably upset by all the arguing and needs comforting."

Aoife's eyes lit up.

"Never rush into a man's arms," Isleen advised. "Let him be."

"I'll just look in on him," the young woman said.

Lochie caught his companion's eye as the young girl left the fireside. Isleen was scowling.

"We're both exhausted from our journey," the Bard explained to those present. "Tomorrow we'll tell our news."

Then the two of them made their way out of the hall toward the guesthouse.

Sárán was seated just within the door and it was he who greeted them.

"We didn't expect to see you both here this night," the young man said in surprise.

"We didn't expect to be here ourselves," Isleen answered and she touched Sárán's hand lightly. "You have the look of a raven about you, my lad," she told him softly.

Sárán blushed.

"Your eyes are bright and clear. Your hair is as black as soot. You'd be a beautiful bird if you had been born of the winged folk."

"I've often watched the birds of the air with envy," the young man admitted. "I have often wished to know the freedom they experience. Indeed, before I took the Druid learning I was nicknamed the Raven. Fineen considers it unseemly for a student to be addressed in such a prestigious manner. One day I'll earn the name."

"Be careful," Lochie warned him. "If you wish for something with a deep heartfelt desire, it may be granted."

Sárán frowned and Isleen laughed.

"Don't listen to him," she mocked. "He met a seal-woman once who stole his heart away and then left him to pine for her. He's ever after been fascinated with the shape-shifters."

"Shape-shifters?" Sárán replied with obvious interest.

"Those beings who have perfected the art of changing from one form to another at will," Lochie explained. "Has your teacher not spoken of them?"

"No. He's never mentioned them."

"We've had more important work to do," Fineen interrupted, looking up from the fireside. The healer scrutinized the pair carefully before he spoke again. "How did you manage to make your way here so quickly? I'd heard you were in the east keeping a watch on the Milesians."

"So we were," Lochie explained. "But we followed the fleet around the southern coast and realized they were making for this place. And so we traveled as quickly as we could, hoping to arrive in time to give warning."

"You're not weary from your journey?" Dalan asked from his seat by the hearth.

"We have been on the road since we were children," Isleen laughed. "Such a trip is nothing to us."

"But there's no dust on your clothes," the healer observed. "And your shoes are clean."

"Our teacher taught us the importance of being well presented when we visit the kings of Innisfail." Isleen shrugged. "That is obviously not a skill imparted by the Danaan Druids."

"Who was your teacher?" Dalan cut in suspiciously.

"Cromlann the Old," Lochie answered without hesitation. "After his death we both went to the lands of the Bretani to conclude our studies. But Cromlann was our first teacher."

"I knew him well." The Brehon nodded. "He was a fine harper. Even up to the day he died."

"There was none finer."

"But Cromlann passed away over forty summers ago," Dalan added. "I was just a boy when he fell ill. You could not have possibly known him."

"Perhaps Lochie and I are older than you might guess," Isleen cut in.

Dalan's eyes narrowed.

"Sit with us then and we will share our tales of the road," Fineen offered in an attempt to dispel the tension. "But I beg you not to distract my student with stories of the shape-shifters. Their day has passed and gone."

"And may we never be plagued with their evil again," Dalan added sharply.

"Now I know who you are talking about," Sárán cut in. "The Watchers."

"There is nothing more to be said on this matter!" the Brehon barked sharply. "We have more pressing concerns."

Fineen raised his eyebrows at this unexpected outburst but made no comment. Instead he picked up the conversation where it had been when the two travelers had arrived.

"Brocan will calm down," the healer assured his fellow Druid. "He is renowned for his outbursts. I forgive him easily for his temper is usually followed by deep remorse."

"The king is a stubborn man," Dalan sighed. "And now his wife is taking opposition to him. I do not imagine he will be convinced easily. And even if he were to enter into an alliance with the Danaans, it is not certain he could be trusted."

"We have no choice but to give our trust to him," Fineen replied.

"Forgive my intrusion in this matter," Lochie interrupted, "but Brocan's reluctance to ally with Cecht is well known. I understand he is a stubborn man but perhaps he has not been persuaded because he has not yet heard the right argument."

"What better argument is there than the survival of his people?" Dalan asked. "What more can we say to him?"

"There is the matter of the debt he owes to Cecht as a result of Fearna's death," Lochie suggested. "I know it has been an overwhelming burden on his people and a source of great worry to the king. If that debt could somehow be laid aside for the time being, you might find him much more cooperative."

"Such a debt cannot be annulled," Fineen pointed out. "It would create a dangerous precedent in future cases."

"Then do not annul it." Lochie shrugged. "Simply change the nature of the fine."

"Are you suggesting I adjust the judgment?" Dalan frowned.

Lochie nodded. "Instead of paying his debt in cows," he suggested, "make him pay with the service of his warriors and the allegiance of his people to the Danaans."

"He would not be able to refuse," Fineen agreed tentatively.

"And it could be stipulated that the alliance only remain in effect until the threat of invasion is ended," Lochie added.

"I will need to think about this carefully," the Brehon sighed, already considering the possibilities. "This has never been done before and I would want to make sure Brocan can raise no objections."

"It is a solution to the problem," the healer admitted with mounting excitement. "Why did we not think of it?"

"Because in the long term such a judgment may cause us more problems than it solves," Dalan countered. "Though I must admit it would solve our dilemma now."

"I have been a close confidant of Brocan's since he was elected," Lochie told them. "Let me present this to him as an honorable way to bring about a settlement."

"I made the judgment," the Brehon objected. "It should be me who makes the offer."

"I fear Brocan does not trust you. You passed a judgment against him which, we both know, revealed the deeper truth of Fearna's death. In my opinion he considers you responsible for his shaming and the debt laid upon his people."

"He must know I would not do anything to endanger the best interests of the Fir-Bolg."

"Nevertheless," Lochie said, holding the palm of his hand up in protest, "I believe he will more likely listen to my advice than yours."

Dalan narrowed his eyes and cast a glance at Isleen. The Brehon could not understand why his suspicions were raised by these two. They seemed to have a knowledge of the Druid Assembly's decisions and to hold the interests of the people of Innisfail at heart. But his instincts screamed out a warning to him.

"I will consider what you have said very carefully," the Brehon told Lochie. "Nothing can be done until morning in any case. King Brocan has gone to bed."

"He has asked that I attend to him after midnight to offer advice," the traveling Bard informed them. "It would be an excellent opportunity to broach the subject."

"Indeed," Fineen agreed immediately. "I can see no other way of placating him and bringing him into the Danaan camp. It is worth a try."

"Very well," Dalan reluctantly conceded. "Broach the subject with him. Make no commitment. Give no assurances. Offer no guarantees. Tell him it is merely one solution and the whole matter is still open to discussion."

"I will do so." Lochie smiled. "Let us hope that at last the deadlock may be broken."

"At last," Fineen repeated with a sigh. "Brocan has become more and more difficult to deal with each passing moon."

"And Riona has turned against him now," the Brehon agreed.

"We passed King Cecht on his way out to find her," Isleen told them.

"Where has my mother gone?" Sárán inquired with concern.

"I have no idea. Perhaps down to the sea to be alone."

"But there are Milesians abroad!" the young man protested. "I must go and see she is safe."

"I will accompany you," Isleen offered, standing up.

Lochie raised an eyebrow. "Don't worry about Brocan, wife. I'll see to him. You go and search for Riona with this young man."

"Thank you, husband," she replied sweetly. "Perhaps between us we will be able to sort this whole mess out and bring the Danaans and the Fir-Bolg together."

"I am certain we will," he assured her. "For now I will sit with our colleagues to discuss the other news of the war. We have been away for a long while and I would like to catch up on the latest developments."

When Sárán and Isleen had taken their leave, Lochie turned to Fineen. "Now tell me about the Quicken berries. I heard a rumor the Druid Assembly is going to plant the great tree afresh to ensure a good supply of the fruit. Is that true?"

Dalan did not raise his eyes from the fire as the healer explained the plan. The Brehon was already trying to understand the strange sense he had that something was terribly wrong.

"Your father is no longer fit to rule," Isleen told Sárán after they had passed the sentries at the gate.

"Then it's up to the Council of Chieftains to replace him," the young man replied cautiously.

"Your brother would make a fine king," she continued as she put her arm through his.

"He is not yet a warrior."

"He is young and strong. With a Druid such as yourself behind him he would be a fine king. You have a good sense of right and wrong, don't you?"

"I have learned much under the tutelage of Fineen," Sárán sighed. "And the most important lesson has been that I have so much more yet to learn. Perhaps one day when I am older I will ask the council to consider me as an adviser to the king. For the time being it would be better if someone like Fergus, who is a skilled warrior and a wise man, were to take my father's place and Dalan to advise him."

"You agree that Brocan must be replaced?"

"If my father refuses to accept this last concession," the young man admitted, "then the council will have no choice. None of our people wishes to prolong the old fight with the Danaans. We all understand the peril facing us. It is just unfortunate my father insists on being so obstinate."

"His pride has been injured," she conceded. "It is understandable he should not wish to compromise himself further."

"I have lived among the Danaans now for a full turning of the seasons," Sárán told her. "I have seen they are a good-hearted people. Their ways are not those of the Fir-Bolg and their customs seem, at first, to be strange. But they are learned and value honorable folk no matter what their origins."

"If you do not mind that they will soon rule over your people, then you have nothing to worry about."

"The Tuatha De Danaan have no intention of ruling the Fir-Bolg. Nor do they wish to see us subservient to their ways."

"You are wrong," Isleen snapped and she stopped in her tracks, grabbing him by the shoulders and forcibly turning him to face her. "Our people were here in Innisfail long before the Danaans, and before they arrived our Fir-Bolg ancestors were the master craftsmen of the Islands of the West. Their work was revered across the known world. It was our forebears who built the stone circles and the hollow hills which the sun and moon visit every midwinter. It was our musicians who first played upon the harp and composed poetry."

She looked deep into his eyes. "Whatever the Danaans know of poetry, music and stoneworking," she went on, "they learned from us. Whatever skills they have as interpreters of the signs, as keepers of the seasons, as manipulators of the four elements, they were given by Fir-Bolg masters."

"But their legends do not mention us as anything but enemies." Sárán frowned.

"Do you know the full tale of the Islands of the West?" she asked him.

"I have only heard snippets," he admitted.

"Then let's go and sit by the ocean and I'll tell you the whole story. Not the legend the Danaans would have you hear, but the Fir-Bolg history which is seldom discussed these days."

"What about my mother?" Sárán protested. "Shouldn't we find her first?"

"The King of the Danaans has cast an admiring eye on Riona." Isleen laughed. "She will come to no harm with his protection. If there are any Milesians about, Cecht is more than capable of dealing with them."

She took his arm again and they continued walking down the rocky track which led to the ocean. When they came to the water's edge Isleen found a large stone to sit on. The moon was new and the sky dark, but Sárán had a good view out over the western seas as Isleen told her tale.

"In the long-ago there was an island," she began, "out there on the horizon it was, so that if we had lived in those times we would have been able to see its snow-capped mountains even now. That was the ancient home of our people."

"The Islands of the West?"

"That was the name our folk gave to it." She nodded. "But the Fir-Bolg were not the only people who dwelt there. The Danaans and the Milesians also trace their roots to this once enormous land."

"It was one land?"

"Oh yes," she confirmed. "But that was before parts of the country began to subside into the ocean. In the final days of the great homeland all that remained was a scattered archipelago stretching across the horizon."

"If the Danaans and all the other folk originated

there, then surely we are the same people?" Sárán reasoned.

"In the dimmest darkest past that is possibly true," she conceded. "But the histories do not commence with such remote beginnings. The first stories of the Islands of the West concern the wisdom which the Fir-Bolg had amassed about the natural and the supernatural worlds. The Danaans were their students in those times and together the two folk surveyed the invisible lines of energy which spread throughout the island."

"What lines?"

"Hasn't that healer taught you anything?" Isleen asked in outrage. "He is a Danaan so I am not surprised he has not mentioned this. Our ancestors revered the earth as a living creature. Those Druids of our folk who understood this best knew that the whole ocean and every land are crisscrossed with lines of energy which lie just beneath the surface. A skilled Druid-Seer can tap into this energy and use it to travel vast distances in a matter of moments. Or to bring healing to the sick, or to find a water source, or to locate the best place to sow a certain crop, or even to discover a doorway to the Otherworld."

"Fineen has never spoken to me of this!" Sárán gasped, feeling let down by his teacher.

"The Danaans were not renowned for their knowledge in this field," the Seer explained. "They sought their wisdom from the trees flowers and herbs of the land, just as the ancestors of the Milesians pursued the study of the animal world. But the Druids of the Fir-Bolg found the most powerful source of knowledge and this made the other peoples jealous."

"So the stone hills and circles were built to mark this energy out?" Sárán asked.

"You are very intelligent." Isleen smiled as she touched his cheek tenderly. "That is precisely what the stone chambers and the standing stones were used for. At certain times of the cycle of the seasons the earth energy surges with great force. These times are usually close to the fire festivals which we now celebrate, but especially at Midwinter's Eve, Samhain, and Beltinne. And every so often the sun explodes with energy which rains down upon the earth to renew its spirit."

"That is why the passages and chambers are lit by the sun and moon at times!"

"Yes."

"But why is this knowledge not spoken of?"

"Because it led to jealousy and war," Isleen explained. "The Fir-Bolg decided it was best to depart from their homeland and colonize the lands to the east rather than divulge the wisdom they had collected. Innisfail was one of the first islands they came to and as a consequence this land has more stone circles and ancient passage mounds than any other above the ocean. If only the Danaans had not dabbled in the wisdom our ancestors had discovered."

"What happened?"

"The Chief Druid of the Danaans decided to plunder the knowledge of the Fir-Bolg so that his people might save the Islands of the West from the encroaching ocean. Our folk knew there was no hope of salvaging the land. It was only a matter of time before the ancient country sank beneath the waves. That is one reason our forebears found it easy to leave their ancestral home."

"They knew the islands were doomed to be drowned?"

"They did." Isleen nodded. "For their wisdom was such they had learned to read the signs in nature. But the foolish Dagda and his Druids were stubborn. They wanted the land for their own and they used what little they knew of our wisdom to try to keep the sea from stealing the land. In the event their meddling with nature made the situation much worse."

"How?"

"The lesser moon which had been in the heavens for many generations came crashing to earth. It landed on the western edge of the islands, causing the land to spew forth hot rock and ash. The destruction was swift and brutal." She paused. "But before it came to that the ancestors of the Gaedhals, who were very warlike, tried to force the Danaans to stop their meddling. The result was war."

"So the Danaans and the Milesians are ancient enemies?" Sárán realized.

"Their quarrel began in those times, though few of their Druid historians would likely admit it. While they fought it out between themselves our folk were left in peace, here in Innisfail, and the ancient home-land finally disappeared beneath the waves in the great cataclysm. Before that happened the Milesians sailed off to find a new home. They traveled for many generations before they found their way here. The Danaans did not depart the Islands of the West until the last moment. To the end they clung to the belief that their Druids could alter the course of nature."

"They believe it still," Sárán noted. "For they have found the doorway to the Otherworld and plan to withdraw all our folk behind that veil to avoid conflict with the Milesians."

"And they have refined their skills as herbalists so they can produce the Quicken berries as their ances-tors once did," she noted. "But they do not know the price they will pay for their immortality. They are an ignorant race." There was bitterness in her voice.

"Make no mistake," Isleen told him. "The Danaans are our enemies. They will misuse their limited knowledge as they did in the past, and they will drag our people into a war which we do not want."

"We must resist them then," Sárán said defiantly, not really knowing how that might be possible.

"You have learned much from them in the time you have been studying with Fineen," Isleen said. "Surely you know their strengths and weaknesses. There must be a way to bring them to heel. What they are planning to do is wrong. Passing through the doorway to the Otherworld is dangerous enough. The forces such a strategy might unleash are beyond their imagination. Look at the terrible mess they made when they tried to raise a tempest."

"The Milesian Bard, Amergin, knew of a song to dispel the storm. That is why it was defeated."

"The tempest was ineffective because the Danaans do not understand the powers they are imposing on the world. We few are the last of our people with the will to resist. Even your sister has been drawn into their web of enchantment."

"Aoife and Mahon are constant companions," Sárán admitted. "I have that on good authority."

"It is Cecht's plan to wed his son to Aoife," Isleen whispered urgently. "Once they are joined, the Danaans will effectively rule all the folk of Innisfail."

"And what of the Druid Assembly?" the young man asked. "Surely they understand the danger. Would they really permit such a deliberate manipulation of the peoples of this island?"

"The Druid Assembly are puppets of the Danaan kings," she scoffed. "They are powerless to speak out against the warrior caste. That is how it was in the ancient days. Nothing has changed. Unless they are stopped, the Danaans will destroy the last remnants of our folk."

"How?"

"They speak of withdrawing behind the veil into the Otherworld," Isleen informed him. "But the Druid Assembly has made no provision for the Fir-Bolg to go with them. Neither have they produced enough of their famed elixir of life to share with any but their own folk. They will abandon us as they would have in the ancient days."

"I can't believe Fineen would be a part of such a plot," Sárán gasped. "He has been so good to me, considering the great wrong I did to him."

"They don't hold the same laws as we do. They hold no respect for the ancient pathways of the earth energy. They do not consider the ancient monuments to be sacred. The son of the current Dagda has set up his house in the great hill at the Brugh!"

"I was told the Dagda granted his son the right to live there as long as he protects the monument with his life," the young man countered.

"Those places are centers of the earth power," Isleen hissed. "They are not meant to be dwelling places for Danaan Druid princes."

She took his arm and held it tight. "Consider this. The Danaans call themselves the people of the Goddess Danu."

"Yes. Danu is venerated by the Fir-Bolg also."

"Do you know who Danu is?"

"She was a matriarch of the Islands of the West in the days before the flood."

"That is correct. But her full title is often forgotten. She is Danu of the Floodwaters. Danu of the Drowned Lands. She of the High-Places and the Low-Places. Goddess of the Falling Stars."

Isleen paused to let Sárán ponder the meaning of those titles for a moment.

"Danu was the Chief Druidess of the peoples of the

West before the land began to subside into the ocean. It was she who advocated the singing of powerful songs to stave off the inevitable flood. Her strategy failed so she gradually moved her Druids to the mountains until there was nowhere left to go. Then the lesser moon fell to earth, trailing its children behind it. The survivors of the ancient homeland were forced through her foolishness to sail off on a voyage of conquest."

Sárán began to shake his head and Isleen realized she had told him too much. He was struggling to take it all in.

"Why is this tale never told?" he asked her.

"There's much for you to learn," she said at last. "You need not hear it all tonight. You are bright and a quick student. If you would know more of these secret doctrines which are forbidden to be spoken of in Danaan circles, then I'll teach you."

"Yes," Sárán decided in a flash. "I want to learn. I want to know everything you can pass on to me."

"That's my lad," Isleen cooed and she leaned forward to kiss him lightly on the lips. "We will be a fine team, you and I."

Sárán swallowed hard and pulled away in discomfort. "I'd like to find my mother now and bring her safely back to the hillfort," he told her.

"Very well then." Isleen smiled. "But she has probably already returned safely to her bed."

Chapter 17

AFTER LOCHIE LEFT, FINEEN AND DALAN, THE TWO Druids, sat for a long while in silence, neither wishing to be the first to shatter the quiet. Both men valued their own solitude and there had been precious little of that for a long time. In the distance the low crash of thunder rumbled menacingly and both heads turned to listen.

"I heard her speak three nights ago at Mag Tuireadh," Fineen whispered. "She sang an ancient song as she washed my hair. And when she struck her flint to light the fire, the spark killed a dozen men."

Dalan put a hand to his chin and considered the healer's words carefully. "The answer to your riddle," he said at length, "is thunder, rain and lightning."

"You have it." Fineen smiled.

Dalan laughed. "Will this brew of yours really do what you claim?" he asked, revealing what was on his mind.

"It will cure the sick," Fineen assured his friend. "And I have seen it bring a man back from the brink of death. The knowledge of it was passed down from my Danaan ancestors."

"Why was it never employed before?"

"Because though it heals all wounds and banishes sickness, it also has an unnatural effect on those who take it."

"What is that?"

"Anyone who drinks this potion and continues to do so once every four seasons will not die. It holds death at bay indefinitely. There may be other unknown effects which develop in time. No one is sure. The Dagda in his wisdom has lifted the prohibition on its use, but I must admit I fear eternal life more than I do passing away to the Halls of Waiting."

"There will be no death?"

"No more dying." The healer nodded.

Dalan turned away to pick up his harp. "I don't wish to live forever," he said quietly.

"You will only live as long as you take the Quicken Brew," Fineen assured him. "If you decide not to take the brew, the effects will diminish within days. The older you are at the time, the swifter the seasons will catch up with you."

"Why take it at all in that case?"

"The Milesian Gaedhals are an unpredictable people," Fineen explained. "We do not know whether they will respect the Druid class in war. We have been ordered to take the brew because our lives and our wisdom are important to the survival of our people. The edict of the Druid Assembly is only binding until peace has been achieved."

"Once the Gaedhals have agreed to a treaty, we each have the right to decide whether we will continue taking the brew?"

"Correct."

The Brehon began to pick out a little tune that would one day make a fine dance melody. For the moment he was still refining it so he did not strike the chords.

"I am uneasy in my mind," Dalan sighed as he strummed.

"How's that?"

"I have a fear the Draoi-Craft of Balor has returned to plague the folk of Innisfail," the Brehon told his friend. Dalan reached into his pack and retrieved a leather bottle. He removed the cork and offered the vessel to his companion.

Fineen took a long draught of the mead and then handed the bottle back. "What Fomorian Draoi-Craft would that be?" he asked.

"It is like a riddle to me," the Brehon sighed, distracted now from his music. "The coming of the Milesians has occupied my thoughts for so long, I have had precious little time to consider there might be some greater and more dangerous force at work here."

"What are you talking about?"

"What drew the Milesians to our land?" Dalan asked.

"Their Chief Bard told me they were led here by a series of dreams," Fineen explained. "Scota, their queen and Amergin's mother, had visions of Innisfail as a wide green but uninhabited land. The Gaedhal Bard himself was convinced they would find a country rich in game and lush pastures for their cattle. But none of them considered for a moment our people would seriously resist their coming."

"He is said to be a wise man," Dalan noted, "this Amergin."

"Indeed he is," the healer agreed. "And he is a Seer of wondrous skill, so I heard tell."

"But a skilled Seer would have scrutinized every detail of a dream. He would have known there would be battles. Visions do not lie. A wise Bard would not have let his people set out on such an expedition without making certain there was not going to be war waiting after a long sea journey."

"That is true."

"And this fight between Brocan and Cecht," the Brehon added. "It has gone on too long. The King of the Fir-Bolg is a reasonable man. He has always been able to put his personal feelings aside and work for the good of his people. It is unusual for him to be acting with such stubbornness and with no thought for the future.

Fineen frowned as he took the bottle back from his friend. "It is simply the old animosity between Danaan and Fir-Bolg coming to the surface again," he reasoned.

"No," Dalan disagreed. "There is more to it than that."

Fineen took another mouthful of mead and once again handed the vessel to his companion.

"There is something about Isleen and her husband that makes me feel uneasy," Dalan continued.

"Go on," Fineen urged.

"Lochie told us their teacher was Cromlann. I knew the old man before he was struck down with the shaking hands and had to give up the harp."

"But you said he had been a fine player up to the day he died!" Fineen exclaimed.

"And Lochie agreed with me without hesitation," the Brehon pointed out. "If he had been a student of Cromlann's, he would have known the old man did not so much as touch the harp for the last ten winters of his life." Dalan stared into the fire in contemplation.

"I must admit I myself have felt uncomfortable around them," the healer confided.

"They are not all they appear to be," Dalan sighed, "that is certain."

"Are they Milesians?" Fineen pressed, eyes wide with wonder. "Sent to cause mischief among our people?"

"I do not believe so."

"Then what do you believe?"

"I fear we may have been seated this evening in the presence of the last of the Watchers."

The healer drew a deep breath and snatched the

leather bottle from his fellow Druid. "I pray you are wrong, brother," he whispered. And then he put the vessel to his lips and drank deep.

"There is some doubt in my mind yet," the Brehon admitted. "And I have no experience of their kind. But all the evidence points to some interference in the affairs of our people." Dalan turned to the healer to present his case. "Is it not strange that the Milesians should appear from beyond the seas just at a time when peace has finally been arranged between Danaan and the Fir-Bolg?"

The Brehon took his friend's arm and held it tight. "And Brocan is not the only one who is acting out of character. Sárán's crazed attack on you last summer was so strange that if you had foretold it I would not have believed the boy capable of such an act."

"Are you saying he was influenced by the Watchers?" Fineen gasped in disbelief. "The Watchers are creatures from the legends. They have not been heard of in generations. Not since the time of Balor. The Druid Assembly established long ago that they had passed into a state of impotent limbo when their lord and master was defeated."

"Two of them were never tracked down," the Brehon pointed out. "The Dagda decided they could not have survived since no word had been heard of them."

"But after all this time they cannot possibly still be trying to influence the affairs of our people . . . can they?"

"Perhaps the Watchers have been here all along, waiting for an opportunity for revenge."

"Isn't it more likely that Lochie and Isleen are traitors?" Fineen reasoned. "Have you considered they may be working with the Milesians to cause conflict within our camp? After all, they have admitted to traveling in the Bretani lands and we both know the Bretani are closely related to the Milesians."

"You could be right," Dalan conceded, taking the bottle back to drain the last drops. "In future we will keep a close eye on Lochie and Isleen. From now on the Watchers will be watched." He sighed and relaxed a little. "If they are Milesians it is only a matter of time before they show themselves for what they truly are. We will wait and be patient."

"You should rest," Fineen insisted. "You've been working hard to convince Brocan to change his mind and you're exhausted. As your physician I must insist that tomorrow you go to the spring and sit in the quiet of the wood for a while to refresh your weary spirit."

"I will," Dalan promised with a yawn. Then he returned to gently touching the harp wires.

"I've a riddle for you," the Brehon said after a short while.

"What is it?" Fineen asked with a smile.

"In the dark we sit," the Brehon began. "Seven lonely sisters. On the hilltop you'll see us each clutching a tallow candle. But our tiny flames don't flicker. Where we sit the wind can't touch us. Won't you come to visit us, young man?"

"Your riddle's too easy," Fineen said with mock seriousness. "And it doesn't flow well."

"I've not been playing this game for very long," Dalan protested. "Riddling is not part of a Brehon's training."

"Were you never a child?"

"Riddling was frowned upon as a waste of time in my father's house."

"But all the world is a riddle, my dear friend," the healer laughed. "And I'm told that when the answer to the great question finally dawns on you it keeps you laughing to yourself for the rest of your life."

"Which could be a very long while if you have taken the Quicken Brew," the Brehon noted dryly. "But you haven't told me the answer to my riddle."

"You are speaking of the group of seven stars in the night sky known as An Tréidín, the little herd." Fineen smiled. "The Fomor knew them as the seven sisters."

Dalan grunted, pretending to be disappointed that Fineen had guessed so easily, then he returned to his harp and his friend sat back to listen.

Lom woke up suddenly and stared wide-eyed at the door to the round thatched house, his whole body tense. He knew he had not been dreaming. He had been sleeping deeply and peacefully, aided by all the mead he had drunk at the feast.

He looked across at Aoife's bed and saw it was unoccupied. He guessed it was only a short while before dawn. Lom started to relax. His head was aching a little from the drink and he could hear rain spattering lightly on the thatch roof.

Lom didn't fancy going out in the cold to look for his sister and he was still very sleepy, so he rolled over and pulled the furs up around his head. He told himself with a sigh that Aoife would be back soon. Then he realized she'd want to talk until breakfast time. He must rest as much as possible before she returned.

Lom had not lain there long when he heard voices just outside the house. He threw the covers from his head, hoping to catch a snippet of the conversation. To his surprise he heard two male voices talking in low tones, but none of it made sense. Then he caught the unmistakable sound of a sword being drawn from a scabbard. This was followed by a low sinister laugh and the noise of footsteps moving quickly across the open ground outside.

His ears bristling, his senses sharpened, Lom stared at the ceiling listening hard. There were no more unusual sounds. But he sensed an unusual tension in the air that set him on edge. Something was not right. Like a harp with one wire tuned poorly or a thudding bodhran with a slackened goatskin, it nagged at him to investigate.

Lom stretched and half sat up, deciding it was time he was out of bed anyway. He threw the furs off, shivered, found his clothes and was very quickly dressed.

The morning was chilly and wet so he grabbed his cloak.

In the courtyard he heard a dog bark and a cow give a long low cry. Nothing unusual just before sunrise. But still, Lom's instincts told him to beware. Cautiously he poked his head out through the cowhide flap of the small stone house.

All was quiet. Perfectly still. Smoke hung low over the ring of a dozen round houses. The air was clear and brisk. There were puddles on the ground and gray clouds filled the sky. A cow had wandered out in the night. She was nudging some clumps of grass by the gate and chewing peacefully.

Lom frowned. He scanned the wall and gate to the hillfort. There was no one about.

He had never seen the gates left unguarded. There weren't any sentries to be seen. The hillfort was all too quiet. His frowned confusion was dispelled a split second later.

The gate swung silently open as if the wind had pushed it. Then a short stocky warrior appeared. The stranger was scarred with deep green spiral tattoos that swirled over his fair skin. These adornments reminded Lom of the body decorations the Danaans wore when they went to war. But this stranger was not painted. He was covered in elaborate tattoos.

The warrior did not notice Lom observing him from his doorway, so when the intruder judged all was clear he slipped silently through the gate. He closed it again without a sound and crossed the settlement to the king's hall, flattening himself against the building as he listened for any noise within. The strange warrior then went to the door and pulled aside the cowhide flap. He peered in for a moment and Lom found his breath to speak.

"Who are you?" the young man stuttered nervously.

The warrior spun around, drawing his bright silver blade from a leather scabbard. Their eyes met. Lom stood tall in defiance at the intrusion.

"Who are you?" he demanded again, his voice firm this time.

The stranger did not take his eyes off Lom for a moment. And he did not reply. He watched the young man hesitate a little and read the alarm in his face. The intruder moved out into the middle of the courtyard, pushing the stray cow out of his way as he approached. When he was no more than twenty paces away the fair-skinned intruder did something completely unexpected.

He smiled broadly at Lom. His teeth stood out white against the fierce tattoos on his face. His bright eyes sparkled like mossy green pebbles in the bottom of a stream and they were full of mirth.

As the two of them stared each other down the gate opened again and other silent forms slipped into the settlement. The strangers spread out in a fan. By the time Lom had managed to break away from the stranger's stare the hilltop fort was swarming with warriors all attired in the same manner as the smiling one. Dozens of intruders ran this way and that, spears at the ready, swords held high to strike, small shields worn tied to their upper arms.

Lom noticed Brocan's aged cousin stick his graying head out from the king's hall looking for his cow. None of the intruders noticed him and in a moment the old man had disappeared inside to raise the alarm.

This brought Lom to his senses. He took a deep breath to cry out, but before the words could escape his mouth someone else called the warning that had been on the tip of his tongue.

"Attack!"

Lom did not recognize the voice. He frowned deeply.

Then the intruders answered as one with a chilling shout. "Eber!" they screamed with delight.

And Lom realized it was not a warning he had heard. It was a war cry. In that instant he noticed that the first warrior was gone, vanished as if he were some apparition from the Otherworld.

"Rise up!" Lom cried, hurrying out into the settlement. "Take arms! The enemy is upon us!"

He had hardly spoken those few words when he noticed the first flaming torch and arrows brandished by one of the strangers.

"Spare us, Danu," he muttered in disbelief.

Suddenly there were a dozen sputtering fires spreading across the settlement. Women, children and warriors of his own clan were running half naked from their homes, awoken by the smoke of burning thatch and the mocking laughter of the enemy.

Lom rushed to his mother's house but she wasn't there. Then he struggled against his panicked kinfolk as he made his way toward the king's house to find his father. No one was offering any resistance. Most folk were stumbling about stunned.

The Fir-Bolg had never been attacked in the dead of night before. It was against the rules of war, unthinkable that women, children and the wise should be subjected to battle. That was a warrior's duty and the battlefield was the only place for fighting.

His uncle's voice could be heard encouraging people to take their children to the safety of the nearby spring. But Lom couldn't see Fergus anywhere. The words were quickly heeded though and many folk started making their way to the second gate where there was a path leading down the hillside.

Lom was close to the king's hall when he noticed the roof was entirely engulfed in flames. It must have been the first house the Milesians set on fire. Lom had left his sword at the door before the feast the previous evening and impetuously decided he would have to retrieve it now before the fire got out of control.

He pulled his cloak over his head to protect his hair from the falling coals. Then, with a quick prayer for a heavy fall of rain, he plunged into the burning building.

What he saw chilled him to the bone. A dozen of the older folk were still wrapped in their furs, too sleepy or too drunk to wake up, even though the roof was blazing. Lom dashed around to stir them, calling to them to awaken.

Brocan coughed as he woke and it took a few moments for him to open his eyes. But as soon as he had looked about him he was on his feet, dressed and helping folk to the door. Lom woke as many as he could and finally carried Brocan's old cousin out to the courtyard.

By this time almost every building was ablaze, the gates were wide open. The livestock were being calmly herded out of the hillfort by the foreigners. Lom remembered his sword and without consideration for his own safety went back inside the hall to find it.

And it was fortunate that he did so. As he was leaving, his arms laden with bronze blades, he tripped over a form in the darkness. It was a body. The young man stuck his own sword through his belt and dropped the other weapons without hesitation. Then he dragged the unconscious form up off the ground, struggling to carry the body step by step to the door, roof timbers falling all about him and the thick smoke choking his lungs.

In no more time than it takes to draw a dozen breaths he was at the door with his burden, but to Lom it seemed like an eternity. He dumped the seemingly lifeless form on the wet ground outside just as his prayer was answered. The rain started to bucket down so heavily that Lom could feel the huge drops pummeling into his head.

He rolled the body over onto its back and pulled away the cloak wrapped tightly about the head. The rain was falling so hard now it was kicking up the mud and he could barely see. Lom pushed his own cloak aside and then examined the face before him. It was his own.

"Sárán!" he cried, fearing the worst. He shook his brother and slapped his cheeks to revive him.

Sárán opened his eyes a little and then was racked with a fit of coughing and spitting.

"Are you injured?" Lom asked anxiously.

"No," Sárán gasped. "The smoke is choking me but I'll surely recover. The last thing I remember was Isleen leaning against me as we made our way to the door. I must have fallen over."

There was a black mark across his head and a little blood on his tunic so Lom reasoned his brother had been hit by falling thatch.

"Where's Isleen?" Lom asked urgently.

"I don't know," his brother replied hoarsely, coughing up a lump of black mucus before he had finished speaking.

"Perhaps she's still inside the hall."

At that precise moment the roof to the king's hall collapsed with a crash that sent splinters, sparks and smoke in all directions. Lom dragged his brother to his feet again as quickly as he could, hoping the Seer had already escaped, for she surely would be dead now if she had not.

"Can you walk?"

"Yes," Sárán replied, but he was doubled over with a fit of hacking.

"Go to the spring at the foot of the hill and wait for me," Lom ordered. "I'll be along soon enough."

"What are you going to do?"

"I must find our mother and father," Lom replied. "And I have no idea what became of Aoife last night."

"She was off to meet Mahon when I saw her last," Sárán told him. "Perhaps they also went for a walk. But our mother didn't return. I was waiting in the king's hall for her. I think Cecht was with her."

"Go now," Lom insisted.

"I'll help you search," his brother protested. "Two pairs of eyes will see better."

"You are a student of Fineen the healer," Lom reminded him. "You will be far more useful at the spring. I am sure there will be folk who need tending. And you may need some attention yourself."

"You're right," Sárán conceded. "I will go. Don't get yourself into any trouble. I don't want to be tending your wounds by the spring."

Lom nodded and hurried back to his own house. Miraculously it was untouched by the flames. But there was no sign of Aoife. Lom turned around to survey the havoc. Somehow he knew his sister was not safe at the spring with everyone else. She was in danger and he had to find her.

Lom drew his sword and made his way to the front gate of the hillfort to begin a search of the countryside around.

* * *

Dalan had woken to the smell of smoke. It was strong in the confined space of the house but he had thought nothing of it. Until he had noticed the fire had died down and was little more than dull coals dying among the ashes.

Only then had he seen the wisps of gray smoke snaking thin fingers across the underside of the roof. At that very instant he had heard a shout outside. This had been followed almost immediately by the noise of people running past the hut.

Fineen, asleep on the other side of the central fire, had stirred, then sat up as the noise grew louder.

As the two Druids stared at each other now in sleepy disbelief a hundred bright embers rained down upon them from the roof timbers as the thatch burst into flame. At the same time the house was drowned in a cloud of thick smoke.

"Fire!" the Brehon yelled. Within seconds both men had grabbed harps, herbs and anything else they could carry and were out in the courtyard among the throng of panicked Fir-Bolg who were making for the gate.

"What is going on?" Fineen gasped, still only half awake. "Is this a dream?"

"The houses have been set alight," Dalan realized. "The hillfort has been breached and raided. It is too hazardous to stay here. We must make for the spring at the foot of the hill."

"Milesians?" Fineen gasped.

"Who else would come upon this place in the night and set fire to the houses?"

"Your prayers have been answered," the healer noted with some bitterness.

"What do you mean?'

"Brocan will not be so reluctant to join the fight against the Milesians now they have openly attacked his own hillfort."

Dalan nodded. "But what a terrible way for his stubbornness to be challenged."

Lom skirted over the rocky outcrops that lined the pathway to the sea. He avoided the track so as not to risk being seen by the enemy. By the time he came to the shore the sun had risen and the rain was beginning to ease a little. But he was drenched from head to foot and chilled to the bone.

At the seashore he stood for a long while struggling to pierce the veil of misty rain, searching for any sign of enemy ships. But the rain still cast a heavy sheet of gray over the strand and he could see nothing. He decided to retrace his steps and climb one of the higher outcrops where he reckoned he would get a better view of the bay. In a few minutes he was standing precariously balanced on the top of a narrow granite precipice that jutted out over the water. And almost immediately he spotted what he had been searching for.

Far out in the middle of the bay at the edge of the encroaching mist was a long dark shape sitting low in the water. At first Lom thought it was some huge monster come up from the depths of the ocean to feed. But as the mist receded he saw another shape exactly the same as the first. Both had high prows jutting forward and both were crowded with tiny black figures running this way and that in a frenzy.

Lom gasped. The vessels were huge, larger than any he had ever seen before.

His gaze fell at last on a third ship and his heart sank. He quickly calculated there must be over two hundred warriors aboard those three ships. The Fir-Bolg of the Burren had no hope of defeating such a force.

As he watched, the young warrior noticed half a dozen small rowing boats made of leather just like the curraghs the Fir-Bolg fishermen used to travel out past the Isles of Arainn. The boats had just set off from a landing place some distance up the rocky coast and they were brimming with warriors who wore shining helms and carried bright swords.

In the leading vessel Lom clearly saw a flash of bright yellow which he recognized as King Cecht's cloak. Then he noticed a woman with red hair seated beside the king and his heart cried out that he had not been able to rescue his mother from the Milesians. The other boats were loaded with cattle, goats and other plunder from the hillfort.

With a sense of hopelessness he sat down on the pinnacle of rock and watched the little boats make their way out to the ships. When they had unloaded their human cargo they made for the shore again to pick up more warriors.

Realizing there were still Gaedhals on the shore, Lom hardened his resolve to find Aoife. With no consideration for his own safety or that the odds may be utterly against him in a fight with the Milesians, he set off down the rocks for the enemy landing place.

The going was hard and slow but eventually he spotted the invaders' landing site, though there were many more warriors milling about than he had expected. Those first few rowing boats had only carried a fraction of the Milesian raiding party.

Lom concealed himself behind a rock and tried to still his beating heart while he took careful note of the enemy. He knew he wouldn't have a chance against so many. Yet he couldn't simply leave his mother and sister to the mercy of the invaders.

The young warrior leaned against the rock and the rain began to pelt down again as if in mockery of his predicament. He clung closely to the stone, oblivious to the cold and damp as he sorted through the options open to him. He edged around to where he could get a better view of the enemy and his heart leaped into his throat. Standing amidst the Milesian warriors was a young woman with flaming red hair. Aoife.

He closed his eyes and cursed the invaders under his breath.

In the next instant his sword was knocked from his grip and he felt a large hand covering his mouth so that he could not call out. Lom tried to turn his head but his attacker was too strong for him and he found himself pushed face first to the ground.

"Don't move," the assailant urged hoarsely, but Lom was not about to give in so easily. With a violent twist of his body he managed to throw the other man off balance for a second, just long enough to launch an attack of his own. The young warrior threw a wild ill-aimed punch that connected with the other man's shoulder.

The assailant fell back against the rock and Lom kicked him hard in the groin so that he fell forward in agony. Then the young Fir-Bolg warrior grabbed his sword and lifted it to strike. The stranger cowered beside the stone with his arms over his head, gasping to breathe through his pain.

Lom was not about to let this fellow live. But he had never killed a man before, and all his training told him that it was dishonorable to take the life of a warrior who could not rise to his own defense. So Lom paused for a few crucial seconds.

And then his attacker spoke.

"Lom!" the stranger gasped. "It's me! Mahon." He lifted his head and then slowly moved his hands down to where the pain was worst. "I've been following the Gaedhals since they captured Aoife," he grunted, still suffering. "I've been waiting for an opportunity to save her. I thought you were one of their scouts. I planned to trade you for her."

"Mahon? I never expected to see you," the young warrior exclaimed as he sank down beside the Danaan.

Both men were drenched, cold and exhausted. The steam poured out of their mouths in great folds and their chests heaved with the exertion of the fight.

Mahon groaned. "That was quite a kick."

"I'm sorry."

"I'll live," Mahon managed to gasp as he caught his breath. "I may never have children, but I'll live. There's two of us now. We have a chance of rescuing Aoife if we're careful and quick."

"It's too dangerous."

"We can't sit here a stone's throw from her and do nothing!"

"Be quiet!" Lom demanded. "I am trying to think."

"Thinking won't save your sister," Mahon spat. "It's action that's called for."

"Your kind of action will get all three of us killed," the young Fir-Bolg warrior replied impatiently, edging his way around the rock so he could observe the Milesian warriors again. "The first boats have returned," he reported, "and they are loading their warriors and spoils into them now."

"If you won't join me I will go down and challenge them myself," Mahon threatened.

"You'd be cut down before you had walked twenty paces," Lom whispered. "Even if you managed to defeat one of their warriors, we have no way of knowing what retribution the Milesians might take against their captives. It is simply too risky."

"Your sister is about to be boarded onto an enemy ship!" the Danaan said in disbelief. "How can you even think in this manner?"

Lom didn't answer but watched carefully as the invaders got into the boats one by one until just one enemy warrior was left ashore with his sister. Suddenly the boats were pushing away and the last Milesian jumped to his position.

"They've left her behind!" Lom shouted triumphantly and in a second he was on his feet running down to the shore. He reached his sister in a matter of moments but the boats were already out of reach of even a well-aimed stone.

In the last boat a warrior with long dark brown hair stood up to observe the unexpected arrival. The two enemies stared at each other without a word passing between them.

"Come back, you bloody cowards!" Mahon screamed, arriving on the scene. "Fight us fairly for our parents!"

"Be quiet, Mahon," Aoife said softly and the warrior was so shocked at her gentle rebuke that he simply stared at her in amazement.

"Who is that fellow?" Lom asked.

"His name is Eber," his sister replied. "He is the brother to Éremon, their chieftain, and Amergin, their Bard. His mother is Scota, Queen of the Gaedhals. Eber is a war leader in his own right and claims to be an honorable man."

"Honorable?" Mahon spat. "Is it honorable to raid an enemy camp in the middle of the night and take captives?"

"He was commanded to do so," Aoife explained. "That's what he told me. Raiding is not forbidden under their laws."

"But if they could bring themselves to attack by

night," Lom asked, "why did they not put everyone to the sword? Why did they take prisoners? And why did they release you?"

"I am only a Druid in training," Aoife told him, "but to them I am a Druid nevertheless and therefore immune to acts of war. I begged to be taken instead of our mother but Eber would have none of it."

"Barbarians!" Lom gasped.

Mahon put a hand on her shoulder and she turned to hold him.

"What do they intend to do with our parents?" he asked.

"They are hostages," she replied, looking him in the eye. "Eber took them to ensure our warriors would meet them in open battle at the next full moon."

"Open battle?" Lom repeated. "What trick is this?"

"It is my duty to pass these tidings on to the Druid Assembly," Aoife replied. "If our warriors gather at the appointed place at the nominated time, our parents will be released unharmed."

"And if not?" Mahon cut in.

"I don't know what they intend to do with them," she answered with a shudder. "But I can imagine."

Chapter 18

THAT EVENING FIRES WERE BUILT WITHIN THE HILLFORT and the tribal chieftains gathered from across the Burren to hear news of the daring raid. Makeshift shelters were erected, food brought in from nearby settlements, and warriors sent to scout the coast to the south in case the invaders had more raiding in mind.

Brocan organized the defenses, whilst the gathering of information and the distribution of supplies were left to Fergus. Both men worked to the limit of their endurance, pressing those under them to their tasks with words of rebuke and stories to inspire fear.

When evening drew its veil across the land they had completed their effort. Night watches were positioned around the violated fort; fresh warriors were called in from the smaller settlements close by and a food store was prepared within the one house untouched by the flames.

When the scouts returned after dark Fergus took them aside to hear what they had to say. Then he went before the Council of the Chieftains and all the gathered inhabitants of the hillfort to give a full report of the enemy's movements.

The veteran's proud features were visibly changed by what he had heard. In the firelight the lines upon his forehead stood out starkly, the wrinkles round his eyes seemed deeper. It was as if a dozen winters had descended upon him, draining his soul of its bright spark. Despite his obvious exhaustion, however, the old warrior still had an air of authority about him which demanded respect.

"In the dawn light they came," Fergus began. His voice was strained and cold. "Two times one hundred hard warriors from the southern lands fell upon our folk in the darkness. They gave no warning. They offered no terms. They asked for no truce."

Fergus scanned the crowd. All the folk who lived within the hillfort walls were staring blankly into the fires. Those of their kindred who had come to their aid from the other strongholds of the Burren were wide-eyed with awe at his speech.

"Our king has no quarrel with these folk," the veteran went on, "yet they burned our houses, our stocks of food and our halls. They drove our precious children from their beds and broke down our walls." The veteran paused, the events of the previous night vivid in his mind.

"And most outrageous of all," he went on, "they

made off with all our cattle save the few that were killed. Our goats were not all taken, for goats are canny creatures and run at the first sign of danger. Many have returned to us this evening."

Fergus took a slow deep breath composing himself for the next part of his tale. He did not want to betray his feelings as he spoke. "Truly these Gaedhals are a savage, unruly people. I find it difficult to believe they are our kin."

"Our distant kin," Brocan corrected him.

"To steal an enemy's cattle is to threaten starvation," the veteran continued. "Battle between seasoned warriors is hard enough to bear. But to involve the entire community by raiding food and stock illustrates the depths to which these folk will sink in order to conquer us. This is not war. It is barbarism."

The gathering voiced their agreement loudly. When they had calmed down Fergus went on. "Our way of life is under threat. The laws we hold dear are being flouted in a manner I never would have thought possible. Two hostages were taken also. They were both of the warrior class but they were unarmed when captured. Who would have thought it possible?"

Once again the assembly vented their outrage at this blatant breach of custom.

"How many of our folk were wounded in this action?" the king inquired.

"Twenty of our kin were injured," the veteran

replied solemnly. "By the mercy of Danu no one was killed."

"For that we can be thankful," Brocan cut in.

"Only two folk are still unaccounted for," Fergus went on. "They are two Druids of renown, Isleen the Seer and her husband Lochie the Bard. No trace of them has been found either among our people or in the ashes of the house in which they were sleeping."

Dalan cast a glance at Fineen. The healer nodded in silent acknowledgment of the point the Brehon was making to him.

"Hardest to bear of all, Riona, the queen of our folk who dwell in the Burren, the wife of our king, was one of the two taken hostage," Fergus stated. "And our honored guest King Cecht of the Tuatha De Danaan was with her. We have no tidings of where they may be now, nor indeed whether they be alive or dead. But the enemy left a message with young Aoife, daughter to the king, and she will speak her news now."

Aoife stood to take her place beside Fergus who waited with head bowed to hear her.

"It was Eber," the young trainee Druid started. "He is the brother of the chieftain of the Milesian Gaedhals. He planned and led this raid. He commanded me to report that his kin are tired of this war."

"Do they seek peace by raiding?" Brocan snapped and there were hums of agreement all around the fire.

"Eber claims he was ordered to make this raid by

his elder brother," she went on. "He wishes you all to know he did this under protest. It is not in his nature to make war on children and cattle."

"What else have they been doing these past four seasons?" someone called out from the crowd.

"The reason the Milesian chieftain resolved to undertake this raid," Aoife explained when the mutterings had died away, "was to force all the defenders of Innisfail into one last battle. The Gaedhals propose that the victor of this conflict gain the sovereignty of the land forever."

There was an immediate chorus of bitter indignation as everyone threw their opinion at the young woman. Fergus stepped forward and raised his hands.

"Silence!" the veteran bellowed. "The cows made less noise when they were being led away from their homes for the last time."

"The Gaedhals did not expect to capture a Danaan king and a Fir-Bolg queen," Aoife spoke up. "Eber was genuinely embarrassed at the captives he hauled in."

"Not embarrassed enough to release them," Brocan jibed. "Or our precious cattle. If it were not for the generosity of my neighbors and fellow chieftains, the Cauldron of Plenty would hold nothing but water this night."

"The Milesian has given his word the hostages will be returned to us unharmed before the battle," she went on. "And this fight will take place in nine nights near the foot of the mountains known as Sliabh Mis."

"Nine nights?" Brocan shouted in surprise. "It is at

least three days' march to that place. And it will take many more days to raise our warriors."

"Eber has thirty ships at his disposal and they are full of hardened warriors, men and women of the land of Iber," his daughter continued, trying to remember every detail of what she had been told. "His brother Éremon also has thirty ships. He is making a similar challenge in the northeast of Innisfail. There they will fight the gathered forces of the Danaans. The two brothers have split the countryside between them north and south."

"So we can't count on the support of the Danaans?" Brocan asked.

"I do not know," she answered.

Aoife closed her eyes to concentrate, desperate not to leave any detail out.

"Eber requests that Druids be sent to witness the outcome of the battle," she recalled, "and to agree on the exact location. He has offered our people the high ground in any such conflict as a gesture to our ancient occupation of this land. There is an apple tree growing on a hill at the foot of Sliabh Mis which he says would easily be defended. Eber said he would respect that spot as our gathering place."

"And what if we should be defeated?" the king asked. "What then?"

"We are to withdraw from the southern part of the island," she replied, "or submit to him as king of this country."

Once again there were expressions of disgust and

cries of anger from the crowd. Fergus tried to still the gathering but in the end he decided it was best to let the fury burn out of them a little before he made any attempt to continue the proceedings.

A bronze pot larger than the Cauldron of Plenty was brought forward and cups were soon dipping into it. Fergus took his cupful of the hazel-flavored mead. Then he sat down by the fire to warm himself. The veteran did not want to waste any time but there were many in the gathering who had some comment to make and he was bound by tradition to let them speak.

When Brocan finally stood up and raised his hands for silence Fergus jumped to his feet.

"We may muster at most one hundred warriors," he told his king and the waiting audience. "It will take seven days at least. Then we will march hard to arrive at the field in time, but I believe it can be done."

"One hundred is only half the number of the Gaedhals," Brocan reminded his steward. "I will not risk that the Milesians have more warriors in reserve. How many more can we raise?"

"Maybe ten or twelve at the most," Fergus admitted. "If we press the aged and untried into service. Any other able-bodied men and women are beyond the reach of the summons. If we had another week I could have two hundred on the field."

"We don't have any more time," Dalan cut in. "Nine nights and that is all."

Brocan turned to face the people seated around the

fire. "And what if we do not accept this challenge?" he asked them.

Most of the gathering fell silent, confused by this question. It was unthinkable that they should ignore the insult leveled at them. Besides, most folk were concerned about the loss of their cattle. If it came to winter and they had no stock, there would surely be famine.

"If we cannot be certain we will defeat the Milesians outright," Brocan reasoned, "it would be stupidity to face them in battle. Their weapons are superior to ours, the Druid Assembly can attest to that. And they may have many more warriors than we can possibly field."

"The lives of Riona and Cecht may be in danger," Fineen protested and there were many who agreed with him. "They are being held as surety. What will happen to them if we do not concede to this demand for battle?"

"I'll not be forced into a fight which we cannot possibly win," the king countered, but it was clear the gathering would not support him in this. So Brocan, ever the one to give his kinfolk whatever they wanted, began to consider the likely outcome of a battle while he continued to argue against it.

"The lives of two are nothing compared to the future of our people. This challenge only has power over us if we accept it. If we choose to ignore the summons, we show our contempt for their claim over our land. If we fight them we legitimize their invasion."

He surveyed the crowd. "I advise that we do nothing. Let the Milesians come to us. Next time we will be ready for them."

Dalan raised his eyebrows. The Brehon could see the sense in this argument but he knew the Fir-Bolg of the Burren would not accept the king's wishes in this. They were stirred up by the loss of their stock. And if Brocan had not, just the night before, opposed an alliance with the Danaans, he may have had their ears. But now the chieftains were muttering that their king simply did not have the stomach for fighting.

"What of the cows?" an old woman called out. "Would you have us starve?"

"Our neighbors will aid us," Brocan replied confidently. "As we have always aided them in times of crisis."

"How will we pay the fines levied against us by the Brehons," Lom interjected, "if we have no cattle to give to Cecht?"

The king narrowed his eyes at his son, wondering whether the boy had said this to turn attention to himself. Brocan decided his son would one day make a fine king. He had an excellent sense of the people's opinion.

"It's the duty of a king to defend his people," Fergus spoke up, voicing what was on everyone's mind. "If a king can't guarantee the safety and security of the folk he is appointed to protect, then he is not entitled to the kingship."

"But if he wastes the lives of his kinfolk in a forced challenge which they have no hope of winning, is he a better king? If he loses the land to which he and his kinfolk were born, is he a wise ruler? There is more to the office of kingship than most of you might think. This is not a time for hasty decisions and heated revenge. The loss of the cows will hurt us, it is true. But the loss of our land will be the end of our people."

"Brocan is right!" Dalan cut in, standing up to be noticed. Everyone gasped in amazement. None of them expected the Brehon to support the king on this matter.

"The odds are against us," he went on, carefully gauging the reaction to his words as he spoke. "We would be dancing to a Milesian tune to engage in this contest."

"Even the Druids see the sense in what I am saying," the king stated with confidence.

"Of all of us Brocan has the most to lose," Dalan went on. "His wife may never return to him."

"And what about our homes and cattle?" one chieftain spat.

"The homes can be rebuilt," the Brehon soothed. "And the cattle will have to be bred from your neighbors' stock. No lives have been lost so far. If we are careful no one should die for this cause. Brocan is right. We have very little chance of victory against these savages."

The crowd roared their disgust but the Brehon simply held up a hand until the gathering was silent again. His ploy had worked. The Fir-Bolg of the Burren were hot with anger and resentment. They would not be stopped in their quest for revenge.

"Poverty is nothing new to the Fir-Bolg," the Brehon stated. "Our folk have survived harder times than this. The war against the Fomor was no less harsh."

"Some of the kings refused to fight in those days also," someone muttered.

"If the king won't fight," another voice suggested, "then perhaps we need a new king."

Brocan raised his eyebrows in surprise. He was already considering how to gracefully bow to pressure.

"The simple truth is," Dalan spoke up, making his move, "we could triumph in this conflict. Brocan is right, we may not win this battle. However, if we fight their contest, we will certainly be victorious in the war."

"How is that so?" Fergus grunted with suspicion.

"They outnumber us," the Brehon went on. "Their weapons will make short work of ours. Their warriors will be well rested. But we have a secret in store they have not even dreamed of."

He paused to make sure he had everyone's attention.

"The Druid Assembly foresaw this day," he went on. "They preserved the Draoi-Music which our ancestors practiced in the days before the destruction of the Isles of the West. The Assembly has decided to use this music to open the doorway between the worlds."

There was a general mutter of awe.

"Will we enter into the Otherworld?" Brocan asked. "I would rather fight than retreat."

"The Draoi-Seers and the Druid musicians are already on their way here from the north. They will arrive in two days."

"I have no wish to leave my home," Brocan stated flatly.

"What will we eat in the Otherworld?" came a call from the crowd. "Are there many cows in that place?"

Dalan smiled until he realized the comment had not been a joke at all.

"I have been entrusted with nine berries of the ancient Quicken Tree," the Brehon continued, brushing over the question. "These are the same berries which grew in the land of Murias in the time of our ancestors."

He removed the pouch from inside his tunic and held it up for all to see. Then he handed it to Fineen. "I give them now into a physician's hands. He will prepare the brew."

Fineen passed the leather pouch directly to his student, Sárán, for safe keeping.

"What good are the fruits of the Quicken Tree to us?" the king scoffed.

"Will they fill our empty bellies?" someone cut in.

"As you know, a potion brewed from the berries will ensure none among our war party perishes from his injuries," the Druid explained. "The Milesians will be so awed by this miracle they will readily make a treaty with us. The first thing we will demand is the return of our cows, for we will take them with us and eat well in the Otherworld. Once the treaty is agreed, our people will withdraw into the Otherworld and remain there in peace for the rest of eternity."

"I will not abandon my land to the invaders!" Brocan shouted defiantly.

"You will not have to," Dalan explained. "The Otherworld is not separate from this world. The two are intricately linked. Our new home exists in the realm beyond the doorway. At the same time Dun Burren will remain here on this side of the door. Our folk will be able to cross back and forth as they wish. But the Milesians will not be able to cross over into the Otherworld unless we allow it."

"I will not be a party to this," the king stated. "I sense Danaan trickery in this tactic."

"It may be the only way to retrieve our cows and keep off hunger come the winter."

"There is no honor in this action."

"You must join the alliance or risk that your chieftains will take part without you."

"Let the chieftains go."

"If they go you will no longer be King of the Fir-Bolg of the Burren."

"It seems to me that will be the outcome no matter which choice I make," Brocan noted wryly. "So I will take the decision which costs me the least affront."

"Your presence and that of your clanhold are essential if we are to make a good impression on the enemy," Dalan reasoned.

"A good impression? I do not go into battle to make a good impression. I go to defeat my enemies and end their threat."

"A Fir-Bolg presence without you and your immediate kinfolk would tip the scales too far in favor of the Gaedhals," the Brehon pressed. "Without you we will not be able to hold our ground for long enough."

"Sixty warriors will stand by me," the Fir-Bolg king countered with venom. "If that robs your force of warriors I cannot be held responsible."

"Do you think by ignoring the invaders they will simply go away?" the Brehon scoffed, unable to believe Brocan's stubbornness in the face of his people's opinion. "Beware, there is an opportunity in that assertion for the composition of a very eloquent satire on the duties of a king."

"Do not threaten me with satire!" Brocan warned. "I don't fear your poetic tricks. Say what you will. I care not. But when you have lost your land and your hope to these foreigners, remember it was because you danced merrily to their tune."

Dalan smiled and nodded, acknowledging the king was quoting the Druid's own earlier words.

"I lift my feet to the melody of my own choosing," Brocan declared.

"Very well then." Dalan hardened his tone. "I had hoped it would not come to this." He took a deep breath and glanced at Fineen to make sure the healer was still supporting him. When his brother Druid shrugged and rolled his eyes, Dalan went on. "Is there anything that could persuade you to take the field?"

Brocan breathed out heavily. At last he seemed to be getting the upper hand in this negotiation. But outwardly he still regarded the Brehon with suspicion. "What do you mean?"

"Is there any price you would put on the lives of your warriors in battle?" Dalan pressed. "To put it another way, what would it take to convince you to aid the Danaans and all the people of Innisfail in their time of need?"

The king tried to hide his joy. One moment his kingship had seemed to be at an end, the next the Brehon had offered him a wonderful gift which would win his people back to him.

"Remission," Brocan replied sharply and without hesitation. "An unconditional remission of the verdicts placed upon us without shame to my people or to myself. Nothing short of the annulment of your judgment of a fine against us for Fearna's death will convince me to take part in this adventure."

There was a collective gasp from the gathering. Some of the chieftains openly praised Brocan's wisdom at holding out for this valuable concession, but most were as surprised as Brocan by this turn of events.

Dalan cast his eyes to the ground in defeat.

Brocan observed the look and read it as unfavorable. "I will consider nothing less," the Fir-Bolg king reinforced. "The debt must be wiped out, now and forever."

Dalan sighed as he raised his eyes to meet Brocan's. When the Brehon spoke his voice was uncharacteristically subdued. "That is quite a concession you are asking the Danaans and the Druid Assembly to make. Is that the only way I can ensure your participation?"

"If the Brehon judges can approve such a remission I will recommend to the chieftains of my people that we form an alliance with the Danaans."

"And what of the Druid Assembly's plan to open the doors to the Otherworld?"

"I will put that to the chieftains in a separate council."

"Very well," Dalan said quietly and without emotion. Then he dipped his cup into the mead pot and went back to his seat. No one uttered a sound as the Brehon sipped his liquor.

Brocan frowned, not understanding what Dalan meant. "You don't have the authority to make such a decision alone," the king protested.

"I am authorized by the Druid Assembly to offer whatever concessions are necessary to gain your support."

"You will truly reverse the judgment?"

Dalan got to his feet again as he drained the cup to refresh his voice. "From this moment your debt is annulled. Any cattle already delivered to Cecht remain his property but there will be no more payments. As long as you honor a treaty with the Tuatha De Danaan and fight in this battle against the Milesians with all your warriors, my judgment is reversed."

The Fir-Bolg king smiled. Then as the full meaning of the Brehon's words hit him, he began to laugh. But suddenly a thought crossed his mind. He did not want it said he had sold the services of his warriors to another king.

"I must consider the situation more carefully before I hasten to give my word on it," Brocan muttered.

"You will be well paid for your skills as a warrior," Danal cut in. And then he turned to face the crowd still listening intently. "King Brocan of the Fir-Bolg of the Burren has agreed to a treaty with the Danaan," the Brehon began. "He will supply warriors for an expedition to fight the Milesians. And in return for their loyalty his people will be freed of their debt to King Cecht. This is my judgment."

"The Fir-Bolg are now mercenaries," Fergus cried out in disgust. Everyone turned to look at him as he removed his cloak and laid it in the midst of the fire. Then he took his leather boots and threw them in to burn as well. The veteran kept nothing but his roughly stitched woolen trousers.

Then the veteran spoke and his voice was weary, angry and cold. "Fergus watched his house and the hall of his king burn down last night. He saw his kinfolk run for their lives. But Fergus is not a mercenary. Fergus will not accept a Danaan king as his overlord. The Fir-Bolg may well lose sovereignty over their land if this treaty is made. The Danaans will become our rulers. I would rather pay the heavy fine to the Tuatha De Danaan, stay out of this fight with the Milesians and see my folk retain their freedom. In fact I would prefer to deal with the Gaedhals than with Cecht's people."

With that the veteran pushed his way past the seated folk and vanished into the night.

Brocan was visibly shaken. He had grown up with Fergus and he understood that frustration had brought this proud warrior to say such things, yet he was shocked his brother would so openly stand against his decision. Nevertheless, he forgave his foster-brother without a moment's hesitation.

Brocan was silent for a long while as voices were raised around him, some in favor of the deal, some bitterly opposed. In the end the king knew the best path to take would be to secure an annulment of the debt and then see what the future held. With luck, he told himself, there might not be any need to go to war.

"I have made up my mind," he said at last. "Since our cattle are gone I must think of the future. The debt will be wiped out so the burden on our kinfolk will be eased. We may even retrieve our cows before this adventure is concluded."

Then he took a mouthful of mead, readying himself to give the orders.

"Tonight I will send scouts to bring in as many of our warriors as possible from outlying duns and forts.

They will meet our main force at Sliabh Mis. I and my warriors march at sunrise for the south. If we arrive early our people will be well rested in time for the fight."

No one dared to speak up against him. Everyone was glad this was not their decision to make.

"I want twenty warriors who are willing to accompany me to the battleground. We will assemble after first light. Now everyone go to bed. There is much to be done in the morning and we all need our rest."

No one moved.

"Now!" he ordered.

Suddenly the courtyard was alive with movement as folk found places to rest for the night or gathered their closest kin about them. Brocan wrapped his cloak tightly around his body to keep out the cold air coming up from the bay. Then he called for the chieftains and the fastest scouts.

Dalan pulled the hood of his own cloak over his eyes and went to the fire to lie down. Fineen touched his comrade's shoulder to congratulate him but the Brehon's eyes were already shut tight. At last Aoife managed to push her way through the crowd to his side. She shook Dalan lightly as she spoke, surprised he seemed to be resting so soundly.

"What do we do now?" she asked.

"Sleep," the Brehon told her. "Tomorrow you and I have a long journey ahead of us."

Chapter 19

By the time Sárán finished cleaning his teacher's herb bowls at the spring it was well after midnight. The water skins were full and all the silver measuring cups packed away in their leather case when he rose to return to the hillfort.

The young novice had shouldered Fineen's bag and was preparing to climb the hill when he noticed the tiny orange glow of a fire on the other side of the valley. He knew he should be getting back to the hillfort to sleep but his curiosity was aroused. Carefully he stowed the bag and the water skins by the holly tree which grew by the spring. Then he made his way off toward the tempting light.

If they were Milesians, he decided, they would surely not harm him. Aoife's treatment had shown they respected the Druid kind, even novices such as himself. Any of his own people would all be within the fortress of Dun Burren, even though the breached

walls offered little protection. Still he walked mind-
fully on, making as little noise as possible. The ground
on this side of the fort was rocky and difficult to cross
under moonlight, so it was some time before the
young man came close to the fire.

To be sure he was not putting himself in danger
Sárán sat back behind a large boulder to survey the
scene. Before him was a perfectly constructed fire,
small but burning brightly. It was well provided with
a stack of kindling and a store of fuel. A few steps
from the fire, lit by the flickering flames and laid out
on a piece of dark cloth, was the body of a cleanly
plucked gosling. The bird had been pierced by a long
bronze skewer. It now waited to be roasted over the
flames.

"Will you sit there among the rocks all night?" a
woman's voice called and suddenly a figure appeared
in the firelight.

It was Isleen.

"Come and share this feast with me, young Sárán,"
she offered. "While it roasts we will talk."

The young man stood up, feeling rather stupid at
having concealed himself so poorly.

"If I had been a Gaedhal," she laughed, "I would
have set out to hunt you when I heard you clambering
over the rocks."

"I thought I was making very little noise," Sárán
replied good-naturedly, accepting the gentle ridicule
as he walked over to the fire.

Isleen placed the cleaned bird high over the flames

so it would roast evenly then searched around in her pack until she found a leather flask.

"Let's have a drink to keep out the cold," she offered, passing the bottle to the young man.

"I am warm enough," he protested but even as he spoke the air seemed to take on a chilly bite.

"Drink," the woman told him firmly and Sárán took the flask without any further hesitation.

"What are you doing here so far from the hillfort?" the novice asked her after he had swallowed a gulp of mead. "What happened to you last night? And where is your husband?"

"He's probably off with Dalan talking of the troubles that have beset us all. Those two must think they are young again. And like young men I'm sure they believe they can solve the world's woes," she replied. "I came out here for some peace after the excitement of the last day and night."

"Are you not concerned there may be Milesians about?"

"Sit down, Sárán, and warm yourself. You know as well as I do that the invaders have sailed south to make preparations for their battle-challenge. Considering everyone will be traveling toward Sliabh Mis in the morning, this may be the last chance I have to be alone with my thoughts. But I don't really mind that you have come to talk with me. I'm sure there is much to be said between us."

"You haven't answered my question," he pressed as he took a seat by the fire.

"I made my way down to the sea when I escaped from the hall," she explained. "What happened to you?"

"My brother found me."

The aroma of the roasting bird filled his senses so completely he was distracted by it. The next thing he knew his mouth was watering and he was staring at the slowly cooking food.

"Have you eaten since last night?" Isleen inquired warmly.

"I've been working alongside Fineen for most of the day. There was so much to do, and since he did not stop to eat I considered it best that I fast also."

"Fasting has its place," the woman told him sternly. "If you are seeking inspiration through dreams, if you wish to discover your limits, or if there is simply not enough food to go around, then it is a helpful practice. But if you are tending to the wounded and the sick you must keep up your strength. If you do not you will fall ill yourself."

Sárán nodded politely to acknowledge the advice.

"If I am to be your teacher you must take my words very seriously. You must never hesitate to do as I bid you," she added.

"Fineen is my teacher," the young man protested. "I am bound to him in payment of my fine."

"Did he not tell you?"

"Tell me what?"

"You are to travel under my tuition for a while," Isleen informed him. "It's all been arranged. I thought that's why you sought me out at my fire."

"I honestly had no idea," Sárán replied, shaking his head. "When was this arranged?"

"Two moons ago. Bless him but Fineen is quite forgetful sometimes." She smiled. "Have you got all your things together?"

"No."

"That's too bad." She frowned. "For as soon as we have eaten we are off to find the Milesians. You won't have time to go back to the hillfort now."

"I left Fineen's bags of herbs and the water skins by the spring."

"They'll be safe there until morning. Someone will retrieve them."

"It'll only take me a little while to take them back to the fort and say my farewells."

"We are about to set out on a long journey," Isleen said sternly. "You have already told me you have not eaten for some time. There will be precious little chance to cook a decent meal once we are on the road. You will stay here and eat with me," she demanded. "And you will rest a short while before we set out."

"Let me go bid farewell to Fineen."

"No. You must become accustomed to accepting orders from your betters."

Sárán's shoulders slumped in disappointment. "I wish he had told me of this plan," the young man muttered.

"Don't look so dejected." Isleen smiled, passing him the leather mead flask again. "You never know what you might learn from me. Perhaps you'll even enjoy yourself. You'll certainly gain the knowledge you need to one day become a High Druid."

"I would rather speak with my teacher, even if it's very briefly."

"You'll see him at the field of contest at Sliabh Mis," she soothed. "You have the Quicken berries, don't you?"

Sárán frowned.

"How did you know that?"

"Fineen told me to guard both you and your precious berries well," Isleen explained. "And so I shall. Now we must rest."

At Isleen's insistence they slept only a short while after they had eaten. Then they made final preparations for the journey. Three hours before the dawn, when all was perfectly quiet around the sacked hillfort of Dun Burren, the Seer and her newly acquired student slipped away to the south.

By sunrise they were already coming to the edge of the rocky ground of the Burren. At midday, with Isleen setting the pace, they could see the mouth of the River Shannon in the distance. The Seer reckoned they'd reach water by nightfall.

At the edge of a forest where the road plunged in among the trees they came to a wide but poorly maintained crossroads. Here Isleen called a brief halt by a standing stone which stood at the edge of a pool. The water fed out of a spring under the upright granite slab.

The Seer leaned against the stone and muttered under her breath a string of words which Sárán could neither hear nor interpret. While she did that her student filled a leather mug with water.

Isleen finished her strange prayer and turned around to look directly at her young companion. "In the ancient days this was a busy place," she informed him. "Though the forest is encroaching on it now, this crossroads was a trading center where Fir-Bolg and Fomor came together to exchange news and barter for each other's goods."

"Were there Fomorians near here?"

"Down that road to the west lies Dun Beg, the last stronghold of the followers of Balor. It's a dangerous path and one not to be traveled by the unwary. Lost souls wander there and the forest has an appetite for the well journeyed. Many folk go missing on this road."

"What do you mean?" Sárán asked nervously, something in her tone making him feel very uneasy.

"I mean it is wise to keep your wits about you. Never go off into the forest by yourself and never trust everything you see or hear while you are passing under its dark canopy."

Then she noticed the cup full of water in the young man's hand. "And whatever you do," she advised sternly. "You must never, ever drink from that spring."

"Why not?"

"Because though it seems sweet in the daylight and looks remarkably fresh, this pool is poisoned. All those who drink from it are doomed to become at one with the ever-living forest."

Brocan lay among his salvaged clothing until the sunlight would not let him sleep any longer. It had been his intention to get the warriors moving early but he was exhausted and demoralized. And his people were faring no better.

"It's all very well for Dalan to speak of my obligations to the Druid Assembly and to the Danaans. But what of the folk we will leave behind?" he asked himself. "Who will defend them if the Milesians should sail back into the bay to indulge in some more raiding?"

He blessed the wisdom of his forebears who constructed storage caves near the hillfort. And he thanked the stars he had the good sense to keep them well stocked. No one would starve, he assured himself, and that was something to be proud of.

Brocan sat up amongst the gathered remnants of his clothing and his singed furs and stretched his arms as he yawned. Dun Burren was beginning to stir. A few cooking fires were smoking with the smell of oats in great pots.

The king stared at the empty space just beyond his feet. He puzzled for a moment, wondering who would have dared to take the Cauldron of Plenty to cook their breakfast without waking him. It was unheard of that anyone would simply neglect to ask him if they could borrow it.

In seconds he was on his feet making his way to each of the cooking fires. But wherever he went folk were using their own salvaged utensils. The cauldron was nowhere to be found. Brocan never once considered it might have been stolen until he found Fergus seated by a fire, stirring his oats as they boiled.

"Good morning, my lord," the veteran greeted him. "Sit down and join me. Breakfast is nearly done."

"Where is the Cauldron of Plenty?" the king asked without replying to the invitation.

Fergus looked up blankly. "I last saw it when you were cleaning it out before bed."

"I can't find it," Brocan whispered, not wishing anyone else to know for now.

"Can't find it?"

"When I went to sleep it was at my feet. When I awoke it was gone."

"Someone has borrowed it without thinking." Fergus shrugged. "Do not think ill of any of your folk if they have forgotten their manners just now. Everyone is in shock."

"I have searched Dun Burren from fire to fire," the king snapped. "It is gone."

"Gone?" the veteran quizzed. "It must be here somewhere. Unless the Milesians crept back into the camp in the night and spirited it away."

His comment had only been half serious but it struck a chord with both men.

"In the name of Holy Danu herself!" Brocan hissed. "Where are the sentries?"

"I'll fetch them," Fergus replied and was gone to wake the warriors who had been standing guard during the dark hours.

When he returned two young men followed him, sleepy-eyed and confused.

"Did you notice anything unusual in the night?" Brocan demanded immediately.

Both men shook their heads.

"Did anyone enter the camp after sunset?"

Again the two warriors shook their heads with certainty.

"But young Sárán, your son, went out after sunset and he did not return," one man offered.

"Sárán?" Brocan hissed. "What mischief is he playing at now?"

The king dismissed the sentries to go back to their rest, then turned to Fergus. "Find that lad and bring him to me," he commanded. Then the King of the Fir-Bolg sat down by the fire to stir the oats and try to clear his thoughts.

To have lost all his cattle and livestock in the Milesian raid was enough of an insult to his pride. But the cauldron had been given into his care by the Dagda of the Danaan Druids as a peace offering. It was his duty as King of the Fir-Bolg to protect it. If the sacred vessel was missing, it would bring shame on him and all the people of the Burren.

When Fergus returned he did not have to say anything. The look on his face told his news for him.

"He is gone?" Brocan asked.

The veteran nodded. "It seems so. There is no sign of him in the dun. Fineen expected him to return last night after he had finished his chores at the spring. But he has not been seen."

"Why would my own son steal the cauldron?" Brocan asked himself. Then he turned to Fergus and looked him in the eye. "Is it likely that Sárán may have been taken by intruders as he worked at the spring?"

The veteran looked away to avoid the king's eyes. "The healer told me he gave Sárán the Quicken berries to guard with his life."

Brocan closed his eyes and bowed his head. "Send out your fastest scouts. I want him brought back immediately. That lad will pay dearly for this crime. He has shamed me and our people. And he has stolen the berries which are our only hope of saving lives in the coming battle."

"I have already dispatched my two fastest runners," Fergus reported. "I sent them south toward the mouth of the great river. If Sárán is attempting to make his way to the Milesian camp, that is the route he will most likely take. At the shore he will probably find himself a boat to cross the water."

"He will then make the Deer Island," Brocan added.

Fergus nodded agreement.

"If the scouts do not find him before he sets off for the southern shore of the Shannon's mouth, they will have no chance of finding him," the king noted bitterly. "Then we will find ourselves in trouble."

"We have no hope of making a good stand against

the Milesians if Fineen cannot prepare the brew in time," Fergus agreed.

"Yet we must go to the battle now," the king groaned. "I have given my word. If only we could have stayed out of this fight."

"I am sorry for standing against you last night," the veteran offered. "I did not reckon without the life-brew of the Druids."

"Find that boy," Brocan ordered. "Bring him back to me with the berries and the cauldron. I will set out with the main body of warriors soon. But you are to take your best trackers and your swiftest runners, five battle veterans, ahead of us. You must stop that lad before he gets as far as the Shannon Waters."

"Yes, my lord."

Fergus bowed, turned around and in minutes had gathered his small team of warriors. Before the oatmeal had begun to burn in the bottom of the cooking pot they were off, picking their way over the rugged terrain, headed for the fishing settlement on the Island of the Deer.

When Dalan awoke, the settlement was already abuzz with the tale of Sárán's treachery. Fineen came over to the Brehon as the news was being discussed by two warriors.

"Is it true?" Dalan asked his friend.

The healer nodded. "One man may be content to listen to the gentle lapping waters of the lough," he sighed. "Another is compelled to toss a stone to hear the splash. I find it hard to believe Sárán would do such a thing, but the evidence would seem to suggest my student has proved to be a traitor."

"Is it possible he was taken by the invaders?"

"The Milesians raid in large groups. It is rare for a small party of their warriors to be abroad alone. And if Sárán were taken it would have had to have been by a party of only a few warriors."

"Because a large group would have been seen by the scouts or the sentries," the Brehon concluded.

"I should not have trusted him with the berries," Fineen rebuked himself. "But over the last four seasons I have grown to trust him like a friend. He is always dependable and accepts the most menial of tasks cheerfully. I don't know what could have inspired him to take this action."

"We both know there is no love lost between father and son."

"But this treachery puts every warrior of the Fir-Bolg at risk of death," the healer reasoned. "I just can't understand it."

"Would you say he follows orders without question?" asked Dalan.

"Absolutely. That is what makes his treachery all the more puzzling."

"If a Druid other than yourself were to give him a command," the Brehon inquired, "do you think he would balk at it?"

"No."

"I think we need look no further than Lochie and

Isleen," Dalan decided. "They are recognized as Druids and they both have an air of authority about them."

"You're right!" Fineen gasped. "They must have tricked him, but why?"

"Many things have become clear to me with the destruction of Dun Burren." The Brehon lowered his voice. "I sense that Isleen and Lochie are the Watchers."

"If this is true there will be panic amongst the Fir-Bolg if the news is made public," the healer whispered.

"Then we must not tell anyone."

"We can't keep it to ourselves!"

"Brocan will surely withdraw his tenuous support if he suspects Balor's seed are still among us. We will be fortunate if his warriors join the fight as it is. When they hear the berries are gone, they will think twice about endangering their lives. And that will make our chances of negotiating a favorable treaty almost impossible."

"What can we do?"

"I'll find Lochie," Dalan declared, "and confront him."

"And if he has disappeared also?"

"I'll track down Sárán and bring back the sacred berries of the Quicken Tree myself," the Brehon declared. "I will meet you on the plain by the foot of Sliabh Mis in three days' time. It is too late to send to the east for more berries. If I have not recovered them by that time, then all is lost."

With that the Brehon grabbed his Raven-feather cloak, slung his harp upon his back and silently took his leave of the healer.

"May the spirit of Danu go with you," the healer whispered after Dalan had gone. "And may the Watchers be vanquished."

Then Fineen went to search for his herbs and utensils down at the stream, all the while marveling at the fact that the famed King of the Fomor had reached out a ghostly hand to strike at his enemies after generations in the grave.

King Cecht of the Tuatha De Danaan and Queen Riona of the Fir-Bolg were taken on board Eber's ship to the south after they were captured. They spent that day and the next at sea out of sight of land until the Milesian fleet came in to shelter within view of the mountains known as Sliabh Mis.

Scota, the king's mother and a queen in her own right, said nothing to either of them even though she recognized Riona from her dream. But she never left their company for the space of a breath unless a trusted and able guard could take her place. And the ochre-painted queen always had her spear at the ready.

The captives were treated as befitted their rank but they weren't permitted to make a sound throughout the voyage. Eber left them to his mother's watchful eye. He didn't approach them until they were all seated in a rowing boat headed for shore.

Ahead, beneath the mountains where the land swept round into a shelter bay, the Milesians had made camp. Smoke from many fires was drifting skyward. The wind had dropped by sunset and the rain clouds were retreating across to the western horizon.

"We two are the rulers of our people," Cecht informed his captor proudly. "Among our folk this sort of raiding would be considered dishonorable."

Eber listened carefully, discerning the meaning behind the strangely accented speech. "My people don't consider raiding a dishonorable practice," he replied. "I'm sorry to have caused offense. I don't wish any ransom for your release. I merely intend to ensure your warriors meet mine at the appointed hour and place."

"You've broken with the customs of war," Riona spat. "This is an outrage against the Brehon laws."

"This land is now under the rule of law of the Milesian Brehons," Eber informed her in as polite a tone as he could muster. "My judges have advised me that as long as I release you before the battle I will be within my rights as King of the South of Eriu."

Cecht frowned to show he didn't understand the last part of the speech. "Eriu is a queen of the Danaan people in the north," he said after a moment. "You use her name as if it belonged to the land."

"It does now," the Milesian warrior replied. "When my brother Amergin the Bard met Queen Eriu to negotiate a treaty between our people she promised to work toward a peaceful solution if we named the land after her."

"Eriu is my mother," Riona said. "She always was self-centered and rather fond of herself," she added wryly. "But this land is and always will be known as Innisfail, the Island of Destiny."

"My people are the rulers of this island now," Scota cut in sharply. "We'll call it what we wish."

"And you are the queen of these barbarous folk?" Cecht cut in.

"I am a queen by right of election and appointment by the Chief Bard of our folk."

"Who just happens to be your son?" The Danaan sneered. "And are any of your ancestors worthy of the office of king or queen? Or is this an innovation that has recently been awarded to your kin?"

"My father was a king of our people," Eber snapped. "My mother is descended from a princess of the eastern countries."

"For one who claims royal descent," Riona noted dryly, "you have the air of an outlaw about you."

"We've been fighting against your kind since the last cycle of the seasons," the Milesian retorted. "I can't help it if I'm forced to fight running skirmishes with warriors who'll not stand and fight like valorous heroes. You should have given this land over to us long ago. It's just foolish, stubborn and wishful to cling on till the last. Why do you think I've had to force your hand?"

"The taking of duly elected rulers in war is forbidden unless they are bearing arms," Riona protested. "That's why we have stewards and champions, so the continued stability and safety of the people are not at risk from overzealous, uneducated, impatient brigands such as yourself."

"You will not speak to me like that!" Eber shouted, losing his temper. "I have seen enough good warriors fall trying to wrest this land from your control. I have had enough."

"Then why don't you go home?" Cecht asked quietly.

"This is our home," Scota replied. "My son is King of the South of this island and you'd better get used to it. My warriors will walk over yours in the coming battle and then we'll see who deserves to claim sovereignty."

"We won't submit," the Danaan king laughed. "My folk won't give in to your demands just because you hold me hostage."

"You may be surprised," Eber answered.

"You are a boy," Riona laughed. "In the land of the Burren you wouldn't be king of a cowshed."

"Be quiet!" Eber demanded.

"Do you know who you are talking to?" Riona asked him in surprise. "Or is it simply too much to expect any decency from you folk?"

"You will be quiet or I will have you gagged."

"Gagged?" Cecht muttered in shock. "The Brehons would demand a fortune you don't have as a blush fine for such actions."

"My Brehons would not make such a judgment." Eber smiled. "Not against me."

"Your Brehons are not versed in the laws of this land and the customs of our people."

"They do not need to be," the Milesian shot back. "You are not the rulers of this country anymore."

"We will still be here when your folk are quoting our laws and singing our songs." The Danaan smirked. "You are not the first people to attempt to take our island from us."

"Let him be, Cecht." Riona sneered. "He's not worthy of our anger."

"Cecht?" Scota repeated, unsure if she had heard correctly. "Your name is King Cecht of the Tuatha De Danaan?"

"Yes."

"You have a son called Mahon?"

"Yes. How did you know that?"

"He's a fine lad. You should be proud of him."

"You've met my son?" the Danaan king stuttered in disbelief.

"I dreamt that a king and a queen dwelt in Dun Burren," Scota admitted reluctantly. "And I was guided to my landing place by that same sleep vision. That's how we came across you. I've been dreaming about this country since my husband died thirteen winters ago."

"You've dreamt about Mahon?"

"I have." Scota's eyes suddenly filled with tears.

"But it was no dream brought you to Dun Burren

on the night of our meeting," the Danaan mumbled as he drew his conclusions from all he had heard. "You came because you were informed I would be there."

Then the king turned to Riona. "There's a traitor among us."

"You're wrong!" Eber protested but he was too sharp with his indignation.

"How did you pay the informer to betray his own kinfolk?" the king asked. "What did you give? Your folk have no laws. You're not civilized enough to hold this land."

Eber ignored the insult and hailed the warriors on the shore. As soon as the boat struck the soft sand of the beach he leapt out immediately and shouted instructions to his people. "Feed them, water them and lock them away where they can't observe our preparations," he commanded. "And if I hear so much as a word from either of them I'll have the head of the sentry appointed to guard them."

Then he turned to his captives and bowed quickly without any pretense at concealing his contempt. "I trust your stay with us will be comfortable, and I pray to the gods of my people it will be short."

Then Eber, self-proclaimed King of the South, stormed off to wash and find himself some clean clothes.

Scota was not so abrupt with the captives. She took Cecht's hand as they parted and held it while she spoke. "Your son won't be harmed in the battle," she whispered. "I've dreamed his part in it. So let him fight in the thick of it if he so wishes. I guarantee his safety."

"Have you truly seen this in a vision?"

Scota nodded. "I have." She smiled.

Then she laid her spear down in the sand and left the two captives with their guards.

Chapter 20

FERGUS AND HIS FIVE WARRIORS HAD MADE VERY GOOD
time to begin with. They had set a solid pace without
running, for the veteran did not want to exhaust his
men's battle-readiness. The search party had just
come to the crossroads marked with a standing stone
when one of the scouts reported a strange sight.

Where the western road turned a sharp bend
about two hundred paces into the forest, he had seen
a tall woman with red hair accompanied by a younger
man who fitted Sárán's description. Fergus had been
unwilling to take this road at first because he knew
where it led—to the ruined stronghold of the Fomor.

"Conor," he told the man, "I want you to scout
ahead down the eastern road for a thousand paces.
The rest of us will sit for a while and take a breath. If
you see anything, blow as hard as you can on your
horn and we will come to your aid."

The scout ran off on his errand while Fergus sat

down by the stone to wait. He traced a finger over the signs cut into the massive tooth of granite but he had no idea what they might mean. In a moment he had taken his leather tankard from his belt and scooped up some water from the spring. As he held it to his mouth to drink there was a strange unfamiliar bird call nearby so he stopped to listen.

But the call was not repeated so Fergus drank a deep draught of the clear cooling water. Following the veteran's lead the others were soon dipping their tankards into the pool. By the time Conor returned each of them had banished his thirst.

"What did you see?" Fergus demanded.

"Nothing," came the report. Then the scout got on his knees to drink up the water in large mouthfuls from the surface of the pool.

"Whoever you saw was heading down to the west," the veteran noted. "If I don't investigate we may regret it. I don't want Sárán escaping with the cauldron. I can't risk that."

Reluctantly Fergus decided to split his force, leaving two warriors at the crossroads. He and the rest of the search party then set off toward the deserted Fomor settlement of Dun Beg. They had not walked far down the ancient path when the two figures appeared again in the distance.

"Run!" Fergus shouted to his comrades. "If we don't we'll never catch them!"

At that pace it was not long before they came to a darker part of the forest where the trees formed a great roof over the narrow road. As they moved on the air became stale and the light dimmed. Fergus slowed his warriors and they walked on more cautiously.

"I don't like this place," the veteran muttered. "I've heard too many tales about the forest of Dun Beg."

Just then the veteran heard voices not too far away in amongst the trees. He turned around, trying to judge their direction, and before he could call out one of his warriors was rushing off to chase the noise.

"Come back, Conor, you fool!" Fergus cried. "This wood is no place to be wandering, even before sunset."

But the man paid no heed and was soon gone from sight and sound. The veteran had to restrain the other two warriors to stop them following.

"It is death to enter the forest alone," he warned them. "The spirits of the long-dead Fomorian sorcerers inhabit the dark canopy. They have been here for many generations and their wrath has not abated in all that time."

On the opposite side of the road there was a shout.

"That is Conor's voice," one of the other men cried in anguish. "We can't let him die alone in the woods assailed by the ghosts of the enemy."

And with that the warrior charged in among the trees. In moments the forest swallowed him like a great beast devouring a morsel of food.

Fergus turned to the last warrior in the party. "We must get back to the crossroads. It is too dangerous to remain here."

"What about those two?"

"They should have listened to me," Fergus replied. "There is nothing we can do for them. They are hopelessly lost by now and by nightfall they will find themselves in peril from all sides."

At that moment there was another cry from the heart of the woods. A shriek of terror that trailed off into a desperate fading whine for help.

Fergus found himself compelled to run to his comrades' aid. He shut his eyes to block out his surroundings, resisting the urge to rescue his men. With his body shaking, the veteran clenched both fists, willing the desire to go away. When it did, it was replaced by a terrible fear, the sort of terror he had felt many times before battle.

"We are safe as long as we stay on the road," he told the other warrior in a trembling voice as he reluctantly opened his eyes again. But the last man was gone. He had vanished as surely as the other two.

That was enough for Fergus. Without another thought for the fate of the others he turned on his heels and ran as fast as his legs would carry him back to the crossroads, cursing that he had been tricked by the evil inhabitants of the Forest of Dun Beg.

As he approached the standing stone he could plainly see that there was no one about. The two warriors he had left behind were gone without a trace. The veteran leaned against the stone for a long while to catch his breath, trying to throw off his fear.

When he had recovered a little he dropped to his

knees to scoop up a drink. But when he brought his hand up to his mouth there was a terrible stench to the water. He put his face close to the pool to examine it. All across the top of the pool there was a thin multicolored film of liquid.

The veteran touched this with the tip of his finger and brought it carefully up to his nose. He recoiled from the odor immediately.

"It didn't smell bad earlier," he thought. "What has happened?"

That was when Fergus began to feel very sick. The trees about him started to spin and he had to sit down. He realized the water at the spring had been poisoned, and for that he blamed the Milesians, the Fomor and even Sárán.

But his last thought before drifting off into unconsciousness was that this terrible incident had all been his own fault.

Dalan followed hard on the heels of Fergus and his warriors. Deer Island at the mouth of the River Shannon was the obvious place to head for because there would be fishing boats nearby with which to cross the water and the river mouth was too wide to swim.

This part of the country was well wooded with few pathways through the forests but the Brehon had traveled this way many times before. He knew the main road south had many blind branches which ended amongst the gray ruins of Fomorian forts. These places were reputedly haunted so this country was sparsely inhabited. Dalan realized the Watchers probably knew this area very well. In ancient days it was the seat of Fomor power in the west and the last stronghold of their warriors when the combined strength of the Danaans and Fir-Bolg had forced their retreat.

The woods were silent now. No songs of Balor and his deeds rang out between the trees. Only ghosts walked these paths. And the spirits of the long-dead Fomorians wailed their breathy melodies to the accompaniment of the wind in the high branches.

By noon Dalan had come to a crossroads marked with a standing stone. Incised lines along the western side of the upright granite slab informed the traveler that the western fork of this path led to Dun Beg, last stronghold of the Fomor. The Brehon ran his fingers over the lines. No Fir-Bolg or Danaan had taken that path to Dun Beg in all the generations since Balor's folk had made their final desperate stand at the coastal fortress. The dun was far to the south, too far out of his way. Yet the Brehon was filled with a desire to go there one day and see the fortress for himself.

On the eastern side of the stone the lines told the traveler this fork led to Dun Ruan of the Fir-Bolg. On the southern face the secret scratches directed him to the Shannon, and on the north back toward Dun Burren of Brocan. By sunset, Dalan calculated, he should see the waters of the river mouth.

There was no time for rest so Dalan pressed on at his fastest pace in the hope of overtaking Sárán and the Watchers before they reached Deer Island. He knew if they crossed the Shannon there would be little hope of picking up their trail again. His eyes to the ground in front of him, Dalan trudged step after step through the afternoon. The forest thinned and the land became open hillsides with scattered trees, the mark of generations of inhabitants cutting the timber for their houses and fuel. It was a sign he was nearing the river.

But the Brehon hardly noticed the changing landscape. His thoughts were on Lochie and Isleen. Such was his absorption that he failed to notice the two strangers standing in the middle of the path until he was almost upon them.

It was only his intuition that saved him from walking right into them. The Brehon stopped as soon as he became aware of their presence. Cloaked and covered the two figures waited patiently in the distance.

"Have they been listening to my thoughts?" the Brehon asked himself. "Have I placed myself in danger by traveling in this country alone? What have they done with Sárán?"

All these questions flooded his mind at once as he struggled to make a firm decision whether to go on and face them or to find some way around. He knew they'd seen him. It was useless to avoid confrontation now. At least, he told himself, he would soon discover the truth.

With that Dalan strode on. When the strangers saw him coming closer, one of them squatted down in the middle of the road to wait. The other opened his cloak to reveal a sword sheathed at his side.

Dalan noted their cloaks were too fine for brigands or outlaws.

They did not remove their head coverings as was the custom when strangers met on the road. This alone convinced the Brehon he had stumbled upon Lochie and Isleen on their flight south to the Milesian camp.

Step by nervous step he came closer, heart beating hard in his chest, expecting at any moment to be cut down by these ageless enemies of the Fir-Bolg. The squatting figure stood up again and Dalan discerned immediately by her movement that this one was female. There was now no doubt in his mind whatsoever.

A deep breath and two more paces. Then Dalan stopped just beyond the reach of an unfriendly sword. The Brehon lowered his harp from his shoulder and placed it on the ground ready to dodge the expected blows.

No one spoke. The Druid could feel the sweat running down the back of his neck. He suddenly realized he was very uncomfortable in this cloak of wool and that he should have worn the Raven-feathers. To ease his discomfort he pulled back the hood and then addressed the strangers.

"I am Dalan," he began. "I am a Brehon judge. And I am on the business of the Druid Assembly. Who dares block my path?"

"Dalan!" Aoife cried as she uncovered her red hair.

As she spoke Mahon revealed his face also and for a few shocked seconds the three travelers stared at each other in relief.

It was about an hour before sunset when Sárán and Isleen emerged from the forest close to the coast and the young man was sure he was going to collapse from exhaustion. In all the seasons he had followed Fineen around the land, he had never been pushed so hard as he was now.

Isleen on the other hand seemed as fresh and as energetic as when they had set out before dawn, though her pack was larger and heavier than his. Sárán concluded with admiration that she must be used to this pace of travel, though he was amazed she never suggested they stop for rest.

Once they cleared the forest road the young man was sure Isleen would call a halt, but she carried on with renewed vigor and determination.

"I must stop for a bite to eat," Sárán begged when it was plain she intended to press on.

"We do not have the time," came the sharp reply. "We must be at the mouth of the Shannon as the last of the sun's rays fall upon the land. If we are not at the appointed place the boat will leave without us."

"You have arranged for transport across the river mouth?" Sárán asked in surprise.

"Of course I have. How did you think we would get over to the other side? It is too far for you to swim."

The young man shrugged, catching the inference that Isleen did not think she would have any difficulty in swimming the distance, even after a full day on the road without rest.

"I can't keep going without food and water," he protested.

Isleen laughed as she handed him her water skin. "You may drink," she told him, "as we walk. You will get no food until we reach the shore. A full belly will slow you down. You will appreciate a meal more if you wait until the Shannon is laid out before us."

Sárán took the skin and swallowed a gulp of cool fresh spring water. Then Isleen snatched it off him again before he could take another mouthful.

"Too much and you will double up in pain," she declared. "I can't carry you as well."

Thirst hardly quenched, the young man opened his mouth to argue. But he got no chance to speak. Just at that moment they came to the top of a rise and before them in the distance lay the mouth of the Shannon.

"It will not be long now," Isleen stated. "If we move quickly we will have time to sit by the water and eat our fill before the boat arrives. But I mean to get there in plenty of time. You have slowed me down enough today."

"Who is meeting us?" Sárán asked, trying to take his mind off the emptiness of his belly.

"People from the south."

"The Cairige? The folk of the southern Fir-Bolg?" he pressed.

"There are more tribes in Innisfail than the Tuatha De Danaan and the Fir-Bolg," she retorted. "Have you not traveled in the south?"

"Fineen is of the northern Danaan folk," Sárán replied. "He is a brother to the present Dagda."

"So you have spent much time in that exalted company?"

"I have."

"But your people were put down by the Danaans in the ancient days," she reminded him. "How can you bring yourself to bow down to the Danaan Druids?"

"I have never been made to feel less worthy simply because my kinfolk are not well represented at the Druid Assembly," he replied.

"Save your breath," she snapped. "I have a mind to walk hard now since our destination is in sight. I want you to think carefully on all that has happened in the past four seasons. And to consider the changes which are about to engulf this land."

"What changes?" he inquired but Isleen did not answer him. Her eyes were on the mouth of the river and she had picked up her pace so that he was stumbling to keep up with her.

When they finally came to the water's edge the Seer held up a hand to the sky. The sun was one hand's breadth away from touching the horizon and this made her smile with satisfaction.

"You have done well," she told her traveling companion. She pointed to the flat piece of land out in the middle of the river mouth. "Over there is Deer Island. When the sun touches the rim of the world in the west we can expect to see a boat coming across from the southern shore."

"May I sit down now?" Sárán gasped, barely taking in her words.

"Yes." She smiled. "I'm proud of you and impressed. Not many men can keep pace with me."

The young man dropped down on the soft grass at the shore and stared up at the sky as he caught his breath. He lay like that for a little while until he had the strength to ask again, "What changes are about to overtake this land?"

"There is no doubt that the Milesians are going to be victorious," Isleen explained. "Our people may be forced into the dark places of the earth in order to preserve our way of life. The Danaans have already hatched their plan to open up the ancient system of tunnels and underground caverns that were used in far-off times to shelter from the wrath of Balor. But I for one do not trust them to invite the Fir-Bolg to join them."

"Our people have their own caves and tunnels," Sárán reminded her. "The depths of Aillwee are not far from Dun Burren. Those caves are still used to store winter forage for the cattle and dried meat for the clanhold."

"The point I am trying to make," Isleen said tersely, "is why should we have to withdraw underground at all? It was the Danaans who came up with this proposal. Perhaps they are happy to spend the rest of their days in a dark pit only emerging into the sunlight when there is no enemy about."

"But you said yourself the Milesians will surely take Innisfail for themselves."

"That doesn't mean we have to submit to them completely. If your father were a wise man he would have sought a separate treaty with the invaders instead of wasting his time with a Danaan alliance that will surely cost Fir-Bolg lives. But he was too frightened of what the Danaans might do to him and to the last of his people. Do you recall what happened in the ancient time when the Fir-Bolg formed an alliance with the Fomor against the Tuatha De Danaan?"

"I had no idea there was such an alliance!" Sárán retorted in shock. "The Fomorians were an evil race. I can't believe my ancestors would have allied with them."

"The Danaan Druids would have you think that the Fir-Bolg have always been a little people," she told him. "But it is not so. Your ancestors once ruled this entire country from the western ocean to the eastern strand. The Druid Assembly long ago forbade the telling of that part of the history because it could have inspired a continuing rebellion amongst the Fir-Bolg."

"Continuing rebellion?"

"The Danaans have kept the truth of your folk quiet for many generations. Now is the time to reclaim your birthright."

"A separate treaty?"

"Precisely." Isleen smiled, reaching out a hand to

brush the jet black hair from his forehead. "And since your father is too frightened to negotiate such a truce," she went on, "you must do it for him."

"Me?" Sárán gasped, sitting up.

"You are better than a king," she told him in her best instructional tone. "You are a Druid."

"I have not finished my training," he protested. "I am a student. I would not know what to say."

"Then you had better start thinking seriously about it. The boat will be here soon and the Milesians expect to be able to speak with you on this matter."

"What?"

"That is what I have arranged for you," Isleen told him. "If all goes well there will be peace between the Milesians and the Fir-Bolg. There will be no need for your father and his warriors to attend the battle-contest at Sliabh Mis. You will save many lives."

She pointed out across the water now lit by the setting sun. It was as if a goldsmith had pressed gold leaf down upon the land and the river and then held a candle to it to bring out the honey hues and sparkles. In the midst of this gorgeous expanse of light there was a black speck moving slowly toward the northern shore.

"Here they come." Isleen pointed. The boat was not one of the simple fishing curraghs Sárán had expected, but a wooden rowing boat such as the Milesians were famed for.

"Why should they listen to me?" he asked her. "I am nothing more than a king's son. I am not the ruler of my people and I have no right to negotiate on their behalf."

"They will listen to you. Have no fear of that."

"But even if they agree to a separate treaty, my own folk will never ratify it," he argued. "I am only the student of a healer."

"The Fir-Bolg will agree," Isleen stated confidently. "On the one hand there is much sense in making peace before lives are placed unnecessarily at risk. And on the other hand there is this," she added, placing a hand on her pack.

"What is that?"

"Last night after you lay down to your rest I went to speak with your father, hoping to reason with him. I found him in a deep sleep from which I could not wake him. I knew the situation demanded urgent action. I knew his people were already regretting his leadership in this matter."

"What is that in your pack?" Sárán repeated, fearing the worst now.

"Since he would not wake," Isleen answered, "I lifted from him the symbol of his authority and honor. I took the Cauldron of Plenty."

"The cauldron?" the young man cried. "That is treachery! You could be banished for such a crime. And the fine against my father's dignity would indenture your kinfolk to the seventh generation. How is this going to make the Fir-Bolg accept a treaty?"

"If they do not favor such an arrangement"—she

shrugged—"they will not see the cauldron again. In turn they will have to recompense the Dagda for its loss."

"You have risked your life and liberty for this?" Sárán muttered, still disbelieving. "When the Druid Assembly finds out they will hunt you down to impose their justice on you."

But they will not think it was me who stole the cauldron," she sighed.

"What?"

"Eber of the Milesians believes that you stole the cauldron. He thinks it entitles you to negotiate with him. The word will get back to the Assembly that it was you not I who arranged this meeting with the invaders."

She brushed his hair again gently with her hand.

"So," Isleen advised him, "you had better start thinking about what you are going to say to Eber. He will be expecting nothing short of your full cooperation."

Dalan was the first to smile broadly.

"I didn't recognize you," he laughed. "What in the name of Danu are you doing here?"

"We heard Sárán had stolen the cauldron," Mahon replied. "We've come to find the lad before Brocan can get his hands on him."

"My father would kill him if he found him first," the young woman added.

"You must return to the Fir-Bolg camp immediately," Dalan chided. "You have no idea of the danger that is abroad in the land."

"We are not far from the cost," Mahon reasoned. "I believe Sárán and Isleen will be making for the river mouth near Deer Island. That is the only place a boat could be landed safely."

"What do you know of Isleen?" the Brehon snapped.

"Only what I overheard you and Fineen discussing the other night," Aoife admitted. "You suspect that she is one of the Watchers. You have come to find her."

"And destroy her if I can," Dalan rejoined.

"You cannot do that on your own," Mahon noted, "and be sure that Sárán is safe."

"Sárán is a traitor and an outlaw. He will surely suffer banishment for this crime."

"You don't believe he stole the cauldron," Aoife asserted. "You know Isleen is responsible. At the worst she put him up to it."

"That is yet to be proved. For the time being Sárán must be considered an enemy."

"We are not far from the cost and we have outrun Fergus and the warriors," Mahon told him. "They took a track to the east on the forest road. Perhaps the old veteran knows a quicker way to Deer Island, but I think it more likely they have become lost."

"You saw them?"

"They were about five hundred paces ahead of us. We heard them."

"And why did you not hail them?"

"Because they will suspect the worst of Sárán,"

Aoife cut in. "If my brother is fool enough to put up a fight, they will surely kill him, trainee Druid or not. There was great anger at Dun Burren when we left."

Dalan turned to scout the road behind them. There was no movement and the sun would soon be setting. Fergus and his warriors had almost certainly missed their chance to apprehend Sárán and recover the cauldron.

"I am beginning to wish Fergus was with us now," the Brehon sighed. "If we are really dealing with the Watchers, then we are going to need help. Three of us alone will not be able to overpower such a being."

"So we can come with you?" his young student asked eagerly.

"It would not do if I sent you back to Dun Burren and some evil befell you. How would I explain that to your father?"

"If we cross through the forest just ahead we will come to where the trees end and the hills roll down to the Shannon," Mahon suggested.

"No," the Brehon replied quickly. "We will stick to the road. I would rather be out in the open at sunset. This forest is full of the undead spirits of the Fomor. I would not like to be amidst them when darkness falls."

"It will be a longer journey."

"Then we will have to stop talking about it and get a move on," Dalan decided. "I trust you will both be able to keep up with me?"

With that the Brehon picked up his harp and

stepped out along the path toward the coast. Mahon and Aoife stood for a moment in surprise but before Dalan had gone ten steps they were at his heels.

A thousand paces brought them to the edge of the forest with still enough daylight left to make the landing place at Deer Island. Here the road became a narrow cow track, rough and rarely used. But by chance they had come a quicker way than Sárán and Isleen. This path descended to the river mouth very steeply so the going was shorter.

"How do we know they will be at the landing place?" Aoife asked.

"We don't," Dalan replied. "We can only hope that was their plan. But in truth there is no better place to find a boat at this time of year. The people of the island come here to collect whatever treasures the sea washes up. That storm of a few nights ago will have them out in numbers combing the shore for crabs and cuttlefish."

As he spoke they caught their first glimpse of the water. And out upon the river mouth they saw the dark speck of a boat making for the shore toward them.

"That's the place." Dalan pointed. "Down there. We must hurry now for I fear we may already be too late."

Chapter 21

Sárán looked out over the wide mouth of the River Shannon as the boat came steadily closer. He could clearly see the red face paint of several of the enemy. The man who stood in the prow had long hair painted with lime to stiffen and whiten it. All along the man's arms there were bold red lines. His feet were red. His palms were painted red. And a broad stripe of red ran across his face from ear to ear so that his eyes stood out in contrast.

Behind him at his shoulder was a woman completely caked from head to toe in a thick coating of red ochre. Her clothes were red, her hair was red, even the sword she carried had been smeared with ochre.

"That woman is the Queen of the Gaedhals," Isleen explained. "Her name is Scota."

"I'll not betray my people," Sárán said with determination.

"You already have," Isleen told him.

"When the Druid Assembly discovers what you've done they will banish you," the young man warned. "You stole the cauldron of the Dagda and you would deliver it into the hands of the invaders."

"You stole the cauldron," she sighed sadly. "No one is going to believe a young man who is already paying for a terrible crime. Not when a well-respected Seer such as myself speaks against him. If I testify I knew nothing of this whole misadventure, they will take my word for it. Everyone will assume your story to be a desperate lie invented to save your skin."

"Why have you betrayed your own people?"

"I am merely trying to bring this war to an end without any further bloodshed," she reasoned. "Can't you see that?"

Isleen smiled in such a way that Sárán suspected she was lying.

"You could have done this differently," he replied. "If you really wanted peace."

"You must argue the case," she explained. "You must ask yourself whether you wish to save the lives of your kinfolk who will surely fall in this coming battle. One day you'll understand that what I'm doing is for the good of everyone."

The boat was closer now. The warrior in the prow was standing in readiness to jump onto the beach. The woman behind him had passed her sword to him. She now held a long slender spear at the ready.

"Please," Sárán pleaded. "It's not too late to change your mind. Give me the cauldron and let me go."

"And where would you go? Half your father's warriors are out searching for you. Imagine what would happen if they found you with the cauldron? I would expect their rage to be almost uncontrollable. I don't want to put you at such risk."

This last comment had such a flavor of contempt about it that the young man flinched. And at that moment he remembered he carried the Quicken berries in a small bag at his belt. He had completely forgotten they had been given to him to carry. He could do nothing but curse his foolishness in believing the Seer. Then he understood the cauldron had to be abandoned if he was to have any chance of returning the berries to Fineen in time to prepare the Danaan brew.

As those thoughts were passing through his mind the boat scraped ashore. The queen and four warriors stepped out.

"Sárán, son of King Brocan of the Burren," Isleen said, making the formal introductions, "this is Scota, Queen of all the Gaedhals, and her son, Eber, King of the Southern Milesians."

The warrior nodded but did not speak. The queen smiled and nodded. Sárán moved his head slightly in acknowledgment.

"Do you have the cauldron of which you spoke?" Scota asked Isleen.

"I have it here," she answered proudly, patting her pack.

"We'll make a good pairing you and I," the Milesian king stated with a grin.

Sárán's expression dropped away and his jaw slackened in surprise. "You're going to marry him?" he gasped.

"It will help the Fir-Bolg people accept their new rulers," Isleen explained, holding out her hand to be helped into the stern of the little vessel. "Their king will be a Milesian but their new queen will be one of their own. And so will all my children."

"You're no queen," Scota scoffed. "And you're no Gaedhal. My folk won't accept you while I live."

"Then I'll be patient. Surely you haven't much time remaining," the Seer retorted as she sat down beside the tillerman.

"Enough," Scota said in such a manner that Eber wasn't sure if his mother was ending the conversation or assuring Isleen she'd be around for some time yet.

"Are you coming boy?" the queen asked.

Sárán didn't answer. Instead he turned and ran as fast as he could back up the path toward the road.

"I knew I could rely on you to do that," Isleen sighed to herself. "You'll not escape the disgrace I have arranged for you by running away from it, young Sárán."

The young man didn't look back when he heard shouts behind him. Nor did he turn when these were followed by a loud horn blast. Thinking only of putting one foot before the other he was soon back up near the road, running toward the forest as fast as his aching legs could carry him. The further he went the more convinced he became that he would not be cap-

tured by the Milesians if he took shelter in the woods.
Then a gut-shivering sound assaulted his ears, sending
an icy rush through his blood.

Ahead of him in the forest the answering call of another horn reverberated through the trees. It brought
him instantly to a halt. Sárán was still bent double when
yet another blast, this time from the left, brought him
to his senses. He must hide.

Ahead of him was a fork in the path. He ran toward
it, struggling to recall which branch they had come
down on the way to the river. By the time he reached
it he still had no clear memory so, more out of hope
than anything else, he chose the right-hand fork.

He was soon blessing his luck for this part of the
path was familiar to him. The black soil in the forest
had turned to mud along this part of road. Sárán
dodged between the puddles, leaping where there
was no dry footing. He hadn't gone far along this difficult path when he saw three dark figures on the road
far in the distance. They were running as fast as they
could in his direction.

It was too late to turn around, and Sárán had no
idea who was lying in wait for him back down the
path. He looked to his right. Fifty paces beyond the
road's edge lay the forest planted by the ancient
Fomor. The young man drew a deep breath then and,
preparing himself for the worst, darted into the cover
of the enveloping canopy of darkness.

He had not walked ten paces when the world was

plunged into utter black and he had lost all sense of direction. In a mood of despair he finally sat down where he was and prayed that the Milesians would not find him in this dank, heavy forest.

As Dalan, Mahon and Aoife had descended the steep path toward the shore they had witnessed the landing of the Milesian boat. They had plainly seen Sárán standing on the sand as Isleen was helped to her seat. Her distinctive red hair had given her away immediately.

It was Aoife who had noticed that her brother did not follow the Seer into the boat straightaway.

"Something's frightened him," she told the others. "I think he's going to try to escape."

She had just spoken those words when Sárán turned around and ran. In moments he was out of sight. One of the Milesian warriors blew a blast on a short carved cow's horn. Two of the invaders set off after him and then another horn blast sounded as if in answer. The sound came from the direction of the forest, an urgent stuttered call like that of a frightened bird.

"There are more Gaedhals lurking around here," the Brehon decided. "We must hide until the danger is past."

Mahon was about to protest when a third lowing bellow from further down the riverbank announced the presence of more warriors.

"Get down," Dalan demanded. "There must be ten

or twelve armed Milesians looking for Sárán. We are no match for so many."

"We must help him!" Aoife protested. "We can't simply abandon him to those barbarians."

"There is nothing we can do," Dalan repeated, "but wait until the danger is past. Then we will be in a better position to aid him."

"What better position than the one we are in now?"

"We will have our lives and our liberty," the Brehon retorted tersely. "If these invaders have such a disregard for the law that they could arrange the theft of the Cauldron of Plenty, I doubt they will have a care for our status as Druids. Especially not since we are accompanied by the son of the King of the Danaans, whom they also hold. I would prefer not to deliver any further prizes into their hands at the moment if you don't mind."

"He's right." Mahon nodded reluctantly. "If Sárán is captured we will have a chance to rescue him."

"And what if they decide to kill him?" Aoife shot back. "What chance will he have then?"

"They want him alive," Dalan pointed out. "He is no use to them dead."

They all hushed suddenly as the Milesian warriors returned to their boat, pushed off from the shore and began rowing with swift strokes out into the middle of the river. The sun had almost set and a sea fog was appearing around the opposite bank.

"Why are they running away?" Mahon gasped in surprise.

"Because the search party from Dun Burren has been sighted."

"That must have been who replied to the other two horn blasts," the Danaan surmised.

"Come on," Aoife begged, dragging them both to their feet. "We have to get down to the shore and follow Sárán. We cannot vouch for his safety if Fergus and the warriors come upon him before we do."

The two men traded glances for a moment, then followed after her as quickly as they could. By the time they reached the sandy riverbank the invaders had already rowed a good distance.

Dalan rushed down to the water's edge. There he stood for a long while, sending his thoughts across to Isleen.

"If you knew the trouble you have caused," the Brehon whispered, "or the strife that is about to break out all because of you, you would probably be overjoyed."

As if she had heard every hissed word the red-haired woman stood up in the stern of the vessel and turned around, holding a lantern to light her face. And there she stood staring defiantly back at him until the boat passed through a drifting bank of fog and vanished into the night.

"I will hunt this country from mountain to deepest valley until I find you, Isleen," he promised. "I'll find a way to put an end to your mischief."

Then he was away up the hill headed for the forest, hard on his companions' heels.

He soon caught up with Mahon and Aoife who had
paused at a fork in the road.

"Which path do we take?" the Danaan asked in
confusion.

The Brehon looked about and quickly realized
Sárán could equally have chosen either direction. He
summoned all his instincts, calmed his racing thoughts
for a second, and then made a decision.

"We'll take the right-hand path," he told them and
without another word they were off.

It was not long before they came to the muddy
stretch of road where Sárán had dived off into the
woods for cover. They could still see his footprints in
the deep sludge and it was obvious where he had
gone.

"We're too late," Dalan sighed in despair. "He has
gone where few folk would dare to tread and where I
would not go if my life depended on it."

"Why do you say we are too late?" Aoife inquired
hesitantly, dread in her heart for the answer.

"Because the forest is haunted by the ghosts of the
Fomorian sorcerers who died at the siege of Dun Beg.
He is beyond our help now. The cauldron has been
lost to the Milesians and the Quicken berries are
gone with Sárán. We are too late."

"What shall we do?" Mahon asked.

"Build a fire while there is still enough light to collect kindling," the Brehon told him, "and then sit by it
all night without straying for an instant. A good

bright fire is our only hope of surviving the night to come."

"What about Sárán?" Aoife sobbed, seeing Dalan was ready to abandon her brother to the demons of the forest.

"I will have to think very carefully about that question," her teacher admitted. "Right now I have no idea what we should do, other than stay out of the forest and get a fire going to keep the spirits of the night at bay."

Brocan and his advance party of warriors arrived at the standing stone which marked the Dun Beg crossroads just as the sun went down. The king ordered the war party to halt for the night but Fineen intervened, giving him the same warning about the spring at the foot of the stone that Isleen had given to Sárán.

"I would rather we did not stop at all," Brocan admitted. "But the road passes through the Fomorian forests before too long and I would not risk traveling that part of the path by night."

"The woods are no more dangerous after sunset than they are during the day," Fineen laughed. "I have heard tales of the most terrible events which took place here. Many of them bathed in the bright warm summer sunshine. Daylight does not keep evil at bay, though it may seem to."

Brocan gestured for the healer to keep his voice

down. He did not want to make his warriors any more concerned than they already were.

"Could we make it to the landing place at Deer Island before dawn?" he asked in a low voice.

"I have traveled this road many times," Fineen replied. "I guess we could expect to arrive there shortly after midnight if we did not stray from the road at all."

"Why would we stray from the path?"

"The spirits entice folk into the woods with little temptations," he whispered so that only the king could hear. "Those who answer the call are never seen again. The forest devours them. It takes them in and they become food for the trees as their bodies putrefy."

Brocan swallowed hard and then glanced at the healer. "How do you suggest we resist the temptations of these spirits?"

"I haven't got the first inkling of an idea," Fineen told him with a friendly hand on the shoulder. "I've never seen them."

The king narrowed his eyes, unsure whether the Druid was playing some sort of game with him.

"Hadn't we better be on our way?" the healer asked, breaking the silence.

"Yes," Brocan agreed and then with a wave of his hand he sent the scouts out again. The remainder of the warriors waited a short while and then followed, marching on by moonlight, the path a silvery band of earth laid out before them.

At length they came to the edges of the forests. Here the trees which had flanked their eastern side joined with another wood on the west. And the tops of the trees seemed to have intertwined their branches overhead to form a natural roof.

Fineen approached the king before they marched on and spoke a few words to him. Brocan held his hand up, calling the war party to a halt.

"We could camp here until dawn if you prefer," the healer told Brocan. "There is no safe place to stop after we enter the forest. Once we take the first step under that canopy we must go on until we reach the other side."

"We will march on to Deer Island tonight," came the cold reply. "I am not afraid of the ghosts of a defeated people."

"I am," Fineen retorted. "May I suggest that every second warrior light a torch?"

"One or two torches will do to lead the column on," Brocan declared. "I don't want to burn them up unnecessarily."

"My lord," the healer cut in, "if you want to make it to Deer Island by dawn you will need at least thirty torches. The demons will not approach a fire. It is one of the only precautions you can take that may prevent or forestall an attack."

"You seem to know an awful lot about the demons of this place," the king remarked with suspicion. "I thought you said you had never seen one?"

"These beings cannot be seen, my lord," Fineen

said, eyes lit with a recollection of terror. "They find a way inside your thoughts. The world becomes a dream. They will croon to you and you will curse your ears for hearing their songs. They are not like us. I don't know anyone who can truthfully say their eyes have beheld the demons of Dun Beg. You will not see them."

Brocan was suddenly very uncomfortable. There was sweat trickling down his forehead. His hands were shaking.

"I would not think any less of you," the healer said at last, "and neither would anyone else, if you decided to wait here until sunrise."

The king would have agreed to this straightaway, yet something told him that if Fergus had found Sárán and they were somewhere within this forest, they would stand in need of assistance. Besides, he did not want to look weak in front of the warriors when his popularity had only just taken a turn for the better.

"We will go on," the king said with quiet decisiveness. "Everyone is to carry a lighted torch!" he ordered at the top of his voice.

"If we must go, then let us be well lit," Fineen sighed with acceptance.

"If the Milesians see us they will wonder at this mysterious procession through the ancient forest in the middle of the night," the king laughed.

"We will be a fearful sight," the healer agreed. "But

not as fearful as what we are likely to encounter before dawn."

Tinderboxes were quickly brought out, resin-tipped torches set afire. Then the company of warriors from the hillfort of Dun Burren set off into the darkest, most frightening journey of their lives.

Chapter 22

IT WAS A LONG WHILE BEFORE SÁRÁN'S EYES ADJUSTED to the utter darkness of the woods. But all he glimpsed were confusing shadows, frightening shapes and the occasional scurried movement of some small creature.

Despite this he managed to remain calm and quickly decided to keep moving to prevent the Milesians' stumbling over him in the dark. But he had to wonder whether they would have been so foolish as to dart into the trees as he had.

He turned a full circle, searching desperately for any sign of light or life. But there was nothing to guide him in the eternal night of the forest. Then he realized that in turning around he had completely lost his bearings. Now not only was he blinded but he had no idea which direction he had come from.

Berating himself for the mistake, he carefully felt his way forward step by step. He went on like this for a long while, counting his paces to help keep track of time.

When his count reached one thousand he stopped still and sat down to listen. The first thing he realized was that the woods had become gradually hotter. The air was stale and sticky. He must be near some stagnant water, he reasoned.

Sárán touched the ground beneath him and sure enough it was soaking wet. This reminded him that he was very thirsty. He found the leather bottle at his belt, uncorked it and drank the last few drops of precious cooling liquid. He had not filled it since the night after the Milesian attack when he was washing at the spring.

Far off the young man could hear the cries of night birds. Above him the leaves rustled in an imaginary wind.

Then faint and in the far distance he heard a voice.

Sárán strained his ears, focusing on the sound. A shiver passed through him. There was someone else in the forest with him, far enough away that he could just hear the sound of them speaking but not close enough for him to understand what was being said.

His first thought was that he should move as far away from the voice as possible. But he soon came to his senses. He had no water, no way of knowing where he was or how to get out of there. No way of making a fire. Nothing to eat. He could be lost in this place for days. Better to risk capture by the Milesians rather than perish alone in the woods.

Just then the voice in the distance turned to laughter. Wild, hysterical and unrestrained. Sárán swallowed hard. He could discern no joy in the sound, no mirth.

His resolve wavered. Then a whiff of smoke caught in his nostrils.

"Fire," he thought. "Light. Food."

The laughter ceased abruptly and by the time the last echo had died Sárán was making his way toward the source of the sound.

The going was slower because he had waded into a pool. He didn't realize until the water was up around his knees that it had been getting steadily deeper. Mud on the bottom of the pond sucked at his boots so it was a great effort to lift his feet.

The young man was near exhaustion by the time his feet found dry soil again. But the voice was louder and closer. Sárán sat for a while to catch his breath. There was only one voice doing all the talking. A man whose tone indicated despair but whose words were still unintelligible.

The smell of smoke was stronger so Sárán made his way forward again. He did not know how long he went on, struggling in the darkness to gain ground. Time lost all meaning in a place where the sun had never visited.

When he first saw the light of the stranger's fire it stung his eyes. He looked again and his heart began to pound. The trees seemed to be the dancing shadows of mighty demons twisting about in the yellow radiance. The forest was turned from black to a rich sweet green. The stranger's voice went on in an unnerving monotone. And Sárán finally admitted to himself just how frightened he was.

It was a long while before he could coax himself on. Fifty paces he counted before he came to the edge of a steep ridge that descended to a cleared, brightly illuminated space. The trees still blocked his view but now he could catch a little of what the stranger was saying.

Sárán heard his own name and froze to the spot.

"Who is this?" he asked himself, struggling to recognize the voice. It could not possibly be a Milesian warrior, so it must be one of his father's people sent out to find him. Suddenly he was emboldened.

With a breath of relief he began the climb down to the clearing. The voice grew louder; the scene unfolded slowly. Before him was a grassy cleared circle about thirty paces across. The clearing was encircled by a perfect ring of masterfully carved standing stones such as Sárán had never seen before. Each granite needle was covered in the most intricate patterns. Not just the familiar spirals that Sárán had so often seen but also symbols which he could make no sense of at all. At each quarter of the circle there was a larger stone, taller and broader than the rest. On either side of these pillars there was enough space for a man to enter the clearing.

The stranger was still hidden from view. Sárán decided he must be sitting at the foot of one of the stones. He continued down until he was sure the man must be able to hear him but still the voice carried on.

Sárán stopped to listen and the sound that came to his ears filled him with terror.

"When I find him I'll kill him. That Sárán, curse him. If it hadn't been for his treachery we would never have come here. I would not have been drawn into the woods. I would not be lost in this demonic kingdom."

There was no emotion or hope in the voice. The speaker was dispirited, exhausted, spent to the point of madness. But he talked on.

"That's right, boys," the stranger said as if addressing his companions and at last Sárán recognized the voice.

"Fergus!" he cried. His call echoed through the forest, stirring the night birds to screech back their challenges and wakening creatures that should have been allowed to rest.

The voice had stopped. Sárán made his way as quickly as he could down into the clearing. There a merry little blaze had been built up out of fallen timber, twigs and dry leaves. There was no sign of the veteran.

Then the young man heard something that would be with him to the end of his days. It was the sound of Fergus sobbing quietly to himself. The veteran had managed to wedge himself in between two stones. He was cowering in debilitating terror.

Straightaway Sárán began to feel his own heart beat louder. "What are you frightened of?" he demanded.

The veteran just screamed back at him. Sárán ran to his side but the battle-hardened warrior slunk back out of his reach, retching with fear.

"What has scared you so?" the young man cried, looking all about him for the source of danger.

"You!" Fergus shrieked. "It's you!"

Sárán reached out a hand and placed it on the old warrior's shoulder to calm him.

"I won't hurt you," the young man assured him gently, dismayed to see his uncle in such a state. "Come out."

Slowly the veteran calmed down until he was finally able to emerge into the firelight. Sárán gasped to see the man's face. It was completely covered in blood. His hair was matted with it, his cloak stained with it.

The veteran's hands found Sárán's and the old man looked directly into his nephew's eyes. "Are you going to take me?" he asked with a tremor in his voice.

"Take you where?"

"Has my turn come?"

"Your turn for what?" Sárán begged in confusion. "Where are your warriors?"

The veteran did not speak. His mouth was dry, he gasped for air. And then he pointed to the opposite side of the stone circle. Sárán looked across to a low rock just on the other side of the fire.

The young man had to turn away as soon as he realized what he was looking at. And it was a long time before he could bring himself to cast his eyes in that direction again.

"I don't believe it," he stammered. "What happened?"

On the rock before him lay the severed heads of five warriors. And to Sárán's horror he could put a name to every one of them.

"The owls did it," Fergus whispered. "I saw them trap each man and kill him. Then they gnawed the heads from each warrior and set them on that stone."

"Owls?" Sárán repeated, astonished. "How did you get here?"

"I don't recall," the veteran replied. "We were at the Dun Beg crossroad. The scouts saw something on the road. The next thing I remember is finding myself here. I gathered together what kindling I could in the dark and lit a fire. The next thing I knew I was watching the birds butcher my comrades."

Fergus let the tears well up in his eyes as he grabbed Sárán's hand.

"They are going to kill us," he said. "There's no doubt about it."

"Then we will have to defend ourselves," the young man decided.

"We can't fight them off," Fergus wept. "They are too many."

"Why didn't they take you?"

"I sat close to the fire. They don't like the flames. They can't abide fire. Makes them fly away."

"Then we'll set their home ablaze," the young man declared, holding his uncle's hand tightly. "We'll burn our way out of this forest."

Dalan struck the two pieces of flint together. A spark sailed gracefully up and into the midst of the dried leaves he had set down for tinder. In a moment his skilled hands had the blaze burning brightly. Then he sat back against his harp case and looked about him.

The landscape seemed to have changed dramatically. He was sure the trees were taller, their trunks broader. Mahon and Aoife seemed suddenly to have become tiny. They huddled together like two skittish creatures, eyes everywhere, on the lookout for danger.

An owl chanted a steady, even call which ended on a high-pitched squeal then started all over again. Dalan wished he knew something of the speech of birds. He was convinced they were passing news about this unwelcome intrusion into their home.

"They are watching us," Mahon whispered with dread. "I can almost feel their eyes burning into us."

"This is their world." The Brehon nodded. "We are invaders no less than the Milesians are trespassers on this island of ours."

"They want us to be on our way," Aoife stated. "I can hear the hatred in their cries."

"Spirits long gone from this world is what they are," Dalan told them both. "They take joy in our fear. They are taunting us."

As he spoke a bright red ball of light rose slowly up from the road two hundred paces away. This inexplicable light danced about erratically them plummeted to the ground again and disappeared.

None of them could find words. The strange light had been at once terrifying and magnificent. The owls started up a great chorus as they moved through the forest. Their powerful wings beat with the sound of a rushing squall surging between the trees.

"Play the harp for us," Aoife begged. "That would surely quiet their howling."

"I dare not," the Brehon replied. "These are the spirits of the Fomor and their folk had no love of the harp. Their music was the piper's tune. We have already attracted their attention. I do not wish to invite their wrath."

Another light appeared as he was speaking. This was a bright green so powerful that they each had to shade their eyes from its glare. The glowing orb danced about, sailing high up to the canopy of trees and then round in endless circles and spirals that trailed behind after it.

"What is that?" Mahon asked in wonder.

"I haven't any idea," Dalan admitted. "I've never seen anything like it before in my life."

"It is beautiful," Aoife gasped in awe. "It is calling us to dance with it."

"You will sit still and turn your gaze away," the Brehon commanded in a soft but firm voice.

"It will do us no harm," she replied.

"Do as I say," Dalan insisted. "I am your teacher. You will obey me."

Aoife frowned and pushed away from Mahon. "A thing of such splendor could not possibly be of any threat. I will show you," she said and stood up. Mahon reached out a hand to stop her but she was already beyond his grasp.

"I demand that you turn your eyes away!" Dalan shouted.

Aoife stopped. Slowly, reluctantly, the young woman shifted her gaze and looked directly at the Brehon. And as she did so the light went out.

In the next instant Aoife was back in Mahon's arms.

"I would have run off into the trees chasing it," she sobbed. "I was ready to follow that light to the end of the earth."

"We must not look upon them if they come again," the Brehon decided. "They are sent to seduce us into leaving the safety of our fire."

The owls suddenly began a noisy, boisterous exchange that soon became a deafening cacophony. The sound was speeding through the treetops above them like thunder traveling across the land.

"Whatever you do," Dalan called out loudly above the noise, "don't move from this fireside. They are trying to frighten us into the darkness."

At the edge of the firelight they could see the swooping owls, dark birds with white faces and huge eyes. Aoife and Mahon ducked their heads as the creatures sailed in close to them. The Brehon felt a wing brush his head and he lay down flat on the roadside to avoid being attacked.

"We must get away!" Aoife cried out. "They mean to do us harm!"

"Be quiet and still and all will be well," Dalan told her sternly. "If we let our fear get the better of us, we will be defeated. We must stay together if we are to have any hope of making it through this night."

And so they huddled close to their fire as the owls continued their diving attack. Gradually the creatures became bolder, flying in through the flames, crying with chilling angry voices. When one bird caught a feather in the fire and screeched off into the night like a shooting star, the intensity of their wrath doubled.

Suddenly the air was full of thousands of screeching birds, talons extended, falling down upon their cowering prey. The three frightened travelers could only lie flat and hope the fire would keep them at bay.

Dalan felt the urge to fight back building up inside of him. His throat was dry and his patience was wearing thin. The owls were playing a game with them and the Brehon was not about to let them win. He got to his feet, ignoring his own advice. In seconds he was thrashing about at the owls as they swooped toward him. The birds cried triumphantly. This was the moment they had been waiting for, when one of their victims would weaken.

Dalan realized his mistake even as he was getting to his feet, but he knew this attack would go on for hours unless he gained some little victory. He dodged about, avoiding the creatures as they spread wings and dived at him. Choosing his moment carefully, he enticed the birds to come closer and closer with each assault. And then he struck. When he had eyed his victim Dalan followed the creature carefully. The owl made one pass at him, flew out into the darkness and immediately swooped in again. This creature was full of malice and reckless in its approach.

Then the owl sailed high in the air, making a graceful turn near the treetops and falling down upon the Brehon with full fury.

Dalan wrapped his cloak about his right hand to protect it, then he stood defying the owl to attack him. Just as he expected the bird singled him out, screeching with all its might as it flew directly at his head.

At the last possible moment the Brehon dodged out of the way, at the same time reaching out with his cloaked hand to grab at the creature. And then he blessed his luck as his fingers found the owl's leg. He grasped it tightly and swung the bird down at the ground with the power of its own descent. As it headed past the fire the bird slipped out of Dalan's fingers and hit the ground near Mahon, who jumped on it quickly to stop it escaping.

Dalan threw his cloak over the stunned owl and held the makeshift trap up to the other birds. "If you do not leave us in peace," he announced, "this bird will roast over the fire for our supper. Do you hear?"

The effect was immediate. Just as abruptly as the attack had begun the owls went quiet, withdrew to their perches in the surrounding trees and the air was clear again. Dalan tied the cloak with a leather strap from his harp case and then laid his prisoner down by the warmth of the flames.

The owl soon regained consciousness and as soon as it did began to kick and scream to its comrades. But the great gathering of owls sat silent and sullen around the edge of the forest, each bird staring intently at its comrade. Their hate was growing. Their outrage building.

It was long after, when the captive owl had finally settled down, that the birds made their next move. Without a call or cry having passed between them, they rose from their perches and flew off into the night, leaving the travelers to wonder whether they had won this battle.

"You will sleep now," Dalan told the other two. "I do not think we will be troubled again tonight. But I will keep the watch just in case."

With that an exhausted Aoife pulled her cloak over her head and snuggled close to Mahon. In a very short while they were both resting warily. Much later when all was still they fell asleep, leaving Dalan alone with his thoughts and his fears.

Brocan, Fineen and the warriors of Dun Burren marched for a long while before they heard or saw anything unusual in the forest. The king was beginning to believe they would experience no trouble at all on this journey.

But he was wrong. The spirits of the forest were waiting until the band had traveled too far to be able to retreat. The Fir-Bolg war party was being drawn into a trap.

Torchlight illuminated the edges of the road and the wall of the forest but no one could see into its depths, so close together were the trees. Everyone was silent, expectant and nervous. And each was lost in his own thoughts.

So when the first sign of danger revealed itself only Fineen took any notice. The healer heard the owl hooting in the distance and immediately called the band to a halt.

"We must form ourselves into a defensive circle," he urged Brocan. "The enemy will be upon us very soon."

"What makes you think that?" the king laughed. "There hasn't been a sign of danger and the forest is quiet."

"Do as I say!" Fineen insisted. "I know a little of the language of birds. They are passing the word among their number to attack us in force. If we are not ready for them we will suffer for it."

Brocan did not waste any more time arguing. Even though he thought it foolish to fear a flock of owls, he did as Fineen suggested and formed the warriors up into two circles, one within the other.

The outer rank knelt down, spear points level with

their bodies. The inner rank held their weapons high in readiness for assault from above. Every warrior still held a torch in one hand as they waited to see what form the threat against them would take.

They did not have to wait long. In an awe-inspiring wave thousands of birds appeared out of the dark, screeching, screaming and diving in every direction. At first even the disciplined warriors of Dun Burren were almost scattered, their formation penetrated by the ferocious birds.

The wounded who fell in the first wave were dragged into the center of the circle, eyes gouged, cheeks ripped open or faces scratched. But these were only a few. And the outrage of the remaining Fir-Bolg warriors soon outstripped their fear. They fought back with vengeance in their hearts and in a short while many owls had been struck down, impaled on spear points, cut open by swords or scorched by torches.

Before long a hundred feathered shapes lay flapping helplessly at the feet of the formation. And for each one of the owls that was wounded another two birds lay dead. Those warriors who only had minor injuries soon stood up again to join their comrades as the air became thick with shrieking creatures.

Wherever a gap appeared in the defenses, wherever a warrior fell back injured or overwhelmed, Brocan was there to fill the space. From his mouth poured a constant stream of encouragement, gentle reprimand, determined vitriol and, when necessary, violent abuse. Although at times he could barely be heard above the noise of the winged war cry, he did not stop.

Fineen, tending the wounded in the center of the circle, screamed out in agony as an owl tore at his ear with its beak. Brocan heard the healer's cry and struck the bird down with the point of his spear. Then he cast the body into the darkness.

Before the carcass had landed the birds began their withdrawal. The main force of owls retreated to the trees on either side of the road, while a rearguard kept up a steady harassment of the defenders.

As these assaults gradually tapered off, the rearguard of the feathered war party remained on the wing while their companions rested out of reach of spear and sword. As these owls flew their chaotic circles up among the treetops Brocan realized they were marshaling themselves for a concerted attack.

Now that the king knew his warriors could defeat such an enemy he was emboldened. He reckoned the owls had no chance of breaking through his defenses or of scattering his warriors.

"We've beaten them!" he cried in triumph but none of his war party cheered. They kept their stations, grim-faced and ready for the coming assault.

"They know they will not make us run," Brocan continued. "They are retreating!"

The warriors picked up on his enthusiasm and cheered loudly. This was an old tactic used when an enemy was doing badly and it often led to the end of a battle. Only Fineen among all of them was silent. He was busy trying to staunch the flow of blood where the top of his ear had been sheared off.

"Keep your formation tight," he told Brocan when he had wrapped a piece of torn cloak tightly around his head. "They do not mean to attack us again until their allies have arrived."

"Their allies?" the king asked in confusion. "More birds? We will make short work of them too," he added confidently.

"This fight is far from finished," the healer explained wearily. "We have just witnessed the first sting of their wrath."

It was then the king caught sight of a strange red light rising off the road a hundred paces further south.

"What is that?" he demanded of Fineen.

"Those lights signal the arrival of the armies of the Fomor," the healer answered solemnly. "Your warriors must hold their ranks no matter what befalls them. The Fomorian host intend to attack us from the road while the birds assault us from the sky. We are only eighty. They have thousands."

"The Fomor are a dead people, aren't they?"

"These are the spirits of the dead. They cannot harm us unless our fear deprives us of all sense. They intend to frighten us into forgetting our discipline. They want us to run into the forest where we will surely die. If anyone breaks rank the owls will pick them to pieces. And what the birds don't get hold of, the woods will certainly devour."

Brocan turned to his warriors to speak. "We will prevail if we stand our ground. They can only defeat us if we break formation and make for cover. Hold fast and we will have the victory."

As he spoke the hosts of the Fomor marched into view. And even Brocan, who had confronted many enemies in his day, was shaken to the core by the sight. These warriors did not look like ghosts to him. They wore bright colors on their cloaks and carried polished swords and spears. Their faces were painted in the purple Brocan had heard described in the ancient legends. Their shields were long, rectangular and heavy. Their helms had crests of white horsehair and their eyes shone with red fury.

"Hold your ranks steady!" Fineen cried out to the now silent and stunned warriors of Dun Burren. "This army will not harm us. They are nothing more than spirits. We must not yield any ground or we will all be slaughtered."

The Fomor closed in steadily, marching with short quick steps and humming a battle chant in time with their movements. Sixty paces away they halted just as any real war party would do, out of range of spear cast.

Brocan recognized this ancient tactic. Display your superior force. Taunt your enemy with the discipline of your warriors. Then dangle the threat in front of them to strike despair into their thoughts. Compared to this elaborate dance, the battle itself was only a small part of the engagement. It would be won and lost now in the hearts of his war party. If their spirits faltered they would all be scattered to the four winds. If they held firm no force of this world or the other would move them.

As the ghostly enemy stood silent on the road they began their war song. And it chilled Brocan's blood to hear it. A slow chant, deep and mournful, it rose gradually in intensity until it filled the air. The owls high in the trees joined in with long steady calls that complemented the melody.

Then the Fomor began a rhythmic beating of sword and spear against shield. This was the infamous song their warriors had sung in the ancient days whenever their folk came raiding Innisfail from across the sea. Fineen knew the tales well enough to be able to conjure a clear picture in his mind of their mighty ships rowed by banks of hardened fighters. The healer heard a drum join in the performance, then another, until it seemed to him there were hundreds of drummers accompanying the music.

No Fir-Bolg warrior flinched. None made any sound in answer to this challenge. They each stood with eyes wide and hearts beating hard, waiting for the attack that would surely come. Brocan looked about him. He could see his war party were balancing on the fine line which separated valor and terror.

The song grew like a budding flower, spreading out into three distinct melodies that vied with one another but always kept perfect harmony together. The Fomor took one step forward and then another. And

the Fir-Bolg watched, fascinated by this timeless ar-
chaic ritual, a dance that had not been seen on this island for three generations.

The leading rank of the Fomor ran forward five
paces and all in Brocan's war band gripped their
weapons in anticipation. But this was just a taunt to
put their nerves on edge. The enemy halted and sang a
line of their song. Then the rest of their number ran
forward to join them.

They continued in this manner until they were
barely twenty paces away. Then Brocan stirred as if
woken suddenly out of a sleep.

"They are close enough to cast spears," he muttered to himself, surprised he had been so enthralled
by their dance that he hadn't noticed. "Form two
ranks!" he ordered. "Spears at the ready for the rear
rank to cast."

The front line of warriors knelt down, pushing the
points of their spears forward, ready to repel the
enemy. The warriors in the rear held their weapons at
their shoulders, raised ready to throw.

"Don't be fooled," Fineen warned the king. "Your
spears are useless against this enemy. If you order
them to cast their spears they will be defenseless
when the real attack comes."

"How will we defend ourselves then?"

"Stand firm to the last and all will be well."

"Stand firm!" Brocan repeated. "No weapon is to
be thrown unless I give the command."

The Fomor took another step forward and their

voices rolled through the Fir-Bolg ranks like thunder passing over the land. This close Brocan could clearly see the strange attire of the enemy. Their armor was very light, mostly constructed from shaped leather with some bronze reinforcing and rivets. Helms were of polished bronze that shone like pink-tinted gold. Their spears were long and heavy, good for stabbing but difficult to throw.

Shields of leather, bronze and wood protected the front rank troops, but they were huge and cumbersome, spending the vigor of the warriors before the first blow had been struck. Brocan was beginning to understand how these once undefeated warriors had eventually been overcome.

The king noticed a few warriors in his own front line looking back at him for guidance. He steadied them with a gesture and a strong voice.

"Hold!" he ordered. "No move until I give the order."

Then, just as the Fomorian war song was reaching a fever pitch, and as their lines came within striking range of a handheld weapon, the noise of their battle chant ceased. The sudden and unexpected silence which followed spoke of devastation, of emptiness, of annihilation.

The tension was too much for many of the Fir-Bolg to bear. Some were allowing the tears to roll down their cheeks, others were shaking uncontrollably. A young man in Brocan's front line stood up and before anyone could stop him he had rushed forward at the enemy, his spear level in front of him.

As he approached the Fomor lines the enemy jeered at him, raised their weapons and disappeared. He ran on, slashing with his spear point at the shadows, striking nothing but empty air.

The other warriors in Brocan's war party broke their ranks to observe this wonder. Some simply stood gaping, others retreated, muttering amongst themselves.

"They must stand their ground," Fineen insisted, grabbing the king by the sleeve. "They are falling into the enemy's hands."

Brocan looked up at the treetops and suddenly understood this diversion had been intended to split his defenses. If all discipline faded, the birds would be able to single out his warriors and pick them off one by one.

"Form a circle of two ranks!" he screamed and for the most part his warriors obeyed the command without thinking.

But the young man who had charged out heedless at the ghostly Fomor did not hear the order. He was in the middle of the road, wildly thrashing at the empty air, defying the enemy to return and do battle with him. It was then he made a costly mistake.

In his attempts to strike out at the spirits, he dropped the flaming torch from his hand. In moments it had sputtered out on the wet road, filling the air about him with curls of its dying smoke.

By the time his comrades were standing in their circle the young man had begun to calm down but by then it was too late. Countless owls as irresistible as the waves of the ocean began to surge down upon him. Before he could raise his spear to fend them off, he was engulfed, completely lost among their feathers and wild cries.

The ground about him was gradually soaked in blood as hundreds more birds joined in the frenzy of the kill. If he called out for help or in anguish he was not heard above the jubilant hooting of this Otherworldly foe.

Brocan watched the scene helpless to save the careless warrior, but his resolve hardened.

"They shall not get any more of us," he declared to his war band above the din of the slaughter. "Now you see what will become of you if you break from your ranks. We will hold firm and we will survive."

The young man was still invisible to them, cloaked under the great bulk of birds. Abruptly the seething mass toppled forward and spread out upon the road and the king knew the young man was finally beyond pain.

"What do we do now?" Brocan asked the healer.

"We march on in a tight formation guarded front and back by flame and spear," Fineen replied. "They will continue to assail us but they will have no chance of breaking through if the warriors do not flinch at their duty."

All eyes were now full of hatred and most hearts ready for vengeance. The king knew how warriors could change when these two emotions showed upon their faces. While the owls were still picking at the young man's corpse he gave the order to march.

Past the bloody mess in the road the war party trod, weapons at the ready, torches swinging at any owl foolish enough to come too close. But the birds knew their strength lay in their great number. Wave after wave descended upon the Fir-Bolg so that after they had marched one hundred paces twice as many of the winged creatures lay dead behind them.

Now the warriors knew their opponents. They understood their methods and their weaknesses. A thousand steps they trod and then an anguished cry arose from the bird folk. Their steady attack dwindled and their numbers, still in the countless hundreds, began to decline.

Before the war party had marched another twenty paces the air was cleared of owls. Only the trail of scattered dead and wounded birds behind them remained. The king called the band to a halt again and they took up the shape of a defensive circle once more.

And they waited.

"What is happening?" Brocan asked the Druid.

"I don't know," Fineen admitted. "Some catastrophe has befallen the woods. All the bird folk are retreating to safety."

"What calamity could cause them to break off battle and fly from us when they were so determined?"

As he spoke the forest to his right began to rustle. The rustling soon turned into a rumble as the trees began to shake. The air was full of the cries of thousands of animals leaping, charging, screaming as they left the cover of the woods. Like the banks of an overflowing river they burst out from their cover, flowing all around the startled Fir-Bolg.

"They mean us no harm!" the healer shouted. "Let them pass."

All the path before the warriors and after them was a panicked assortment of creatures. Badgers, boar and wild dogs, mice, squirrels, rats, otters, wolves, foxes and every tribe of bird passed by, ignoring the war party entirely as they crossed the road and ran on.

Among the last a great brown bear, Brocan's own totem animal, loped its way across and disappeared into the trees at the other side.

"What is going on?" the king demanded.

"A warning has passed through the ranks of all the creatures who live here," Fineen replied. "The forest is on fire."

Chapter 23

LONG AFTER MIDNIGHT DALAN AWOKE WITH A START. It had been his intention to stay wide awake by the fire but the hours had passed by slowly and silently. Eventually he had dozed off. The Brehon stretched his arms high into the air and moved his toes in his boots. He glanced over at Mahon and Aoife still fast asleep in each other's arms.

Only then did he notice the countless owls sitting wide-eyed and silent all around them, waiting for the fire to die down. In an instant the Brehon was on his feet but the birds were not intimidated by his sudden move. Dalan grabbed the last of their supply of fallen timber and stacked it neatly on top of the flames.

Soon the little blaze was burning away merrily again but the Druid knew the fuel would not last them until dawn. He looked down on Mahon resting so peacefully and considered whether it was worth waking him. He decided to wait until the flames had almost finished their work. Let the young warrior rest for now.

Then Dalan took up his seat, leaning against his harp once more. After he had settled he took out his little black-handled knife, a tool which all Druids carried no matter what their specialist craft. He turned it over in his hand.

"I have never taken any life with this blade," he confessed quietly to the nearest owl. The bird stared back without any sign of recognition. "But I will slay as many of you as I can before you overwhelm us," he went on. "Do you understand?"

The owl cocked its head and took a step closer.

"Stay back," the Brehon warned and the bird nested itself down again to wait. Twenty paces away there were owls landing to join their comrades. More and more arrived by the minute. Dalan was beginning to despair.

Suddenly there was a great stirring at the back of the assembled birds. Owls were hooting loudly and flying off in different directions. Only those closest to the fire seemed determined to stay put. Dalan quickly surmised the birds were about to launch an assault, despite the flames which had kept them at a good distance for so long.

"Mahon!" the Druid called. "Aoife! Wake up! We are about to be attacked!"

The pair stirred immediately but already many owls had disappeared into the night. The birds nearest the ring of the fire were also withdrawing reluctantly and this puzzled Dalan.

He looked around, then gasped, "Torches! Coming from deep within the forest!"

"Who would be traveling the forest road at night?" Mahon asked.

"I have no idea," Dalan replied. "But I fear we are in real trouble now. The birds we could keep away with a simple fire. Armed warriors are a different matter entirely."

"The fire will give us away," Aoife pointed out. "Shouldn't we put it out?"

"Then we risk being attacked by the owls," Mahon countered.

"Aoife is right," the Brehon sighed. "But I fear they will have already spotted our tiny blaze. If we can plainly see their torches at this distance, there is no doubt they have seen our shadows moving about in front of the fire."

"We must escape!" Mahon exclaimed.

"It is useless to run," the Brehon told him wearily. "There are too many of them. And in any case where would we go? The road to either side of us is a muddy trap. We would not get far. And I would rather take my chances here, waiting for these warriors to come upon us, than venture into the forest of Dun Beg."

It was then Mahon saw a little flash of orange in the forest. "Look!" he cried. "More of those strange lights are coming upon us."

The Brehon frowned. There was a light, but it was not an Otherworldly fire like those they had seen earlier. This was a single orange torchlight flickering from view as it passed between the trees.

"I fear we are surrounded," Dalan muttered, down-hearted that the end had come upon him so soon.

"Are they Gaedhals?" Aoife asked.

"I hope so," the Druid replied. "For if they prove to be the folk I fear them to be, we are in deep trouble."

"Fomorians?" Mahon gasped. "But all the Fomor are dead and gone, their dust scattered to the winds."

"Their spirits live on in this place," Dalan told him. "Many of them have taken the form of those owls. The remainder march in ghostly company to harass any travelers passing through their realm."

No sooner had he finished speaking than two fig-ures stumbled out of the forest and fell down on the soft earth. Their torch dropped to the ground and was soon extinguished. Mahon drew his sword in readiness but Dalan, his eyes wide with surprise, held the young warrior back.

"You will not be needing that yet," he said, hardly able to believe his own eyes. "They are not our ene-mies."

"Who are they then," Mahon inquired in confu-sion, "if not the spirits of the Fomor?"

But the Brehon did not have a chance to answer. Aoife had already recognized her brother and was running toward him before either Dalan or the young Danaan could stop her.

"Aoife!" Sárán cried, overjoyed to see her. "How did you know we would come out of the forest here?"

"This was the spot where you entered the woods," Dalan replied for Aoife as she cradled Sárán's head in her arms. "It is no more than chance brought us to stay here the night."

"Dalan," Fergus coughed, "is that you?"

"Is that the king's brother?" the Brehon asked incredulously. "How did you come to find Sárán?"

"He found me," the veteran admitted. "And he saved my life."

"We must get you both to the fire," Dalan told them. "You are soaked through to the skin."

Sárán and Fergus looked at each other with concern.

"Fire!" they said together.

"There is a fire sweeping through the forest," the veteran gasped. "We barely escaped it by diving into a stagnant pool. The flame front was whipped up by the wind and swept away down a valley. We are not far ahead of it."

"A fire?" the Brehon repeated, finding it hard to believe there was yet another danger descending upon them. "How on earth did a fire start deep within the woods?"

"We lit it," Sárán told him.

"You lit a fire in the forest?"

But before the young man could tell any more of his tale Mahon put a firm hand on the Brehon's shoulder.

"The warriors are almost upon us," he declared. "What shall we do?"

"Warriors?" Fergus asked with sinking heart. "Are you going to tell me we trudged through that hell just to be captured on the other side by the Milesians?"

"Come to the fire," Dalan sighed. "There is no escape for us. Even if we were all fit to run, there is nowhere left to flee. We will wait and warm ourselves by the light of the flames. Are you thirsty?"

The veteran nodded and with his arm around the Brehon's shoulder managed to walk to the fireside and sit down. And there they all waited with resignation for the enemy.

But as the warriors drew closer, making their way laboriously through the mud which blanketed this part of the road, Fergus noticed a familiar form at the head of the column. The veteran stood up so he could get a better view of the approaching war party.

Then, to everyone's surprise, Fergus cried out triumphantly and ran down into the mud, slipping and sliding as he went.

"What is it?" Dalan called after him. "What's the matter?"

"It's Brocan and the warriors of Dun Burren!" the veteran sang. "They've come to rescue us!"

The Fir-Bolg war party covered their heads with their cloaks to fend off falling sparks as they marched, managing to escape danger before the fire consumed the southern edge of the forest completely.

Dalan, Aoife, Mahon, Fergus and Sárán marched among the warriors. Brocan didn't speak a word to any of them until they were safely beyond reach of the flames and the spirits of that haunted place.

Where the road came out of the woods at the top of the hill overlooking the mouth of the River Shannon he finally halted his people then commanded cooking fires be lit and food be apportioned out. Two casks of mead were opened. Everyone took a cup to ease their discomfort and exhaustion.

"We'll rest here till noon," the king told them as the eastern sky behind him was lit by the red glow of the forest blaze. "Then we will press on to the river."

He sent two scouts ahead to arrange with the Cairige folk who fished the waters around Deer Island for boats, enough to carry his warriors to the southern bank. Then, when all were settling down to rest and he had eaten a few mouthfuls of bread washed down with mead, he sent for his son, Sárán.

"Do you have the berries which Fineen gave into your care?" Brocan asked the young man in a quiet but demanding voice.

"They're here," Sárán replied, handing the little leather pouch to the healer.

Fineen took the bag, checked the contents and then spoke to the king. "The berries are safe. I will be able to prepare the brew in time if we make it across the river today."

Brocan nodded and sighed heavily. "And what of the cauldron?"

"The Milesians have it," Sárán replied, head bowed in shame.

"You delivered it into their hands?"

"I had no idea Isleen was carrying the cauldron in her pack," the young man protested. "If I had known it was her intention to betray her people by this action, I would have stopped her. I did not discover her real purpose until it was too late."

"Nevertheless you left your duties and your teacher to go off with this woman," Brocan growled. "You deserted your kinfolk in time of trouble. You led us into danger by taking this road south."

"I was following Isleen," Sárán pleaded. "She told me that Fineen had granted his permission for me to travel with her."

"And why didn't you ask your teacher about this yourself?"

"There wasn't time."

"What do you think, Dalan?" Brocan asked. "You are a judge and I have decided to bring charges against this lad."

"He's your son," the Brehon began.

"I didn't ask you for a lesson in genealogy," the king snapped.

"If you charge him formally, there is a risk he could be banished," Dalan explained. "Would you want that?"

"If he's guilty he should be punished," Brocan answered coldly.

Dalan looked hard and long at the young man standing before him. "Do you understand the nature of the charge being brought against you?" he asked after considering the matter.

"Yes. Theft and treason," the young man shot back with vestiges of his old arrogance in his voice.

"And your defense is that a Seer convinced you to desert your teacher and your king to travel with her to the south?"

"That's correct."

Dalan turned to the king. "I've been suspicious of Isleen and her husband for some time. I should have said something publicly. I should have challenged them. If I had, this problem would not have arisen and the Cauldron of Plenty would be safe."

"Are you trying to shift the blame?" Brocan asked with suspicion.

"Sárán could not have known of my growing distrust of them," Dalan observed. "He simply followed the orders of a respected Seer. He had no reason to question those commands."

"Sárán is a traitor and a thief. I demand the harshest penalty under the law," Brocan countered.

"I cannot oblige you," Dalan breathed. "It was youthful foolishness, that's all. You said so yourself."

"And is there no punishment for foolishness?"

"The sentence which I pass upon fools," the Brehon replied, "is that they should learn from their mistakes."

"You're afraid," the king decided. "You, the last of the Fir-Bolg Druids. You're frightened to upset your Danaan masters." Brocan took a deep breath and looked the Druid in the eye. "Very well. Sárán will be cast into chains and dragged along with us to Sliabh

Mis. After the battle I will try him with another judge until a fitting punishment is meted out."

"You can't do that," Dalan protested. "It is the role of the Brehons to institute such things. You don't have the authority."

"It seems that treachery among the Fir-Bolg Druids is not so uncommon," Brocan noted bitterly.

"A king has no right under the law to hold anyone against their will," the Druid maintained calmly.

"I no longer recognize your authority," Brocan hissed. Then he turned to Fergus. "Take Sárán and bind him well so all he can do is walk. He will come with us in shame for his actions."

The veteran did not move. "My lord, your son saved my life in the forest. If it weren't for him I'd still be there staring at the lifeless heads of my five scouts. His tracks into the forest led us out again. I owe him my life."

"It was because of Sárán that you were led to the forest in the first place!" the king cried. "He is responsible for those five deaths as surely as if he had murdered them himself."

Fergus nodded. "I spoke up against you once," the warrior declared. "I vowed I would not do it again. And so I will be true to my word as long as you are legally the elected king of our people."

Fergus turned to Sárán. "Come then, lad. Submit to your fate and trust that your innocence is genuine."

The young man stepped forward and Fergus led him away to be bound.

"That is enough talk," Brocan commanded. "I will rest now before we set out for the river. No one is to approach me on this matter until we reach Sliabh Mis. Then I will tell you my decision."

"Your decision?" the Brehon asked.

"I will make up my mind about this battle when I have judged the Milesians' strength."

"You have already made a commitment to fight with the Danaans against the invaders."

"I have changed my mind."

Isleen and Eber arrived at the Milesian camp around the same time as Sárán was being bound in chains by the veteran whose life he had saved. On a long stretch of seafront known to the Cairige people as the Beach of the Bright Sands their boat landed and was dragged ashore by many hands.

The Gaedhals cheered their war leader as he went around the crowd, greeting those who had just arrived from the east.

"So you have deserted my brother then?" he asked one man.

"Éremon is a good leader but he drives the people too hard," the man replied.

"I will drive you hard also," Eber told him. "But I will reward you handsomely. We have barely six days to prepare for this contest. This evening I will speak with the clan chieftains and we will discuss our strategy."

Then the Milesian leader made his way through the

crowd to a roughly built stone shelter set aside for him. Isleen followed after, hardly noticed among the adoration heaped on Eber.

Once they were inside the stone hut Isleen spoke. "The King of the Danaans is here?"

"He is my prisoner," Eber told her proudly. "I give you my thanks for letting me know he would be at Dun Burren. He will prove a valuable bargaining point."

Eber offered her a cup of mead flavored with liquor made from hazelnuts. She took it and drank the cup down in one gulp.

"And will you want me for your queen when you are King of the South?" she asked.

"I am already King of the South," he sniggered. "This battle contest is merely a formality. I have the symbol of kingship delivered into my own hand."

As he spoke a warrior appeared at the doorway carrying the cauldron.

"Set it down by the fire," Eber directed.

The man did as he was told then left immediately.

"So this is the renowned Cauldron of Plenty?" he said almost to himself as he ran a finger around the richly decorated rim. "I imagined such a magical vessel would be far more impressive. There is no gold adornment or silver trimming."

"This is not the only cauldron," Isleen laughed. "This is merely one of the Druid vessels held by the Danaan and Fir-Bolg."

"And each has the power to feed a multitude?"

"Oh yes," she assured him.

The king approached her so that they stood close enough to see the patterns in each other's eyes.

"Prove it to me," he urged softly.

"What food would you have me cook in it?" she inquired. "What meal takes your fancy?"

"Salmon," the Milesian told her without hesitation. "Baked salmon."

"Very well," Isleen laughed, obviously enjoying this game. "Then eat your fill."

Eber frowned. "What do you mean?"

"Your fish will be getting cold," she told him gesturing with her eyes toward the cauldron.

Frowning with disbelief the Milesian went over to the vessel to look inside. To his astonishment it contained a single salmon the size of a newly born calf. He took his meat knife and sliced away a piece of the fish to taste.

"This is delicious," he exclaimed. "Cooked with herbs and honey the way I have always liked it."

Eber reached his hand in and grabbed as much of the fish as he could hold. Then he stuffed the food into his mouth, laughing at the wondrous miracle.

"Perhaps you would rather roast goose?" Isleen offered, and when Eber looked again the salmon had changed into a roasted goose browned to perfection. The enticing aroma filled the stone hut as Eber dropped the remnants of the salmon and took to the bird with his meat knife.

"How is it done?" he begged her.

"Druid knowledge," Isleen explained. "Only one of my kind can bring such foods out of the cauldron."

"So I will have a use for you after all, wife." Eber grinned.

"Without me the vessel is useless."

"Beef broth," the Milesian challenged with a hint of mischief in his voice. The words were hardly out of his mouth when thick brown soup began bubbling away inside the cauldron.

"I can't wait to show this little prize to the Fir-Bolg king," Eber chortled. "Now he will know who owns this land."

"You are not so smart as you first appear," Isleen chided.

"What?"

"You will not earn his respect by showing him this prize. You will earn his eternal hatred. He will vow to destroy you for desecrating one of the most sacred treasures his people possess."

"But his folk no longer possess it," Eber pointed out.

"Show it to Cecht. Let him return to Brocan with the cauldron as a gesture of your goodwill," she suggested.

"Are you mad? This vessel could feed my people without the need for foraging and raiding. It will remain with me."

"There is a greater prize than this," she teased. "The Quicken Tree."

"A tree?" Eber shrugged. "And what is so special about this Quicken Tree?"

"It is a symbol of the law," Isleen lied. "A powerful bargaining tool which you would be advised to use to your advantage. It is so sacred the merest mention of it will give you the upper hand in negotiations with the Danaans."

"I don't intend to negotiate with them," the Milesian scoffed. "I'm going to defeat them in battle and take their country for my own."

"As you wish." She shrugged. "But you will gain more if you come to an agreement."

"I will keep the magic vessel," Eber decided.

"Then I will leave and the cauldron will be useless to you. You are a fool. You've forfeited a friend, an ally and a wife in one stroke."

With that Isleen made for the door. The Milesian leader made no attempt to stop her.

"Please pass on my respects to King Cecht of the Danaans," she said as she left the hut. "My business with you is at an end."

Eber smiled to himself, well pleased with this prize and unconcerned by Isleen's threat to withdraw her support.

"She will see that I am right," he thought as he fetched a bowl to taste the soup. "And she will not leave this place. After all, how far can she get without a boat?"

When he had found a wooden bowl he went back to the cauldron to try the broth but the vessel was empty. He reached into the depths of it with his fingers and it was cold to the touch. In moments he was outside calling for his guards to fetch the Seer to him. Eber went back inside to sip his mead.

A long while later there was a cough at the door.

"My lord?" the guard ventured.

"Yes."

"The Seer called Isleen is nowhere to be found."

"How is that possible?"

"I cannot say, my lord. She is not anywhere among our people or our campfires. She has disappeared."

"Search again!" the Milesian bellowed. "And do not dare show your face until she has been found."

The guard was about to leave when Eber realized Isleen had escaped from him, and he cursed his foolish tongue for upsetting her.

"Bring the Danaan king to me," Eber demanded of the man. "And the Fir-Bolg queen also."

"Yes, my lord."

The Milesian took up a fur to cover the cauldron, deciding it would be best if he did not reveal his prize for the moment. Then Eber returned to his drink and to pondering the strange nature of the people who inhabited this land.

By the time Cecht and Riona arrived at his hut the Milesian was beginning to understand that he would achieve nothing without the help of these people. Three summers of war had proved that he would not be able to hold the south under his sway alone. He simply did not have enough followers.

"Welcome!" Eber offered as the King of the Danaans entered the hut.

Riona followed after, showing her contempt by not wiping her feet at the door.

"I beg you to sit down," The Milesian said, ushering them both to a flat stone beside the fire. "So what do you think of my assembled army?" he asked as he handed them cups of mead from a jug.

"We will accept your hospitality," Cecht told him ignoring the question, "because after the cowardly manner in which you took us captive you owe us some recompense. But please do not expect polite conversation. You are an invader who has no regard for the high and sacred Brehon tradition. If you were a barbarian from the eastern lands or one of the foreigners who sail occasionally from the west, I could excuse you."

Cecht took the cup and drank a mouthful of the sweet liquor.

"But our peoples share a Druid tradition," he went on. "We understand the same laws. We come from the same source, the sacred holy Islands of the West."

"You are right," Eber agreed. "Like a great stone that has been split up, we all share a common origin. And the pieces may easily be fitted together again."

"That remains to be seen," Cecht replied skeptically. "We have grown a long way apart. Our origins may be the same but the paths we have all walked since have sent us in different directions."

"The fact is," the Milesian said, coming to the point, "my people are here now. We have superior weapons and skills as warriors."

"We have better laws," Riona told him. "We have fine musicians."

"And my folk have the Draoi arts of healing and song making," Cecht added. "So perhaps we should be speaking of sharing this land between us so that each benefits from the talents of the others."

Eber nodded. "I have something I would like to show you," he said and reached over to remove the fur covering from the cauldron. "My warriors brought it to me."

When Riona saw the vessel she stood up in dismay. "Is my husband dead?" she cried.

"Brocan is alive as far as I know," the Milesian told her.

"Then how did you manage to steal this from him?"

"That is not important. The point is I now have this miraculous vessel. I possess some of your Draoi art. I have the power to feed my warriors endlessly without diminishing our supplies and livestock. I now possess the famed Cauldron of Plenty."

"This is not a Draoi vessel." Cecht smiled. "This is a symbol granted to the King of the Fir-Bolg by the Druid Assembly. It has no Draoi about it."

"It produces whatever food one desires," Eber protested. "I have witnessed this myself."

"Who told you this tale?" Riona laughed. "Its only value is the honor that goes with it. It represents the reputation of a king's generosity. Any who sit at his table are fed from the Cauldron of Plenty. This is a recognition of Brocan's hospitality."

"There is a Cauldron of Plenty," the Danaan king

went on, "but that resides with the Dagda, the Chief Druid of the Danaan folk. It is one of the four treasures my people rescued from the Islands of the West before they sank beneath the waves."

"Isleen showed me!" Eber spat. "You are lying. This is a trick to make me believe the cauldron is worthless. I know it can produce whatever food is called from it and I demand to know the secret."

"Isleen?" Cecht repeated. "She brought this cauldron to you?"

"Yes."

"That is treachery of the worst kind," the Fir-Bolg queen declared. "I cannot believe that one of our own people would do such a thing."

"She asked me which food I desired most," Eber explained. "I requested roasted salmon. And there it was. Then she produced a finely flavored goose and last of all a thick beef broth."

"Isleen is a Seer," the Danaan protested. "The Dagda himself does not have the knowledge to turn a ceremonial bronze cooking pot to such uses."

Riona touched the cauldron and examined the inside. "It is cold now and empty," she noted. "Are you certain you did not imagine the whole episode?"

"I am certain."

"This riddle is simply solved," Cecht remarked. "Call for Isleen and we will see for ourselves. Where is she?"

"My guards have been unable to locate her," Eber admitted. "She has disappeared."

"You must return the vessel," the Fir-Bolg queen urged him. "It was not yours to take. And if I know my husband, his rage will be overflowing already. There is little chance that we will negotiate any treaty if this matter is not resolved."

"A treaty?" the Milesian queried. "The sovereignty of the south is to be decided in battle. That is the challenge I placed before your husband. There was no mention on my part of any treaty."

"But a treaty makes much more sense," Cecht replied. "Our peoples have skills which could be beneficial to each other."

"I will not be a party to any treaty. This land is mine by right of conquest."

"We shall see," Riona sighed. "We shall see."

Chapter 24

THE EASTERN HORIZON ADORNED ITSELF IN A MISTY blue-gray. At the very summit of the sacred hill at the foot of the Sliabh Mis mountains, around the spreading apple tree, ninety warriors of the Fir-Bolg stood shoulder to shoulder with twenty Danaans, awaiting an end to this adventure, one way or another. Dawn clouds announced good tidings for the defenders on this the appointed day of battle.

Rain would surely soften the surface of the earth. Then the hillside would become slippery. By the time the Milesians were ready to storm the Fir-Bolg position they would doubtless find the going heavy. Even a light fall of rain would guarantee more than a few casualties among the attackers before they even reached their enemy.

Brocan waited with a lightened heart as the drizzle turned to a downpour. Cloak wrapped close about his head, he blessed this change of fortune. For the first time since he accepted the battle challenge he was daring to hope for victory.

"If I win the field today," he told himself, "the Danaans will owe me a great debt. We will drive the invaders out of the south with their tails between their legs."

Pungent smoke from Fineen's fire caught at the back of the king's throat, distracting him from his thoughts. Brocan turned around and walked briskly over to the fireplace, stepping carefully to avoid the muddy patches of ground.

The healer was stirring a great bronze cauldron not unlike the Cauldron of Plenty in its design. This one was smaller and burned black across the bottom from endless use. Fineen never seemed to have time to polish his cooking vessel properly.

"Will the brew be ready on time?" the king asked casually, as if the answer didn't really matter to him.

"Of course," the healer replied in an injured tone. "Do you think I was up all night idly counting the stars? I was here with my ladle stirring the pot while you and your warriors slept soundly."

Brocan leaned over the pot, surprised at the small amount of liquid bubbling in the bottom.

"Will there be enough for all my people?" he asked.

"Enough and more."

"And you say this brew will keep all harm from my folk in battle?"

"It will heal any who are injured. It will restore to life those who fall dead on the field. And it will prolong life, bestowing new vigor, sharpened senses and increased strength upon the healthy."

"We may not stand in need of it," the king chortled. "The weather is on my side."

"You would not consider forgoing the brew?" Fineen asked in shock. "Your people have earned it. And it is freely given by the Danaan folk in recognition of your alliance with them."

"I've never taken charity from your folk," Brocan snapped, mildly insulted by the healer's tone. "And my warriors don't need any Draoi tricks to help them stand against the foe. I don't believe this battle with the Milesians will be more frightening than the fight in the forest. If my warriors could defeat the very spirits of the air, then a handful of barbarians from across the sea will not bother them."

"If we defeat the Milesians here today," Fineen countered, "the war will not end. They will not simply turn their backs and go home. They will continue to raid and harass the countryside until they wear us down. Do you want that?"

"If I defeat them it will be a resounding victory," Brocan stated confidently. "I won't leave them the strength to raid eggs from a wren's nest."

"The Druid Assembly spent one full cycle of the seasons planning for this fight," the healer pressed. "They know we can't drive the enemy from Innisfail forever. Can't you see the wisdom in seeking a treaty? Don't you understand that this is the only way to achieve an honorable peace?"

"Honorable?" the king scoffed. "Druid trickery and potions. I don't see the honor in that."

"Your people will retain their lands." Fineen shrugged. "They'll keep their own rulers. And they'll not be harangued by the invaders. All my folk and yours will withdraw behind the ancient veil which guards the Otherworld."

"Will we be ghosts like those spirits we battled in the forest?"

"No," the healer replied. "Those poor Fomor souls are disembodied creatures doomed to wander until they accept the next stage of existence. We will have life, free from sickness, pain or death."

"I wonder whether life would be worthwhile without those things," Brocan mused.

But his thoughts were cut short when a hand came down firm upon his shoulder. It was Fergus.

"They're coming," the veteran announced.

"Are they alone?"

"It seems so," Fergus replied. "And Cecht is carrying the cauldron on his back."

"The cauldron?" Brocan hissed. "How in the name of Balor's Evil Eye did that Danaan get hold of the cauldron?"

"I have no idea."

"And Riona is with him?"

"Yes, my lord," the veteran answered with bowed head. "They're walking hand in hand."

Brocan did not flinch at this piece of news. "I expected no less," he said without any hint of emotion. "Let's go to the summit and wait for them. With this rain the Milesians won't start the fight before noon. We've plenty of time."

The king led the way to the place where he intended his warriors to stand. The two old friends sat down on their cloaks in the rain and watched as Cecht struggled up the muddy slope bearing the cauldron. Riona followed after, often helping the Danaan king to his feet when he slipped on the hillside. Brocan looked on patiently. His wife and his old enemy were still a long way from the top.

"The Gaedhals will have as much trouble gaining these heights," he stated to his steward. "We probably won't need the Danaans. I'll honor my obligation to Cecht. Though not perhaps in the manner he expects."

"And what will become of your wife?" Fergus inquired.

"I have no wife or queen any longer," Brocan grunted. "She may go where she will but she won't fight among our folk today."

"She's a warrior," the veteran reminded him. "We need every sword hand and spear point we can muster. And she has a right."

"Let her stand among the Danaans. She is no

longer Queen of the Fir-Bolg as far as I am concerned."

"Our warriors would likely disagree," Fergus advised in an urgent whisper. "Only the Council of Chieftains has a right to strip her of titles and responsibilities. It's not given into your hand to take such measures."

"I'll answer to the Council of Chieftains when the time comes," Brocan retorted. "If we win a victory today the chieftains won't care what was said between me and her. They'll be too busy rejoicing at our new-found peace and prosperity. She'll fight alongside her new king. And the Danaans will take up position at the rear. They are to engage the enemy only if some disaster befalls our warriors. Do you understand?"

"I do," the veteran sighed. "Will you come now with me to take the brew? Fineen told me the Dagda's musicians from the east will gather soon to bless it."

"No."

"No?"

"I'll not be sharing the Quicken Brew with everyone else."

"Why?"

"Because we have a chance to beat the Milesians on our own without treaties or Draoi tricks to save us."

"Brocan!" the veteran pleaded. "If we win there won't be a treaty."

"I realize that. And I am beginning to believe it

would be a good thing if the Fir-Bolg were able to hold their own with the Danaans. I don't trust Cecht."

"No man would blame you," Fergus sighed, his gaze straying back to Riona and the Danaan king.

As the veteran watched, Cecht stumbled forward in the mud, dropping his burden. The cauldron, still wrapped in the blanket Isleen had carried it in, rolled back down a little way until Riona caught it.

"We'll win this battle," the king laughed. "The Gaedhals won't have any easier a time of this hill than the King of the Danaans."

"Will you truly place your own life at risk in the wild hope we will win the battle?"

"Yes."

"The Druids have offered us eternal life and healing from all wounds," the veteran reminded him.

"And they claim we will all be young again," Brocan added, spitting on the ground in front of him to show his contempt for that promise.

"Will you ask your people to follow your example?" Fergus ventured.

"They'll do as I ask," Brocan stated. "If I present this strategy to them as the last hope for the sovereignty of the Fir-Bolg."

"They may not take up this cause as willingly as you might expect."

"If we take the brew we may as well surrender our future to the Danaans," the king reasoned. "Once we come to rely on the Danaan Druids for the Quicken Brew we lay ourselves open to coercion. If we reject the brew and gain the victory we will be in a strong position to bargain with the Danaans."

"And what of the promise of eternal life?" the veteran asked. "The Danaan brew can provide a life free of pain, sickness and death. Would you deny that to your people?"

"I don't know about you, Fergus, but I have always expected to die one day," Brocan quipped. "I have grown used to the idea after all the battles I have fought. As for pain, it is just a warning to us to be careful. I like to be warned of my carelessness whenever possible. And as for sickness, everyone knows it emanates from the depths of the soul. The signs of the illness may be healed but the causes will remain. Until they are eliminated there can be no true healing. This brew will deal with the symptoms well enough."

"We have been offered life," Fergus repeated. "Without the necessity to pass on to the Halls of Waiting."

"I have seen enough of life to be more than curious about death." Brocan smiled wryly. "It holds no fear for an old warrior like myself. Indeed the prospect of returning to this earth in a new form has me intrigued."

The veteran shrugged, unconvinced by his king's argument.

"You and I have been like brothers," Brocan went on. "Though you were fostered to my family we have shared everything from the moment you tasted my mother's breast milk. My eyes have seen what yours have. Tell me the truth. Are you not tired of fighting? Are you not weary of this world?"

Fergus dropped his head. "I am, in some respects."

"Would you truly wish to live forever? Would you be willing to shun the prospect of death forever?"

"It is an attractive thought. It would be a revival of the senses."

"But would you be so enthusiastic if you knew that no matter what you did you could not die? Would you still yearn for the things that make life worthwhile now?"

"What do you mean?"

"Life is sweet because at any moment it could be snatched away from us." Brocan smiled. "There is something sacred about our vulnerability. It inspires folk to love with all their hearts while they have the opportunity. The true value of ourselves, our lifelong achievements, our ambitions, our loves, all depend on this simple premise."

The king took a deep breath and sighed before he went on. "There is nothing surer but that one day we must depart this world for a short time. Then we go to the Halls of Waiting to shed our memories before returning refreshed like the new buds in spring."

The veteran stared into his friend's eyes. He was beginning to agree with Brocan.

"If we charge down onto that battlefield today," the king went on, "after partaking of the brew, we may as well give up our souls to be consumed with boredom. There will be no value in the victory if there is no risk to our lives. This battle will be the start of a long tedious time without rest. Our lives will become futile."

"I have many memories of my long life," Fergus sighed. "And among them are too many saddening recollections. I know there are loved ones waiting for my return. And surely time spent in the Halls of Waiting would wash my sins and sadness away forever. There is no other remedy for the dark remembrances of days gone by. It is true that many good memories will be cleansed away with them, but to avoid the path of nature is worse than foolish."

"The Druids often speak of the way our ancestors tried to bend the forces of nature to their will," Brocan added. "The Isles of the West were destroyed because of the greed which grew from such stupidity."

"We have everything we need at Dun Burren." The veteran nodded. "Our lives may be hard compared to the Danaan folk of the east, but we are a happy people, well provided for. Our clanspeople are honest and hardworking. They are honorable, gentle, loving folk who value a good heart. It would break my spirit to see them changed all for the sake of a clever Draoi trick. The Quicken Brew would cause us more problems than we can imagine."

"Now we must convince our people," Brocan ended, clapping a hand on his friend's shoulder.

Fergus nodded as Riona and Cecht reached the summit of the hill. The exertion of the climb had shortened their breath but the Danaan king wasted no time in getting down to business. The veteran got to his feet and bowed. Brocan, however, did not stand.

"I bear news from Eber, King of the South, war leader of the Milesians," Cecht began.

"I don't recognize a king in that barbarian," Brocan jibed. "But I see a king before me transformed into a lowly messenger."

Cecht straightened his back and stood to his full height as the insult struck home. "Here is your cauldron," the Danaan spat as he dropped the vessel with a thud onto the wet ground. "Eber sends it to you with his compliments."

"That does not cancel the insult of stealing it in the first place."

"He didn't take it," Cecht explained. "It was the Seer, Isleen, who brought it south."

"Aided by Riona's boy Sárán no doubt," Brocan spat.

"He's your son also," the Fir-Bolg queen cut in.

"Not anymore," Brocan informed her. "He awaits the judgment of a Brehon court. I've disowned him."

"Eber sends you an offer," the Danaan king went on. "If you yield to him now and accept him as overlord of the south, he will allow you and your people to keep your lands. He has also promised he will not levy tribute greater than one third of all your produce if you lay down your arms and come to his house in peace."

"And did he make this offer to you also?" The king sneered.

"He did."

"How did you answer him?"

"I told him this land had been held by my folk since before my great-grandfather's time. I told him he would have to take it from me in blood or leave this island forever."

Brocan smiled. "Then we'll fight him together."

"We will fight," Cecht agreed. "And when the moment is right the Druid singers will open their doorway. The dead will rise from the field of battle and the wounded will be healed."

Brocan held his tongue and Cecht noticed the uneasy silence immediately.

"What's happened? The Druids have made the Quicken Brew, haven't they?

The Fir-Bolg king nodded.

"And the Druid musicians?"

"They're waiting to perform their task," Brocan assured him.

"Then what's the matter?"

"I must tell you I have a mind to win this battle."

"Win?"

"I intend to inflict heavy casualties on their warriors and drive them into the sea."

"You always were self-centered but such an act would be selfish even for you," Cecht replied coldly. "The strategy of negotiating a favorable treaty has been carefully planned by the Druid Assembly. There is no other way to ensure we hold an advantage against the Gaedhals. This very day in the north Eber's brother Éremon is to fight a battle against the Danaan hosts. The whole plan relies on a common outcome which will leave the invaders awed at the skill of our Druids."

"I'm not a Danaan," Brocan began.

"You've brought our warriors to this field." Riona frowned. "You have agreed to enter into a covenant with the Tuatha De Danaan. Would you compromise the honor of our people by breaking your word? What are you doing here then?"

"A great deal has happened since you were taken hostage." Brocan shrugged. "The Fir-Bolg are here to do their part, but I haven't decided what part that will be because I have changed my mind."

"You cowardly, treacherous old liar!" she jeered.

"You'd do well to clean the dirt from under your fingernails before you advise me to wash my hands," Brocan snapped. "A queen who is disloyal to her own folk and her king has no right to advise in matters of diplomacy. She is no longer considered a queen."

"Now I see what you've been planning!" Riona exclaimed. "If the Milesians are defeated here today you'll turn on the remaining Danaans and slaughter them. To rid yourself of two troubles at one stroke!"

Brocan gave no sign, no indication of his thoughts, nor did he show the slightest hint of emotion. Then his eyes fixed on his wife's for a space of several breaths. Suddenly the king turned away from her, and

Fergus realized the accusation must have had some truth in it. The old veteran frowned, then swallowed hard.

"I divorce you," Riona said in a low emotionless voice.

"What did you say?" the king asked, matching her tone.

"I divorce you."

"So be it," the Fir-Bolg king replied with a wave of his hand. "Fergus will be our witness as he was at our wedding. When this battle has been won I'll gladly discuss the details of your share of our holdings."

"I want nothing but to be free of your stubbornness and my shame," she told him. "Keep our common holdings. May they serve you well."

"Done," Brocan spat. "You'll not stand the field among our folk this day. If you've a mind to engage in battle, stand with your new-found family. Only twenty Danaans answered the call to fight. I am sure they will appreciate an extra sword hand in their midst."

"You'd better think twice about turning on my folk," Cecht advised.

"I never intended that," Brocan replied. "If you think about it, your people will have had their share of the Quicken Brew. So it would be rather stupid of me to attack them."

Fergus looked up from the ground, ashamed that he had doubted his king. "Then what's your plan?" he asked.

"The Danaans intend to retreat behind the veil of the Otherworld. Let them. They'll leave the land to us."

Riona strode off for five paces or so, cursing under her breath.

"I'll go to my people now," Cecht stated, his voice hard. "I've heard enough. Think well on your decision to turn this day to your own ends. We've never been anything more to each other than bitter enemies so I won't flinch at threatening you. If you betray my people I'll seek you out wherever you may hide and I'll put an end to your miserable life as I should have done last summer on the battleground."

"You'll not find me hiding," Brocan challenged. "But you will need to raise more than a mere twenty of your kindred if you wish to murder me. The Fir-Bolg are loyal, even if their queen is not."

"I'm loyal to my people," Riona hissed. "But I can't respect their king."

"Your mother was a Danaan," Brocan spat, as if that explained her attitude to him.

"Would you have Eriu come here to settle for that insult?" Riona asked.

"I'd welcome her as I always have. With a prayer she will not be visiting for very long."

Riona laughed. "It's always been a wonder to me that with a wit like that you could have such faith in your own decisions," she mocked.

"Most of my warriors are off in the north," Cecht cut in, coming between them. "The Milesians have fielded a force of many hundreds there. Every fighting hand is needed if the Danaan folk are to give a good account of themselves. That's the only reason so few Danaans are assembled here today."

"This alliance of yours doesn't seem to serve both sides with the same share," the Fir-Bolg king noted archly. "Go make yourself ready for the fight. Since I'm in command here today your folk will fight with the reserve. You've missed one skirmish while you enjoyed the enemy's hospitality. My warriors won a victory a few days ago against a fierce foe. They'll not meekly withdraw from battle and sue for peace."

"Be it on your head," Cecht said finally. "But don't blame my people if many Fir-Bolg lives are squandered as a result."

"Where's Sárán?" Riona asked abruptly.

"He's chained to a cow near Fineen's fire," Brocan replied. "I would prefer it if you would leave him alone. Under your influence he has committed a treacherous act."

"Under my influence?" she shot back. "You are a little too free with your accusations! It was the king, Sárán's father, who taught him the art of serving the self first," Riona noted with bitterness. "You nurtured his greed and that emotion is always the root of treachery."

Cecht took her arm then and led her away before any more harsh words could be spoken. Brocan would have followed after, taunting her in his anger, but Fergus put a hand on his shoulder to restrain him.

"If you really wish to win this fight," the veteran told him, "we need to talk to our warriors and consider a battle plan."

The king nodded, shook his shoulders to ease the tension in his body, and then the two of them went to assemble the warriors of the Fir-Bolg.

Fineen had already unchained Sárán while the brew was undergoing its final boil. The healer needed all the help he could muster so he ordered the young man to fetch him some water.

"The healing potion must be watered down before I can dole it out," he explained to the young man.

"What if my father catches me walking about freely?" Sárán asked with concern. "I have provoked his anger enough. I wouldn't like to see him really lose his temper."

"You are a Druid in training," the healer reminded him. "And I am still your teacher, no matter what charges have been brought against you. Now go and do as I bid. I don't have time to argue."

The young man nodded, picked up a bronze bucket and went down to the nearby stream to collect the water.

He had not been gone long when Dalan and Aoife came over to the fire and sat down by its warmth.

"The brew smells sweet," the Brehon commented.

"I was forced to add a lot more honey than I planned, just to make it palatable," Fineen admitted. "There are other herbs mixed in which were not mentioned in the recipe. To leave them out would have meant the potion would be nearly impossible to drink."

"I hope there will be some bread with it," Aoife commented. "I am very hungry."

"Warriors do not eat on the morning of battle," the Brehon informed her. "That was why there was no breakfast prepared."

"Do Brehons break their fast before they witness a fight?" she asked.

"They do." The healer smiled. "Dalan does in any case. I have seen him put away enough for three men before a battle."

"It is a delicate duty," the Brehon protested. "If I miss the slightest detail of a fight I could cause offense or misrepresent the facts. Food aids the memory." He turned to his student. "Always eat a good meal before you sit down to remember a fight."

"That is good advice." Fineen nodded. "But you will not find any food here. I have some bread but only enough for those who will not be fighting to take a small piece with their brew."

"We will make do with whatever is available," Dalan assured him.

"Is the potion ready?" Aoife inquired.

"It is," the healer replied.

"May we have ours now?"

"As soon as your brother returns with water from the stream I will call the ritual. When that is done everyone will take their portion. You may go to your father if you will and tell him it is time to assemble the warriors for that purpose. And then go to Cecht and tell him to bring his Danaans to the fire."

Aoife was gone before the healer had even finished speaking.

"And make sure they have their weapons ready," Fineen called after her. "It is almost noon and the Milesians will be upon us soon." Then the healer turned to Delan. "Are the musicians ready?"

"The singers have their melody well rehearsed," the Brehon informed his friend. "And the trumpeters have polished their instruments so they will seem to be all the more magnificent."

"Will the song-making truly open the doorway?" Fineen queried.

"I believe it may," Dalan replied with obvious reservation. "I have never witnessed this song before and my experience of the Draoi arts of music is limited. But I have reason to be hopeful."

"The Druid Assembly would never have entrusted the task to you if they did not believe you would rise to the challenge."

Dalan shrugged his shoulders to show he was not convinced.

"I have heard you were nominated to be among the candidates for the position of Dagda," Fineen commented.

"I was nominated," Dalan admitted. "But I have little chance of winning enough support among the Danaan Druids to gain the vote."

"Do you really think they would reject a talented Fir-Bolg in favor of a mediocre Danaan?"

"Since the days when my people were first joined with yours in the Druid Assembly no Fir-Bolg has held the office of Dagda," Dalan reasoned. "It is unlikely that will change, especially in these turbulent and unsettled times."

"You have the skills and the knowledge for the position. I'll cast my support behind you."

"Thank you," the Brehon said, taking his friend's hand. "But I'd really rather stay by Brocan's side after this business is concluded. I may be the only person who can reason with him. And that will certainly be necessary in the coming season."

"Brocan can look after himself," the healer argued. "You can't put aside the highest office in the Druid Circle simply because of one stubborn old king. You must think also of your own fulfillment."

"True, but I have another, greater problem. I fear that if I do not find a way to defeat the Watchers," Dalan admitted, "a greater peril will come to this land than the Milesians."

"Those Watchers have become an unhealthy obsession with you," Fineen stated bluntly. "I acknowledge they are very likely abroad in this land, but what can you do to fight them? There are none now living who keep the lore which related to them. You would be giving a greater service to the Druid Assembly with your leadership than by tracking down a pair of spirits whose day will soon be past."

"I wish I knew for certain they were fading from the world," the Brehon said wearily. "But the truth is they are becoming stronger. They feed on the fear and suffering of our folk. Soon they will have a new race of people to prey upon. The Milesians have no tales about the Watchers. Their Druids have no experience with them. Whereas I—"

"You are a gifted judge."

"I have a duty to find some way of dealing with the Watchers," Dalan insisted. "I stumbled across them and I must track them down again. With the threat from the Milesians the Druid Assembly has released much old lore about the Draoi-Music. Perhaps I will discover a song which will rid us of the Watchers before they bring more havoc upon us."

"Let us talk more about this when the current crisis is resolved," Fineen suggested.

"The Milesians are here because the Watchers drew them to our island home. If we do not defeat these ancient servants of Balor, other invaders will be summoned to our door before too long."

"Help me finish preparations for the brew," the healer said, trying to distract his old friend. "The musicians will be here soon to begin the ritual blessing. Could you stir this pot while I see to them?"

"I would be happy to," Dalan replied, relaxing a little.

"Steady and slow," the healer advised, handing him the wooden ladle.

"As you wish."

"You shall have the first helping," Fineen told him. "And then you must administer it to me."

"Very well."

With that the healer was gone to find the Druid musicians, those singers, drummers and harpers who would lay the blessing of their craft upon the Quicken Brew.

Brocan's warriors listened in stunned silence to his reasoning. But when he had finished speaking the king knew every one of them was behind him. After the victory against the owls in the forest the Fir-Bolg would have battled the flow of the River Shannon if he had asked them to.

"If any among you have doubts about refusing the brew," the king assured them, "I'll not judge you if you decide to take it. But any warrior who accepts the Quicken Brew will fight alongside King Cecht. I won't have them with the Fir-Bolg."

No one moved among his warriors. This brought a smile of gratitude to Brocan's face. Then there was a cough from the rear as someone pushed forward through the ranks. In moments a young man stepped out from the gathering. It was Lom.

"I will take the Quicken Brew," he announced.

Brocan was speechless at his son's gesture. "Why are you doing this?" he managed to mutter finally.

"I can see Dalan's argument," Lom explained. "If we beat the Gaedhals today, they will only return again. Eventually they will come in such numbers that we will have no hope of standing against them. We cannot always expect to have weather and landscape on our side."

"You would submit to the Danaans?" Brocan gasped.

"It is not submission. It is common sense."

"If you do this," Brocan stated coldly, "you will join your brother as an outcast from our people. You will be banished forever."

"You've been unjust to my mother and my twin," Lom countered.

"Your mother has divorced me to take up with Cecht. Your brother is a traitor who stole the Cauldron of Plenty from me. Is this the kind of company you wish to keep?"

"Sárán did nothing wrong," the young man protested. "He was tricked by the Seer Isleen."

"You are not yet tainted with the sins of your brother. If you leave my company now you should realize you will never be able to return. You will have no place among us."

"Then I'll live with my mother among the Danaan who do not make and break their word whenever the whim takes them," Lom replied with a coldness in his voice to match his father's.

"What word have I broken?" Brocan asked. "I am a servant to my people. I must do as they wish. My office depends on them. A king cannot always do as he wishes. A king is merely the protector of his kinfolk."

"You've been dishonorable!" Lom cried.

"I have bargained our kin into a very favorable position," Brocan pointed out. "If the Danaans get what they want from this battle, we'll still need to hold our own against the Milesians. If the Gaedhals gain the victory our position will be even less secure. But it is still my intention to win this fight and assert the strength of my people again."

"I can see there's no sense in arguing with you," Lom sighed.

"You may have a little wisdom about you after all," the king snapped.

Lom walked off in the direction of Fineen's fire where the musicians were gathering to perform their ritual.

"Go to your mother then," the king called after him.

Lom didn't have the opportunity to answer. At that very moment the choir of Druid musicians began their chant. Three bronze horns each as long as a man sounded their deeply sonorous bellows.

Then Lom was gone to join the ceremony, leaving his father to ponder the loss of another son.

The rain was still pelting down as the singers began their strange melody based around the low notes of the bronze horns. Lom felt his guts begin to shake as he approached the assembled Danaans. All doubts he may have had about taking this step were banished from his mind.

Around the fire where the brew had been cooking

the choir had assembled in the shape of a crescent moon. At the two horns of the formation sat the musicians with the long bronze horns, facing in toward the singers. In the center of the choir three harpers were positioned to guide the singers in their melody. Lom had never heard music like it before in his life. The strange tune floated in the air all around him, filling his every breath with excitement. It penetrated his body like a sharp prickling tingle that started at the top of his head, traveled down his spine and spread out into every muscle and fiber of his being.

Lom noticed Aoife standing hand in hand with Mahon among the Danaans and he wondered what his father would make of that. But he soon found he had to close his eyes to take in the music and all such thoughts left him.

Somewhere along the way the melody transformed into a soothing embrace which enlivened his spirit. Lom held a hand up to his face in wonder, half expecting the tips of his fingers to be glowing with energy. There was no visible light, just an ethereal prickling sensation, warm and relaxing.

As the music gradually gathered momentum Lom found his twin brother and his mother standing silent with Cecht and Dalan. He approached them without offering a greeting because he did not want to break the spell of this gorgeous music. Riona nodded to her son and reached out a hand to take his. At the very moment they touched Lom perceived a more intense and moving sensation flow through him. His mother released his hand and the feeling subsided a little, but the effect of it burned fiercely in his mind as if the contents of his head had been seared with the heat of a divine flame.

As his breathing began to quicken Lom started to feel uncomfortable. He knew there was nothing to be afraid of, but the intensity of the experience was decidedly unsettling. An urge came over him to run back and join his father, to abandon this wild scheme of the Druids. But Lom could not bring himself to move his feet. The choir lifted up their voices in a glorious harmony that brought vivid pictures of the mountains and the sea to his mind. But Lom instinctively knew this landscape spread out in his imagination would be found in Innisfail. Somehow the music had given him a glimpse of the ancestral land of his people.

By this time the young man could feel sweat gathering in the palms of his hands. The sweet voices held only a rising terror for him. Lom was faltering in his resolve, ready to run. And he would have done so too if something unexpected hadn't happened just at that moment.

As if they all shared common thoughts, the choir, the harpers and the horn players ceased their song at once and a heavy silence descended on the hilltop.

Lom breathed more easily and risked a glance around him. Dalan's eyes were shut tight, his face covered with perspiration. Fineen was shaking almost imperceptibly as he stared ahead with empty eyes.

Riona swallowed hard, struggling to catch her breath. When he realized everyone about him had been as deeply moved by the experience as he, Lom felt suddenly comforted.

He had no sooner begun to settle though when a steady drumbeat struck up from the midst of the choir. Among the thirty singers were nine men and women who bore goatskin drums. The beat was strong like the pulse of a heart. And it was soft, comforting like a lover's gentle embrace.

As the drummers meted out their rhythm Lom felt compelled to close his eyes. And as he did so the landscape that had filled his mind earlier returned in striking colors. Just as the song had entered his body through the top of his head, so too did this steady drumbeat. But now the young man could sense the music journeying up and down his spine with a warmth that left him refreshed, enlivened and intensely aware of every pore of his body. This, he told himself, must be a similar experience to that state the Druid kind called ecstasy, which their Seers strove to attain throughout their lives.

The drumbeat became more urgent; the singers raised their voices again. But now their song was not so harmonious. It was filled with distracting little phrases which did not seem to suit the melody at all. Then suddenly, in a grating conflict of notes which fought violently against each other, the music ceased.

Lom opened his eyes, noticing the rain had begun to fall a little heavier. Dalan stepped solemnly toward the cauldron. Fineen followed after him a few seconds later. Both men were pale and somber.

"In the days of our ancestors," the Brehon began, "the Druid kind held much wisdom at their command. They knew such skills and crafts that we can only wonder at. And yet for all their learning, for all their knowledge and for all their understanding of the ways of the earth, they allowed their craft to be used for ill deeds. They turned their skills to greed and avarice. At first it seemed they had tapped into the source of all the abundance of the universe. The chief Druids among them sanctioned the use of song to bring riches to the Islands of the Blest."

The Brehon paused to allow his audience to consider his words.

"In time they no longer held the earth in any esteem for it appeared they had the power to produce all they needed for their survival, and more. But their conceit blinded them to the destruction they had brought upon this world by upsetting the delicate balance of all life."

Dalan took a deep breath as he looked around at the listeners. Most had bowed their heads. Some seemed to be praying.

"So it happened," the Brehon went on, "that one day the Druid-Seers declared that a great tragedy would soon be visited upon the world. The lesser moon that had for generations sat in the heavens beyond the greater moon was slowly edging closer to the earth. The wise ones calculated it would come down upon the Islands of the West and obliterate them as it fell."

Fineen stepped forward then and took up the tale from his companion. "That's why the Danaans abandoned the ancient homeland to come here. It was our own Druids who brought this disaster down from above because they had not learned to stem their greed or tempered their cleverness with wisdom. The Islands of the Blest were swallowed up entirely by the floodwater and all those who had remained behind, their beautiful cities of glass, their fine roads paved with sparkling stone, their palaces and sanctuaries, all were washed away as if they had never been."

It was Dalan's turn to speak. "The first Quicken Tree, a rowan of exceptional beauty, grew in the mountains of the Isles of the West. It was a tree of healing, a tree of life. When our ancestors departed their homeland they took with them nine berries of the fruit of that bough. And in secret a new Quicken was planted so that if ever our folk stood in need of its healing, they would not be denied."

"Each of you," Fineen continued, "will taste the brew of the Quicken berries today. And in so doing you will ensure not only the survival of our people but the continuity of our laws and customs. This responsibility is not to be taken lightly. If we are successful in implementing the plans of the Druid Assembly, the Milesians will, in time, adopt our customs as if they were their own. This is the surest way we know of preserving peace on this land for all the folk who live here."

"Now you must each make a vow," Dalan stated. "To uphold the Brehon laws with every measure of your being. To never waver in your compassion for the Gaedhals, who are like children compared to us. They need our guidance. They must be taught there are better ways to conduct themselves. To that end it is the duty of all of you who take the brew to act as counselors, as teachers, as advisers to these newcomers in the hope they will learn from our example. For one day they will be the guardians of our knowledge and this island."

With that Dalan stepped back to the fire where the cauldron was simmering gently in the glowing coals.

"If there are any among you who cannot make these solemn promises," Fineen declared, "let them withdraw from this gathering."

The healer paused to see if anyone would leave. No one moved.

"Very well," he went on. "It's time to take on the mantle of immortality. Now let us shake off the endless cycle of birth and death and rebirth. We will live in the world of the senses for as long as we desire, and our kin who tarry in the Halls of Waiting will not see us again until the world has changed entirely."

Fineen went over to where Dalan was waiting for him. Then the healer took a small piece of oat bread with a cup of steaming liquid from the cauldron and handed them to his friend.

"Just drink it straight down and eat the bread afterward," Fineen whispered.

Dalan did as he was told. No sooner had he taken a mouthful of the liquid than his face screwed up. He swallowed the brew quickly and stuffed the bread into his mouth as fast as he could to take away the strong flavor.

"Did it really taste that bad?" Fineen asked under his breath.

"That was the foulest concoction ever to pass my lips," the Brehon coughed, keeping his voice down so no one would hear. "You may be a fine healer but your cooking skills need some improvement."

"I'll water it down," Fineen decided, tasting a spot of the brew from his finger. "That'll make it more palatable."

"Are you going to have your portion?"

"I'll wait if you don't mind," the healer replied.

"You were trying that out on me, weren't you?" Dalan groaned. "I can't believe I let you do that to me."

"You may be a fine judge but you're very gullible." Fineen shrugged with a grin.

"I can't banish the foul taste of it," the Brehon complained as he gulped water from a bucket.

"It could be worse," the healer told him. "Stop your whining and go to your work. You have a battle to observe today. And this tale is one you'll be asked to relate a thousand times over the rest of your life."

Then Aoife stepped up beside her teacher to receive her portion.

"Have you taken your brew?" she hummed.

The Brehon signed to her silently that he had.

"Now the Milesians can't defeat us. Not even time will wear us down."

"We shall see," Dalan replied with a sigh. "We shall see."

CHAPTER 25

To Brocan's delight the rain was falling heavy by noon and his hopes rose higher when the Milesians appeared to be late for the contest. He scanned the ground at the foot of the hill and tried to judge the time, but as each moment passed the king was becoming more confident.

"If Eber doesn't arrive soon, he will forfeit the battle," Brocan confided to his steward.

"He's put himself to too much trouble to simply walk away," Fergus remarked. "He and his warriors will be here. And my instincts tell me we are in for a harder fight than we expected."

"You are getting old," the king joked. "There was a time when you would have been as relieved as I am not to have to fight a battle."

As they were speaking a large group of figures appeared out of the sheets of rain to stand silently at the bottom of the hill.

"Here they are," the veteran observed, pointing at the gathering of ragged-looking Milesians.

"How many?"

"I would guess there are only forty at the most," Fergus laughed. "This must be some sort of trick."

"Have all the Danaans taken the brew?" the king asked.

"Yes."

"And are they waiting in the rear as a reserve force?"

"Cecht was none too happy about that," the veteran noted. "But he agreed this was your fight to command as you wish."

"Good. Their swords will see some work before this battle is won," Brocan said confidently. "When our warriors begin to tire we'll send in the Danaans to finish our work."

Brocan looked down on the field before him and silently puzzled at the small turnout of Milesians. After a long while he voiced a doubt. "What do you think this Eber is playing at?"

The question was answered almost immediately as the rain began to lift. There, concealed by the heavy downpour, were standing many more warriors than the forty Fergus had estimated.

Both Brocan and his foster-brother sounded groans of disappointment.

"Three hundred and fifty I would guess, or thereabouts," the veteran said before Brocan had recovered from the shock of their sudden appearance. "And another thirty or so over there in a line." He pointed.

"They might be reserves," the king hoped.

"A strange place to put them then," Fergus grunted with suspicion. Then he moved closer to the king and spoke in a low voice no one else would hear. "The weather is on our side, but even so we have no hope of stopping so many before they reach the top."

"Each man has a throwing spear and a fighting spear," the king calculated.

"And most have a sword as well," the veteran added.

"We are one hundred and twenty," Brocan sighed. "This will be a hand-to-hand fight after all. But if we can catch them on the slopes we'll have the day. And if we have the day we'll be rid of Gaedhal and Danaan at once. We'll have our land back."

As the king spoke Fergus noticed movement among the thirty warriors standing to one side of the Milesian line. He watched and his heart sank. He could barely believe what was before his eyes.

"They have hunting bows," he gasped.

"No warrior brings arrows to the battlefield," the king scoffed. "The rules of war don't allow it."

"They used fiery arrows during their raid on Dun Burren," Fergus recalled.

"It's one thing to use arrows against a house. Another entirely to employ them against enemy warriors in battle."

As they were discussing this point Dalan was already making his way onto the field to confront the enemy war leader on the issue. Eber came out to meet him and the two of them engaged in a heated discussion while the king and his steward looked on. Brocan scratched his head, wondering what they were saying to each other.

When the two men had finished, the Brehon made his slow way back up to the summit to speak with Brocan.

"What did he say?" the king called out.

"Arrows are customary among his people in war," came the reply. "He claims we should have objected earlier and that it's too late for him to change his strategy now. Do you accept these conditions?"

"This is truly barbarous!" Brocan bellowed, hoping the Milesian would hear him.

"He doesn't expect to lose," Fergus stated. "And he's not afraid of a legal objection to such tactics after the battle. Eber intends to slaughter us all."

"Then he's in for a surprise." Brocan smiled. "We won't submit quite so easily." Then he turned his attention back to Dalan. "So be it!" he cried. "Let them throw what they will at us."

With a nod of encouragement to his steward the king went to give his warriors final instructions as a wave of Milesians approached the foot of the hill.

He had walked only a few paces when the first arrows fell among the Fir-Bolg. All around the king the shafts struck soft wet earth. Brocan turned to face this threat, a weapon he had never seen used in battle. But he treated the barbed missiles with no more attention than he might the raindrops.

"We are not wild game to be hunted in this manner," he complained bitterly.

Four warriors were struck, none of them seriously wounded.

The next fall of arrows was caught up on the wind and overshot their targets to fall in the rear of Brocan's battle line. The Danaans bore the brunt of this attack and Cecht called out a warning to his warriors to fall back out of range.

As the words left his mouth an arrow struck him hard in the shoulder.

The king cried out in shock. Riona quickly led him to where Fineen was standing by his fire.

"Take it out!" Cecht screamed, twisting his body about in agony. "Take it out!"

Fineen was there by the king's side in moments with a knife to cut the iron barb out.

"Hold him down," the healer told Riona, and three warriors stepped forward to help. Fineen worked quickly, slicing open the flesh to ease the arrow out. As soon as it was free he threw the offending missile behind him in disgust.

"This is not war!" the healer spat but his anger was soon forgotten as he saw the change taking place around the wound in Cecht's shoulder.

As if many weeks were passing by before his eyes Fineen watched the wound begin to fester and dry out, and the torn flesh knit together again. In no more time than it takes to boil water on the fire the injury was gone, leaving a scar but no other sign.

"I can't feel any pain," Cecht muttered. "Is the wound bad?"

"Take a look for yourself," the healer advised with wonder in his voice. "I've never seen anything like it."

The king looked down at the spot where the shaft had penetrated his shoulder. There was nothing but a line of seared skin where the wound had healed completely.

"I don't believe it," he mumbled to himself, touching the scar with his fingers.

"I'm not sure I believe it myself," Fineen added. "But we now know the Quicken Brew will do what was promised."

"Is there any pain?" Riona gasped in awe.

"No more than if you had pinched me," Cecht replied as he pushed the warriors out of his way and stood up. "This is a miracle."

"It's the workings of Draoi healing," Fineen corrected him.

"Stand in your ranks!" the King of the Danaans ordered, addressing his people. "And don't fear the enemy. They can't harm you."

He went through his assembled warriors, showing off his scar, and everyone marveled at it.

"Listen to my orders and heed them well," Cecht bellowed. "If you are struck by sword, spear or arrow, fall where you stand and wait until the healing has taken effect."

"The musicians will begin their chant at the height of the battle," Fineen declared. "When you see the doorway to the Otherworld open have no fear but march boldly in. Let no Milesians follow you and don't look back. Dalan and his student will remain behind to open negotiations on our behalf."

Cecht leaned in close to the healer so that only he would hear what was said. "What do we do if Brocan turns his warriors against us?" he whispered.

"To stand against him would be pointless," Fineen explained. "His warriors can do no harm to your people now."

The king nodded, then he returned to his warriors, Riona holding his arm to give him support, though he didn't need it.

When they were gone Fineen made ready to destroy what remained of the brew. He had only just lifted the cauldron from the fire when the next rain of arrows fell. Soon he had six Fir-Bolg warriors seeking his help with their wounds.

Queen Scota gulped, frightened by the intensity of her own heartbeat. As the Milesian Gaedhals raised their battle call and moved forward, she silently blessed their song. But all the voices of these people could not drown the thudding in her ears.

The rain eased a little more as they advanced up the muddy slope but the mist was not thinning. Then, as the warriors dropped their voices almost to a whisper, the clouds parted high above. A golden beam of sunlight, a great heavenly sword of light, swung down across the ground before the Gaedhals. Scota could almost imagine the ethereal weapon to be carving the land open before her.

"It's a sign!" she cried out at the top of her lungs as her warriors rushed on past her. "The Children of Míl will have the victory!"

Scota was certain her own fate was sealed. Her thoughts went to those she would never see in this life again. Her sons. Her dearest friends. All the terrible struggles of life were finally going to be absolved from her soul, washed away in the waters of the Well of Forgetfulness. The journey had ended. The voyage was about to begin.

The Milesian queen breathed in the sweet rain-soaked air and savored the scent one last time. Then, with an unburdened soul, she took the steps she knew would lead to the end of this life. And they were the slowest, longest, most intense steps she had ever walked.

Each intake of breath seemed to last an eternity. Her heart thumped hard, working its hardest now at the last. The queen's head pounded with a slow, steady rhythm; every sense was accentuated.

The sunlight was suddenly swallowed up in the clouds and the landscape darkened once more. Where the grass had been flattened by the feet of her warriors Scota could smell the freshness of the rain and the musty odor of the earth. She heard every cry, every jangle of weaponry, every grunt, every curse among her advancing warriors.

Colors intensified as if a magical veil had been drawn over her eyes, deepening her perception. Scota noticed her arms ached as they did after a day at the oars. Her tongue caught on the roof of her mouth. It was coated in ochre war paint that had washed off her face. The pigment tasted rich and raw like the aroma of freshly gathered mushrooms.

With each sense demanding such attention the Milesian queen began to feel overwhelmed. She staggered a little before deciding to halt for a moment. Warriors pushed past her in their rush to the conflict. Already the clash of swords, spears and shields could be heard.

A shower of stones flew down, pelted from slings behind the Fir-Bolg lines. One sailed gracefully high and then fell at a sharp angle. Scota sensed the little missile before it had even reached the top of its arc. She followed the dark speck in the sky as it hurtled toward her, never doubting for a moment it would strike her but unable to bring herself to move out of its way. It loomed larger and larger by the breath, falling slowly, gracefully, spinning down on its mission.

When the stone hit Scota the queen heard her helmet fall to the ground. At the same moment her knees buckled under her and the muddy earth crashed into her face. Her mouth filled with wet soil but the earth held her like a little child in its embrace.

Scota was suddenly more comfortable than she had ever been in all her life. And she felt the nagging tug of exhaustion holding her down, stripping her of the will to rise. The queen spat mud from her mouth but otherwise she did not move.

"I am so tired," she whispered feebly.

Then she lay on her stomach for a few breaths more before she willed herself to roll over onto her back.

The move was surprisingly easy and painless. Scota realized she was not seriously injured, but she had no mind to get back up and join the fight. Death would come to her today, perhaps she should just lie here and wait for it.

But Scota's mind was full of images from her vision of this battle and they would not let her be. To fulfill her destiny she must go willingly to her death, not passively.

In moments the queen sat up and was soon on her knees reaching for her helm. It was badly dented and her head was ringing but Scota was determined to press on. She found her sword lying in the mud nearby, wiped its blade and looked about her.

All the Milesian warriors had passed by. The queen was alone and everything immediately around her was still.

"I've been left behind," Scota berated herself. "Get on your feet, Queen of the Gaedhals, you have not many steps to walk now before you may take a longer sleep."

She stood up, slowly checking her body for wounds. That was when she noticed a man who looked very much like her husband standing a little further up the hill, beckoning her to hurry. But this man was as young as Míl had been when they had first met. His hair had no touch of gray in it. It was shining brown, long and flowing. His beard was neatly trimmed and his shirt the brightest saffron, like the one he had been buried in.

Without question Scota trudged on, her heart lightened by the hope that her departed partner had come to guide her to the Halls of Waiting. She concentrated all her attention on her husband, blocking out the bitter fight that swirled about him.

He was remarkably calm; his eyes were as warm and inviting as they had been the first time she had seen him all those years ago. Scota laughed aloud and the spirit smiled back. He was so real to her it was incomprehensible he had passed over nearly thirteen winters ago.

As the ghost gently beckoned to her, Fir-Bolg warriors were pressing down on the Milesian line. Despite having more troops on the field the Gaedhals seemed to be losing ground. Míl pointed toward their son Eber, and Scota reluctantly tore her eyes away from the image of her beloved.

From where she stood the queen immediately saw that a disciplined effort at any point along the enemy line would cut the Fir-Bolg force in two and scatter the warriors. But the Milesian fighters locked in the thick of the battle had no idea victory was so easily within their grasp.

She turned her gaze back to where Míl had been standing. But her husband was gone. Scota realized he had come to give her a message.

"I must lead the charge," the queen told herself with a hardening resolve. "If I don't act, our warriors will be pushed back into the sea. This is my destiny. It was my dreams brought the Gaedhals here to this hill. Now I will buy their future with my blood."

Then Scota was off with renewed energy, fears forgotten, to give up her life for her people. At the top of her voice she screamed the air out of her lungs.

"To me! To me!"

Her warriors instantly rallied as they fell back toward her, fending off the enemy in their disciplined retreat. The Fir-Bolg did not follow at first, hesitant lest they should fall into a trap. But the battle fury had taken hold of them. And they did not stand their ground long before one young woman among Brocan's warriors ran forward to hurl a spear at the Gaedhals. Other Fir-Bolg followed her lead, tossing their weapons at the enemy in futile assault. Most of the spears landed short of their targets. A few young warriors drew their blades and stepped out from the ranks to taunt the enemy. Their scorn was answered by a hail of arrows from the enemy rear. Only one man fell, for mercifully the shafts mostly overshot their mark to land harmlessly behind the Fir-Bolg war party.

Fergus could see there was little holding the younger warriors in check. It suddenly seemed to him that he and Brocan were the only calm ones among all their people.

"We're losing them!" Brocan cried to his friend.

The veteran nodded then bellowed with all the force he could muster, ordering the warriors to stay in line. Either they could not hear him or they would not. The king quickly sized up the situation and sent a runner back to the top of the hill to call on the Danaan reserve.

By now Brocan had realized he could not possibly hold his warriors back. They were full of the spirit of war and would not be turned way from this reckless charge. With a glance of resignation at Fergus he held his blade up high above his head. "Forward!" the Fir-Bolg king commanded. "We'll chase them to their ships! We'll hound them back to the shores of Iber!"

His warriors answered his order with a joyous shout. Scota felt the force of their voices rolling down the hill at her like a tumbling boulder of sound. The queen quickly formed her troops into an arrow shape with the point facing back down the hill.

They barely had time to perform the maneuver before the first Fir-Bolg ran into the waiting arms of the Milesian battle lines. As Brocan and his warriors clashed with the Gaedhals the outer arms of the arrow closed in and the Fir-Bolg were suddenly surrounded.

A battle horn sounded from the top of the hill as Scota found herself in the thick of the fight. A sword flashed by her face but there was no room in the press to raise her weapon to parry a blow. The queen staggered backward to avoid another attack and was on her back in the mud before she knew what had happened.

But Scota soon regained her feet and rushed back into the fight. It was then she noticed Eber struggling with an enemy warrior not five paces away. Her son's face was covered in sweat; his hands, red from the ochre war paint, seemed to be stained with the blood of many. Just as she had resolved to go to Eber's side she felt a hand firmly grasping her wrist.

"The line is not holding," a familiar voice told her urgently. "The enemy have called in their reserves. They are attacking your people from behind. Break the circle and withdraw or the Gaedhals will be slaughtered."

The grip on Scota's wrist loosened and she looked on the spirit of Míl now standing beside Eber.

"I will watch over him," the ghost assured her. "You must concentrate on winning the day."

Scota filled her lungs, ready to give the order. "Fall back!" she bellowed. "Fall back into a long battle line!"

The cry was taken up along the hillside by all the Milesian warriors. Soon they were withdrawing in good order, fighting a defensive retreat as they moved. But Scota had to be dragged away by her son. The very moment she had issued the order the queen had glimpsed in the distance a face she had been dreading to see. The face of the woman who was destined to send her on her way from this weary world.

CHAPTER 26

SÁRÁN, FREED FROM HIS BONDS, HAD WATCHED THE
fight begin from the top of the hill, standing with the
musicians and singers of the Druid-Seers. All those
who were not of the warrior class had gathered
there, unsure whether the Milesians would respect
the immunity they were guaranteed under Danaan
laws.

It hadn't taken Sárán long to spot his brother Lom
in the thick of the fighting. His twin was very conspic-
uous. Long jet-black hair tied at the back of his head
gave him away. Sárán had felt more strongly than ever
that bond which is said to exist between two identical
twins. In all but body he had been beside his brother,
parrying each blow, swinging his blade in fury and
shouting to his comrades.

"You will be king one day," Sárán had whispered,
blessing Lom from afar. "I'll serve as your Chief
Druid. It's well you took your portion of the Quicken

Brew. Now we will rule our people together in the hidden world behind the veil."

His brother had ignored their father's banishment order. Even though he had partaken of the brew, Lom was determined to fight among his own people. None of the Fir-Bolg had even noticed when he joined their ranks moments before the charge down the slope.

The air had been full of arrows falling down all around the warriors. It had seemed the Gaedhals didn't care if their own warriors were struck down by the missiles. Many Milesians had fallen to Fir-Bolg blades. Sárán had felt himself shake with revulsion every time he heard a warrior cry out in pain. Several times he'd had to turn his eyes away. At last he had been able to watch the carnage no longer. He had walked back to where his sister and teacher were watching anxiously with Dalan as the Milesians formed the shape of an arrow and surrounded the Fir-Bolg.

"The king can't see the battle from our perspective," Fineen was muttering. "He has no idea of the danger he is in."

"We must warn him!" Aoife cried.

"That is not permitted," Dalan told her sternly. "We are Druids. We are observers and no more. To interfere with the ways of warriors is to break the law. Remember well what you see here today. When you are old, folk will ask you the details of this battle and you will be expected to call the story to mind without a second thought."

"I don't intend to grow old," Aoife replied.

Dalan frowned for a moment then realized she was referring to the effect of the Quicken Brew.

"Teacher," Aoife began, "so many Fir-Bolg have fallen. And now they're charging into an ambush. Are you certain anyone who has taken the brew will be safe from harm?"

"Mahon will return to you without a scratch on his body, I assure you," the Brehon told her.

"Someone has to warn them!" Sárán yelled, finding it difficult to believe such a conversation was going on at a time when all their people were in danger.

"Would I be hurt if a Milesian struck at me?" the young woman asked.

"You certainly won't be harmed," Fineen promised.

Aoife grabbed her brother by the arm. "Come then!" she cried. "Let's lend a hand to the Fir-Bolg. This'll be the only real fight we're ever likely to see!"

Without a second thought Sárán began barreling down the hillside, screaming a warning to the warriors of his kinfolk.

"Come back!" Dalan commanded, but his words were blown away on the wind. "You are Druids! You are forbidden to take part in war!"

"They've not taken their vows yet," Fineen reasoned, holding his friend by the shoulder to restrain him from following off down the hill to catch them. "There's nothing we can do to stop them. Let them go to warn Brocan before too many Fir-Bolg are killed."

"That girl will go too far one day," the Brehon muttered. But then something caught his eye out on the battlefield.

Quickly Dalan removed his Raven-feather cloak and handed it to Fineen. Then he grabbed at the healer's blue Druid cloak.

"I must borrow this for a while," he said, distracted. "I don't want to be mistaken for a warrior."

"What is it?" Fineen asked.

"Isleen and Lochie have returned," the Brehon replied. "And I must go down to the battle to meet them."

Aoife ran down the hill as fast as she could in the mud and rain. The clash of weapons grew louder as she approached the place where the Danaan warriors were making their stand. It was now impossible to tell which side had the upper hand. Everything she'd seen from the top of the hill was now a jumbled mess of constantly shifting battle lines.

Aoife shook with fear as a tall muscular Gaedhal staggered through the Danaan ranks unopposed. Her blood ran cold when he caught her eye and stared directly at her with an intensity so powerful her feet were rooted to the spot.

All around her, shouts of pain and hatred filled the air, making her breathe in short, sharp, terrified bursts. Aoife couldn't call for help; she couldn't run either. The foreigner raised his shining silvery sword to strike at her.

His face was expressionless, calm and determined. Aoife wished he'd make some sound. His silence was far more terrifying to her than a battle yell would have been.

In the next breath he lunged forward at her, thrusting the tip of his blade toward her heart. As if in slow motion Aoife watched the weapon approach but somehow she couldn't move to avoid it. The next thing she knew the Gaedhal was at her feet and she was standing just out of his reach, shivering with terror. The enemy warrior had a Milesian arrow in his back. He'd been cut down by one of his own archers.

Aoife reached out a shaking hand to touch the stranger on the crown of the head, silently blessing him and sending his spirit on its way.

"What are you doing here?" Cecht yelled at her. The Danaan king was shaking her by the arm to get her attention. "You're a Druid!"

"I was blessing him."

"He's a Gaedhal!" the king exclaimed.

"I know," Aoife replied, still in shock.

"Go back up the hill. There are arrows flying everywhere. You might be hit. And I wouldn't count on the Gaedhals respecting your Druid status."

"Where's Mahon?" she cried above the din of the battlefield. Then, suddenly jolted out of her fright, she blurted out her warning about the enemy tactic.

By this time, though, the Milesians had fallen back into a single battle line and Brocan had ordered a withdrawal. In moments her father too was standing at her side demanding to know what foolishness had brought her to the thick of the fight.

"Go back!" the Fir-Bolg king commanded her. "This is no place for you! You have no weapon and I can't watch after you."

"I'll stay," she answered defiantly, catching sight of Mahon amongst the Danaan warriors.

Brocan shook his head, let his sword drop to the ground and, quite unexpectedly, hit Aoife across the face with the back of his hand. The young woman fell into the mud and did not stir.

Without prompting, Fergus sheathed his sword and bent down to pick her up. As he threw Aoife over his shoulder he stopped to look Brocan in the eye.

"All I seem to do is carry your children off battle-fields," he grunted. The veteran looked back up to where Dalan and Fineen were standing. "And why does it always seem to be uphill?" he added, setting off with his burden.

Just then the Gaedhals raised a war cry and strode forward at the defenders, their spear points lowered. In their red war paint they looked like a swarm of strange unearthly wasps defending their hive with a forest of stingers.

"At them!" Brocan shrieked triumphantly and his warriors lowered their spear points to create a bristling row of weapons.

The Gaedhals, goaded on by Brocan's daring, were tempted into advancing. The going was hard up the muddy slope. Many warriors were already exhausted. A small number simply sat down where they were to catch their breath. But the rest struggled on.

Before the Milesian warriors had gained ten paces of mud-soaked ground, another shower of arrows pelted down. A dozen Fir-Bolg men in the front rank fell back wounded. But their comrades didn't flinch.

The Gaedhals halted ten paces in front of their enemy. Eber was at their head. Some of the Fir-Bolg warriors, thinking the enemy had stopped to rest, retreated a little up the rise to aid their fallen friends.

"Hold your line!" Brocan bellowed.

But as soon as a few had retreated, the others followed. The Fir-Bolg lost twenty paces then as the warriors instinctively moved out of range of the Milesian arrows. Eber made no move to chase after them. He held his ground, waiting for the right opportunity.

"Stand!" the Fir-Bolg king ordered again.

He was now certain the Milesians would have the upper hand until their archers were dealt with. Some Danaans hurried forward to take up position in the front rank, and Cecht found a place beside Brocan.

"We can't win the field," he told the Fir-Bolg king bluntly. "Their foot soldiers outnumber us two to one. And those archers are picking your warriors off too quickly. It's only a matter of time."

Brocan breathed deeply and stood tall. "I'll have

this day," he promised as he turned to face the Danaan king.

Another fall of arrows plummeted out of the sky. Brocan swiftly sheltered behind his shield but Cecht did not flinch for a second. When the assault had passed Brocan lowered his shield again and noticed the Danaan king's sword lying before him on the ground. He looked up at the Danaan in disbelief.

An arrow had embedded itself in Cecht's left shoulder near the bone.

"There's no pain," the Danaan muttered in wide-eyed surprise as he reached up to touch the shaft. "This is my second arrow today."

With a great effort he grabbed the arrow and pulled it out. The barbs tore at his flesh, leaving a gaping red wound. There was blood everywhere, the king's hair was spattered with it.

Cecht tentatively touched the wound with shaking fingers. "I can't feel anything this time," he whispered.

Then, as Brocan watched, Cecht's wound began to heal. The blood dried and became a brown dust which washed away in the rain. Before another fall of arrows had come down, the wound was no more than a star-shaped scar on the Danaan's shoulder.

Two more Fir-Bolg warriors fell in the latest hail from the Milesian archers.

"The enemy won't bring missiles down on their own people," Cecht suggested. "If you're so determined to fight, then let's charge down the hill side by side and fight this battle together."

Brocan laughed out loud at the absurdity of that offer. These two old kings had often fought but never on the same side.

"With an immortal standing by my shield, how can I refuse such a challenge?" The Fir-Bolg king shrugged with a grin. "Forward!" Brocan cried. "I want a steady pace with no running!"

His warriors needed no further prompting. They readied their spears and marched down toward the waiting line of Gaedhals. They advanced slower than usual so none would slip in the mud and become an easy target.

The steady fall of arrows ceased as soon as the Fir-Bolg came close to the Milesian line. Bright silver spear points bristled on the ends of long ash-wood staves. In between the spears there were sword-wielding warriors with wicked-looking blades.

As the two sides met with a mighty resounding crash each side raised a chant. But the war songs soon degenerated into wild yells and grunted curses and then the ranks began to disintegrate. In less time than it takes to strike at an enemy twice, the battle had become a confused melee, more pushing and shoving than anything else.

Brocan's shield was of bronze but it was covered in hardened leather. Not even the Milesians' silvery steel could puncture it. The king pushed spears aside as if they were nothing more than sticks. But in the press he couldn't deliver a worthy blow to any of the Gaedhals.

Cecht managed to push through the enemy ranks as well and he was slashing at the front ranks with a wild fury. His face was on fire, filled with hatred. His strong sword arm beat down upon the Milesian shields like a blacksmith's hammer at the forge. Blow after blow he landed so swiftly no enemy warrior could slip in between to strike him.

Suddenly Brocan found himself standing alone. The warriors of the Gaedhal had faltered and fallen back down the hill in the face of such a determined assault.

"We have them!" the Fir-Bolg king sang as he tasted victory in the air.

Before he had finished speaking the enemy line collapsed and suddenly the Milesians were on the run. Brocan tossed his shield aside, raising a cry of triumph to his people.

"To the sea!" he urged them. "Chase the invaders back to the sea!"

His people were so exhilarated many simply charged forward, screaming at the top of their lungs. There was laughter in the air also, amid the cries of pain, the strong coppery smell of freshly spilled blood and the slimy squelching mud.

Before Cecht realized what had happened and could call out to the Fir-Bolg king to stand his ground, the war party had moved forward. The Danaan king lifted the battle horn secured at his waist and blew three sharp bursts. His own warriors recognized the call immediately and dutifully fell back to stand by their king. Moments later arrows began to fall again.

But Cecht's signal was ignored by the ecstatic Fir-Bolg. They were eager to drive their enemies out. Not even Danu herself, had she appeared before them in all her light and majesty, could have convinced Brocan's people to turn around.

When the other Danaans retreated toward King Cecht's standard Mahon made his way into the ranks of the Fir-Bolg. Before King Brocan's men twenty Milesian spearmen stood their ground refusing to retreat when all their comrades ran. What encouraged this brave action none could tell, but it held the Fir-Bolg advance as Brocan's people dodged around the bristling weapons.

Mahon quickly grew impatient with this impasse, screaming to the nearby warriors that they had nothing to fear. Finally in frustration he pushed forward, a broadaxe at the ready, to strike at any of the enemy who came within reach.

His heart beat wildly in his chest, pumping exhilaration throughout his body. No battle had ever been like this, no foe so deadly, no cause so just. And all fear had left him for he was secure in the knowledge no weapon would harm him this day.

A gap opened in the Fir-Bolg ranks and he spurred through it toward the forest of spears raised on the Milesian side. The enemy saw him coming with determination in his eyes and a war cry on his lips. A few faltered then turned to run. In moments panic had spread among this small group of defiant foreigners.

By the time Mahon reached the place where they had been standing the Gaedhals were already fleeing. Only one warrior among them made no move to retreat. She was a woman with gray locks stained red with ochre. The Danaan prince turned all his attention to her.

In the next instant the woman beckoned mockingly toward him, daring him to take her on.

"Do you think you can better me, lad?" she laughed. "You're barely out of your mother's arms."

And then a chill coursed through her body as she recognized his face.

"Who are you?"

"I am Mahon, son of King Cecht of the Tuatha De Danaan."

Without another word the queen raised her sword to strike but the young warrior hooked her blade under the haft of his axe to parry her blow. Then, before she had the chance to recover, he pushed her back into the mud.

As Scota fell she watched the Danaan raise his weapon once again to strike and just as in her dream an arrow fell from the heavens to thud into Mahon's chest near the collarbone. The warrior's eyes grew wide with fear for just a second as the shock of the sudden injury struck him.

"You will not die," Scota told him. "I have seen this. Your wound will heal."

The warrior looked down when he heard her words and all fear passed from his face. He grabbed the arrow with both hands and plucked it out of his body, tearing the flesh as he did so.

Scota looked on in horror. Though she had witnessed this incident before, her eyes refused to believe what was being presented to them. She felt the hilt of her sword heavy in her hand and knew she must raise the point to stab at this young man. Before she understood what was happening, her hands were covered in his blood and the weapon was buried to the hilt in his stomach.

Still lying on her back Scota put her feet up on his thighs to withdraw her sword. It slipped out with a great gushing of red liquid then she crawled back a short way to watch what happened next.

To her utter dismay and horror the wounded man stood his ground, though he had received a wound that would have rendered a weaker man unconscious.

"How can this be?" she asked him, though Mahon never heard her above the din of battle.

The answer came in an unexpected manner. And what she witnessed confirmed all the details of that dream she'd had so long ago.

The Danaan held his guts with both his hands to stop them falling out at his feet. But he needn't have bothered. Within moments the arrow wound high in his chest near the collarbone had festered, closed and healed. Before he drew ten more breaths the young man's stomach was closing over also. In twenty the wound was gone.

Scota scrambled to her feet as Mahon smiled at the miracle. But before she had a chance to strike him again a blow rained down on her head from behind and she teetered forward.

The world all around the Milesian queen became a blur of motion. Scota found herself on her back once more in the mire. Tears filled her eyes so that she could just make out the shape of a woman standing over her. The queen wiped her face with a bloodied hand.

The strange woman before her was a Fir-Bolg warrior. Scota reached for her sword but it was beyond her grasp so she slowly edged her way up onto her elbows until she was half sitting in the mud.

"I am Scota, Queen of the Milesian Gaedhals!" she panted. As the words left her mouth a spear thrust into her body. She felt the thud as the weapon struck her and she looked up to see Riona standing over her. This was the vision she had seen in her dreams.

"I can't feel any pain," Scota whispered.

The warrior woman knelt down beside her and took her hand as if they were sisters. Scota looked into the eyes of her killer and squeezed the woman's hand hard. Then, as the life slowly drained out of her, the Queen of the Gaedhals heard a woman's voice.

"Do you remember? I am Riona, daughter of Eriu. I was once the Queen of the Fir-Bolg of the Burren."

"Once?" Scota whispered but her senses were already giving in to the long sleep her soul yearned for. Her heart was beating slowly now and every breath was a struggle.

"It is time to let go," she mumbled.

"Not long now," a man's voice assured her. "Soon we'll be at peace."

With the last of her energy Scota managed to focus on the face before her. It was a man of her people. He was young and dark-haired. His mischievous eyes sparkled with a blue the same color as the sky on a clear morning.

"Míl!" She smiled.

In that instant she was bathed in warmth as if she had stepped into a hot spring in wintertime. All her worries left her. The last breath departed. And then Scota, Queen of the Gaedhals from the lands of the Iberi, passed on to the Halls of Waiting, guided by the spirit of her dear friend and husband.

Sárán had followed Aoife down into the thick of battle, somehow managing to stay out of his father's way. The young man had dodged among the warriors, narrowly avoiding injury, trying to find his brother Lom. Taking in the carnage all about him Sárán had decided it would be wise to bring his twin to the rear where he would be safe. If they had a future together as rulers of the Fir-Bolg, Lom would have to be protected. There were strict laws about the suitability of a candidate for kingship. A man or woman with an injury was not considered worthy of the office.

Sárán had made his way through the melee, and at last he managed to get close enough to his brother to grab him by the sleeve.

"Come with me!" he urged. "This is too dangerous a place for the likes of you."

Lom turned to see who was tugging at his sword arm. "What are you doing here?" he sputtered in shock. "You're placing yourself in great danger."

"I'm just as worried about you," Sárán told his brother urgently.

"No harm can come to me!" Lom laughed as he pulled open a savage tear in his tunic to reveal a wide scar. The injury began near his neck and extended down toward his belly.

"Weren't you hurt?" Sárán gasped.

"I felt strange for a few moments," his brother admitted, "but I am fine now. You should have seen the look on the Milesian who cut me! He couldn't believe his eyes when I lifted my blade to strike at him after he thought he had dispatched me."

"Then it is true!" Sárán gasped. "We have become immortal."

"It is true."

Sárán found a sword made of Milesian steel lying in among the tangled bodies. He raised it up as he stood beside his brother. "Now we'll drive the Gaedhals away from our shores forever," he declared and the two of them advanced side by side toward the retreating enemy.

Sárán in his green cloak and Lom in his saffron brown had boldly struck down all who came within the arc of their swinging blades. But the Gaedhals had already begun falling back to the field below the hill where their archers were still loosing arrows toward the retreating Danaans.

Now the brothers heard the battle horn of Cecht sounding out.

"You should go back," Lom told his brother. "The fight is almost over. The Fir-Bolg will finish the task. You are a Druid in training. It is not fitting that you be found here among the slain enemy."

"I'll go," Sárán conceded. "But only because I do not want to risk my future career as a Druid. One day you and I will rule the Fir-Bolg and our people will thank Danu for sending us to them."

"You will never rule," Lom pointed out blindly. "Father has banished you. And Druids, even the most renowned Brehons, are not entitled to kingship."

"I will be your adviser," Sárán retorted. "Every king needs a trustworthy counselor."

"I would be surprised if the chieftains ever allowed it," Lom answered.

Sárán frowned. He had not considered the chieftains would hold the same opinion of him as his father.

"Go back now," Lom urged.

"Come with me," Sárán sulked. "Surely the doorway to the Otherworld will be opened soon. We who have taken the brew should be ready to retreat toward the hill."

"I'll be along in a minute. I want our father to see that I have fought among my own people today. And I want the chieftains to know it too. You are right. One day I may have a chance to be elected to the kingship. It will not hurt my chances if it is well known I stood with our people in the Battle of Sliabh Mis."

With that Lom ran up toward the pennant which marked Brocan's place on the battlefield. But he had not quite reached his father's standard when his attention was drawn to the top of the hill. At the very summit, behind the spreading branches of the great apple tree, the choir had assembled in their distinctive crescent moon formation. And the horns were blasting out as the singers began a new chant.

This song was so different from the music they had performed at the dedication of the Quicken Brew, Lom at first thought they must be a different group of musicians. This melody was strong, vibrant and taunting. The rhythm echoed the strident humming of the Danaan war chant.

Suddenly the warriors fell into an uneasy stillness as the song drifted out down onto the battlefield. Danaan, Fir-Bolg and Milesian alike stopped whatever they were doing to look up at the choir.

A subtle golden light could be discerned all around the spreading branches of the apple tree. It reminded Lom of the glow of turf coals in winter. On the tree the small green unripened apples began to swell and turn to red as if time were passing by swifter than ever.

In a sudden burst of intense song the choir raised their voices in a tremendous uplifting phrase which gradually built to a crescendo. At the same moment the golden light around the apple tree burst into a bright explosion of fiery illumination. Everyone who watched was forced to turn away as the light stung their eyes.

The land all about was brought out of the gray shades of cloudy drizzle. Above the battlefield a broad-banded rainbow emanated from the top of the hill and stretched its arc of breathtaking colors toward the sea.

A few folk whose curiosity dared them to open their eyes saw this marvel in the heavens. Lom was one of them. He still could not look at the apple tree for the light was too intense, but he could plainly see the effect that light was having on the world about him. The grassy hill was a beautiful shade of green; clouds on the far horizon took on hues of purple and red. In the distance the sea was a deep enticing blue topped with wave crests of brilliant white.

Then unexpectedly the song stopped, the light receded and the vibrant colors drained away to become the dull grays of rain once more. All around the tree there remained a dull echo of the golden illumination so that the leaves on the branches seemed to be an impossible shade of green. Apples ripe and heavy fell to the ground. A few rolled down the hill until their progress was halted by the mud.

As Lom looked with wonder a battle horn sounded and all the Danaans began to retreat toward the summit. Moments later the apple tree erupted in another fiery display which quickly burned out again. And then in its place there stood a wide stone doorway with two massive solid oak gates. The gateway swung open and the same intense golden light that had surrounded the tree poured forth from behind the doors. Lom shielded his eyes, realizing he now had a difficult decision to make.

"The Danaans are deserting the field!" Brocan cried out and the Fir-Bolg warriors raised calls of derision. "The cowards are leaving us to fight the invaders all alone! Fergus, take up your battle horn and call them to return."

The veteran did as he was told, blowing a blast that shook the stomach of every warrior close by. But the Danaans did not turn from their march up the hill to the doorway.

Lom saw his brother among them; his mother was there also. Aoife was walking with her arm around Mahon's waist. Lom knew he would regret it if he stayed behind with the Fir-Bolg, even though they were his own people.

Another fall of arrows rained down from above, daring Brocan's warriors to advance toward the Milesian lines. The king took up the challenge.

"This fight isn't ended yet!" he cried out.

Lom ran to his father's side in time to join the charge toward the enemy. But to his horror Brocan stumbled in the mud before they had gone twenty steps. The king rolled over and lay face down on the slope. His warriors noticed his absence immediately and their attack soon began to falter.

Lom bent down over his father and saw he had been struck by an arrow. Fergus came running over and eased the shaft from his brother's chest. The king coughed and then fell into unconsciousness. His skin was very pale and his breathing strained.

The veteran slumped down by his foster-brother, eyes staring blankly. Lom tore off his own tunic and pressed it down hard on his father's chest to staunch the flow of blood. All around them Fir-Bolg warriors were trying to keep the Gaedhals at bay.

"We have to get him to safety," Lom told Fergus urgently.

"He's finished," the veteran choked. "I've seen better wounds than that which were fatal. He doesn't have more than three hundred strong breaths left in him."

"We must carry him to Fineen," Lom insisted. "The healer may have some of the Quicken Brew. It'll save his life."

Fergus looked up at his nephew and shook his head. "Your father would prefer it this way," he said wearily.

"Would you let him die? With healing so close at hand?"

"It was his decision to risk his life by not taking the brew. He knew the danger." The veteran shrugged.

"He'll die!" Lom shouted.

This was enough to wake Fergus out of his shock. "I've carried you and your sister up hills away from bloody battles. Now it's his turn."

With that he carefully picked up the wounded king and, with Lom's help, settled the body over his shoulder. Then he carried his burden to the top of the hill in search of Fineen.

CHAPTER 27

Dalan the Brehon had run as fast as he could down the hill toward the Milesian lines, certain he'd spotted Isleen and Lochie moving around among the press of warriors. But by the time he'd reached the center of the fighting the Watchers had disappeared.

As an unarmed Druid marked by his blue cloak he had been ignored by the combatants, free to move unharmed among the melee. In the thick of the fight he had found himself kneeling beside a wounded warrior. The man had received a terrible slash across the throat and was clutching the wound as he bled to death.

"If only Brocan had let his warriors drink the brew," Dalan muttered.

"Help me!" the warrior gasped, straining to make any sound at all.

"I'll do what I can," Dalan soothed. "Don't speak. Save your energy."

The warrior nodded his understanding, closed his eyes and sank back into the Brehon's protective embrace.

Dalan sat in the mud on his knees, cradling the man until his pain eased with his last breath. Dalan looked into his lifeless eyes and shook his head in sorrow.

"There was nothing you could do," a soothing feminine voice pointed out.

Dalan looked up with tears in his eyes to see Isleen and Lochie standing before him.

"You did this!" the Brehon stuttered, rage filling his heart. "You're responsible for all this misery and bloodshed."

"That warrior you just nursed into the afterlife is fortunate to have found his peace," Lochie noted. "You've no idea how fortunate he is. One day when you're weary of this world you'll understand."

The Brehon didn't hear a word. All he could think of was that the Watchers were responsible for the many deaths on this field. If they hadn't interfered in the lives of mortals the Gaedhals might never have been inspired to set sail from their homeland and there might still have been peace in Innisfail. They were callous and selfish to be using ordinary folk with good hearts and kind souls for their own purposes.

"It's true." Lochie smiled, reading the Brehon's thoughts. "We care nothing for your people or the Danaans or the Gaedhal. We're only concerned with our own future, our own fate."

"You brought on this battle. You've destroyed the lives of so many folk in the search for your own contentment and peace."

"Of course we have." Isleen shrugged. "Pain, fear, anger, anguish and despair are our sustenance. If we have to continue our existence we'd both prefer to be well fed and strong."

The Brehon felt a rage boiling in his heart such as he had never felt before. He leapt to his feet and before he knew what had happened there was a sword in his hand. It was made of bright strong Milesian steel and it weighed heavy in his grip. For a moment he held it, feeling the balance of the weapon, and it seemed to him that his fury was flowing down his arm into the blade.

"You're a Druid," Lochie laughed. "What do you think you're doing with that weapon? Your kind are forbidden to bear arms."

But Dalan was shaking with anger. He couldn't speak. He took two tentative steps forward, raising the sword as he advanced.

"Are you angry?" Isleen laughed. "Are you enraged?"

"Rage is so sweet," Lochie added as if savoring the taste of it in the air. "And your rage has a hint of remorse about it. You've no idea how much strength those emotions give us."

"I have nothing but contempt for both of you," Dalan spat.

Isleen closed her eyes and threw back her head.

"You've no idea how wonderful that feels," she said in a low voice.

"Your kind are so weak," Lochie laughed. "Even you, the strongest and wisest of men, are no match for us. Look about you at all we've achieved. And you stand there with a blade and can't bring yourself to use it. You're pathetic."

This was too much for Dalan. In the next second he strode forward and brought the sword down hard on Lochie's right shoulder. The Watcher made no attempt to move out of the way. Indeed the expression on his face hardly changed.

There was a sickening crunch as the weapon split flesh down to the ribs, cracking the Watcher's collarbone. Lochie's arm dropped forward limply but he showed no sign of pain.

"That wasn't a very Druidlike response," Isleen chided as she inspected her companion's wound.

"You'll have to do better than that." Lochie nodded.

As the Watcher spoke the wound completely disappeared, leaving no trace, and the Watcher's torn cloak was restored to its pristine condition.

"You're wasting your time with that lump of polished steel," Isleen advised him.

Dalan was still burning with anger but now he felt powerless as well. He lifted the sword again, surprised at how easy it was to wield now he had found its point of balance. Then he swung the blade around his head and struck Lochie with a devastating blow.

The blade lodged deep in Lochie's ribs but there wasn't a drop of blood to see, no cut, no injury at all.

"You're powerless against us," Isleen told him. "And your rage is simply making us stronger."

"May Balor's ghost haunt you," Dalan hissed.

"I've already cursed Balor's spirit," Lochie sighed. "I'm not afraid of him." Then the Watcher took hold of the sword and flung it high in the air. The weapon landed far away over near the Milesian archers.

"You promised Lochie you'd help us," Isleen reminded him.

"It was you then?" Dalan gasped. "It wasn't a dream."

"You've let us down," Lochie replied, wagging a finger in mock rebuke. "Now we'll have to think of some appropriate punishment for you."

"I don't know how to free you from your bonds," the Brehon shouted in desperation. "If you give me time I'll find out. But stop this terrible carnage. These folk don't deserve to suffer for your selfishness."

"Your kind mean nothing to us," Isleen told him flatly, then pointed a finger at a Milesian warrior who had just dispatched a Fir-Bolg opponent. The Gaedhal's eyes widened with shock and he dropped dead in his tracks. Lochie was obviously amused at this because he turned around to pick a warrior for himself.

Before Dalan could comprehend what was happening the two Watchers had begun a frenzy of killing. Twelve Milesian warriors fell without a weapon touching them. Their comrades began to fall back in fear, believing some Danaan spell had descended on them.

"They can't see us," Lochie explained. "It helps increase their fear."

Dalan couldn't control his revulsion a moment longer. He rushed at Isleen, grabbing for her cloak to wrestle her to the ground.

"Stop this!" he screamed. "Stop!"

The Watcher threw back her head and laughed in a rasping, rattling cackle. She pushed her face close to Dalan's and he smelled the sweet incongruous scent of lavender. Then Isleen was gone and he was tumbling forward.

"Now you will witness our true nature," Lochie told him as Isleen reappeared beside her companion. "The doorway has opened and your folk will never be able to close it again."

Then, in a gradual, frightening transformation, the two Watchers began to change form. Their clothes disappeared. They stood naked before the Brehon, their bodies covered in blood and gore. It was matted into their hair and dripped from their mouths. And their eyes stood out like shining pebbles on a fine red cloth.

They had taken on the war paint of the Milesians. But instead of red ochre these foul creatures had bathed themselves in the blood of the slain.

"You've disappointed us, Dalan," Lochie announced. "Now you'll know what real havoc is. Your people won't rest until we have our freedom."

"We've only just begun our work," Isleen gloated. "This is our revenge on your kind for all we've suffered through the generations."

"I won't let you continue your bloodbath," Dalan vowed. "I'll find a way to defeat you."

"There's only one way to defeat us." Lochie smiled. "You must find a way to kill us. We're too strong to be sent into the stones."

"I'll find a way."

"You'd better be quick," Isleen hummed. "We can cause an awful lot of damage and heartache when we've a mind to."

The both of them laughed uproariously and then, in less time than it takes to blink an eye, they had vanished as if they had been nothing more than a product of the Brehon's imagination. The next thing Dalan knew someone was gripping his sleeve, dragging him back up the hill.

"Brocan's been wounded!" the Fir-Bolg warrior told him urgently. "Come, we need your help."

The Brehon took a moment to shake off his horror, then he turned and followed the warrior to the top of the hill.

Fineen examined the Fir-Bolg king carefully. Brocan's breath was already a low rasping at the back of his throat. It was obvious he'd been severely wounded. When the healer had finished looking at him he shook his head mournfully.

"I saved a cupful of the Quicken Brew in case the

need should arise," Fineen told Lom. "But I can't be certain it will do him any good. He's lost a lot of blood and his rib cage has been shattered by the force of the arrow and the manner in which it was removed. It may already be too late."

"You said the brew could heal any hurt," Lom protested.

"I don't have enough experience of its properties to be certain. All I know about it I learned from hearsay."

"Give him the Quicken Brew," the young warrior demanded.

"Your father chose to reject it," Fineen reminded him. "It wouldn't be right to administer it to him now."

"You have the power to save his life," Lom insisted.

"But should I exercise that power? Can you be certain that's what he wants?"

As the healer spoke Dalan arrived at the fire. "How bad is it?" the Brehon asked, breathless from the climb up the hill.

"He's not long for this world," was the solemn reply.

"Give him the brew," Dalan commanded.

"Fineen refuses to," Lom cut in.

"We'll stand in need of his experience and wisdom after all this trouble is sorted out," Dalan pressed. "If he passes away now, who'll lead the Fir-Bolg?"

"I will," Fergus offered. "Brocan chose me as his successor four seasons ago. I'll be King of the Burren if he passes away."

"You're already the king," Lom pointed out. "My father might as well be dead."

"The decision is yours to make, Fergus," Dalan advised. "If Brocan dies, it will be your duty to lead the Fir-Bolg into the future. If he lives, there'll be another hand to help you guide the tiller."

Fergus lowered his eyes to the bloodied pale form on the ground. Brocan wheezed painfully but there was no sign of consciousness from the Fir-Bolg king.

"He's my brother," the veteran murmured at last. "How can I let him die when the means to save his life are readily available?"

"Give my father the brew!" Lom shouted.

Fineen put aside his reservations and went to the fireside to fetch what was left of the Quicken Brew. He stirred it with a wooden spoon as he brought it to where Brocan lay.

"It's gone cold," the healer noted. "I was advised only to administer it hot, or at the very least warm. But I left it standing too far from the coals. I'll give it to him but you must not expect too much."

"Hurry!" Lom demanded.

Fineen knelt by the dying king while Fergus held Brocan's nose and tilted his head back. The brew spilled into the slack open mouth and much of it dribbled down his chin. Then the veteran tenderly laid his foster-brother back on the ground and spread his own cloak over the injured man.

"How long before we know?" Lom asked.

"Not long," the healer replied.

Brocan's breathing became suddenly easier. His whole body relaxed as the pain seemed to drain away from him. Fineen touched a finger lightly to Brocan's throat.

"His heartbeat is slowing," the healer announced after a pause. "He's weakening."

Brocan's breathing was less strained but it was also more shallow. His face was a deathly white now and his lips were changing hue to a gray blue. As they watched the king drew in a deep breath with great effort. And when he exhaled it seemed that all the worries of the world were expelled from his body.

Fineen lifted Brocan's eyelids to check the color of his eyes. Then he turned to Lom and Fergus, the disappointment apparent on his face.

"There's nothing more I can do." The healer shrugged.

"He's gone?" Fergus asked in a whisper, not willing to believe his brother was dead.

Fineen nodded.

But just then Brocan drew another deep breath and opened his eyes. The healer watched with surprise as the bloody wound in the king's chest began to bubble with activity. A flat scab formed over the gaping hole and in a few minutes there was no sign of the injury save for a large scar of soft new skin.

Brocan looked up at the expectant faces gathered around him and frowned.

"I've just had the most astounding dream," the king said.

Fergus smiled and brushed a hand through his brother's hair.

"I am tired of fighting," Brocan said softly.

"I know."

The king lifted his eyes to his friend and the veteran saw they were full of sadness. "I want to go home and rest," Brocan sighed.

"What of the battle?"

"Send word to the Milesian king. Tell him I'm ready to sue for peace."

In the chilly autumn morning air representatives of the Danaan folk and the Fir-Bolg waited around a large fire on the hillside thirty paces from the entrance to King Cecht's fort at Dun Gur. Druid counselors, Brehons in their blue robes, Seers, Poets, physicians and harpers stood around the king, arranged according to their professions.

Cecht, Riona and the Danaan royal household remained at the gates of the hillfort awaiting the arrival of the foreigners. Brocan stood by the fire dressed in the formal cloak of his office with an eagle feather in his long gray hair to signify his status.

The Fir-Bolg king was a changed man since the battle of Sliabh Mis. His manner was more friendly and jovial. And his generosity to those who had suffered in the sack of Dun Burren was unsurpassed. Brocan gave all his cattle away to the needy folk of his kin and kept only goats for himself. He had worked tirelessly for nearly two moons building a new home for his people in the ancient caves of the Aillwee on the coast of the Burren.

More importantly, he accepted Lom back into his house with all the forgiveness his heart could offer. Riona, Sárán and Aoife had not approached him since, but Brocan seemed very understanding of their feelings.

In the days after the battle he never spoke of the dream that had come to him as he lay dying at the healer's fire. And he never once expressed any regret that the Quicken Brew had been administered to him without his consent.

Fergus noticed the foreigners first. He pointed them out to his foster-brother and soon everyone was peering off into the mist to catch a glimpse of the Gaedhals.

Over the hillside track in the distance the brightly colored train of King Eber of the Milesians made its way toward them. For here on this day the treaty conference was to be held which would seal the future of Innisfail.

"It would seem the Druid Assembly has achieved its aim," King Cecht declared to Dalan as the Brehon stepped up to report the Milesians' arrival. "Will the Dagda be satisfied with what we've achieved?"

"We still have a good way to go," the Brehon conceded, "but I imagine he is pleased so far. In the north he has met with Éremon the brother of Eber. The treaty negotiated there was a simpler matter. There was no dissension between the Danaans and their allies. We must do everything right, then we'll be able to rest peacefully."

"I've never felt so rested in my life," Cecht hummed as he held Riona's hand tightly in his. "I have never been so content."

"And at the same time," Riona cut in, "I have never looked on this world with so much contempt. The Otherworld is a paradise where colors are more vibrant, emotions deeper, honesty easier and the cares of this world insignificant."

"I've decided on the concession which you suggested to me," the king confided.

"You will relinquish Dun Gur to the Gaedhals?"

"I see the wisdom in such a move," Cecht sighed. "This place has been the home of my family since the Danaans first arrived in Innisfail. But we have a new home now. A better home. It would be churlish to cling to this place knowing such a gift might earn us the peace we all yearn for."

"The most important thing," Dalan assured him, "is that we can in time win the trust of the Milesians so they see the value in adopting our Brehon laws. If they don't change their ways, it will be only a short while before new conflicts arise. Already Eber's brother Éremon is demanding that the southern Milesians pay homage to him as high-king of the entire land. The gift of Dun Gur will win Eber's confidence in the art of diplomacy over the devastation of warfare."

"This hillfort will be a secure settlement in which

to establish himself," the king added. "These walls have never been breached. No besieging enemy has ever managed to bring the garrison to its knees. If his people are secure Eber will have time to listen to reason."

"When will you join us in the Otherworld, Dalan?" Riona asked and the Brehon was surprised to notice her expression was gentler, her voice warm and welcoming.

"I have duties to fulfill before I can consider retreating behind the veil," the Brehon replied.

"You've been nominated, I hear, to the office of Dagda," she teased. "You'll make a great High-Druid."

"Indeed I've been nominated," Dalan sighed. "But I find I am unable to accept the honor."

"Unable to accept!" Cecht gasped. "Do you realize what you are saying? Few Druids are ever considered worthy of such rank and responsibility. And now more than ever the Druid Assembly needs wise counsel from such as yourself."

"The current Dagda will serve for a while yet," the Brehon assured Cecht. "He took the Quicken Brew. It's no longer so urgent that a replacement be found as his health is not ailing him any longer. And in any case there are others who could just as easily fill those shoes when the time comes for him to stand down."

"But you've a unique talent," Cecht pressed. "You've always been comfortable in the world of the spirit. You know the ways of the Otherworld. I may be a king among my people but I have no idea how I'll face the challenges which lie before us. Your guidance would be a great reassurance to me."

"I'll offer you whatever advice I can." Dalan smiled, acknowledging the compliment. "But there's a task I must perform which is more delicate and more urgent than any other challenge which may beckon."

"What would that be?" the king asked in surprise.

"The Watchers are still abroad in the land," the Brehon answered solemnly. "Neither Lochie nor Isleen has been sighted since I encountered them on the battlefield. I feel it's my duty to deal with them before they cause more havoc. We've not yet achieved a certain and lasting peace. And I don't believe it's possible until these ancient troublemakers are released from their imprisonment."

"This may turn into the work of a lifetime," the king cautioned. "Are you willing to take on this quest in the knowledge there may not be an answer to this riddle?"

"Fineen has taught me well." The Brehon smiled. "I've learned there is a solution to every puzzle. One just has to look at the question in the right light."

"You know best what is right," Cecht sighed. "Let's hope your skills as a mediator can bring Brocan back into the fold. I am frightened he will cause trouble of his own even if we come to an agreement with the Milesians."

"I have spoken with the King of the Fir-Bolg," the Brehon said. "It is his wish to remain independent from any decisions you and the Gaedhal may negotiate."

"Independent?"

"Brocan wishes to broker a separate peace with the Milesians in order to retain some of his people's land and titles. Eber has been informed of this and has proved himself favorable to such an arrangement."

"Why was I not informed of this?"

"It was a delicate matter," Dalan soothed. "In any case, you were aware Brocan was reluctant to throw in his lot with you."

"He is still fuming that his wife left him for me," Cecht whispered so no one else would hear.

"That's not quite true. The Fir-Bolg king is a changed man. Anyone who has their life snatched away from them then unexpectedly given back will grow from the experience. Given time he may even prove an ally."

Cecht coughed in disbelief.

"I'll believe that when I see it with my old gray eyes."

"You'll witness everything through young blue eyes in future," Dalan corrected him. "It would be wise to remember that or you may find the gift of everlasting life becomes tedious."

"Brocan shouldn't have arranged his own separate peace," Cecht frowned. "And you shouldn't have agreed to negotiate it."

"The Gaedhals are not far off now," Dalan noted. "They'll arrive before a cauldron of fresh water boils.

I suggest very strongly you don't attempt to interfere in the agreement between Eber and Brocan. They're not joining in alliance against you. Each is ensuring his own people are well served by these treaties."

"You should have told me."

"Be content," the Brehon snapped, tiring of the conversation. "Brocan has been given a gift he never desired. His life won't be easy. His kinfolk will pass away to the Halls of Waiting before you have even begun to grow tired of your endless life. He'll be alone. You'll have those about you who care for you."

Then Dalan touched the Danaan king's arm to draw his attention to the approaching delegation. On the other side of the water Eber and his party were already embarking in the cowhide curraghs that would bring them to the island in the middle of the lough.

"Enough of this talk," the Brehon said firmly. "You must remember your place in all of this. Brocan never disclosed the secret of the Quicken Brew in all his discussions with Eber. The Fir-Bolg king has acted honorably to preserve your advantage in these negotiations. I trust you will treat his position with the same respect."

Cecht grunted but the Brehon was already striding down to the water's edge to greet the Milesian delegation.

Brocan had stood all the while a good distance away from the Danaan king but now he moved quickly to stand by Dalan. The two men nodded to each other as Cecht waited with his own retinue. His welcome would be much more formal because this island still belonged to his kinfolk.

"Thank you, Dalan," Brocan whispered as they both watched the curraghs cutting through the water past the houses built on reeds in the middle of the lough.

"I've only done my duty."

"I know I've been difficult," the Fir-Bolg king admitted.

"Danu knows that!" Dalan replied.

"Now all I want is peace," Brocan stated. "I've seen what a waste my life has been. I have no wish for petty warfare anymore."

"You have no bitterness for the manner in which your life was saved?"

"I only refused the Quicken Brew through stubbornness," Brocan sighed.

"You mentioned a dream when you were waking from the effects of the brew."

Brocan stared blankly out across the lough. "I dreamed I was a drop of rain. I imagined I was falling from on high, passing down through the clouds on my earthward journey. Beneath me I saw a lake and my yearning heart wished to be absorbed completely into it. The wind took me and guided me toward the sparkling water. Just before I dived in I perceived there were many others like me, all wishing for the same ending to their lives."

"To become one with the great lough," Dalan echoed. "Your dream reminds me of an old poem."

Dalan paused, bringing the verses to mind. Then he recited them, his voice suddenly formal.

"Raindrop, hurtle down. Surrender yourself to the lough. Flow on with all your kinfolk to the river. Onward to the sea, at one with the ocean. Where will Danu take you when you have merged with her? My soul is a raindrop."

"Yes," Brocan breathed. "To unite with all my brothers and sisters. To be lost in the unfathomable beauty of this lake. I don't know whether my spirit will ever know such peace. But in my dream I was aware it was a fleeting experience, that I would be a raindrop again one day and the endless cycle would carry me on whether I wanted it or not."

"The most sacred places on this earth are where the waters meet," Dalan agreed. "Danu is the Goddess of the Flowing Waters. She is the force behind the turns and changes in our lives, just as she is in the origin of the seasons and cycles of nature."

"I pray every day to her for peace and the opportunity to join again in the great lough of souls."

"May you be granted your wish," the Brehon sighed and placed a hand on Brocan's shoulder. "You've learned a lot and you deserve to find your peace."

"Is it too late for me to take Druid orders?" the king inquired.

"It's never too late." Dalan smiled, pleasantly surprised.

"I'd like that," Brocan decided. "My spirit has been neglected."

"You still have some work to do as leader of your people."

"When that's all finished then." Brocan nodded. "I'll take the orders and seek healing for my soul."

The Brehon nodded, gaining a new respect for Brocan. He might have been stubborn, even unreasonable at times, but he was not too pig-headed to admit he still had a lot to learn.

"I've one more request to make of you." Brocan coughed.

"Another? What?"

"Aoife."

"I don't understand." Dalan frowned.

"I've lost my wife and one of my sons," the Fir-Bolg king began.

"That is not entirely out of your hands," the Brehon reminded him. "You could still accept your sons back."

"Sárán is not likely to return to my hearth."

Dalan shrugged. "Perhaps you're right," he agreed. "You treated him harshly and he's as proud as you once were."

"Aoife and I have had our disagreements but I don't think she would shun me," Brocan said.

"Lom and Sárán are going to be careful with you in future." Dalan nodded. "Perhaps even distant. Aoife will certainly prove easier to influence. Would you have her back?"

Brocan turned around to glimpse his daughter laughing at Mahon's side. "With all my heart," the king replied, the emotion choking his words.

"She's my student," Dalan reminded him. "She's bound in duty to go wherever I would take her."

"Then I beg you to consider my hall at Aillwee your own and to bring her there whenever possible."

"You've abandoned Dun Burren forever?" the Brehon asked, knowing the answer.

"All my people have already moved into the caves of Aillwee," Brocan replied. "Dun Burren will be covered in grass before three summers have passed. In three generations no one will remember it was once the stronghold of the Fir-Bolg in the west."

"The Bards and Brehons will recall Dun Burren in song," Dalan offered. "I'll come to live for a while at the bear caves and I'll bring your daughter. She may be the only person living who can heal the rift between you and your sons."

"Thank you."

The first curragh touched the shore as the Fir-Bolg king spoke, and the oarsman jumped out to lend a helping hand to his passengers. The first Milesian to set foot on the island of Dun Gur was Eber, son of Míl and King of the Gaedhals of the South.

"Welcome," Dalan said in his most formal tone.

Brocan exchanged nods of recognition with the Milesian but they didn't speak. Their business was largely concluded.

"As Chief Brehon of Western Innisfail," Dalan went

on, "it is my duty to present you to the king of this island, whom you have met only on the battlefield. Cecht of the Danaan has invited you to his stronghold to speak to you of peace. He wishes you to know that until this day no enemy has ever set foot on this soil. It is his hope when you leave here you will no longer count yourself among his foes."

"A fine speech," Eber complimented the Brehon. "I'm sure with your guidance this business will be concluded satisfactorily."

"Then let us go to the fire. It's our tradition that such talks be held outside the walls of the stronghold. When all parties are agreed the celebrations commence within the fort."

"A wise custom."

With that Dalan led the way to where Cecht stood waiting by the fire just beyond the outer wall of his hillfort.

"Greetings, cousin," the Danaan king exclaimed for all to hear. "I trust you will find my hospitality more generous than I found yours to be."

"I am humbled by your words," Eber replied politely. "A war camp is no place for feasting. I hope you understand there was no ill intent in the lowly state of your lodgings."

The Milesian signaled to one of his retainers who handed over a dozen cowbells to his king. Eber held the heavy bundle by their leather straps, examined them quickly, then handed them to Cecht.

"I present you with a gift to soothe our friendship,

cousin," the Gaedhal declared. "Twelve cows. These are their bells. They wait for you on the other shore of the lough."

"Those are my cows!" Brocan hissed to Dalan under his breath.

"It seems Cecht will be their keeper," the Brehon whispered in reply.

"Is it not enough," the Fir-Bolg King sighed, "that the Danaan stole my wife, two sons and a daughter? Does he have to take my cows as well?"

Then Brocan smiled at the way things had turned out. "That's the price of stubbornness," he muttered under his breath.

Dalan didn't hear the comment. He was listening carefully for the Danaan king's reply to this generous gift.

Cecht looked hard at the bunch of cowbells. It was plain he had noticed the workmanship was Fir-Bolg. Dalan thought the Danaan king might raise a protest. But Cecht's mouth began to curl into a smile which mirrored Brocan's.

"It is with joy," Cecht began, his face beaming with happiness, "that I accept your offer of peace and friendship."

"There's more," Eber went on, bolstered by such an encouraging reception. "I've brought with me game, fish, butter, a barrel of honey, four oxen ready for roasting, a dozen casks of mead, one hundred skins of the same honey brew, six goats, two barrels of dried apples, a cask of fresh cream and three sacks of dried herbs of many varieties."

The smile dropped away from Cecht's face as he realized much of what the Milesian king had brought with him was probably plunder.

"You don't have much experience with kingly duties, do you?" Brocan noted, addressing the Gaedhal.

Before Eber could protest, Dalan stepped forward.

"Food is the greatest gift of all," the Brehon declared. "When we share our food with friends we share their company, their dreams, their sorrows, their joy and all their stories. There is no more holy act in veneration of the Goddess Danu. For she is our Mother who provides all our needs."

Cecht curled his lip at having to accept Dalan's judgment. But the Brehon had spoken and his word was law unless another judge of equal status could convincingly refute the statement. And there was no such Druid in all Innisfail except the Dagda himself.

The Danaan king closed his eyes, thought hard for a moment and quickly decided to ignore the origin of the gifts and to accept them in the spirit in which they had been offered.

"It's only fitting our peoples celebrate their treaty with food gathered by my folk and tendered by yours," he said slowly.

Dalan gasped with admiration at the Danaan king's wit. By choosing his words carefully Cecht had managed to accuse Eber of theft, brush off the offense as unimportant to future relations and offer his forgiveness. All in one breath.

"Now we should begin our discussion," the Danaan

king went on. "It's the custom of my people that all such talks be conducted in the open. There are clouds gathering for a downpour so I would like to finish as quickly as possible."

"Will you cede the land to my people?" Eber asked, getting straight to the point.

"Under certain conditions," Cecht stated.

"So your folk don't intend to abandon the country to us?"

"I'm sure you are aware of the skills of our Druids," Cecht said in a low voice full of implied threat. "We intend to live within the Otherworld created for us by the Ollamh-Dreamers."

"But are you going to vacate the land?" the Milesian repeated.

"I propose that your people take all the land of Innisfail above the soil," the Danaan king informed his guest. "My people, however, will retain all that is under the soil. We will withdraw into our underground palaces forever."

"Never to walk above the ground again?" Eber pressed.

"Never to make our homes in the territory set aside for your folk," Cecht stressed. "It may be necessary for some of our folk to travel across the land of the Gaedhals from time to time."

"There will be no war between us?" Eber asked.

"No quarrel will sully our friendship," the Danaan confirmed. "As long as our Druids are permitted to instruct your Brehons in law. And only if the Milesian clans follow the Brehon laws established by Danaan precedent."

"I have no Druid to advise me on this matter," the Gaedhal protested. "My brother Amergin is away with King Éremon in the east. I cannot agree to a condition if I do not have a full understanding of all its implications."

Dalan stepped forward. "My lord, I am a judge. The law has been my life. And the laws we maintain in this land have been passed down from the Council of the Wise which presided over the Islands of the West in ancient days. These are laws applicable to Innisfail. The customs of your people are suited to the Iberi lands. But you are living in Innisfail now, where life is very different."

"The laws we have suit us well," Eber countered. "I have no wish to change them."

"In the Iberi lands there is much cattle raiding." Dalan shrugged. "You have told me yourself it's the only way many poor clans survive."

"That's true."

"There is no cattle raiding here."

Eber looked hard at the Brehon to see the faintest hint of a lie showing on his face. There was none.

"There's no cattle raiding here?" the Milesian asked, confused.

"There is no need. The land is rich and fertile for the most part. Grass grows lush. The rains fall regularly. And there is an abundance of game, so only small numbers need be slaughtered for food."

The Brehon could see Eber was thinking through the repercussions of this.

"Without the necessity to raid," Dalan went on, "wars are uncommon, disputes settled quickly. Killing is rare. Treaties are many. Hunger is unknown."

He waited for his words to hit the Gaedhal. Then he went on.

"Your laws pertain to a different set of circumstances; though they seem reasonable to you now, in time they will seed conflict among your people."

"I understand," Eber ventured. "But I can't agree to such terms until a Brehon has advised me."

"I am a Brehon," Dalan stated.

"I realize that," Eber replied with uncertainty. "How will I explain this to my people?"

"It is a sign of the cooperation which will continue between our kin from this day onward," Dalan suggested.

Eber searched the Druid's face then turned to Cecht. Both men were expressionless, refusing to give their thoughts. The Gaedhal felt trapped. This was wrong, he thought to himself. No king had the right to barter the customs of his people.

"I can't agree to this term," the Gaedhal said at last.

"If I gave you a gift to seal our treaty, would you consider accepting the terms?" Cecht asked, with a faint smile.

The Gaedhal thought carefully for a few moments. "It would have to be a substantial and generous gift," Eber conceded, intrigued by what might be on offer.

"You are standing on it," the Danaan declared. "This island, the lough, the lands all around and the fortress of Dun Gur. I give them to you to vouch for the sincerity of my terms."

"You would have been vacating these lands in any case." Eber frowned, sensing some trick.

"By the power of the Draoi-Music this settlement was to have been withdrawn into the Otherworld," Cecht cut in. "The lough and the island were to remain within the confines of this world but the walls of Dun Gur were to disappear forever. I am offering my fortress and my friendship."

"I must think on this," the Milesian stated, touching a hand to his chin. "There's much to be considered."

"I'm glad you have decided to be so careful," Cecht told him. "These are weighty matters which deserve deliberation. Go to the shore of the lough and look upon what will be yours if you accept my offer. Taste the waters which will protect your people and soothe the dry throats of your cattle. Walk all around the shore at your leisure. But you may not enter Dun Gur until this treaty is agreed."

"Very well," the Gaedhal replied. Then Eber turned on his heel to walk to the pebbled shoreline. He wandered about for a while and afterward sat staring into the waters, oblivious to the rain which began to pelt down.

Dalan, Cecht, Brocan and all the assembled Danaans waited on the hillside, forbidden by tradition to move until Eber agreed to the terms.

The afternoon passed by. The storm clouds grew heavier. And those who waited for the Milesian king were wet through. A cold wind blew up off the lough. Folk began to shiver. The fire danced about so wildly no one could get close enough to it to be warmed.

Then at last, when the sun was low in the sky, Eber walked back up the hill to face the Danaan king again.

"Your people have many skills in the Draoi arts," the Gaedhal began. "I demand an assurance those arts will not be raised against my kindred again."

"You have that guarantee," Dalan replied without hesitation.

"Yet there may be times when my folk stand in need of that same Draoi craft," Eber went on. "Will you willingly provide it?"

"When you request our aid we will do whatever is in our power to help," Dalan affirmed.

"You must promise me, however," Cecht cut in, "that the waters of this lough will be respected and protected by your people forever. The lake has been a defender and a comfort to my folk. I would not see it desecrated."

"I will keep the lough as your kin have kept it," Eber vowed.

"Then it's settled?" Dalan ventured.

"The hillfort of Dun Gur would be a fine gift to give as the security for a treaty." The Milesian nodded.

The Brehon sighed with relief.

"But it is not enough," Eber went on. "If I am to accept your Brehons instructing my Druids in the law, I would require another assurance also."

"And what did you have in mind?" Cecht inquired.

"I have heard there is a sacred tree which your people venerate above all others," the Gaedhal answered. "I have been told it is named the Quicken Tree."

Dalan gasped with surprise. "Who told you about this tree?" he demanded.

"Isleen the Seer."

"And what did she say of it?"

"That your folk hold it in great esteem. It's the symbol of your kindred. It's a place where oaths are sworn and judgments made. It's a place of sanctuary."

Cecht opened his mouth to speak but Dalan hushed him. The Milesian had not mentioned the Quicken Brew.

"Why do you raise the matter of the tree?" the Brehon asked. "It has no bearing on this treaty."

"If the Gaedhals are guardians of a sacred tree where the law is enacted," Eber reasoned, "they will be more likely to accept the laws which it represents."

"The Quicken Tree stands for the old ways of Innisfail which after this treaty will blend with the new," Dalan declared. "Let there be a new Quicken Tree planted to symbolize the friendship among all our folk. Around about where it grows will be a sanctuary safe from conflict, dispute, revenge or insult. And beneath its branches our people will meet in their councils openly. Danaan, Gaedhal and Fir-Bolg will share this neutral territory forever."

At last Eber seemed satisfied.

"That would put my mind at rest." He nodded. "But my warriors would be the guardians of the place and Milesian Druids would preside over all lawsuits brought before the tree?"

"As long as your Druid judges are trained by our Brehons," Dalan confirmed.

"Very well." The Milesian shrugged. "Then I can see no other impediment to this treaty."

Dalan could hardly believe his luck. Then he realized it was not good fortune. Isleen may not have revealed all she knew about the Quicken Tree, but she would have had her reasons. Still, the Brehon did not have time to consider her motives for the moment.

"As a seal on our agreement," Dalan decreed, "let us share our drink from the Cup of Welcome."

Once more Eber turned to his retainers and gave a hushed order. Before Cecht had produced the silver cup which his kinfolk traditionally offered to guests, Eber held out a magnificent silver bowl with exaggerated spirals etched into its surface.

"This is the Cuaich Cup," the Milesian announced. "It has been with my family since the days when my ancestors served the priest-kings of Maat on the eastern shore of the Middle Sea. I give this as my last gift to King Cecht as assurance that I and all who rule after me will honor the Treaty of the Quicken Tree."

Cecht took the Cuaich Cup, handed it to Dalan to

fill from a mead cauldron and then passed over his own cup.

"Take this, Eber," the Danaan king intoned. "It was crafted in the days before the Danaans came to Innisfail. It is known as the Cup of Welcome. May it always speak of your hospitality and generosity and spread the fame of your bountiful table."

Eber took the vessel, laid it to his lips and drank deep. Then he passed the cup around his followers.

"So by these acts," Dalan asserted, "we do solemnly swear our treaty as agreed. And I propose we meet here at Samhain to decide a place best suited for the site of the Quicken Tree. At Beltinne it will be planted and a great feast held in celebration of this perpetual truce."

"Aye." Eber nodded.

"Aye," Cecht agreed.

"I'm your witness," Brocan cut in to remind everyone he was there.

"So for now let us forget all disagreements of the past," Dalan continued. "All strife is put to rest. All disputes settled. Let us look forward to the peaceful future. Let's dance, drink and welcome our cousins from across the seas."

Everyone at the wall, Danaan, Milesian and Fir-Bolg alike, raised a joyful "Aye!" And then the gates of the fortress swung open to admit the new master of Dun Gur.

* * *

On the western edge of the Forest of Dun Beg, in the center of a clearing where the grass was well tended, there was a small and ancient hill. Sárán's fire had destroyed the southern and eastern reaches of the woods. Here there was a strong smell of charcoal on the breeze, but the forest had escaped unscathed.

At first sight this little knoll seemed no different from any other one might encounter anywhere on the island of Innisfail. But within this grassy mound were stone foundations, a passage and a large chamber.

And there Lochie found Isleen. Under the earth she had waited for him while the Milesians and the Danaans sealed their futures together in bonds of promised peace.

"You're welcome in my house," Isleen declared when she sensed her companion was hovering silent and invisible nearby.

Lochie hummed. Then he began to take on a physical shape. First his outline was discernible, then his long black cloak, boots and finally his face. Isleen turned up her lip when she saw he had taken on his old form with a perfectly bald head.

"I liked you much better as a Bard," she told him.

"It suited me," Lochie agreed with a shrug. "But it's time I returned to what I know."

"Is the treaty agreed?" Isleen inquired.

"I've just left the lough. All I set out to do has been accomplished. Now we can go about tearing their precious peace to shreds."

"To what end?" she grunted.

"Are you not enjoying yourself?"

"It was very entertaining," Isleen admitted. "But I'm in danger of becoming bored with the petty affairs of these folk."

"Then we shall have to make things more interesting for you," Lochie declared.

"How?"

"It's time we set to work on Dalan," her companion informed her. "We must compel him to act on our behalf."

"How can we do that?"

"The game has just begun, my dear friend." Lochie smiled. "Now it's time for us to really cause some havoc. And we will continue to bring strife to this island until Dalan finds the way to set us free from our fate."

"We'll have to work hard to wear him down." Isleen nodded, starting to feel a delicious thrill of excitement at the prospect.

"It'll be fun. And we still have a wager to win."

"Aoife will marry the Danaan prince." Isleen shrugged. "You've already won that bet."

"I can't in all honesty claim that," Lochie admitted with a grin. "Anything could happen between them yet. Their fathers could hardly be considered to be the best of friends, and Brocan may need to marry her into the Milesian royal house if the safety of the Burren is to be guaranteed."

Isleen's eyes lit up with mischief and she smiled.

"Now," Lochie whispered like an excited child, "let's forget this nonsense for a while. Would you like a little game of Brandubh?"

His companion laughed as she turned to hold him in her arms.

"What a wonderful idea," she sighed.

Epilogue

Think about this, then I'll let you alone for a while. Wisdom is better than knowledge. An old Druid taught me that. And he should have known, he learned his lesson the hard way.

The Watchers were cunning, there's no doubt. Mischievous, scheming, intelligent and ruthless. The least of their crimes was that they enticed the Milesians to Innisfail which brought on a terrible war.

The coming of the Gaedhal distressed the Danaan kind and Fir-Bolg both. But the Watchers wanted a greater revenge on their ancient enemies. They had a far more subtle strategy in play.

The Quicken Tree.

Vengeful they were, like no other creature on earth, and that includes all of mortal kind. In equal measure they were cruel, callous and creative. They devised a manner in which to pass their own agony on to their old opponents.

And, for all their wisdom and great learning, the Druid Assembly fell into the Watchers' trap. The bait was eternal life without sickness or pain. The trigger was the disaster of the Milesian invasion.

No mortal tastes a hint of true pain until loneliness takes up residence in his soul. Not until he's lived long past his peers, or tarried far from his kindred for too long, does sorrow taint the spirit. But that torment is no more than a minor discomfort compared to what the Watchers suffered.

I know something of the torture they endured.

The first one hundred summers after the Quicken Brew I spent in joyful celebration of the bounties life may bring. The next hundred were slightly less enjoyable. The next hundred were tinged with discomfort in the spirit. And so on forever until my life has become a burden carried like a heavy stone lashed to my back.

Without a task to keep one busy the mind fogs over, goes stale like a piece of wheat bread left forgotten on the shelf. Eventually thoughts become less frequent; memories rule the imagination, and a yearning fills the heart. I have no name for this longing of which I speak. I know not its source. And yet it rules me even now. Even in my Raven form.

When the Watchers inspired the Dagda to use the Quicken Brew they understood their revenge would be a slow, agonizing affair. They observed the Danaans and the Fir-Bolg who had shared the brew. And they savored the steady decline which overtook so many. A fate worse than death. Unending life.

The Milesians were but one stream issuing into the swirling lough. The Danaans and the Fir-Bolg were another. And the Watchers, they were Fomor who came from far-off times. I prefer to think the Watchers were in fact the instruments of a greater force which guided their hands, though they knew it not. There was a subtle design in all of these events that surely could not have been of their crafting. I would like to believe that Danu the Goddess of the Flowing Waters brought these folk together.

Whatever the truth, four streams poured into Innisfail and at their confluence there was a confusing swirling whirlpool which only much later became tranquil again. The streams became a river which flows even today, though other tributaries have joined it since.

There you have the first part of my story, named afterward in the story-poems as the Meeting of the Waters.

CAISEAL MÓR WAS BORN INTO A RICH TRADITION OF Irish storytelling and music. As a child he learned to play the brass-strung harp, carrying on a long family tradition. He spent several years collecting stories, songs and music of the Celtic lands during many visits to Ireland, Scotland and Brittany. He has a degree in performing arts from the University of Western Sydney and has worked as an actor, a teacher and a musician.

Visit
❖ Pocket Books ❖
online at

··

www.SimonSays.com

··

Keep up on the latest new
releases from your favorite
authors, as well as author
appearances, news, chats,
special offers and more.

SIMON & SCHUSTER
A VIACOM COMPANY
www.SimonSays.com

Pocket
Books

2381-01